dream wheels

also by

⊰ **RICHARD WAGAMESE** ⊱

Keeper'n Me
For Joshua

DREAM
WHEELS

RICHARD WAGAMESE

St. Martin's Press ♏ New York

www.stmartins.com

ISBN-13: 978-0-312-35926-3
ISBN-10: 0-312-35926-8

First published in Canada by Doubleday Canada,
a division of Random House of Canada Limited

First U.S. Edition: September 2006

10 9 8 7 6 5 4 3 2 1

acknowledgements

There's a young Indian cowboy I met in the summer of 2003. His name is Maynard McRae Jr. and he's a bull rider. He was also studying for medical school when I met him and I hope that he made it because the world needs more doctors with the grit and gumption and heart of rodeo folk. I spent a couple days with Maynard and his family and they became the impetus for this story. They live in the Upper Nicola Valley in the heart of British Columbia and they showed me what loyalty, courage, faith, love and unqualified support can engender in a young man, in a home, in a community. This book would not have happened without their story and their inspiration. Thank you, extraordinarily, Maynard McRae Jr. and your family.

To Blanca Schorcht and Vaughn Begg, Ann and Carole Merritt-Hiley, Libby Yandon, Spencer Powell, Alison Powell, Ross McEachern, Lydia Cheng, thank you for gracing me with your friendship. To Dolce 67 in Burnaby for the best Americano coffee in the world, the Boston Red Sox for the love of the game,

Bruce Springsteen for the poetry that inspires me and the Richards, Ford and Russo, for setting the bar so high and filling me with the desire to reach it.

A very special thank you to Dr. Lyn MacBeath for the time, guidance, encouragement and friendship that has enabled me to overcome and carry on.

To my agent, John Pearce of Westwood Creative Artists, Maya Mavjee, Nick Massey-Garrison, Martha Leonard and all the folks at Doubleday, Ben Sevier at St. Martin's Press, a hearty thank you for overseeing this book from beginning to end.

Most importantly, to Debra Powell (Woollams), I could not have done this without you. Thank you for all that you have taught me and all that you exemplify, by comparison my life is shoddy mimicry and I can ever only hope to shamble gratefully along in your footsteps. This book is for you.

Sometimes we arrived back separately
but still seemed inside the borders
we crossed by accident
and went there if we think it real
but we do not think it real
There is one memory
of you smiling in the darkness
and the smile has shaped the air
                    around your face
someone you met in a dream
has dreamed you waking.

AL PURDY, *Borderlands*

dream wheels

the Old Ones say that fate has a smell, a feel, a presence, a tactile heft in the air. Animals know it. It's what brings hunter and prey together. They recognize the ancient call and there's a quickening in the blood that drives the senses into edginess, readiness: the wild spawned in the scent. It's why a wolf pack will halt their dash across a white tumble of snow to look at a man. Stand there in the sudden timeless quiet and gaze at him, solemn amber eyes dilating, the threat leaned forward before whirling as one dark body to disappear into the trees. They do that to return him to the wild, to make all things even once again: to restore proper knowledge. The Old Ones say animals bless a man with those moments by returning him to the senses he surrendered when he claimed language, knowledge and invention as power.

The great bull sensed it and it shivered. The loose skin draped across its bulk belied the tough muscle and sinew that gave locomotive strength to its movement in the chute. The smell was in the air. The ancient smell. It gave a new and different air to the harsh light and dust of the arena. This was old, this scent, causing something to stir in its Indian and Spanish blood that it had never encountered before. Not death, not threat, not challenge because the bull had faced those many times. No, this was more than that. This was more a bidding than an urge, a call forward, an invitation to spectacle, a beckoning to an edge the bull had never approached before. The bull shifted its eighteen hundred pounds and there wasn't much room to spare on either side of its ribs. It didn't like the feel of the wood, the closeness, the thin prick of rough-sawn board along its sides. The rage of others was dribbled into the board against its nose, and the bull shivered again and stamped its heavy cloven feet into the dirt of the arena floor. The noise of the crowd beyond the chutes rose and fell awkwardly against the babble of the cowboys tugging and rubbing and plying leather in preparation amidst the jingle of metal, the snap and rub and crinkle of hard rope and the clomp of booted feet and the whinny and nicker of horses unsettled by the turn of the air, the high, sharp slice of the ancient order that called to them now too. A moment was coming, a confrontation. The bull bellowed once and banged the sides of the chute.

Man feet scraped on the boards at its side, the side facing away from the open ocean of the infield: the man side. Out there, in the packed brown dirt rectangle pressed together by high wooden fencing, was his world, the one the bull controlled, the one they entered with the smell of fear high in the air. The men talked, their voices strained, tight in their throats, and the bull felt the abrasive itch of rope start around its shoulders. Just as the dull clank of cowbell rang beside him the bull caught the flare of action between the boards of the chute as another bull and rider exploded into the arena. The noise of the crowd swelled incredibly and there came the bashing and buckling sounds of leather, rope, bell, skin and bone crashing against each other amplified by roiling clouds of dirt that held it, gave it the shape and tone and snap of electrified energy. It didn't last long. A long, drawn-out sigh accompanied the rider suddenly slammed into the dirt, the sound rising again as bright-costumed men raced about attracting the bull's anger, diverting it away from the rider who scrambled to his feet, eyes ablaze with a strange mix of indignation and fear, and leaped for the security of the fencing. The great bull bellowed to its cousin in the infield and shook the sides of the chute in celebration of another display of power. The men around it spoke bravely to each other but the bull felt the anxiety creeping just beneath their words. It enjoyed that and it bellowed again.

The movement around the chute increased. Men in front of it were pulling rope against the gate that would soon fling open and send the bull careening into the light and heat and dirt of the battle. The men over top of its back moved silently, deliberately now, and the bull stamped and rolled back and forth, side to side, front to back in the chute forcing them to agitation, their words harsher to each other. The rope about its shoulders was secured and the clank belt set in place. The heavy clink and rattle of the bell angered the bull. It dangled beneath it heavy as another testicle but irksome, foreign, and as its weight settled the bull smelled the ancient smell again and rolled its eyes in their sockets to look upward at the men, rolling its head while it did so and giving the topmost boards a solid thwack and shiver.

It watched the young man climb the fence. Saw the set of his face, determined, calm and strong beneath the fear and felt the firm slap of his gloved hand on its neck as he leaned over, feet straddled on each side of the chute. The man bore the smell too. The bull shifted in the chute, made a small bit of room to accommodate the legs of this man who smelled so richly of that ancient call. It felt the dull rounded rowel of spur against its flank as the man slid into place and it shivered, the loose skin unsettling the man, feeling him grip with his thighs searching for hold, finding it and relaxing again. The bull snorted and half rose on its hind feet, twisting its head side to side and trumpeting the acceptance of this challenge and hearing the buzz of the crowd rise in time with its huge head over the top of the chute. The men spoke quicker, shorter words snapped at each other, and the bull felt the waxed rope being pulled tighter and tighter about its girth.

This was the call. This was the ancient order of things, the primal encounter, the scent of the coming together, bone to bone, blood to blood and will to will. The bull understood this. It knew that the man straddling its back answered the same urge. The scent was high in the air now. Fate. Destiny. Life itself, keen as the wolves' call in its blood. The great bull bawled its challenge again and felt the air contract as the crowd drew breath, sensed the man tighten his grip, felt the pull and yank and strain of rope and the ripple of gloved fingers in the small hollow behind its shoulders. It reared again in the chute. Wild. Raging. The call driving it back into primordial time.

He planted his feet on the third rail of the chute and allowed himself one quick look at the arena. It never failed to amaze him. People of all sorts gathered together to witness a part of his life that he had never quite learned to equate with spectacle. Joe Willie had always ridden as a matter of fact. From the time he could remember he had been straddling something, from his father's bouncing thigh in the living room to the pony at three, the sheep at mutton busting at four, the horses at six, the steers at eight and finally, the bulls at ten. Sticking and staying had come to him as naturally as walking and riding, lunging out of the chute on a bareback horse, a saddle bronc or a bull like the champion Brahma cross beneath him now was merely the definition of a life, a cowboy life bred in his Ojibway-Sioux bones as surely as this rodeo grew out of the old Wild West shows his great-grandfather had whooped and hollered and ridden in alongside old Buffalo Bill himself.

Joe Willie shrugged. Too busy for those thoughts now, too busy to entertain anything but the feel of this great bull, the ribs of it through the loose skin against his calves and thighs telegraphing twists and jumps and kicks in a microsecond, reacting to it, sticking and staying. He needed to think ahead to that first mad plunge out of the chute. The dervish beneath him whipping him forward eight seconds in time to definition, truth, life itself.

The bull was called See Four after the powerful military explosive and the number of seconds a rider would likely see on its back before its energy detonated completely and he was blown skyward to crash and eat arena dirt. Up to now that name had held true. See Four was a living legend. Unridable, they said. Bred of bloodstock that had proven to be champion rodeo stock as well, See Four was the draw a cowboy didn't want in any short go or preliminary round. He was a money killer. Eighteen hundred pounds, nearly six feet high at the shoulder, with a hump from his Brahma roots swelling into a neck and head wider than a horse's haunches. Only the space behind the shoulders allowed a rider any chance at all. Only there was there purchase, the slim chance to exist there a tumultuous eight seconds. Behind that slight margin the bull owned everything. To slip beyond it a cowboy could only hope to be thrown clear enough to escape the fury of the hooves and horns when he landed. Behind it was cataclysm.

Joe Willie measured it from above. He rubbed the tough leather glove on his left hand against the inside of his thighs, allowing a little of the rosin to stick there. The bull had reared suddenly, causing him to lose his concentration, and he'd stepped up and off to reclaim his focus. Now, he could feel the world narrowing in scope. He heaved a deep breath, heard the sound of the crowd shrinking, diminishing, the yells of the cowboys pulling backwards out of the air until only a thick, heavy, muffled silence remained where the creak of leather, the huff of the breath of the bull, his own tattered breath and the thudded stamp of hoof on ground existed to be heard. Then he slid downward onto the brindled back of See Four. Everything was slow motion now, from the clenching of his hand under the bull rope to the steady hauling in of tension on the same rope from his father's hands. His eyes unblinking, he saw nothing but the squashed, elongated U of the bull's horns. Peripherally the slo-mo preparations of his friends and supporters keyed him up, excited him, edged him closer to the moment. He felt his father's hand on his shoulder and allowed himself a brief second to look and caught his steely-eyed nod.

"Suicide wrap," he said.

"You sure?"

"Gotta be," he said, gritting his teeth.

His father nodded grimly, then began looping the bull rope between the fingers of Joe Willie's gloved hand. The wrap made it easier to hold the rope but also made it three times harder to free the hand during or after the ride. Joe Willie watched as his father tended to the latch. This ride was everything. This ride was the ride to the top of the world.

The rodeo announcer's voice seeped through.

"Coming out of chute number three, a young cowboy who can take over the number-one ranking for the title of All-Round Cowboy with a successful ride. He's already a champion in the saddle bronc and the bareback riding and he's matched up here with the undefeated, unridden legend, See Four. Ladies and gentlemen, boys and girls, as tough as they come, a true cowboy, Joe Willie Wolfchild!"

He heaved a deep, rib-expanding breath and let it go slowly. Beneath him the bull shuddered once then settled into a curious quiet. They sat there connected by the bull rope and one gloved hand, waiting. There was a smell in the air. Joe Willie shook his head once quickly to clear it, shivered his legs against the bull's sides, raised his right arm slowly to clear the top rail of the chute and nodded solemnly to the rope man at the front of the chute.

And the world exploded.

The great bull was true to his name. He detonated. The rage in him was complete and perfect and whole and when the gate flew open he felt it blast apart into a shrapnel of motion. There was no reason to it at first, just an explosion out of the chute, just a relinquishing of boundaries, just a launch into a space he understood the order of. Implicitly. His eyes rolled back and upward and he caught the flare of the lights as he raised his shoulders and then drove them downward with a powerful kick of his back hooves. The man's weight stayed where it was supposed to. He felt it settle into the pocket of flesh behind the bone of his shoulder and he felt the twin kick of spurs against the bottom of his neck. When he landed after the first kick out of the chute the bull began to reason.

He felt the hand against his back. He felt the man's bulk pinned to that point and the greater part of his weight leaned toward it. Left. The bull understood the direction intuitively and knew that the man would struggle to maintain his position, the rest of his body, toward the hand. He twisted violently the opposite way.

See Four spun, once, twice, three times, four times in a delirious circle, kicking, bucking, head and shoulder rolling away from the strength of the hand on his back. Just at the height of the spin's energy he halted it, kicked twice, arched his back and bucked before spinning back to the hand side. The clank of the bell spiked into the centre of his head, frenzied him, enraged him further, and he knew when the man was gone the sound would disappear. So he spun. He spun and kicked and bucked against the bright whirl of the lights, the roar of the people far away across the ocean of dirt and the splash of colour of the other men bounding and leaping around his mad tear. He rolled his great head at them, bawled loudly and thrashed his horns from side to side while kicking and throwing his rear the opposite direction.

That's when he felt it. The slip, the loss of contact. The feel of air between the slamming buttocks of the man and his spine. He began to work the air. He ignored the man and focused his rage on that pocket of air, trying to increase it, stretch it, enlarge it, use it to separate the man from the rope around his shoulders. He drove all four hooves clear of the ground in a wild, hurtling leap that drew screams from those faraway people and a deep grunt from the man on his back. When his hooves slammed back into the earth he spun again and as he did, he kicked out, leaned away from the glove and felt the air pop open and he knew he'd won.

He spun twice then reversed it. When he did he felt the man float free, felt him take to the air except for the hand that stayed tight to the rope. This confused the bull. The weight was suddenly gone from his back but presented itself now, unpredictably, at his side with a hard knock in the ribs as the man slammed into his flank, the pressure of the hand pulling fiercely to that side. He kicked and spun the other way, determined to end this. He felt the man dragged along. There were others now. The brightly coloured men were racing about screaming in man talk and waving at the bull and others yelling and running and flailing their hats in his face.

The ancient scent was high in the air and the bull knew that this moment was the moment of challenge, of change, of fate and destiny. Every kick, every rise and fall of shoulders and haunches and torso was reduced to a silent roll, a trickle of motion, and even the terrible bawl that erupted from his throat spread across the air like the wave of tall grass in a light breeze. He felt the man's feet slump along through the dirt, dragged, hauled, torn along, and still the pressure of the hand in the rope around his shoulders stayed where it was. He felt blood in his nostrils, behind his eyes, and he kicked as never before to free himself, then rose and fell in silent time and the bull felt the body twist around the arm, felt the back of the man's head thump against its shoulder, felt a tearing, a separation somewhere above the hand and it worked that separation like it had worked the pocket of air before. It rolled its back toward the man and then away and it felt the hand give, felt the rope slip and the horrible clank drop away to be smothered in the dirt.

The bull kicked and spun in celebration of its freedom and the men raced around it trying to get to the man who lay in a heap on the ground. They disconcerted him. He wanted the quiet of the chute that led out of the arena now but the men darting around his head made it hard for him to find it. He speared his horns at them to clear them from his way. He kicked. The crowd roared and he saw the man he'd flung from his back try to stand. A hat was waved in his face and he charged at it. When his vision cleared all the bull could see was the man he'd thrown and the chute he wanted into beyond him. He charged toward it. He felt the puffy give of flesh and the snap of bone as he charged over the man and he kicked backwards once when he was past it and felt the dull thunk of contact. The crowd noise was shrill and hard on his ears and See Four trotted heavily into the chute to escape. As he moved deeper into the shadowed recess he felt time regain itself, reassert itself, and he calmed gradually, glad of the escape.

In the arena time was still in disarray.

book one

THE ARENA

they came up through the draw and he watched the dog run rabbits. He ran low to the ground, his nose skimming the grass, ears flat against his head, tail straight out behind him like a rudder, back paws kicking up tufts of dust so that even in his stealth the flushing of rabbits from the brush took on the illusion of speed. When a hare bolted the dog gave a short burst of pursuit, then idled back into the low prowl again. The man admired the old sheepdog's determination even though time had erased the speed and agility of its youth. The twenty yards or so of chase was all the dog could manage now, but fourteen years would do that to a dog.

The man wouldn't mind a smidgen of that exuberance himself if he could get it. It was the best he could do sometimes to saddle up the old buckskin mare and take his evening ride. Old. Geezer. Coot. Funny how when you arrived at that marker, when you finally, irrevocably qualified for it, everything in your life arrived there with you. Old dog, old horse, old saddle. He laughed to himself. Eighty-four and he could still ride, still saddle his own mount, still muck out the stall and never suffer any ache. He never galloped though. Not anymore. No, him and the old dog and the old horse merely walked now, walked for an hour or so every night down the draw, along the river, through the trees awhile and then back up to the equipment shed to watch the sun go down behind the mountains then moseying homeward before it got too dark to cause the old woman any worry. The dog loped back and walked beside the horse, looking up at the old man as if looking for affirmation.

"I seen ya," he said. "Them rabbits never had a chance."

The dog skipped off a few steps and they eased out of the draw and onto the flat where the equipment shed sat at the far end of the main pasture. When they got there he dismounted, dropped the reins so the horse could graze, gave it a rub along the neck and walked toward the shed. He'd built it out here on purpose. It was his place. The one place on the whole ranch where no one interfered. Hell, no one ever really ventured there but him and the dog. It wasn't much more than boards and beams but it didn't need to be. Inside it was a maze of gear; tools, tack, saws, plowshares, whiffletrees from the draft team he'd broken the ground with, engine parts, dead radios, a 1950s television, toys, snowshoes, rope, fishing gear and rusted guns. Most people might have labelled it a mess, a confusion of junk, but to him it was a museum. His story was here; the whole range of him in the hump and cluster and shadow and odour of the place. He loved the smell of old leather, oil, rope and wood. The way he figured it, smell was the one sense that allowed you to hold on to things, to remember, recollect, reassemble a life, and he came here to do just that. The dog and him would climb up into the cab of the old truck and he'd roll down the windows and sit there staring at the line and curve and lurch of everything, remembering with small, satisfied nods of the head. Eventually he'd focus on the panorama laid out beyond the door and he'd sit and smoke and watch the sun go down, the dog's head laid across his lap.

When he'd first come to this valley there was nothing here but open pastureland and the woman's dreams. Her family were descendants of the gold miners who'd first opened the valley, and the property the ranch sat on had been hers from the day she was born. Her brother's and sister's places were on the adjoining sections. When she brought him here he was incapable of seeing anything but she saw it all. It was like she could see directly into the future, and as they stood there, on a night pretty much like the one he'd just rode through, she told him how it would be. It turned out almost to the word and he loved her for that, though in the beginning he had his share of doubts.

Back then an Indian man and a white woman was still considered a strange union. The fact that he'd been nothing but a rodeo vagabond all his life and she was the product of a settled family with land and money and a local name did nothing to stall the talk when they got here. He drew back some when he was around people but she strode right into a room, daring anyone to say anything to her or about her, and when she introduced him it was with pride and a fierce, visible loyalty. He smiled. Folks never knew enough at first to avoid antagonizing her but they learned quick enough. Couldn't help but. It took a year or so but when the neighbours and the townsfolk saw his industry, the dawn-to-dark routine he put in building and clearing and stocking the place, the fact he never drank like they expected him to and the fact that he and the woman clearly, outright loved each other, they mellowed and eventually, slowly, invisibly, they crossed the line into acceptance and, later, admiration. Now, sixty years later, they were merely Lionel and Victoria and the ranch was merely Wolf Creek and the talk was merely about their grandson, Joe Willie, the rodeo champion. Three generations of Wolfchilds had lived on this land and he nodded in satisfaction. She'd known all along that it would work. She'd known all along that love was enough to pan the gold of family out of the rough pastureland of this valley. She'd known all along that the lanky Indian cowboy she fell in love with at the Cheyenne Rodeo was the man she wanted to build it with, and he thanked her in his heart for that wisdom.

The busted kneecap he got in Mesquite in '42 never healed up right, and after a season of trying to get past it, the bucking and falling got to be too much and he'd had to hang up the spurs. They'd driven here in the truck, with his tack and gear thrown in the back. Rodeo was his blood though, and once they'd got the place up and able to run, it was a natural choice for him to look at how he could still keep a hand in. Stock contracting was the easiest and surest way. With all his connections in the chutes and on the back lots they'd had a built-in market. They'd made the rounds of local rodeos looking for brood stock and the first bull they'd gotten turned out to be a prolific sire of rough-and-tumble bucking bulls. The horses were her concern and she'd proven to have a keen eye for the wild, unpredictable nature required for good bucking broncs. It hadn't taken long. A few seasons later they were turning out prime rodeo stock every year. He'd given up the trucking end of things when they started to ship too many head and it kept him from the rodeos. He ached for it then, yearned for it like a lost love. But Birch took care of that.

Birch had been a solid rodeo rider. He knew the ins and outs of sticking to a bronc and he understood completely the narrow hunk of territory he needed to sit to ride a bull and how to stay there. He had a good career. The old truck had gotten Birch around the circuit too, and remembering that the old man reached out and rubbed a small circle of dust from the dashboard. Good truck. Loyal, like it knew its role in the Wolfchild scheme of things and had played it as long as it could. It died about the same time as Birch's career.

Even though he was in the money more times than not, Birch never made the championship rounds. He was just a good, solid rodeo cowboy, never spectacular, never the whole deal. Not like Joe Willie. Nope, his grandson was a pure natural. Tall and lean, wiry, he was built to ride and from the moment he rode his first sheep you could see that this boy's butt and the ground were not meant to meet up very often. He rode his first steer at five and from there it was plain to see where he was headed. Birch and he had coached him on the bulls and the woman had taught him horses. He could ride anything. He was a national teen champion every year and when he finally went fulltime with the men it was largely no contest at every rodeo he entered. With a few good rides at the National Finals that night he'd be World Champion All-Round Cowboy: champion in the saddle bronc, bareback and bulls. It took a whole heap of cowboy to accomplish that, and Joe Willie was the purest rider the old man had ever seen. Joe Willie had made it possible for the ranch to become what it had. The championship money, endorsements and appearance fees went into turning the ranch into a successful family enterprise. Wolfchild stock was regarded as the prime rodeo stock to be had, and the family worked hard to maintain both the bloodline and their connection to the sport. For him it was the pleasure of all pleasures to look around him and see his family together in one place bound by the dust and dirt, the scent and sound of rodeo; family ties snug as a latigo strap.

The dog barked and the old man looked up to see her trot a horse up to the door of the shed.

"There's been an accident," she said.

"Joe Willie?" he asked.

"Yes. It's not good, Lionel. It's not good at all."

Around him the light faded into night.

Claire Hartley barely moved. She kept her breathing small, short, measured, each dollop of air gauged to keep her awake and maintain the calm, the stillness, the safety of the scant space between the top of her thighs and the back of the man's. Heat. The radiant warmth of her skin against his offered him sufficient assurance to sleep, snoring rhythmically, one hand thrown backwards, draped over her hip bone, the fingers contouring the curve of her buttocks. The whiskey smell spewed into the room with each snore. It seeped from his skin, hung in the air like the curses from an hour ago, and her throat constricted from its sour, sickly richness.

The sex had been rough. It always was. He'd been demanding from the moment he reeled through the door, sweeping her into a fierce bear hug, feet off the floor, twirling her in a clumping caveman dance around the kitchen, his coarse, unshaven cheeks scraping against the sensitive skin of her neck, chafing, his tongue darting lasciviously against the back of her ear. Then he'd plopped her down on the counter, spread her knees with one large hand and inserted himself there, pulling her closer, plumbing her with his tongue, the tang of ferment from the after-work beers cloying, nearly gagging her, and his hands kneading the press of her rump on the counter. No words. There never were. Only the grunt and moan and mutter of lust and her silence. It's what hurt the most, her silence, the utter inability to even scream, protest, challenge the brutish intrusion, the invasion of her. She felt his hardness as he slid her off the counter, wrapped her legs about him only to keep from tumbling them both to the floor and felt the solid urge of him. The pots burbled gently on the stove, their wafted promise ignored, and she reached for the knob as they stumbled past but it slid beyond her outstretched fingers.

He'd thrown her onto the couch. She landed square on her back and bounced twice before her weight settled into the cushions. He'd stood there, unbuckling, unzipping, leering at her, talking now in a garbled mélange of curses and loutish description of her body, his desire, his intentions, his control. She didn't move. That was her part, the one he wanted her to play, the one he needed performed in order for him to move into the realm he needed to inhabit. Acquiescence. Surrender. He needed surrender. The black woman silent before his power. She waited wordlessly and when he reached upward along her thigh and groped for the thin fabric of underwear, the humping of her rear was a preventative move more than invitation. He yanked them from her. He pulled apart the zipper along the back of the thin sundress and threw it from her. He forgot about the shoes. He always did. Instead he raised her heels above his shoulders and speared downward.

She went places after that. She closed her eyes and travelled to the places she'd gone to all her life when the noise and the motion and the vision got to be too much for her. She went to the imagined freedom of the mountains. She went to a splendid day with the wind bringing the scent of juniper and pine and sage to her as she rode along a trail dappled with shadow. She felt the gentle bump of the saddle pommel against her womanhood. She felt the sway and step of the horse's girth between her thighs. She felt the polished leather rub rhythmically against her rear. She felt all that languid, sensual motion, the antithesis of this savage pummelling of her vagina. Then she went to the boy's birth; the joy of it, the agony of bringing him to the light. The terrible hurt followed by the most incandescent beauty lying nestled in her arms. She went there.

The boy was out. He always was. It was an unspoken pact between them that he would stay away until nine or so before phoning and getting her mumbled coded reply that all was settled there. She was glad of that. Glad that they knew enough of survival to engage in this alliance of deception, to allow the venom to spew before coming home to perform the perfunctory roles of home and family for his convenience. She went to the life the boy and she had shared, the measure of his company the benchmark of what she knew as happiness.

The man arched and bellowed like a great whale. He turned her, lifted her into the position he required, slapped, gripped, squeezed, bit and battered her with his penis until the false stamina of booze gave way and he groaned loudly before collapsing on top of her, murmuring gentle noodlings of love in her ear on clouds of boozy vapour. Then he'd sleep. If she woke him he'd be angered and the sullenness would last all evening, taken out on her and the boy in spiteful looks and curses before the booze took over again and he slumped to the bed and gave them reprieve. That's where she lay now. In the amnesty of orgasm.

Soon, when he made even the smallest of moves, she would rise and repair dinner, serve it to him at the coffee table where he flicked through the channels seeking a ball game or action movie to fill his night. Dinner, laundry, neatening was the dance she did each night. The avoidance dance that got her to the place where he slept and she could relax, think, plot the escape she craved but felt helpless to effect.

But tonight he turned. Turned and slipped a hand to her throat, pushing her back into the pillow and rising like an assassin in the dark. She closed her eyes and waited. Waited for the light of memory to take her back again to sunlight and space and freedom. It never came.

Foley had never seen anything like it. The arm had been torn from the socket and only the strength of the muscles had kept it from being separated from the torso. From the paramedic reports, he gathered that the young bull rider had been unable to free the latching hand from the bull and had been flopped about mercilessly for a good thirty seconds. It didn't seem like a long time, but when Foley considered the prospect of being whipped about by a ton of animal it must have been an eternity. It must have seemed that way to the young cowboy too. All of the muscles had been ripped savagely. The deltoids, subscapularis, subspinatus and infraspinatus muscles were shredded. *Shredded.* The rotator cuff was gone. Just gone. Disappeared. Vanished, vamoosed, as the cowboys would say. Right now the shoulder sat completely out of joint, and Foley suspected that the whiplash effect of the bull's thrashing coupled with the twisting of the cowboy's body had done the same to the ligaments as well. But that wasn't all that worried him.

The young man's leg was fractured. Not merely broken but stomped, pulverized. Foley suspected the break had happened when the legs had been slammed to the ground and then the bull had galloped over him. The femur was a mess. When they'd rolled the gurney in through the doors the cowboy was conscious. That surprised Foley. Normally people in that much pain went into shock and lost consciousness, but the cowboy gripped his hand when he stooped to look at him and Foley had felt the coiled strength of his grip.

"Bad, Doc? Huh?" he'd asked.

"We'll see," Foley had told him.

What he saw he didn't like. All the normal attachments that connected the arm to the shoulder were gone. The joint could be pinned perhaps, but the pinning could easily render the arm immobile, incapable of the normal round operation that allowed the arm to be lifted, turned inward and outward, swung. The leg would never be the same. He'd walk, but with a severe limp, and Foley knew he'd never ride again. At least, not as a competitive rider, not as rodeo bull rider. From the initial X-rays Foley determined that the only solution appeared to be a rod down the middle of the bone itself and then a series of screws to attach the bone fragments. Six months down the road, after the cast was off, the cowboy could start strength exercises to build back muscle in the thigh, but the leg would never, ever bear the pounding of bull riding, perhaps not even riding a horse easily.

The young man slept. The morphine had defeated his gritty hold on consciousness, and Foley's next move was to call in the bone specialist and prepare him for surgery on the leg. The arm would take some consultation, and Foley suspected the young cowboy was due for a lot of surgery over the next twenty-four hours. It was going to be tough, but from the tensile grip he'd felt earlier he believed the young man possessed an inordinate amount of strength. He'd need it.

A half dozen cowboys milled about in the emergency area. Foley had treated a number of them over the years and was always impressed with the way they shrugged it all off and began healing in their minds even before the necessary surgery. For them, it seemed, a broken bone was a way of life, and even the concussions, the fractured ribs, punctured lungs and assortment of other results of allowing yourself to be thrown about at will by a wild horse or bull were the price of admission to a lifestyle he couldn't, with his Ivy League background, comprehend. This was different, however. This was being taken right out of the life. This was the end of the trail.

"Are there family members here?" Foley asked when he approached the group.

"I'm Birch Wolfchild, Joe Willie's dad," a tall, lean, dark-haired man said, standing and reaching over to shake Foley's hand.

"Mr. Wolfchild, your son's in pretty bad shape."

"Well, he's been in pretty bad shape before, Doc."

"Not like this."

Birch Wolfchild looked over his shoulder once at the other cowboys and then stepped closer to Foley. He put a hand on his shoulder and began walking slowly down the hallway, and Foley was surprised at how easily the man had gotten him to move along beside him. "Now, Doc, I'm gonna have to tell his mother something and it's gonna have to be something she can take in. So give it to me straight. No gobbledygook."

Foley grinned despite himself. "Goobledygook aside, Mr. Wolfchild, I've never seen a shoulder so completely devastated. The thrashing of the bull ripped everything, and I mean everything, that once resembled a shoulder and left nothing. His leg is crushed and it's going to take major surgery just to allow him to walk again. It's as bad a scenario as I've seen."

It was Birch Wolfchild's turn to grin. "You give it pretty good when you give it straight, don't you, Doc? Well, that's plain enough, I suppose."

"I'm sorry to be so blunt," Foley said. "But the truth is, Mr. Wolfchild, your son is going to need a whole lot more than the surgery."

"Like what?" Birch asked.

"Well, therapy. Physiotherapy—and a lot of it—as well as therapy for the emotional scars of the injury."

"Emotional scars? Head stuff?"

"Yes. Head stuff. He's not going to be able to ride rodeo anymore."

Birch slumped against the wall.

"Frankly, putting that arm back together again is going to require specialized surgery, and right now I don't know for sure how long it will take to rebuild it or even if it can be rebuilt. The leg needs a steel rod to give it strength and there's no way it will ever be safe to take a tumble to the ground again. Now, as far as I know you can't ride anything without strong arms and legs. When Joe Willie comes out of this he's going to have to learn to cope with not being able to ride again. Can he do that?" Foley asked.

The cowboy stared at the opposite wall for a long moment. Foley could see the mind working at registering what he'd just heard, and then the slow welling of tears at the corners of his eyes.

"He needed three seconds. Three seconds on that bull and he was World Champion. Just a clean ride like the thousands he's had before. Me, I figured it was a surefire thing. Hell, Doc, I was even helping to spend the money in my head. It's all we've done. All we've done since he was three was live for this day. You know what All-Round Cowboy means, Doc?"

"No. I have an idea but no, not really."

Birch pursed his lips. "It's like reaching for the hand of the prettiest woman at the dance. A cowboy's gotta be mighty lucky and mighty good. Joe Willie was mighty, mighty good."

"I'm sorry," Foley said, recognizing the emptiness inherent in the words.

Birch nodded solemnly. "I appreciate that. Hardest part for all of us now's gonna be not being at the dance."

He walked slowly back to the group of cowboys, and
Foley watched them talk. Foley could see the shock register but
become replaced almost instantly with a collective look of hardened composure—grit, Foley thought. They circled around
Wolfchild, and Foley knew that the family would have the support it needed to get through this. And they'd need a lot.

Silence was the rule. She knew that. She knew that passage
through moments like this, moments when his lust was a raging
thing, his need for control, dominance and authority drove him
to gripping, twisting, hitting, meant she needed to lie back and
suffer it. Suffer it so it would end. So he could spend himself,
roll off and move into the stilted semblance of home life that he
pulled around himself for the community's eyes. Why she spoke
suddenly she never knew. Only that for the briefest of instants
she saw herself beyond this, beyond the city, the routine, the per-
formance piece her life had become and the freedom, maybe, of
a horse on a trail in the mountains. Back to the dream she'd once
held out for her life. The word spilled from her from her like
dream words do, all languorous and distracted sounding.

"Eric," she said.

He froze. "Shut up," he said and continued his humping.

"Eric, no."

He froze. Slowly, he pulled himself out, got off her, then
stood above the couch, slid his shorts over his thighs and stood
there looking down at her. Then he lit a cigarette, took a swallow from his glass on the coffee table and sat down at the edge
of the sofa. He smoked and she wondered what this turn of
silence from him might mean.

"No," he said in the darkness as if the word puzzled him.
"You tell me no. Funny. I thought you loved me."

"I do, Eric," she said. "I do love you."

"Do you?" he asked the darkness. "Do you?"

He walked over to the small lamp stand and clicked the light on. The room was bathed in a soft yellow glow. He walked to the window and drew the shades across, walked back toward her, and stopped to drain the glass before he spoke again.

"Love says no?"

"Sometimes."

"Yeah?"

"Yes. Sometimes it's not nice what you do."

He grinned. "It's not supposed to be nice."

"That's not love then," she said.

"It's called making love," he said, stepping closer. "Making love. It's how a man does it and you . . . Well, you just have to learn to like it."

"No," she said. "I don't."

He sat on the edge of the couch. She felt the weight of him, the bulk, the heft and girth of him and she swallowed hard. He poured another shot of whiskey and held it up to the light and gazed at it, studying its amber colour, swirling it a little. Then he tilted it back and swallowed it. All of it.

"Nice," he said. "Hmm."

He reached back and slipped one large hand around her neck, not gripping, not squeezing, just placed it there while he put the glass on the coffee table with the other. "How's that? That nice?"

"No," she said.

"There's that word again."

The grip tightened. He turned as he increased the pressure, and Claire's hands went to his thick wrist. He brushed them off with the other hand, grabbed her around the neck with both and pulled her toward him. She was small. Five foot two, a shade above a hundred pounds, and he hauled her like a toy. He stood and dragged her across the couch backwards so that her feet slumped to the floor and he pulled her to stand in front of him, his hands still clenched about her neck. "There," he said. "That's nice."

She looked at him. Steadily. Don't show fear, she thought, even though the tentacles of it snaked through her belly. Whatever he wanted she would do. Quietly. Wordlessly. Just to get it over with and out of the way. Just so she could move on to the zombie dance, the ritual evening, just so she could get to the sleeping part of her life, the normal part. He smiled at her and she saw the man she'd run into at Smokey's Bar and Grill, the smooth talker with the laugh lines that punctuated his talk. The salesman that talked her into this new and better model of a life. The one who'd told her that she needed a businessman and not the run-of-the-mill tradesmen and workaday slackers she'd run with until him. The one who'd promised her and the boy a shelter and a rest from all of the endless, tiresome searches she'd been on for love and home and belonging. The one who dressed her up and moved her through her life like a doll in a fancy doll's house, placing her here, placing her there, telling her how it was going to be until the lights went down and he threw her wherever he wanted. They weren't laugh lines after all. She saw that now in the light and the strain of his anger. They were wrinkles. Old, tired wrinkles, and he was an old and tired man struggling to stay young through this staged life with a beautiful younger black woman. She saw that clearly right then.

"You know what else is nice?" he asked.

She shook her head.

"This," he said, sliding the shorts down and pushing her to her knees in front of him.

She stared at his engorged need and the revulsion was thick in her.

"Now, be nice," he said.

"No," she said in a whisper.

His fist crashed into the back of her head and drove her to the floor. She only had a moment to interpret what was happening before he kicked her in the stomach and hauled her to her feet again in front of him.

"Be nice," he said again, firmly.

"No," she said.

The world exploded.

Victoria Wolfchild placed the telephone back in its cradle and walked to the picture window that looked out over the pasture. The horses were looped to the hitching post at the edge of the veranda and the dog lay panting on the step beside them. She could see the back of him, leaned against the rail fence looking across the valley at the mountains. Smoking. She watched his ribs move out with the inhale, then contract slowly as the plume of smoke streamed out in a long, thin cloud, mushrooming at its end and disappearing into the purple-pink scalloped edges of the evening. Right now he was learning to digest the disappointment and the worry. Las Vegas was thousands of miles away and the distance felt even greater when you were landlocked and helpless at home. He'd want to be doing something, anything. Now, as she reached into the closet for her shawl, Victoria Wolfchild knew he'd be more wrought with anxiety once she told him the extent of the injuries. A star had fallen and the sky was suddenly emptier and colder. Joe Willie had ridden higher and further than either he or Birch had ever dreamed, and the old man wanted that championship for him more than he'd wanted anything these past few years.

Still, it was the fact that the boy was hurt, and hurt bad, that agonized him now. As she stepped through the door onto the veranda she heard the faint syllables of the old prayer song they'd learned together many years ago. His face was raised to the sky now and she knew his eyes would be closed and his throat open to beseech blessings for the grandchild far away.

He hadn't had much use for the old ways when they met. Lionel had been raised in missionary schools. He never spoke of that. Victoria had made it a point to read what she could find of the experience and she'd felt a well of shame for that part of her country's history. She knew that they had removed the language and the culture from those poor children and that once a tribal person had lost those they were pretty much at sea. So, after they'd been married a few years, she started taking him to local powwows and tribal gatherings. He was reluctant at first, not so much for the encounter with his cultural way but more because, even though Lionel loved her immensely, there was a part of him that felt embarrassed being married to a white woman. A cultural embarrassment that only played itself out when they walked among his people. Victoria sensed it in the way his hand let go of hers some when they walked. Not completely, not in any obvious way, but enough. She knew it in the way he looked beyond her when they talked, as if he needed to see who was looking. She knew it by his retreat into shorter sentences spoken lower than usual or by his rapt interest in the ground. It was something else he never spoke of but she knew it in her bones and she also knew that she didn't blame him or hold it against him. The world sometimes held a big eraser in its hand and it didn't care much whose life it skimmed over, didn't consider the impact of its movements. Those whose lives were smudged by it went on with a hunger for the edges, for definition, for completeness. Lionel needed detail, and she helped him find it.

They'd found an old man and his wife and they'd become regular visitors. The old couple spoke to them of the traditions that had once flourished, told them of the ceremonies and rituals that had once guided the lives of the people. Little by little they had filled out the edges of Lionel's life. They filled out the edges of their marriage too. Together, they had found a spirituality that fit both of them like an old pair of moccasins: loose, familiar and comforting. She didn't know when it changed for him, only that there was suddenly a time at a gathering in Montana that he'd stood there in a circle of his people and draped an arm around her shoulders while he sang along with a round dance song. They'd danced the Owl Dance together that night and the Rabbit Dance, and as Victoria looked out at the faces watching the couples step proudly by, she saw only joy and love and acceptance in their faces and on Lionel's too. By the time Birch came around in 1950 they both spoke a smattering of Ojibway and knew various prayer songs like the one the old man sang now with his face raised to the darkening sky. They didn't do so much ceremony anymore. The old bones couldn't take the cramp of the sweat lodge and they'd settled for some time now on smudging with the sacred medicines, prayers and meditation in the morning and the songs they'd sing sometimes with the old hand drum that graced the wall of their living room. She stood on the veranda steps and listened to him sing. The syllables, rich and healing, seeping into the air, the grass and the mountains like blessings.

When he finished he put one foot back onto the low rail of the fence and put his hat back on. She walked down the steps and along the crushed-stone pathway. He heard the crunch of her footsteps and turned. When she reached him she took his hand wordlessly and began to stroll along the fence line. She felt his gaze and his anxiety.

"Geezhee-go-kway is happy tonight," she said.

"Sky Woman?" he asked, looking up and around at the sky. "Yes. I guess she is. It's beautiful."

"I never tire of it. This land, this sky, the mountains."

"No. Me neither," he said.

"We've grown strong here, Lionel."

"Grown pretty damn old too."

"Nice when it happens at the same time, isn't it?"

"What are you telling me, woman?" He looked down at her.

"Joe Willie's bad," she said, turning to him and taking both his hands in hers. "He won't ever ride again. The bull destroyed his shoulder and crushed his thigh."

She watched his eyes change. He looked up across the valley and heaved a deep sigh. Then he looked at her and nodded.

"He'll mend here," he said.

"Yes."

"Gonna need a lot of mending."

"Yes," she said again.

"Bones'll set," he said. "Hard work to mend a busted life."

They walked together back to the house to make a room ready for their grandchild.

He sat on the edge of the bed and watched himself in the mirror. He practised lowering and raising his head, keeping the eyes firm on themselves, then turning slightly to the right and to the left, the eyes, even in the narrowed peripheral field, cold, flat, emotionless, empty of everything but the idle threat, the danger lurking just beneath the surface. When it got so he could sweep the look across the room and not break the intensity he stood and practised leaning. All the weight on the flat of one foot, a hip thrust out and the shoulders canted at an angle to match the hip and the arms dangling loose, casual, and the hands just slightly to the front of the hip pockets with the fingers cupped inward slightly, just so, the thumbs angled toward each other, giving the impression of fists forming in readiness, the will slouched and insouciant, prepared for battle. Then he walked. He ambled slowly toward the mirror, watching. He kept his eyes flat, his head tilted slightly and walked, rolling the shoulders easily with each step, the hands never moving from their position. The plant of each foot was resolute, as if he was going somewhere important but a place of his own choosing, at his own time, his own tempo, the laziness of it a measure of his purpose.

He walked until he perfected it. Over and over, back and forth, watching himself, the look cast back across his shoulder as he spun slowly toward himself again, catching his own eye and seeing the warrior there, the unyielding ambivalence he needed to carry to the street. He was fifteen but he walked nineteen. That was important. In the neighbourhood she'd moved him to this time he couldn't afford to be mistaken for a slacker, a mark, an easy number. The boys played rough here. There were four gangs in the area, and as a half-blood he didn't really fit into any of them: too light for the blacks, too dark for the whiteys and Latinos, and definitely too exotic for the Asians. There were no mulatto gangs. He was alone here, and he felt the weight of his isolation every time he hit the street, the disdain, the anger his obvious mixed blood caused in people. It was a dangerous place to be without backup. But he wasn't the type to roll over. He'd been alone all his life and he'd come to prefer it that way. Every time there was a man they moved and there was always a man and there was always a new neighbourhood, a new school, a new set of faces and attitudes, a new challenge from the bully of the block or the leader of the local crew. But he'd survived. He'd made it to fifteen in his aloneness and preferred it to the unpredictable volatility of the gang. So he practised. He taught himself to walk.

He walked to the mirror over and over again. Slouching, the roll of the hips and shoulders less pronounced than the gangbangers, more a suggestion really than a salute, and when he neared the glass he stepped slowly up to it, his face mere inches away and the eyes steady, empty as a promise from the revolving door of instant dads he'd known all his life. When he said his name it was with the coolness of the hoods he'd watched on video, the detachment itself a threat, a devil-may-care shrugging off of responsibility, conscience, association.

"Aiden. Aiden Hartley," he said to the mirror, his voice low in his throat.

He said it again. Slower. Then he smirked. Just enough.

There was a plate of food on his bedside table. He sat there and ate slowly, watching his movements in the mirror. He always ate later. Once they were tucked away in the bedroom he'd come back and slip up to his room to watch TV late into the night. He hated the sounds, and even the dopiness of late-night TV was better than the slap and grunt and squeaking from across the hall. For a fat fuck the guy could get it going every damn night, and he wondered if she liked his doughy whiteness jiggling above her in the dimness of their room. Probably. Sometimes he carried a wish for his mother. He wished that she could just float away, float right the fuck away from the endless searching and hoping and coming and going: the relentless to-and-fro of her life. Other times, most times, he resented her. She'd stick it out here though like she always did, hoping against hope that this guy was the guy and they would have a home and a history. He never could figure that one out. History. She went after it like she believed their life would start when she found it and he figured they'd been having one all along. Not much of one in the long scheme of things but it was a history nonetheless.

So he found himself hoping that the fat guy with the money, the big car and the nice house would be the one for her. Personally, he didn't care one way or the other. New guys were like new starts, same old same old, all buddy-buddy in the beginning until they got in her pants, and once the thrill of that was gone the slow downward tilt to the dump that always came. He'd picked himself up off more sidewalks than a wino by fifteen and he was tired of it. All he knew for certain was that this last stop on the long train ride to wherever they were meant to get to was another brief disembarkation, a whistle stop, and he hated it like he'd hated all the others. He ate. Then he switched on the television and sat in its glow and watched one show after another until sleep allowed him a reprieve and he floated away himself.

Birch Wolfchild had never really liked his name. He could see the strength of it. He knew that birch was a sacred thing with his father's people. He knew that the ancient legends and stories of the Ojibway were inscribed on birchbark scrolls and that the talking stick used in community ceremony came from the birch tree. He knew all of that and appreciated the fact that his was an honour name, but it was still no name to lay on a rodeo kid. Cowboy kids had no head for elaborate ideas, and their guffaws and snickers irritated the hell out of him. He'd even talked of taking on a nickname, something more appealing to a cowboy's sense of things. Rusty, Slim or Tex would have worked for him, but his mother had told him all his life that Birch was a storyteller's name and he was meant to bring stories forward. What kind of stories Birch never knew, but now, waiting for Johanna, he hoped that he had a few in store for his boy.

His wife was a Sioux woman, a barrel racer and composed of the no-nonsense way of her people and a competitive rider. She'd brook no stories, and Birch had learned over time to lay everything out simple and direct. It was sure a lot less stressful on him that way. Johanna Wolfchild was a fiercely protective mother, and from the beginning she'd wanted the straight goods on every bump and bruise Joe Willie had suffered. There never had been any way either Birch or his son could "aw shucks" their way past Johanna's scrutiny. Now, she'd want it as straight as the doc had given it to him, and Birch knew that she would be the one to take it to Joe Willie when it was time. She always had. She'd raised her boy to face life head on and to teach him that she'd never once shrunk from the truth of things no matter how hard that truth might be. That was the Sioux way, Birch figured. Warrior people. The whole "today is a good day to die" thing always puzzled him, but he saw it in his wife and he loved her for it. When you knew who you were, all of it, the good and the bad, the pretty and the plain, you could face anything and never bend, bolt or buckle. She'd taught him that. When it became clear that Birch was never going to live in the big money on the circuit she'd just handed him his bag, got into the truck and drove them home to the valley. Hardly even stopped for gas on the way, Birch joked, and she hadn't. Their marriage was the same no-nonsense deal. When Johanna knew what she wanted she just roped it, tied it down and took it home. She had with Birch and he was the better man for it. From the moment she'd walked him away from his friends and out onto the dance floor at the cowboy dance in Pendleton, Johanna had moved him and his life onward and upward. He'd always been strong and tough, but Johanna had found a way to make him graceful. Birch grinned at that. Graceful. You didn't learn to cowboy by being graceful but you learned to be a man that way. First thing you had to learn in order to cowboy well was how to fall. First thing you had to learn to be a man was how to stand up, dust yourself off and move on. The grace was in the dusting off.

He waited as patiently as he could, but the closeness of the walls and the sickly pale green made him ache for air. His friends had headed across the way to a restaurant, so Birch stepped outside for a quiet smoke. She hated that. Johanna had been raised in the traditions of her people and for her tobacco remained a sacred plant, a medicine as she called it. Birch figured he could use a little medicine right about now. He'd just fired up the cigarette and had a first good long haul when the cab pulled up at the door.

Johanna Wolfchild always made Birch feel helpless. Not helpless like he couldn't move without her but helpless like the feeling he got the first time he delivered a foal and felt its life warm and wet in his hands. Helpless because the magic in that left him in awe, silenced by its purity and the unrestricted beauty that radiated through his hands and filled his body. That kind of helpless; always. She was regal. Tall, slender but moving with a sure strength that caught a man's attention and held it. Long black hair, greying some now, framing hazel eyes that Birch called cougar eyes for their mystery and lazy sensuality. Those eyes looked at him now and he ground the cigarette out under his heel.

"You'll want to pick that up and put it somewhere," she said over her shoulder as she paid the driver.

"Directly," Birch said, bending to retrieve the butt.

She walked over and stood in front of him. When he looked at her Birch felt opened up, like any secrets he might have held at all got laid right open in the air. Known. Seen. Appreciated. She held the look a long moment, then offered a small crinkle of smile at the corner of her mouth before reaching a hand to Birch's face and laying a palm softly against his cheek.

"How are you?" she asked.

"All right," he said. "Well, as good as can be expected."

"It's not good, is it?"

"No, it's not."

Birch put a hand on her elbow and guided her through the doors and down the hallway to the small waiting area. People stopped what they were doing to look at her. They always did. Whether it was in the back lot at a rodeo, a stock auction or a shopping mall in some huge city, Johanna always got their attention. He sat her down in a chair and got her a cup of water. She took a small sip and straightened herself in the chair.

"Okay, so what is it?" she asked.

"It's his left shoulder and his right leg," Birch said, and for the next few long, hard minutes he repeated what the doctor had told him. Johanna never moved. She sat and watched Birch as he spoke. When he finished she raised the cup to her mouth and sipped from it until it was empty. Then she placed it delicately in the wastebasket beside her, put her hands in her lap, pursed her lips and looked away across the room to some vanishing point far away.

"Suicide wrap," she said.

"Yes."

She nodded and looked at him solemnly. "I'd have gone the same way," she said. "I'd have made the same choice and so would you."

"Yes," Birch said again, quieter, more deliberate.

"So don't go harbouring any thinking in your cowboy head that you might have changed this or that you're to blame because you didn't talk him out of it. We raised a man, Birch. We raised a cowboy. Joe Willie wanted this as bad as he ever wanted anything and he made the choice. Not you, not me, not anybody. Now he's gotta heal and we're going to help him. Simple as that."

"Yes," Birch said.

"Where is he?"

"Bed five, in there," Birch said, pointing.

"I'll see my boy then," she said.

"He's doped out."

"No matter. I'll see him anyway," she said.

He strolled toward the youth centre, catching his image in the storefronts as he passed. A few gangbangers checked him out as he passed. He kept his eyes front, and when they moved he flipped them a sideways look, casual, unperturbed, and they let him pass. He'd had his share of fights and the thought of violence didn't scare him but he was sure he didn't want to be swarmed. No one needed that. So he worked on giving off the persona of a stand-up guy. To be known as a stand-up guy, someone who could take care of his own business, who had a mouth, who could fight but take a trimming too, someone who knew the code of the street and stood by it, was all he wanted. That and to be left alone. One of the Asian gang caught his eye and they nodded solemnly to each other and he grinned when he'd passed.

The youth centre was tucked in at the far edge of a large park. Generally, it was a neutral zone, and since none of the gangs claimed the park as their own it was a family place with dogs and strollers and games being played. He watched the people as he passed and wondered what the glue was that made them all fit together, to stick, to stay and be a predictable thing. It was a mystery to him, and when he felt a longing rise in him he lit a cigarette and clamped it down firmly. The longing always made him mad and the anger had a bitter taste in the back of his throat. He didn't trust that. It was dark there and the darkness held things, ill-defined things, scary things, and he had no time for being scared. Instead he had a plan. A plan for moving beyond the gypsy life of tagging along behind his mother, a plan that would show her and everyone that he had the balls and brains of a stand-up guy, standing on his own and calling his own shots and definitely someone who did not need anybody. Ever. When the time came they would all know that he was no one to mess with, the gangs, his mother, the school and all the hollow men who'd come and gone leaving nothing behind them but the stale smell of their cigars and booze and sex. Especially them. He'd show them. He'd show them all.

The youth centre was less than a hub of activity. Inside a handful of kids played basketball and ping-pong while another clump of them sat twitching anxiously in front of a large-screen TV where some action movie played. He watched for a while from behind them but the movie didn't hold his attention for long and he opted for roaming about idly. The staff members merely nodded to him and no one approached to introduce themselves or to make him feel any sense of welcome at all. Eventually he wandered out back to where four picnic tables made up the smoking area.

"Got a smoke?" a lanky kid asked.

"Yeah," he said and flipped him the pack.

"You're new here."

"Yeah. Kinda dead though," Aiden said.

"Get used to it. Anyone who comes here's not hooked up. It's the only place that's not someone's turf," the kid said.

"So what's to do?" Aiden asked.

"Ah, they give us passes to the movies, bowling, sometimes coupons for the arcade, lame shit like that."

"How long you been coming here?"

"About a month."

"Long time to be bored shitless."

"Any time's a long time for that."

"You know it. I'm Aiden."

"Cort," the kid said.

"Cort?"

"Yeah. Funny, eh? Gave me a name for the place I'd spend most of my time."

Aiden sat on the picnic table beside Cort and they smoked without speaking, settling for watching the young kids playing on the swings and jungle gym. "You got a beef? Is that why you're in court?" Aiden asked.

Cort blew a smoke ring up into the air and they watched it swirl away. "Nah. The old lady. Her and the old man are scrapping all the time. He hits her, we go to the shelter, he comes around whining and snivelling to get her back and we're doing the fucking courthouse two-step trying to keep me and my sister out of foster care. It's bullshit. Sometimes I wish they'd just take us. Make more sense to me."

"Sounds tough," Aiden said.

"What's tough is moving all the fricking time. It's like they think a new worker's gonna make different moves. A new fucking flop is gonna make everything different. I hate that shit."

"I hear you," Aiden said.

"You too? The pop's an asshole?"

"Yeah. But not like that. We just move a lot. I had a lot of different pops. But yeah, they were all assholes."

Cort sniffed. "Having an asshole for a pops makes me ashamed that I gotta be a friggin' man someday, you know? I don't wanna be anything like the shithead."

Aiden shot him a sideways look. "So what's to do around here?" he asked.

"You asked me that already," Cort said.

"I know but I mean, what's to do?" He gave Cort a cool look.

"Oh. Okay. Well, I got a little hash. You into that?"

"It'll do," Aiden said. "For starters."

It was starting to look like a better place already.

They sat together in the chapel. Neither of them was particularly religious but they felt a need for the solace of a space beyond the austere brightness of the hospital. Johanna sat with her hands folded together in her lap and Birch slumped in the pew beside her, one arm slung around behind her, fiddling with his hat with the other hand. The chapel was spare, as though its designers had not wanted to offend anyone's religiosity by including any iconic reference at all. There was just a fake stained-glass window on one wall with a light placed behind to pretend the light of the world. Birch stared at it with mild curiosity. There wasn't a lot of pretend in his world and for the life of him he couldn't understand how people so desperate for some sort of salvation could find comfort in a pretend chapel. Neither could he figure the absence of stuff. Stuff defined things for him, let him know where he was and who ran the show. Here, you couldn't tell what cloth God was wrapped in, and Birch found it real hard to hold out any trust for a God that couldn't make up his mind about furniture. He supposed, if there really was any figuring out to do about it, that God was probably happier out where Birch had always found him or her or whomever—out among the hills and trees and rivers where the great spirit of it was all the furnishings a believer like him had a need or a hankering for. All the deep ideas about it were for bigger and busier heads than his. Still, the chapel was peaceful enough and he was grateful for the break.

Johanna thought about her pregnancy. Joe Willie was the only child she ever had. When she learned about the impending arrival of her child she'd gone to see the old women. Victoria and she had travelled to South Dakota to hear the motherhood teachings of her Sioux tradition. Her mother-in-law was steadfast in keeping the flame of tribal fires alive in her family, and Johanna had loved that about her from the beginning. A lot of white women either wanted their Indian husbands to become less so or else they busied themselves with recreating themselves in an Indian motif, totally abandoning their white history and beginnings. Victoria did neither. Instead, she was the force behind the presence of ceremony and ritual and the tribal way in the Wolfchild family. The only nod to adopting a tribal persona was the old, worn moccasins she wore, a present from the early days of her life with Lionel. So they'd set out together to discover what Johanna needed to do to honour the old way in her motherhood.

They'd camped out with a trio of grandmothers. She'd heard amazing things. She'd heard that a pregnant woman was not supposed to see fresh blood, nor was she to kill anything, in order to honour the life she was carrying. She'd heard that she was always to go completely through a door or completely down a set of stairs, never to turn back halfway. The child within her would see this and might decide to stop halfway down too. A pregnant woman was to rely on her man to help her. A new mother should walk purposefully and in as straight a manner as possible to any destinations she set out for, to not deviate or change plans. She heard many such things and they puzzled her. To Johanna they smacked of old wives' tales, charming folksy bits of whimsy and not anything like what she had expected to hear.

So she asked them. Directly.

"You don't do those things for your baby," she was told. "You do them for yourself."

She learned. She learned that if she was willing to carry through and do all the things suggested to her to do while she carried the baby, as farfetched as they might seem, she would cultivate the necessary willingness to be a good mother. If she could learn to set aside her rational thinking and do these things willingly, she would learn to set aside her rational thinking when the child arrived and learn to exercise her woman's gift of intuition in raising that child. If she could learn to become more intuitive in her responses to that child, she could learn to teach the power of strong choice in directing its own life. If she could allow her child to choose strongly, she could learn to give that child back to Creator each and every day of its life. When she learned to do that, they told her, she would be a good mother.

Most of all, she supposed, she'd learned that there is a backbone in life, a spiritual spine that undercut everything, and that finding it in yourself, learning to feel its pulse, was salvation in its purest sense. She'd listened intently as the words rolled easily and eloquently from those old women and she had found her strength and she'd done all that they asked.

Her child lay in a bed two floors above her. When he came to he would need her, all of her, and she would be there. She looked at Birch, his lanky frame slung casually in the pew, and knew that he would be there too. The thing with cowboys was, that in the laconic, ambling, shrugging casualness of them, there was backbone too, a grit-your-teeth tenacity joined with a wild, wide-open lovingness. She saw it in the way they treated animals, the way they moved on the land, in the way they loved their families; everything equal and deserving.

She squeezed his hand and he broke off whatever reverie he was engaged in and they rose without speaking and headed back upstairs.

When the phone rang Darlene thought it was a joke. Smith and his friends at the Longhorn knew she'd tied it on pretty good that night and that she started her regular shift at the Valley Grill at six a.m. Smith was cute enough. Smart too in a cagey sort of way, and it's what made him a good contractor, but he had a heap of learning to do about what was funny and what was not.

"This ain't terribly humorous so get it on over with," she said, sitting up, wrapping the sheet about her and reaching for her cigarettes.

"Darlene, it's Johanna Wolfchild."

"Oh, geez, god," Darlene said. "What time is it?"

"I apologize for calling so late, but I thought you'd want to know right away."

"He did it, didn't he! That doggone whelp. Made himself All-Round Cowboy at the National Finals, didn't he? Didn't he?" she asked.

"No," Johanna said.

"No? Well, what then?"

"He's busted up, Darlene."

She lit a cigarette, exhaled and set the lighter down beside the photo of her and Joe Willie at the Yuma Rodeo two years back. "He's been busted up before," she said.

"Not like this."

"Like what?" She reached for the beer tucked under the edge of her bed.

"It looks like he'll never ride again."

Darlene laughed, then took a gulp of beer. "No way," she said. "We're talking about Joe Willie Wolfchild here. That son of a bitch's got rodeo for blood. He'll mend."

"He'll mend, Darlene, but he won't ride again. Ever."

"Ever's a long friggin' time, ma'am," Darlene said.

"It can be. But it doesn't need to be," Johanna said.

"What does that mean?"

"It means he's going to need you now like never before."

"I'm here. I'm here," she said, draining the beer and looking at the can puzzled and wanting another. "When have I not been? Been four years off and on."

"Well, it has to be on now," Johanna said firmly.

"I'm Joe Willie's girl. Everyone knows that."

"Just as long as you know, for absolute and for certain."

"I know. I definitely know. So he ain't world champion this year. There's always another go-round. You'll see," Darlene said and flopped back on the bed.

"Understand this, Darlene," Johanna said.

"I understand. You told me when we first started going out that getting busted up was part of the life and that I had to get used to it. Well, I did. I always been in the corner when it counted. I ain't never been no buckle bunny."

"There's more than bones to mend this time."

"Yeah. Okay. Can I go to sleep now? I gotta work."

The phone went dead in her hand.

"Frigid bitch," Darlene said and went in search of another beer.

She was standing at the kitchen window when he came in. He didn't see it at first but when she stepped away from the window and into the light the bruises stood out on her face like remnants of the shadow she'd just moved out of. The black around her eyes shocked him. She reached out her hands to him, but all he saw was the hurt there and he couldn't move and he couldn't think of a response so he just sat on a kitchen chair and stared at her.

"What the hell?" was all he could say.

"Aiden," she said, stepping closer to him.

"No," he said, backing away from her in a half crouch.

"Aiden, I'm okay."

"You call that okay?" He stood in the doorway now, pointing at her.

"It's not what you think."

"It's not? What is it, then?"

"It's a mistake."

"A mistake?"

"Yes."

"Bullshit. Where is the fat fuck? I'll show him a mistake."

She slumped into the chair he'd just vacated and sat there, leaning on her elbows with her head bowed and she didn't speak again for a long time and for a moment he wondered whether she was even breathing. Finally, she lifted her head and looked at him through a silvery sludge of tears that looked slick like oil through the purple of her face. She sniffled. She wiped at her nose with the back of one knuckle. "I need you to do something for me," she said.

"What?"

"Don't do anything."

"What?" he said again, harder.

"Don't say anything to him. Just be neutral."

"Neutral? What the fuck is neutral?"

"Let me deal with it. I know what to do."

"Yeah? What's that? Call the cops?"

"No."

"No? The asshole beat you."

"I know."

"You better fucking know because your face is a mess."

She stood up and walked to the counter and reached down to the carousel where he kept his booze and poured herself a large shot of bourbon that she drank straight down and then placed the glass carefully back on the countertop. He watched her, and the dull clunk of the glass on the counter seemed like punctuation to it all. Recessed, empty, flat. When she turned to him again he could see her trying to be strong, could see it working in her face and he wanted to step toward her and hold her. But he just stood there. They both just stood there and the distance between them seemed like a living thing suddenly, breathing, growing larger by the second.

"If we say anything he'll kick us out," she said quietly. "Even if we go to the police we'll be homeless. I let everything go to come here. Everything. He said he'd take care of us. He'd take charge and we wouldn't have to worry. So we need to be neutral. For a while. Just for a while until I figure out what to do."

"What if he beats you again?"

"He won't."

"Right."

"He won't."

"Why not if he knows he can get away with it?"

In the shadow she stood in, the features of her face seemed to slide downward slowly, and he understood then what outright surrender looked like and it angered him. "Because I'll give him what he wants," she said, and this angered him even more.

In the dream Joe Willie saw the bear. He was straddling the chute, the bull beneath him, pale dust yellow, horns like fists at the side of the great wide head, breathing, taking in huge gulps of air, preparing for the battle. He raised his eyes from the bull and scanned the arena. The crowd was boisterous, filled with a nervous energy that prompted chatter, the ludicrous banter of spectacle. As he took in the familiar motions of the infield, the cowboys leaning over the rails, the clowns stretching, running in place, the pickup riders talking to their horses, he saw the bear, a grizzly the size of a Brahma bull staring at him through the slats across the infield. When he met its gaze the sound of the arena died and he could hear only his own breath and the huff of the bear's. There was no threat in the look. It seemed only curious about him. Joe Willie wondered why the rough stock hadn't flown into a panic over the bear or why the horses weren't rearing. The grizzly stood there like part and parcel of the whole deal, as if it was going to reach back and rosin up for a ride. The bear tossed its head and then slowly began to rise on its back legs using its forepaws for balance on the fence. Joe Willie could see the bend in the boards as they caught the great weight of the bear. Finally, it stood looking out over the fencing, lifted its snout to sniff the air and then levelled its gaze at Joe Willie again. Joe Willie closed his eyes and shook his head to clear it of the hallucination and then turned his attention back to the bull in the chute. Except it wasn't a bull. It was the bear.

As he leaped up higher on the rails the dream changed.

He was in a tent in the mountains above the ranch. It was early morning and there was a wavy curtain of fog over everything. He'd slept with his head facing the open door, and as he looked around him he felt comforted and peaceful. He knew this spot. It was a small glade where he'd often camped. It was a private place where he went to heal aching bones and muscles in the chill of the glacial stream at the glade's northern edge and to refresh his mind from the disruption of the road, the cities, the sometimes jarring world of rodeo. He craned his neck to stretch it and peered out at the fog. It moved. At the far northern edge, where the glade dipped to the stream, the fog moved. It parted, and a large black shape began to emerge.

The bear walked slowly out of the trees and toward the tent. All Joe Willie could hear was his own breathing and the bear's. It came closer, slowly, its gaze squarely on Joe Willie, who lay frozen in place. Time slowed to the rhythm of the bear's walk, and Joe Willie felt captivated by it, entranced and somehow, strangely, unafraid. When the grizzly got to a point just beyond the fire, fifteen feet, perhaps, from the tent, it stopped. They stared at each other. Then the bear rose up, presented itself to Joe Willie in its tremendous size, dropped to all fours, turned and padded away toward the trees. It turned its head every four or five steps and looked back at him. All the way across the glade it did this, and Joe Willie kept expecting to hear it speak to him, maybe in the ancient voice of his grandfather's people or his mother's. But it merely looked at him. Joe Willie squinted at it, trying to discern what the message was. The bear reared up on its back legs once more and rolled in bear walk toward the edge of the trees and the fog. When it reached the point where the fog was about to enshroud it, the bear turned its great head to look back at Joe Willie one more time. Except it wasn't a bear. It was an old woman wrapped in a bear robe. She held the gaze briefly, then stepped into the fog.

Joe Willie moaned once in his sleep and rolled back into the fog himself.

At least the fat prick was good for cash. He slipped an envelope with a twenty-dollar bill under the crack of his bedroom door every morning. The money was supposed to let him go to the movies or whatever distraction he could find for himself until moneybags could get his mother into the bedroom at night. That was fine with him. He didn't want to have anything to do with the fat prick. The day when he did would be the day the fat bastard paid out on everything. Everything. Aiden felt the bile of his anger against the back of his throat and he shook his head violently to clear it. The money was good, and even though he never went to a movie with it he'd put it to good use. Not like the fat prick thought. Instead, he'd saved it. Kept it in one of the envelopes and stuffed it under his mattress until it had built up into a nice little stash. He'd kept his eyes and ears open enough on the street so that he knew who to talk to. Making the purchase was easy, and as he walked down the street he felt secure, settled, carrying the knowledge that things were moving in the direction he had chosen and that there was nothing in the world that could halt it now. When he showed up at Cort's they slipped up to his bedroom and locked the door behind them.

"Did you get it?" Cort asked.

"I said I would, didn't I?"

"Yeah, well, sometimes guys just say stuff."

"I'm not one of those guys." Aiden looked hard at his friend. He walked over to the bed, reached behind and pulled it from his belt and threw it down on the mattress.

Cort smiled. He picked it up and gauged the weight in his hand. "Kinda small, ain't it?"

"Glock 26," Aiden said. "Subcompact. They call it the Baby Glock. Still a nine-millimetre though. It's perfect for us."

"So what do we do now?"

"Look for a score, case it out, take it down. You sure you wanna do this?"

Cort nodded solemnly. "Yeah," he said. "Yeah, I wanna do it."

"Me too."

"Aiden?"

"Yeah?"

"You done this before, right?"

"No. Not this."

"Me neither. You scared?"

Aiden gave him a level look, and Cort could tell that the question irritated him. He pursed his lips and studied the floor before he spoke. "Scared? Yeah. Maybe. Some."

"Me too. But that's good, right? Keeps you sharp? Keeps you ready for anything?" Cort's head bobbed nervously as he spoke.

"Something like that," Aiden said. "But I give it a different name. Something I can handle."

"Like what?"

"I don't know. Like ready. Or pumped. Tell yourself you're ready, you're pumped, not scared, not that, not ever."

"Yeah," Cort said. "Okay."

"I'm gone, pal. Can you stash the piece?"

"Yeah, sure."

"Mum's the word, right?"

"Yeah. Count on it."

They shook hands solemnly, and Aiden made his way out of the apartment and out to the street. The gun was his ticket. With it he could change everything, and when he thought about it he felt a raw excitement. There was a charge to this, the idea of walking into a place, bold as brass, pulling down on somebody, raking in the loot and then backing out, gun pointed, threatening. Jesus. His pecker was getting stiff just thinking about it. He grinned and looked in the windows as he passed. No one knew. To them he was just another kid walking home after school. But they'd know soon enough. All of them. Especially the fat prick.

Coming out of the darkness was like being pulled backwards into the world. He felt the back of his head first. Then his face. Then, slowly, inch by inch, the rest of him. It hurt. Bad. There was a cottony numbness to everything that told him they'd shot him up with morphine. It was always morphine. When guys got trampled, morphine was the only thing that could kill the agony left by hooves, horns and arena hardpack. When he tried to move he felt the tightness of the body cast. He tried to recollect the ride to find the moment when it all went to hell so he could meet it, find his peace with it and start mending. His hand. The wrap. He relaxed and remembered. The son of a bitch reversed himself quickly and kicked out at the same time so that there was daylight between his butt and leather. Only the wrap held him, and as he struggled to reclaim the narrow seat behind the bull's shoulders the wrap and his hand became the swing point for his whole body. When he felt the pocket of air grow with the successive twists and jumps he tried to let go, to kick out and save himself, but the bind was too strong. He remembered yanking at the bull rope and then flat spinning off the bull's back with his hand still strung to the rope and the vision of the arena roof with all its banners. Then it became a series of images: colours, screams, the smell of fear in his nostrils, the hard haul on his arm, the toes of his boots clunking on the hardpack, the slam of the bull's sides against his chest and then his back and ribs as he twisted on the fulcrum of his gloved hand. Then the ripping, the tearing, the burn of muscles stretched beyond their limit and the funny white pop in the head born of sudden pain. He tried to squeeze his left hand together but it wouldn't move. In fact, he had a whole lot of trouble even feeling the whole arm. Only a sodden kind of heaviness told him it was there. As he came farther back into the world he felt his right leg. It was elevated. All he could feel of it was the terrific heaviness of it sitting in its sling. He tried to shift to relieve the weight on his lower back. He groaned.

"Joe Willie?"

He should have known that hers would be the first voice he heard. He'd never had the slightest scratch or bruise his entire career without his mother either doing the doctoring or harassing the poor sawbones who was.

"Water," he said.

She brought the glass to his lips and he sucked through the straw. He moaned. The pressure of drinking that way caused his head to hurt.

"Open your eyes, son."

He looked at her. She was standing beside the bed as proud and as tall as ever. She moved a hand down to his chest and rested it there, watching him. He couldn't feel the pressure of her hand but was comforted by the motion nonetheless.

"Hey," he said, weakly.

"Hey yourself. How do you feel?"

"Not worth a shit," he said. "I'm broke good, huh?"

"Pretty good," she said and pulled the chair closer to the bed. When she sat, her face was level with his. They looked at each other, and Joe Willie could feel her worry.

"Well?" he asked.

He watched her gather herself. It was a familiar thing and he'd always been impressed by it. It started somewhere at the back of her eyes, a movement but not really, more like energy pulling itself together like a fist, positioning itself for maximum release. He'd seen it the first time when he was four, and her favourite mare had broken her leg. She'd looked at her lying in the stall and Joe Willie had seen the same rallying happen before she'd marched to the house and returned with his father's pistol. Then she'd knelt at the horse's flank and rubbed her with the flat of one hand, spoken to her calmly, lovingly, before standing straight and strong and shooting her through the head. Her arm had slumped to her side and she leaned into his father, who took the gun, laid it on the stall rail and gathered her in his arms. She'd pulled him close too, and as his face had pressed against his mother's ribs that day he'd felt the sheer strength of her, the breath huge in its swell of emotion, the hand on his back warm, glowing like a branding iron, searing him with all of her vital energy.

"The bull broke you as bad as I've ever seen, son," she said. "They worked on you a long time and you have a big decision to make in the next while."

"What kind?"

She breathed out. "The change-your-life kind. And there's no one can make it for you. It has to be your call."

"Well? Let's have her, then."

She stood and looked squarely at him. He tried to breathe deep to prepare himself but his ribs wouldn't allow it, so he settled for quick, shallow breaths. She described his injuries and the hard fact of his condition.

"Lord."

"You'll limp, son. There's no getting away from that. It's broke too bad to fix perfectly."

"Ride?"

"I don't know."

"What's the decision, then?"

"Your arm is shredded. Some of the muscle is ripped clear of the joint and the tendons are snapped. The muscles that help to hold your shoulder in place are gone and the glue that keeps the arm in the socket is gone too. They can fix it, but the choice is yours."

"What choice?"

"They can pin the joint—pin the arm into the socket so it will hang properly. But if they do that it might take away your ability to turn it normally, lift it, use it completely. Or they can let it hang in the socket. You can move it around like normal but it'll always be pretty much held there by skin. Either way it'll never come back to what it was, son. Ever."

He looked away. It took a few moments for the message to sink in. He would never rodeo again. The weight of that thought forced him back into the bed with a groan and he wanted the blackness again. He'd always respected his body, trained it, taken care of it, but now, suddenly, he felt betrayed by it, abandoned. Lying there staring at the wall, he felt a great cold well of lonesome course through him and he wanted away. Her hand on his was steadying and he opened his eyes.

"Morphine," he said.

She reached for the flow control on the IV.

He waited for the feeling of warm honey on the brain. He felt his limbs grow soft, vague, less defined until his whole body and the whole world was one warm pliant thing and all thought vanished.

He wouldn't speak to her. In the rare moments when they happened to occupy a room together he pretended she wasn't there and the weight of that silence hurt her as badly as a punch to the ribs. He came and went from school in silence and she found the words he used to tell her where he was going short and sharp and chopped off and blunted at the ends like corn stalks. They hurt to walk through. But at least the man was pacified. No one spoke of the beating. He seemed content with the situation, and if he never asked about the boy at all it was okay with her because in an odd way she felt she was protecting him by excluding him from their talk. The two of them only looked at each other when they happened to meet. Aiden was sullen and Eric looked at him wide-eyed, expectant, awaiting any kind of word at all. Aiden merely offered him a flat, unyielding stare that started and ended nowhere. He moved deliberately, and when he crossed the room he maintained the look, never taking his eyes off Eric until the man would throw up his hands, arch his eyebrows and ask, "What? Say it. Whatever it is say it, kid." But he never did.

Instead he became less and less of a presence.

"Are you okay?" she asked him one day.

"Why?"

"I'm your mother."

"Really?"

"Yes."

"My mother was proud. My mother had guts. My mother would never let a man do her bad. I don't know who the hell you are."

"Aiden, I—"

"Save it," he said. "I don't need any explanations. You said enough already."

"I haven't said anything."

"Exactly."

She looked at him. She could feel his defiance. It radiated outward from the dark pools of his eyes and from the solid plant of his feet. There was nothing of what she remembered of her son in him now. He'd moved beyond it somehow and she'd missed the passing.

The thought of a stiff, wizened thing dangling off his shoulder incapable of independent motion angered him. The idea of not being able to rein a horse, curl a rope or even move around a paddock as naturally as he always had frustrated him and he opted for the dangle of an unpinned shoulder. They helped him like they always did. His mother and his father never left him all that time, and when the time for choosing came they went through all the options, all the possible scenarios and all the likely outcomes before they left him holding choice. No matter what, he couldn't bear the thought of life without movement.

"Let it hang," he told Foley.

He awoke in the bright sunshine of a desert afternoon in a warm, hazy stupor to see the four of them surrounding his bed. He grinned, more out of disciplined politeness than any degree of pleasure, and the eyes of his grandmother and grandfather filled with silent tears. If it was going to be like this all the time, people getting weepy eyed when they saw him, people constantly mourning the vision of what he once was, what he almost became, what he lost, it would drive him crazy. But for now he allowed them their fuss.

"How are you, boy?" the old man asked.

"Been better," he said.

"Do you need anything?" his grandmother asked.

"Eight more seconds, different wrap," he said.

She squeezed his hand. "I know," she said, and Joe Willie wondered if she did, if anyone really, truly did.

There were cards and gifts from all sorts of people, and for the next while they helped him open and read them. He was awed a little by the display of emotion, especially from the strangers, the fans, the ones who never even had a chance to speak with him, to know him other than as the being aboard the beast a few hundred feet away. He wondered how it felt to them, to have a hero fall, to see the idol bent and broken and busted up before their eyes and whether they'd give any thought at all to him once the shock of the thing crested and broke. He doubted it. People were fickle. By the time the next go-round came they'd find another hero and Joe Willie Wolfchild would become another used-to-be, another name to be tossed into the air at the tailgate parties when the great names of rodeo were burped and belched for comparison. *Invalid.* The word galloped in like a runaway steer and he turned his head to the window so they couldn't see the rage on his face. Invalid. In-valid. Not valid any longer, not real, empty, useless. One of the slack-jawed, vacant-eyed hangers-on at the chutes and back lots soaking up with their eyes what they could no longer feel with their bodies. He'd seen them. He'd heard them talked about in tones of pity and sorrow steeped in gratitude that it hadn't happened to those doing the talking. Joe Willie choked back a curse. He'd believed he'd never live to see the day when "what a gol-darned shame" and "Joe Willie Wolfchild" would occur in the same sentence. In-valid. No longer acceptable, strong, suitable, appropriate, valuable, whole. No longer whole. No longer a man. He groaned against his gritted teeth.

"Joe Willie? Son?" his father asked. "Do you need more?"

He nodded and watched his father dole out a few pumps of painkiller. It'd have to be a wonder drug to take away the feeling he had in his belly and at the sides of his head, but right now he'd settle for the darkness again. He looked at the flowers and cards adorning the small table in his room. Like a memorial, he thought. Here lies Joe Willie Wolfchild, champion cowboy, baddest bull buster and bronc rider in the business, consigned to the ground, never to ride again. A pity, they would say. Pity. He needed that as much as he needed tears. Pity couldn't grow muscle, and tears could never wash away the taste of loss because there was always going to be a mirror now, everywhere, to show him as he was. Invalid. Beaten. Defeated. A one-armed cowboy who couldn't ride. He closed his eyes on the image and waited for the drug to take him out, out of the room, out of the world, out of the vision.

The crack made him forget. For the time it lasted he could slip a shroud over his anger and let the drug take him higher, upward beyond the things that roiled within him on the ground. They'd walk then. They'd walk through neighbourhoods and not worry about the gangs and the threat of violence that came from being a pair of unaffiliated kids. The crack let them forget. The gun, or at least the knowledge of having the gun, let them disregard it. The crack let them laugh. They'd laugh in the face of everything and as they walked they felt as though they radiated, the energy of the high pushing everything back a yard or so, making it visible, clearer, as if they were seeing it for the first time. They'd drift into the youth centre and play ping-pong or shoot hoops at the far end of the court away from the rest of the kids. As the night fell downward, deeper, they made their way through the streets of their own neighbourhood preparing themselves to walk into the vacuums that were their homes. It was then that the crack lost its effect. It was then that Aiden knew that drugs weren't the answer for him. Being high meant you had to come down, and if all you had to come down to was the same place you left, there didn't seem to be a lot of point to it. Instead, he became more determined to see his own course through. He'd change the landscape.

They came to the doorstep of the building where Cort lived. Around them there were the usual sounds of the city night. People called to each other from their doorways, laughing between the easy distances, and there were the sounds of music from sidewalk cafés and the clatter of dishes and the slushy

sound of passing cars and a levity that made the dimming of the
light and the approaching darkness easier to enter somehow.
They looked at each other. Aiden hooked a thumb toward the
cement steps and they sat there together watching it all. He lit a
cigarette and passed the pack to Cort. He could tell by the way
Cort settled into the smoke, inhaling deeper, holding it longer,
that he was flattened out, the drug easing off and the reality of
the walk upstairs looming like an unwelcome labour.

"Shit when it ends, huh?" he said.

"The stone?"

"That too."

They laughed.

"Feels freer out here," Aiden said after a moment.

"No shit. It's never Howdy Doody time up there. Ever,"
Cort said.

"Fucker beat my mom."

Cort looked at him. Then he looked back out over the
street and thought a long while before looking at the trees and
the sky beyond. "It eats me up that she stays," he said.

"Me too. Can't figure that. No way."

"Me neither. I had my way the miserable pricks'd get a little of their own, you know?"

"I hear you. Maybe they will."

Cort looked at him again. He nodded. "Maybe they will,"
he said.

"We can change things," Aiden said.

"Yeah."

"All it takes is the jam."

"I got that."

"Yeah."

They looked around them at the street. Everywhere they
could see the shape of people wending their way toward their

homes, a casual slouching about them that spoke of a desire for predictability, for rest, for the safety of routine. The moon was a slip of light above them. Aiden grabbed the pack of smokes and handed Cort the unopened half, then stood up and leaned on the handrail. He moved aside to let an old couple shuffle past them. The old man and old woman held hands and when the man reached out to open the door for her he let his other hand rest against the small of her back. Both boys watched them enter the building and disappear slowly up the stairs, the man still guiding her with that light palm. They looked at each other.

"Chivalry," Aiden said.

"What's that?"

"It means being a warrior with class."

"Yeah?"

"Yeah. Honour, man. Stand-alone honour."

"I could handle that."

Aiden gave a small grin and clapped him firmly on the back. "It's the only way to fly, my friend."

The bear walked right through the crowd and people stepped aside easily to let it through. No one screamed and there was no stampede of people trying to get away. Joe Willie wondered how that could be. The bear was immense. A silvertip grizzly like they saw every once in a while in a mountain valley, five feet tall at the shoulder and as heavy as any rodeo bull. But it strolled through the crowd toward him like any other partygoer and people nodded politely and stepped aside. There was a band playing somewhere and the bear moved in counterpoint to the lilt and jump of the two-step they played. It kept its eyes on him as it approached and Joe Willie felt only a deep curiosity watching it watch him. He could hear the sharp click of claws on the floor. Each step it took was accompanied by a metallic rolling tap of claw. Slow. Solemn. There was a smell in the air. Bear smell. Rancid, foul. But above it, mingled with it, were the twin odours of smoke-tanned buckskin and medicine smudge. Sweetgrass, sage, cedar and tobacco rolled all around him, grew thicker, sharper, more poignant as the bear neared him. Click. Click. Click. The tap of claws continued as the music died and the bear came to within three feet of where he stood. Staring. Silent. Then it stopped. The smell of the old healing medicines was rife in the air, and the bear swivelled its great head around as though smudging itself, snorting smoke and huffing with the feel of it in its lungs. Then it rose, stood up with a tremendous lurch, wavered slightly on its hind legs, caught its balance, spread its front paws wide above Joe Willie, who stood rapt in curiosity. All he could see was bear. All the light in the room was absorbed into the immense wall of fur and he felt that if he let himself he could fall right into it and keep on falling, falling, falling, falling, deeper and deeper into this strange and utter mystery. The bear dropped down onto all fours, shook its head and turned back in the direction it had come. People simply stepped out of its way again, laughing, enjoying themselves. The bear took four steps and turned to look at him, took four steps and turned to look at him, the click of its claws rattling on the floor. When it got to the door it turned its head and Joe Willie saw the face of the old woman again. The smell of the medicines and the buckskin swirled about him again and he shook his head to clear it. The bear was gone but he could hear the claws as it walked away beyond the door. Click. Click. Click.

He opened his eyes. His grandfather sat at the table by the window, tapping his fingernails on the tabletop. Click. Click. Click. A thin tendril of medicine smoke rose from a smudging bowl at his elbow. Joe Willie groaned.

"What do you need, boy?" his grandfather asked.

He closed his eyes again and breathed as deeply as he could. Despite the pain it caused him, it felt good, this flood of air. He grimaced and shifted himself as best he could.

"Damn," he cursed.

"What? What is it?" his grandfather asked, moving closer.

"Damn this place," he said.

"Yes. It's surely an uneventful location, that's for sure."

Joe Willie tried to move his arm but it was wrapped tight against his side. "This gotta stay this way?" he asked.

"I suppose. That's how they want you for a while."

"Pretty snug."

"Yes. They coulda fit you with a latigo, I suppose, then we could have eased it off some to give you a rest now and again."

"Sure. And a hackamore to keep me in line."

"Cowboy needs that now and then."

"I could get by without it."

"Yes."

The two men looked at each other. A quiet ran between them. It was a calmness defined in the bonds formed in the dust and dirt and struggle of the cowboy life. Trust. They wouldn't have called it that. The world gives outsized names to simple things and, for Joe Willie and Lionel, trust was too big a loop to throw over the horns of what they felt. It was an elbows-on-the-fence-rail kind of thing, all leaned back and casual, existing without definition or borders, a line of certainty that ran from the edges of what they did to the uncertainty of the risks they took.

"It's done, then? Rodeo?" Joe Willie asked.

"Yes."

Joe Willie nodded. He could feel a bubble of anger rise in his belly. He tried to shift again but the pain almost made him black out. He settled for lifting his good leg and smacking it into the mattress, scowling and sneering at the cards and flowers on his bedside table. The anger rose in him and as it gained its height he recognized it as the bear, its great girth something he could fall deeper and deeper into. When he tried to shift his shoulder the burn there tore at his senses and he jerked suddenly, driving a long spike of agony down the line of his fractured thigh. He edged closer to the bear.

"Boy?" his grandfather said, looking down at him.

"Squeeze the damn pump."

"You sure?"

"Squeeze the damn pump," he said again.

The rage contracted his stomach muscles and he scowled at the effort but pushed against it as hard as he could. It felt good. He felt a wave of sorrow, deep and hot, building alongside the rage, and as it washed over it and he began to feel the ache of the loss, began to see it framed in his mind, began to see the huge black hole in his life, he squeezed his good hand hard into a fist and pounded it on the rail of the bed. Hard. Hard. And as the drug seeped into him, he was glad for it, grateful for the haze he settled into, and he flexed the hand time and time again, raised it to his face, looked at it and poured all the churning vitriol into its clenched tautness until the drug took over and it fell slowly to his side.

"It'll be okay, boy. You'll see," his grandfather said.

Joe Willie looked at him, numbed by the morphine and quieted by the rage. He turned his head. Something inside him kept right on turning and he followed the bear out of the room.

They walked down the alley and out into the hard flat light of the street. Around them the neighbourhood was thrumming with the afternoon energy of shoppers, buskers, joggers. It was a nondescript avenue, a transition zone between seamy and trendy, organic food stores next to the pawnshops, headshops and coffee joints. Aiden and Cort melted into the background, a pair of kids at loose ends, traipsing down the street and stopping to lean against a wall to smoke. They had book packs hooked over one shoulder, and nothing in their manner or their dress suggested anything other than teenagers on their way home from school. They stayed where they were for the length of time it took to smoke two cigarettes, then slouched away casually to a small café on the near corner. In their booth they were studious about the menu, quiet and at ease, looking out the window patiently while their burgers were being prepared.

"Not much action over there," Cort said after they'd been served. "You sure it's worth it?"

Aiden chewed some fries and studied his friend, pressing one hand downward in the air to quiet his talk. "It's perfect," he said.

"How do you figure?"

"Lots of things. But mostly, it's a family store and the girl works regular evening hours on regular days. She's in college and she works alone. No extra staff, no surprise arrivals."

"That's good?"

"Real good," Aiden said. "She locks up at ten, walks two blocks down the street to the bank and drops the cash bag in the slot. The drop is next to the alley that leads to the park that leads to the ravine and gone."

"Sounds good. Where's the hitch? There's gotta be a hitch."

Aiden sipped at his milkshake. "We gamble on the day," he said.

"Meaning?"

"What they turn that day. How much business they do."

Cort took a long look down the street toward the bookstore. "Doesn't look like much of a business to me."

"Trust me," Aiden said. "Bookstore. Never a crush of people, just a regular, steady business. It doesn't stick out. Not to the cops, not to anybody. They feel safe. Nobody robs a bookstore. It's always the liquor stores and corner stores."

"How much?"

"I don't know. I figure a few hundred."

"That ain't much."

"It's enough to slide it down the list."

"The list?"

"The score list. Guys are pulling down scores all the time. Cops are more interested in the big ones, the ones over a grand, the ones with narcotics involved, home invasions, shootings, that sort of stuff. Small jobs like this don't draw much heat. They'll investigate it because they gotta but they're not real hot to trot to solve it."

"Still."

"Still what?"

"Still don't seem like a lot for the effort."

Aiden nodded. When he looked at Cort he did it squarely and he saw his friend blanch at the directness, lower his head to his food and wait for the next words to release him.

"It's all safe. It's way out of our neighbourhood for one thing and nobody knows us around here. It's fast; show the piece, grab the bag, don't make a lot of noise and attract attention, gone. It's a girl so there won't be a scene. And we're not walking around with fistfuls of loot after. I seen guys after a score spending money like it was on fire in their hands. We don't do that. Everything we do is low key. Safe. Unnoticed. No heat. Besides," he said and grinned at Cort over a mouthful of burger, "I'm just a friggin' kid."

Cort smiled back. "Yeah," he said. "I'm just a friggin' kid."

"Who's gonna figure a kid for a stickup?"

"Not me."

"Me neither. Are we good then?"

"We're good. When?"

"Soon," Aiden said.

Cort looked away down the street, chewing slowly. "Soon," he said quietly. "I like the sound of that. I really, really like that."

In the diffused light through the window blinds she could almost convince herself that he was still a small boy. His head turning against the pillow was the same tousled head she'd seen through his door all those nights of his boyhood. Now, though, there was a deep furrow in his brow she'd never seen before. In the light it looked deep as a cut, an untreated gash, and she wondered what territories he navigated in his dreams. She prayed that they took him to happy times. Life as he'd known it, the life that she and Birch had worked hard to provide for him, had been normal—normal as life can be for a rodeo-raised youngster. There was nothing in her experience to equal the intense spirituality that came from the rhythm of horseback. It was where she'd always found proof of God. Something in her blood told her the truth of this, this union of tribal woman to tribal animal forging a bond to everything she moved through, be it valley, mountain, pasture or rodeo arena. Harmony, they called it, the Old Ones. She preferred to call it perfect. One and the same, she imagined, but perfection sat easier in her mind.

She'd tried to pass this on to her son, and in the early years he'd taken to it bright-eyed, attracted by the mystery, the mystical Indianness of it. Later, as he grew more and more into the company of men, the cowboys, he shrugged it off with a grin and a shy "Aw, Mama" before banging his hat against his thigh and heading off to mount up one more time. Still, she knew it stuck like a burr to a saddle blanket. A mother knew these things about her own, and she understood that deep within her boy, down where it counted, there was a well of spirituality, an understanding of mystery, Wakan Tanka, the Great Mystery that presided over everything. Spirit Dogs. That's what the Sioux had called the horses in the purely tribal days. Loyal, intelligent, intuitive and capable of guiding you to the spirit coursing through you, the truth of it born in the gift of motion, the pitch and sway of the ride. Now, watching him sleep, seeing the furrow of strain and worry at his brow, was where the faith came in, the belief that he would move through the pain and indecision of the world and drink from that deep, cool well.

"What are you thinking?" Victoria whispered, easing into the chair beside her.

She took the old woman's hand and they sat looking at him. "I was thinking that it's going to take him a while to get to where he needs to be with this."

"Well, truth is that he's a cowboy," Victoria said. "He'll grit his teeth, gather up his gumption and try to move it alone for a spell. But he'll tire. Eventually."

"Eventually?"

"It's a cowboy word. It means worn down to the last notch in the belt. Then you can start to see the sense of things."

Johanna smiled. "Damn cowboys," she said. "You just have to love them though, don't you?"

"Can't help it, really. I never could."

"So what do we do?"

Victoria turned in her chair until their knees touched. She leaned forward and put her hands in Johanna's lap, cupped the younger woman's hands in her own. They sat silently, watching Joe Willie.

"I've never been on a bull," Victoria said. "But I watched enough to learn something about it. There's a secret to bull riding that only the good ones really ever get. The secret is that you can never beat the animal. You can only beat yourself. For eight seconds you stare down fear, doubt and indecision. That's what you ride. That's what'll buck you off long before the bull does. You can teach them how to stick and stay. You can teach them how to make eight. Give them all the tools, all the tricks, all the tips, I suppose you can even give them the blood for it, like this one here. But you can't give them the secret. They only ever learn that from the ride. At least the good ones do."

"He was the best," Johanna said and she felt the sorrow crease her face.

"Yes. And it's just another ride, Johanna. Maybe a bigger, badder bull than he ever rode before, but it's just another ride."

"Mankiller," she said.

"What?"

"Some bulls are mankillers. Maybe this is one of them."

The old woman squeezed her hands. When Johanna met her gaze she felt the uncompromising steel of her. "You listen to me, girl. You listen hard and you listen well. There's no room for that here. So you just shoo it right out of your head. You raised a champion. You raised a no-holds-barred, spit-at-the-devil roughneck. You raised a *cowboy*. He's got the blood of three proud peoples running through that body—Ojibway, Sioux and Irish—tribal people, all of them. Not a one of them ever ran from a fight. And on top of that he's got everything that you or I or Birch or Lionel ever gave him. I don't know about you, Johanna, but I figure love's a pretty tough hombre and we filled that boy up with it. Now you be doubtful, you be afraid, you be sorry, but don't you ever let him see that. You don't ever let him see nothing but the love you always showed him. If we have to teach him to ride this big, bad bull here, then that's exactly what we'll do. It's gonna take some doing on his part, a powerful lot of doing, but it's him that's gotta do it. It's him that's gotta find the peace with it. It's him that's gotta want to settle it. The rest of us are leaning on the gate here. Whatever it takes to get him past this is what we have to allow him. Whatever that may be."

"I ever tell you about Mesquite in '42?" Lionel asked.

"Only a few thousand times," Birch said.

"Well, you know that Mesquite in them days was the daddy of them all?"

"Yeah. I know that."

"And you know that that old bangtail I drew was a handful and a half?"

"Yeah. That'd be old Prairie Fire."

"Old Prairie Fire. That's right. And you know that I got me a real fine pair of shotguns, them fancy step-in kind of chaps I used to love?"

"I heard that."

"And I told you that my sweet Victoria was mightily impressed with my look that day, standing at the gate eyeballing me like the coyote at the chickens?"

"Yessir, I surely heard that too," Birch said with a grin.

"Well, let me tell you that I was primed and ready that day. That bangtail had been around the circuit awhile and all I needed was a clean ride. I coulda told you every move he was gonna make once I marked him out. Winning Mesquite was a mighty big thing then on accounta every sumbitch worth his salt was there."

"Daddy of them all," Birch said.

"Damn straight," Lionel said. "Glad you're following along. Anyhow, it couldn't get any better for making the money. Horse I rode before, spanking-new broke-in chaps, a hot an' ready woman waiting for me and ten days off before the next draw. I was ready. I told you this, right?"

"Yessir, you did."

"Well, the truth is that that old bangtail had a few more tricks up his sleeve than anyone figured. I mark him out and we're frying the breeze, riding fast and wild, and he's doing everything I expected him to do. It's looking good. Then about four seconds in he throws me a loop. Right when he normally gathers up for a big leap and kick he almost comes to a stand-still. Well, I'm right over his shoulders leaning pretty good when he starts to crow hop around, and that kills all my timing. Then as quick as he does that he springs straight up and comes down spinning. I do the face plant and the crowd groans. I feel crapped out, but when I go to stand up I know it's bad."

"The knee," Birch said.

"Yessir. Landed square and it busted all to hell. Don't know why. The angle, I guess."

"One of those things," Birch said.

"Just one of those things," Lionel echoed.

"It was over."

"Yeah. Done. I didn't know it right off though. I tried to come back, but I couldn't get enough squeeze. Hurt too damn much. So I hung 'em up."

Birch gave him a look. "So why you telling me this now? Why you telling me this story you told me a thousand times?"

"Well, I guess I just kinda remembered it myself, looking at my grandson all wrapped up and broke. Kinda important now for me to recall what I learned out of that."

"And what's that, Daddy?"

"I learned that it ain't the fall that kills you, son. It's the gettin' up that hurts like hell."

Birch nodded. "That knee still hurt?"

"Only if I think about it," Lionel said.

She watched the young man approach her on the darkened sidewalk and felt fear. As he got closer she realized he was just a kid. He was grinning at her. Guys were all the same no matter what the age, she thought, and gave a small sideways glance despite herself. Jesus, Amie, she thought, the kid's all of fourteen, maybe fifteen tops, and you're giving him the eye. Long day, she figured and clutched the money bag a little closer to her body as she neared the bank deposit chute. The kid was still grinning. Horny little bugger, out way too late for his age, she thought as she stepped up to the bank drop.

"Nice night," the kid said.

She looked at him, the silly grin still pasted to his face. "Yes," she said. "Kind of late for you, isn't it?"

"Not really," he said, stepping closer.

"Excuse me," she said, pressing against the wall.

"No. You excuse me," he said.

It happened like the slow-motion roll of dreams. One hand reaching into the pocket of the windbreaker in one long roll of motion. She told the police after that she'd actually expected to see the gun before it emerged into the low light, shimmering like a small fish. She gasped. The kid looked back over his shoulder and down the length of the street almost casually, then raised the gun higher toward her face.

"I'm gonna need that," he said. The grin was gone.

"I can't," she said.

"No time for can't," he said. "Just give me the bag."

"I can't," she repeated.

He stepped back a pace and aimed the gun hard, his arm rigid. "This ain't no game now," he said, so calmly it surprised her. "You have to give me that bag and I'll just disappear. Don't need to be no bigger deal than that."

She started to cry. Loyalty was strong in her and she couldn't bring herself to simply hand over the store's earnings. The kid looked around again.

"Jesus," he said, "don't do that. Fuck. Just give me the bag."

She kept crying, clutching the bag tighter and stepping out into the light of the street.

"Goddammit," the kid said, waving the gun at her.

She told the police that he almost bolted then. She could see it in his thighs, the momentary clutch of muscle ready to spring.

There was a brief blip of siren, high and hard, and they both looked down the street at the unmarked police car easing to the curb, red dashboard light flashing. The kid blanched, pivoting his head back and forth, trying to determine a direction to flee.

"Go down the alley!" she said.

He looked at her, stunned, and stepped away, sidling toward the alley on the other side of the street. She wanted to tell him he was going to the wrong alley, that he should go down the near entrance. The kid moved across the street in small sideways hitch-steps, facing the policemen, the gun pressed to his thigh. She would recall the silvery glint of it for years after. She would recall the rubbery feel of time, watching the drama unfold in front of her. The kid's small steps, the thin thighs of him trembling through the jeans, the shaky plant of each foot edging toward the freedom of the alley in counter-point to the firm voice of the officers, their own guns raised toward him, one of them crouching to aim while the other stepped sideways toward the opposite sidewalk, talking to him, commanding him. The kid's jaw shook and he raised the gun tentatively, the hand shaking too. He was crying. Huge, gulping, chin-shaking swallows made his Adam's apple jump in his neck and when he raised the gun to cradle it in both hands she sensed that it was more to quell the shaking and make a bigger bid for the alley than any real threat. The voices of the officers hit the air like punches, each driving the crazy beat of the action into a herky-jerky staccato. She saw the muzzle flash and the kid's arms kick back high and hard with the recoil. He looked surprised. There was another boom. The bullet drove the kid backwards a few feet, where he crumpled to the concrete and time regained itself.

Immobility was the worst. Joe Willie felt trapped. He understood now how the calves felt when the ropers had them tied. It seemed that sudden. The calf bursts out of the gate and four seconds later he's dazed on the ground, incapable of moving, while the horse maintains a taut line to prevent him from getting away. Four seconds. That's how fast this felt. It didn't seem like any time at all since he'd been straddled over the chute staring down at the deep brown sea of the bull. He recalled the kaleidoscope thrill of the arena spinning crazily around him, the colours flashing and the sound of the crowd like surf crashing on the rocks. Clear, like it was moments ago. Like time melted. He remembered the conscious times, minutes when he lived with the realization of what happened, but they had an unreal quality to them, fuzzy, obscure, hard to hold. Then the dark times, when the morphine sent him under, were empty except for the bear. What the hell was that about? Cowboys told all kinds of funny stories about the things medication had done to them, and right now it felt best to put it down to some addled morphine dream. Still, the bear turning into an old woman was eerie, something a part of him remembered but far too faint to pinpoint.

He tried to move but had to settle for a hitching of the shoulders. He grimaced. The ceiling, flat, empty, still. His life. That's what his life was going to be from now on. Motionless as he was right now.

"Joe Willie?"

He turned his head and saw his grandmother seated at the bedside.

"Hey," he said.

"How do you feel?"

"Like a roped-up calf," he said.

"Can I do anything?"

"No."

"Do you want anything?"

"No."

"How about a TV? We could get you a TV. Would you like that?"

"No. I don't want a television. I don't want a radio. I don't want a newspaper. I don't want anything. Nothing. Nothing but to be left alone."

"Okay," she said. "I suppose we can arrange that too. Except there's a lot of people that really want to see you. A lot of people that care."

He stared at the ceiling while she waited. "There's nothing for them to see," he said. "The show was in the arena and the show's over. Tell them that."

"Joe Willie?"

"What?"

"It's okay."

"What's okay?"

"It's okay to feel the way you feel right now."

"Thank you," he said. "That helps so much."

"We understand. We really do," Victoria said.

"Do you? Good. That's really good that you understand. Because I don't. I don't understand any of it. Eight seconds, Grandma. One life all boiled down to eight seconds. Less really. What'd I make it? Five? Five seconds? So I was three seconds away from being the best, from being the champion. Three ticks of the clock away from the top of the world and now I can't even move into the world. And when the cast comes off and the carving up they done heals, I won't be able to move around it either. Limp, yeah? Hitch-step around, dragging one arm like some cripple, some invalid. You all understand that? You can explain how I'm supposed to handle that? Can you?"

He felt tears but tightened up his insides until the urge left him. When he looked over at her she was nodding. She reached out and laid a hand on his good one, squeezed it.

"It's a lonesome business, riding," she said. "Maybe that's why a man can get to love it so much. Maybe because there's only him. Only him when the gate gets thrown wide and the bull or the bronc busts out into the open. Maybe there's something in that moment that makes a man feel like it defines him, sketches him out, gives him detail. I don't know, I've never done it. But I helped three men do it. Helped three men make it the focus of their lives. And I guess I learned something about it. I guess I learned a little about what it feels like, about how the ride feels, the thrill, the excitement, the danger. And maybe I know a little something about the sound of it too. The thump and grunt and crash of it, and the sound of the crowd. I know a little something about the noise of it all. How that sounds. But you know what?"

She looked at him. Waited.

"What?" he asked.

"I don't know anything about the quiet. The silence. I don't know anything about how the silence feels when it's over. When the lights go off in the arena and you're left there standing with your rigging, the crowds are all gone, the arena's empty and you stand there wondering what to do next. I don't know anything about that. Cowboys always keep that one to themselves. Even your grandfather, even your daddy. So it makes it hard to understand how it must feel to you right now, knowing that those lights aren't ever going up for you again, that the chute won't get thrown open one more time. But if you were to tell me, maybe then I'd have a chance to get it. To know how that feels. Maybe then I'd know how to help you."

He looked at her and she could see him searching for the words.

"I don't know either," he said. "It ain't never been this quiet before."

They looked at each other silently and she nodded.

She put the tips of her fingers to her face and traced the line of her cheekbones. In the mirror she watched her fingers rise and fall as they followed the line of contusion and then dipped into the natural hollow and felt the looseness of her teeth under the skin, and she pushed her tongue against them and felt the push against her fingers and winced at the sudden stab of pain. She dropped her hand and slid the middle finger of the other along one line of her jaw and then the other. There were bumps there and a heaviness at the mandible joint where his fist had landed most squarely and she opened and closed her mouth a few times and heard the crackle of bone on bone. She tried to smile but the split flesh of her lip was just beginning to heal and it held stiffly so that she managed only a grimace, the emptiness of her eyes giving it the perpetual flatness of a catatonic. She felt none of the reassurance the smile was meant to offer her and she tried to wink at herself but the puffed purple flesh around her eyes turned it into a garish tic and she settled for a squeezing together of the eyebrows, leaning in toward the glass and staring into the depths of her eyes. None of them had ever done this. None of the men. They'd always been disarmed by her beauty and the fact that she had actually chosen them so that when arguments erupted or differences became so starkly apparent she'd always been given a kind of immunity from the fallout, a grace culled from her startling exotic look, the half-bloodedness, the mulatto coffee-and-cream complexion and the great hazel sharpness of her eyes.

But he was different. She'd known that from the very start, but there was something in his power that pulled her along despite her misgivings. He knew things. He knew about a woman's body, was fascinated with them, and he'd explored her fully, learning where to touch her, how she liked a finger placed, a tongue, the rhythm that turned her on and how to bring her to a point of release and let her go, building and stoking the fire in her until he finally took her over the edge. She felt plumbed, known and captive, and it was fascinating. The idea of a big, powerful man doing things to her body she'd never felt before was exciting. She'd given back, and that excited him further although he always retained control, always reined her in with a big palm on her buttocks or back. Then it turned mean. He started to take her. He'd simply walk in and have her, leave her limp and aching once he'd satisfied himself and watch television or demand to be fed. Staring at herself in the mirror, Claire wondered why she hadn't left when it became obvious how cruel he could be.

She cursed herself. Stupid. Stupid, stupid, stupid about men. But hope was a strange thing. Hope could make you blind. Hope could tell you that things weren't what they seemed, that some things were just a phase, a mood, a glitch. Hope could even convince you that if you did as you were told it would all smooth out in time and you'd wake up one morning wrapped in the arms of a man who adored you, worshipped you and sought only to fulfill you. But hope bruised too, and Claire fingered her swollen nose and felt the crush of loss that hurt more than the beating. Hope sometimes felt worse than dying.

There was nothing in the mirror of the vibrant, beautiful woman. There was just a hag, beaten into submission, used, discarded, tossed into a corner until it was time to be used again. *Hag.* She felt fury building in her, a raging, bitter fury that flicked against the sides of her belly and seemed to warm the wounds on her face, make them smoulder, cauterize them in the rank vetch of resentment, disdain and hatred she felt inside her for all the men, all the promises, all the heartache, disappointment, disillusionment, new beginnings and random glories that flared briefly for her but became extinguished in the sop of whispered intentions that were only come-ons dressed up in consignment clothes. Claire pounded her fists against the top of the bureau and then raised them to her temples, held them there, squinted her eyes tight shut to excise the memories, then opened them to look at herself again.

She couldn't be seen like this. Not until she figured out what she had to do. Eric had been careful to exercise control over everything. The only money she had came from the weekly allowance he doled out for groceries and household things. It was generous and they ate well, but Claire had never once considered the need for a financial resource of her own. The cellphone in her bag rang at least six times a day with Eric asking where she was and what she was doing. He was always demonstrative, giving her encouragement and compliments during those calls, sweet even, though the whispered niceties always carried a vague sexual undertone. She had no idea of the bank accounts, which bills were due when, or how the house itself was maintained. Eric took care of all of that. He even bought clothes for her, often sweeping in on a wave of whiskey fumes to present her with another dress, suit or some lingerie that he'd ask her to model for him while he sat on the sofa and watched. He gave Aiden money, bought him things, and he'd paid the debts she'd built up before they met. Her role was the dutiful, obedient housewife, and he reminded her constantly about the lack of stress in her life, how he took care of everything, how she never needed to worry, and for the longest time she hadn't. Her reward was the sex. That's what he told her, and at first she hadn't really minded. But this was different. This felt like slavery.

She sipped from the bourbon and pondered what she might do. There was a knock at the door, and she looked over to the bedside table to check the time and was surprised at the lateness of the hour. There was another knock, more insistent, and she reached for the cold cream and spread it heavily around her eyes and along her cheeks to cover as much of the bruising as she could before she ran in small, mincing steps down the hallway to the door.

"Who is it?" she asked.

"Police" was all she heard.

She leaned against the door frame and closed her eyes. She pulled the robe closer to her. "What is it?" she asked.

"Mrs. Hartley? Please open the door."

She was surprised to hear her name and she took a deep breath and patted the cream in again before she slid the bolt free and opened the door. A plainclothes officer held up a badge. There were two uniforms with him.

"It's Aiden, isn't it?" Claire asked.

"Yes," the plainclothes officer said. "I'm Marcel Golec, Youth Division. You're Mrs. Hartley?"

"Miss."

"Well, Miss Hartley, we need to talk."

"Now? It's late." Claire looked about nervously and hoped that Eric wouldn't be awakened by the intrusion. She nodded, and Golec quietly told the two uniforms to wait outside.

Claire showed him to a chair. "What is it? What's happened?"

"There's been a shooting," Golec said. Claire slumped down heavily in the chair opposite him and the shock on her face made Golec wish he'd made a more delicate opening. "A robbery," he continued, "with a handgun."

"Aiden," Claire said. She spoke the name with regret and a woe Golec could feel.

"No," he said. "A boy named Cort Lehane. Do you know him?"

"Cort? Cort is Aiden's best friend. They met at the youth centre. Cort's been shot?"

"The boy's seriously injured. Two officers stumbled on him trying to hold up a girl making a night deposit. He fired at them. There wasn't anything else they could do."

Golec watched the news begin to sink in. "Are you saying Aiden was with him? Is that it?"

"No," Golec said. "He wasn't there. But the boy claims the gun belonged to Aiden. That he'd given it to him and told him how to do the robbery."

"No."

"It's what he says, and if it checks out we have to charge Aiden with accessory, maybe conspiracy to commit."

"Conspiracy? He's fifteen," Claire said. "That's ridiculous."

"Sounds ridiculous," Golec said, "but the fact is that there's a kid in intensive care right now with a bullet hole in him, a young girl with a trauma counsellor and two officers mighty shook up about firing at a kid. Ridiculous maybe, but true nonetheless. Where is Aiden right now?"

"In his room."

"Can you check?"

"Yes."

Golec watched her walk away. She was small and pretty under the heavy splash of cold cream and he wondered about the bruises. The split lip told him all he needed to know. The outline was always the same and the story of the kids never altered much. Even sumptuous surroundings like this proved to him that all the money in the world couldn't purchase a safe home or guarantee a child's immunity from the effects of grown-up immaturity. The non sequitur irked him.

Claire walked back into the living room with a sleepy-eyed Aiden right behind her. He didn't exactly fit the image of a gangster awaiting the outcome of a heist, and Golec felt encouraged despite himself. But when Aiden saw him standing there the sleepiness was instantly replaced with a wide-awake wariness, a shifting to something he'd seen too often in the kids he dealt with.

"What's up?" Aiden asked.

"I need to talk to you about Cort Lehane," Golec said. "He's your friend, right?"

"Yeah. We know each other."

"Aiden, he's your best friend," Claire said.

Aiden gave her a hard look that Claire didn't recognize and it worried her. "Well, we hang out but I wouldn't exactly call him that," he said.

"Nonetheless, he claims you and he are tight, best buds, partners even," Golec said and watched him closely.

"Partners?" he asked. "Partners in what?"

"You tell me."

"I don't know."

"I think you do."

"I think I don't."

"Aiden, be polite," Claire said sharply.

He looked at her again and Claire felt herself pull back from the intensity and the anger in his eyes. "He's doing his job, Aiden," was all she could say.

"Guess a cop doesn't need to be polite to do his job then."

"Aiden."

"It's all right," Golec said, standing. "We can finish this conversation down at the station if you like, Aiden, because I need answers and I need them tonight."

"Are you arresting me?"

"Not yet."

"So what's the big concern? So what if I know Cort? Big deal."

"It's a big deal because Cort's been shot. Shot during the commission of an offence. A robbery, to be precise. An armed robbery. Been to many bookstores lately, Aiden?"

Golec watched his face register surprise despite his efforts to keep it calm. He was still just a kid playing a man's game and even though he'd learned some street sense somewhere in his travels, he hadn't learned enough to lift him over the fact that he was still just a kid in over his head. This was no criminal. Not yet anyway.

"Is he gonna be okay?" Aiden asked finally.

"We don't know. It's touch and go right now," Golec said. "Cort says the pistol he used was yours. He says you gave it to him and told him how to pull the robbery. He says it was your score all the way."

"My score? I was here. I was in bed."

"True enough. But if the gun was yours I've got you for accessory and conspiracy to commit a felony."

"You got nothing."

"I've got a kid caught in the act who claims you got the gun."

"He's lying."

"I'm not so sure."

"Mom?" Aiden asked, downshifting into fifteen again, and Golec watched her. "You believe me, don't you?"

"Tell Detective Golec the truth, Aiden," Claire said quietly.

"You don't believe me?" he asked.

"Tell the truth, Aiden, that's all."

"You don't believe me. You'd rather believe the cop. Well, fuck you, then."

"Aiden," Golec said sharply. "You don't speak to your mother like that."

"Who the hell are you to tell me how to talk to her? You're not my father. You're just a cop."

"I'm a cop who holds your future right here, boy," Golec said, bringing the cuffs out from behind his back.

Aiden faced him directly and cocked his head slightly, and in the stance Golec could see a future hardcase. He'd seen enough of them in his time to know. Aiden had enough of the young turk in him to not back down easily, enough to make him a candidate for a lifetime of these scenes, enough to not hear the fifteen-year-old speaking under the visage of a tougher, older man and enough to guarantee his mother one huge load of grief and guilt and shame. Golec held the look and waited.

"I got nothing to say," Aiden said.

"Fine," Golec said. "You're under arrest."

"Aiden, for god's sake, tell him!" Claire grabbed at her son. "Tell him you had no part in this. Tell him it's a tall tale. Tell him, Aiden."

The boy looked at her blankly, and Golec could see him steeling himself, pulling himself back and away like they all did, getting ready for the game to come. Claire was weeping now, and as she stepped toward her boy he retreated the same number of steps. The cream was dripping onto the collar of the robe and she made no move to dab it and Golec could see the whole visage of bruises on her face. There was another story here and he'd be sure to tell the uniforms to return to check it out. Her shoulders shook and Golec could see the collapse coming, the fall to the floor that would follow their retreat into the hallway. He wouldn't cuff him. Not in front of her now. This was enough of a shock. Aiden just stood there looking at him blankly, waiting.

"We need to go, Miss Hartley," he told her.

She looked at him, trying to comprehend it all. The cold cream was a dripping mess and the tears shone in her eyes against it so that for a moment she looked like she was melting right in front of him. Then she looked at her son. The two of them stood mere feet apart. Claire reached out one hand toward him and Aiden still would not take his eyes off Golec. Her hand shook, the fingers aching for contact, and Golec could see the miles and miles of separation that was happening invisibly between mother and son. As he put a hand on the boy's shoulder and eased him toward the door he saw the light dim in her eyes like the sweep of a lighthouse beacon turning outward and away across the solemn, empty sea. It saddened him. It always did.

the light breaking through the window and the feeling in his head seemed one and the same. Both were diffuse, and there was a sense of timelessness about it so that staring across the slope of his chest and down the line of his body to the cast on his leg and the small tent of sheet that was his other foot gave Joe Willie the feeling of emerging into a dream, the usual benchmarks of time passing lost in the cottony numbness of the drug. He was alone. He was glad of that. There was a cup of water on the table beside him and he turned his head to look at it. The morphine dried him out and he felt parched and flattened as if everything vital had been drained out of him. The water was on the swing-out table to his left and as he stared at it now he knew he'd have to reach across his body with his right arm to get it. He tried, and he almost screamed with the sudden flare of pain in his left shoulder. The water sat there and he could taste its sweetness and he gritted his teeth and made the same move again. There was a searing flame where the fullness of his shoulder used to be and the weight of him felt like something would snap like kindling, and he rocked back to the flat of his back before throwing his right arm across his chest. He knocked the cup off the table and it clattered across the floor and he almost screamed with rage. He settled on his back and stared at the light easing higher into a soft yellowish sheen against the far wall of his room. He couldn't even get himself a drink of water, and the hard fact of that made him angrier and he could feel the heat of it burning in the hollow of his chest so that when the nurse appeared he could only stare at her balefully while she retrieved the cup and filled it and held it to his lips so he could sip at it until he was satisfied. She mopped his brow with a cold, wet cloth and he closed his eyes and tried to immerse himself in the relief that brought. But when he opened them again he could see her look of concern and it enraged him again. She asked if he needed anything and he only shook his head vacantly, and she moved the table over to his right side and left the room. He felt trapped, pinioned to the bed, and his eye drifted over to the crutches they'd left him the day before.

They wanted him to move. They wanted him to make small excursions down the hallway. He almost laughed. All his life he'd been able to envision his body doing the things he asked it for beforehand, like a dream, a vision, a prophetic glimpse, so that when he swung into the motion it looked like second nature to those watching. They called him a natural, and he supposed there was some truth to that. But in the bed, staring at the crutches and being incapable of seeing himself perform the feat of humping down the hallway, however slowly, he felt nothing natural about his body at all. The crutches were symbols of how far he'd fallen, and he wanted nothing to do with them.

The sun climbed higher on the wall and he watched it, remembering how he'd loved the light of morning on the ranch. It never failed to give him a sense of melancholy so deep in the bones that he could swear purple was a feeling. He'd loved sitting on the porch in the early morning, enjoying a coffee and watching the tricks of the light as it broke over everything. It was an old light, ancient and powerful, rich with stories, and sometimes he believed it spoke to him. There was a voice in the cackle of the ravens, the wacky wobbled call of the loons, the hushed whisper of the breeze and the soft moan of cattle. It was a voice he recognized but couldn't put a name to. The Indian in him, he reckoned. The Indian in him heard all of that and it reminded him of something gone but not forgotten, something in the background of everything he knew, something relevant to everything but remaining unseen, unheard except for fleeting moments in mornings when the quiet peeled back slowly to allow it a vague undertone, a beckoning he assumed was something of the Sioux and the Ojibway spirit of things moving through all of it, himself included. He never told anyone that. It was hardly the kind of thing you could bring up in a back-lot conversation with men who were three-quarters grit and one-quarter gumption. But he'd always loved the cool edge of the air and the look of the sky in the early mornings.

This morning was different.

It was the crutches. In his mind he could picture the ride and he could pinpoint the exact moment when he lost it. He could feel the separation between the bull and the seat of his pants and he knew that one slight twist of his trunk the opposite way had caused it. One fraction of an inch to recover balance, a smidgen, a tad. That's what this boiled down to. Nothing big. No huge, looming mistake. Just a point of the shoulder the wrong way. His whole world had spun on a small twist. That's what the crutches represented.

Then there was the arm. The arm lay limp in a sling across his chest. With every ounce of strength he could summon Joe Willie could not get the arm to move. He could raise the shoulder some but the elbow wouldn't bend, and even though he could flex the hand and wrist there was no way he could raise it.

"Fucking thing," he muttered. It lay in the sling like it was boneless, rubbery, wet with weight, limp.

He closed his eyes and saw the ride. He watched it unroll like a slow-motion replay in his mind. He could feel every downward slam, every crazy, sudden elevation and every dervish of a spin in his hips, his neck, butt, thighs and back. Everywhere but the arm. He saw it then, saw the break happen, saw the bull kick out with the rear legs high and powerful, the opposite direction its shoulders were pointed, saw himself make a slight turn with his shoulders to adjust and felt the air slip under his seat like a hand, lifting him, removing him, disengaging him. Then it became a series of snapshots. He saw his legs shoot out to find the shoulders of the bull again, saw himself lean forward to try to find the pocket, saw the air slip open like a door beneath him and then the pop, the release, the spin out of the safety zone. He saw the whirl of the world then, the lights, the crowd, the scramble of the bull fighters, and felt the awful strain at the shoulder, felt it like a searing jet of flame, and he saw himself grimace mightily, face pointed toward the arena roof, mouth agape, pinioned to the bull by the suicide wrap, frozen there, and he snapped his eyes open.

He put his good hand to his mouth and leaned against the side rail of the bed, staring at the blank face of the wall and

imagining himself staring out across the pasture to the mountains in the near distance, craving that, needing it and breathing hard through his fingers. He wanted to cry, felt it build
behind his eyes, and he squeezed his fingers against his face.
Hard. He squeezed until the desire for tears went away. In its
place was the hard plain of anger. He'd left something behind
in the bull rigging that night. They'd carried him away on the
gurney and it sat there in the tangle and coil of rope and
leather calling to him. A voice, a need, the key to this emptiness he felt so completely, and it was then that he knew that all
the replays in the world would never bring it back. It had been
cut off as neatly as they'd cut the shredded remains of muscle
from his shoulder joint. He looked at the arm like an enemy.
He poked it with his finger, felt its slackness, and he set his
mouth in a hard line.

"Dead fuckin' weight," he said and reached for the water
again.

After about two hours Golec made the trip downstairs to let
him know that Cort would be okay. Aiden nodded. Golec
stood there watching him, waiting, as though Aiden would
suddenly break down in teary sorrow and relief to spill the
beans on hatching the robbery that Cort had ruined. Aiden let
him wait. He sat studying the graffiti smudged onto the wall
by burning matches and marvelled at the inventiveness.
Eventually he raised his head and looked at Golec, who leaned
against the opposite wall.

"What?" he asked.

"Just wondering how you felt about your buddy, that's
all."

"He's not my buddy, okay? Not my winger, not my partner. I just know him."

"Yeah. Right. I could forget all about opposing the bail thing, you know."

"So?" Aiden said. "You still got nothing."

"There's enough," Golec said. "And it strikes me that anyone who had nothing to hide might do himself a big favour and get everything into the clear so he could go home."

"Keep fishing," Aiden said.

"This isn't a game, Aiden. It's tough business. Here's how it'll play." Golec stepped closer to stare at him through the bars. "Cort's already given you up. There's a statement that tells all about you buying the gun, casing the store and telling Cort how the job should go down. I've seen kids like you pull a couple years when they're in this deep. That's two years, Aiden. More maybe, given the fact that a boy was shot and nearly killed."

"So?"

"So? You want to waste two years? You cough up on this and I'll speak for you myself. I know what's been going on with your mom and you."

Aiden looked steadily at Golec through the bars. The cop waited for something to break in the gaze but the kid held whatever moved in him tightly and his face retained its smooth lines, a coldness that Golec recognized all too well.

"My mom's got nothing to do with this," Aiden said.

"She better," Golec said.

"Why?"

"Because she's all you got, son. When push comes to shove, no matter how this turns out, your mother is all you're gonna have, now or after two years of time."

Aiden just looked at him again. Golec stood there for a moment, scratching at his chin, then turned and walked away. Aiden watched him go and for an instant almost broke, almost called his name. But he'd heard enough promises from men.

He'd been lied to before about how things would be better, how things were going to be different, how life would be a dream, how the man was going to make everything that happened before go away and everything that would come after better than he'd ever known. But they all just wanted to hump his mother. He was just the lever they used to jack her into the sack. Men. All the same. All of them. Whatever happened to him he wouldn't turn out like any of them. He watched Golec leave, watched the steel door at the end of the corridor slide heavily shut and heard the firm, unflinching click of it locking behind him. He pursed his lips. He'd push through this himself. Golec was wrong. He didn't need anyone. He was the only one he could trust. Cort had proven that. He was the only one solid enough to get him through it. He'd prove it. He'd say nothing. He'd take whatever came his way and he'd walk through it. But he wouldn't break. Not to a man, not to anyone. The resolve settled in him with a firm, unflinching click.

"I have to get out of here," he said.

"What's that?" his grandmother asked.

"I can't be here."

She studied him for a long time, and he let her look right into him. When he was small it was her he'd always run to for the explanation of things. He'd never known why. She was simply the one who seemed to be the bearer of knowledge, and even though he trusted both his parents and his grandfather implicitly, the old woman was the one he went to when the world begged clarity. Now he could feel her measure him, and the level way she regarded him told him that she saw beyond the cast and bandages and the sickly austerity of the hospital room. He held her look. After a time she nodded and raised the glass to his lips, and he sipped at it while she brushed his hair back with the other hand.

"The land," she said.

"Yeah."

"Sight more useful to the eyes than here."

"A sight," he said.

"You won't have the nurses running at your beck and call."

"Don't beck and call 'em now."

"Doctors won't be around."

"They're never around now."

She offered a small grin. "What if there's something you need that me or anyone can't get for you?"

"I'll get it."

"How?"

"I'll get it."

She brushed his hair a final time and then went to the window to look out across the skyline of the city. There was desert there and mountains and somewhere off to the far western edge of them an ocean, and beyond that another vast stretch of territory she'd never visited. She let herself imagine how it all looked from space and she understood completely how he felt, like a planet impaled against a huge blackness, the light of it dependent on a distant sun that blazed unceasingly. She would be that sun. She turned back to him, and when he looked at her she nodded solemnly and he watched her gather her things together.

"I'll see to it," she said.

He humped his shoulder to find a comfortable position and let himself sink deeper into the mattress, and then sleep arrived without the help of the drug and he drifted off into space.

The shower took some of the sting away. Claire let the hot water run over her body and felt it soothe her bruises. When she was finished she patted herself dry and made her way to the kitchen and helped herself to some of Eric's scotch. She wanted the warmth of it. The beating had left her cold, and even the shower had failed to provide enough heat to chase the shiver she felt in her belly and along the inside of her legs. Damn. She ached, but the scotch left a trickle of fire that ran down her throat and into her belly, and she began to feel more pliant. She stepped out onto the patio and lit a cigarette and stared around at the houses that surrounded her. For the most part they were big two-storey homes with the same small swatch of grass in back that held a patio and a storage shed and the array of kids' bikes and toys and clutter. There were families here. Inside these houses were lives that moved, swung between varied rhythms, separated and came together again like a musical theme, and she wondered how they ever held it together long enough to make a history. At times like this she felt like she had a gene missing, a vital chromosome that held the stuff of family and home and security. She'd mutated into something and someone that didn't fit the parameters of a regulated life.

As she smoked she envisioned all the places she'd moved through, the buildings she'd called home at one time or another, and the line went far back into her memory, into her girlhood, and she began to sense an idleness, a detachment of sorts that had never allowed her to set her feet down anywhere, feel them sink into the ground and take root. When she became a woman she was fourteen and her body had raced far ahead of her emotions. Even grown men were attracted to her, and she felt the first tingle of power that comes from a body both buxom and petite, the swells and curves of it mysterious and alluring even to her. She ran a hand along her side from the push of her breast at her ribs down the swoop of her waist and outward along the wide plain of her hips and stopped at the firm, rounded ground of her buttocks. She'd always been proud of her body, but now it felt as though it had failed her. By virtue of its very lushness it had denied her entry into the vague world of the homes that sat around her in the darkness. Men had promised. Men had undergone the process of buying them for her. Men had even abandoned homes in order to attempt to rebuild one with her.

But there was a gene missing, and the mitosis necessary for growth into a home, a family, a history had never had a chance to begin. Instead, it felt as though she wandered to and fro mindlessly, almost like a guest in her own life, hoping someone somewhere would explain it all for her, guide her, show her the next careful plant of her foot. But no one ever had, and she'd become this beaten woman, incapable of deciding whether to stay and suffer the abuse or cut her own path and leave. She felt the absence of that gene like an old pain.

When the phone rang she startled. She was quick to run back into the kitchen and grab it before it rang again and had a chance to wake Eric.

"Miss Hartley?"

"Yes."

"Detective Golec."

"Yes?"

"We have a hearing in front of a magistrate in one hour."

"One hour? That quickly?"

"Yes, I pushed it."

"Okay. I'll be there."

"Good. Miss Hartley?"

"Yes?"

"Is there anything else you want to talk to me about?"

Claire stared at her reflection in the glass of the French doors. She couldn't see the bruises, only the outline of herself, only the shape of her body and only the memory of what that body had been through all her life. She ran a hand down her side again and breathed deeply. Her son needed her now and she would be there. That was all that mattered. She saw the keys to Eric's Cadillac on the counter and a thick roll of bills he'd forgotten in his passion.

"Miss Hartley?"

She pressed her lips tight together and and reached out to grab the keys and the money and then answered Golec as deliberately as she remembered doing anything. "Yes, Detective," she said. "There is something I want to talk to you about."

"Good," Golec said. "I'll see you in an hour."

"You will," she said and hung up the phone.

"He's better off at the ranch."

The others just looked at her, waiting, it seemed, for her to flesh out the comment. But when she stood there saying nothing more they exchanged glances and rustled about some.

"Tough getting help for him," Birch said. "Small town and all."

"It just takes money. I figure we got enough of that," Lionel said and removed his hat to sit.

"He can have the spare room on the main floor so there's no stairs, but if you ask me, he won't like it," Johanna said. "He'll take it. At least until it angers him enough to make the moves himself."

"He's a cowboy," Birch said.

They all looked at him and he arched an eyebrow in return and the words hung there between them.

"Did he ask for this?" Johanna asked.

Birch looked at her, surprised. "Does it matter?"

"Yes, it matters," she said, and Birch folded his arms across his chest and leaned on the wall to await her explanation.

"If he asked for it, it means he's yearning. Missing something. Feeling a gap he doesn't know how to fill, and that might not sound like a lot to any of you but it's a whole lot to me," she said.

"How so?" Lionel asked her.

"Because he feels," she said. "He hasn't shut down everything. The anger in him hasn't blackened everything. There's a powerful lot of anger in my son right now and that frightens me because I'm not sure I know how to deal with it, but the yearning tells me that there's more in him than rage. I'll take a little sorrow and melancholy right now. I'll take a heap of woe over nothing now."

"Home's best," Lionel said.

"Where it all come together," Birch said.

"It's the land more than anything." Victoria sat beside Lionel and took his hand. "It's constant. It sits there and remains, and despite all the things we might ever do to it, it stays the same, always feels the same on your feet, the wind always a little sharper in the lungs, the smell of it richer and older than anything you ever smelled. Constant. Always makes coming back to it special."

"Because it's regular," Lionel said.

"That and we all need a place we can come back to."

"He needs it to fill that gap you're talking about," Birch said.

"For now," Johanna said. "It'll do some for now. The rest he'll have to fill on his own when he's ready."

"Or when we help him get ready," Victoria said, and they all stared at her and the words hung there between them again. The ebb and flow of the hospital passed about them and they sat together on a short line of chairs and watched it happen. Eventually they came back into themselves and looked at each other, each wondering what the next move should be or who should tend to it.

"I'll see to it," Victoria said.

Johanna rose with her and the two women walked away toward the nursing station. Birch and Lionel watched them go, then turned and looked at each other. Birch grinned at his father and patted the chest pocket of his jacket.

"Guess we might as well smoke," he said.

"Guess," Lionel said, and they rose and walked together toward the smoking area.

Bail denied. Claire couldn't believe her ears. Two words that shocked her so terribly that when she stood in protest her legs wobbled beneath her and she had to lean on the bench seat in front of her for support. Golec turned and looked at her, a profound sorrow on his face. He shrugged, held his hands out at arm's length with fingers splayed, and Claire felt a hot wave of resentment wash over her. The judge had sat passively through the proceedings, staring at the papers in front of him so distractedly that Claire doubted whether he'd even heard what had been presented to him. Golec hadn't pressed, hadn't said anything above a quiet, polite timbre in order to snare his attention. Now, judgment passed, the judge stared at his desk in the same disaffected way.

The bailiffs came and stood on either side of Aiden. The boy looked at her and she saw how small he was, how much a little boy he was, and despite the pinched-lip gaze he levelled at her, she could see a small tremor in him. Aiden just looked at her, then turned when the bailiffs touched his elbows and walked out of the courtroom between them. Claire closed her eyes, dropped her head and leaned hard on the seat back, hands shaking and hot tears flowing down her face. She gasped for breath and sat down hard. She cried openly. Soon, she felt a soft hand on her shoulder, a hand that pulled her close and held her, and when she opened her eyes Marcel Golec was looking at her. She pulled away.

"Come with me," he said and led her out of the court-room.

He didn't try to speak to her, didn't try to offer any words of consolation or attempt to cover up for himself, and as Claire followed the broad back of him through the courthouse, she appreciated that. There weren't any words adequate to cover the feelings running through her, and Golec was astute enough to know that, sensitive enough to leave her with her thoughts. They stood silently in the elevator and the only time he spoke to her was when they arrived at the reception area for the cells. "I'll bring him," he said.

Aiden looked small against the steel and concrete. He tried to walk as tall as he could, but Claire could see the shrinking that the circumstances effected in him. His eyes were hardened and blank, but she could sense the fright he walked in.

"Are you okay?" she asked.

"I'm all right," he said stonily, casting a look at Golec. The policeman moved out of earshot.

"What can I do?" she asked.

"Nothing."

"Are you sure?"

"Yeah."

"Aiden?"

"What?"

"I'm sorry."

"For what? You didn't do anything," he said, shifting his feet.

"I feel like I did."

"Yeah, well, you didn't."

"Did you?" Claire asked, and he gave her that hard look. She stepped closer to him and he allowed her to put her hands on his shoulders. "Because if you tell me that you didn't, I'll fight for you. I'll stand beside you and do whatever it is that needs to be done to get us past this mess."

"And if I did it?" he asked.

Claire eased him to her and felt his stiff resistance. She held him. She closed her eyes and felt the warmth of him. "Then I'll still fight for you. I'll still stand beside you and we'll get through this together. No matter what it takes. You just need to tell me either way."

Claire smelled the cellblock on him. It was in his hair and on his clothing, and she remembered how he'd smelled as an infant, that rich, ancient, almost burnt-dust smell, and as she heaved a deep breath she could still catch a shimmer of it rising upward through the dankness of the cellblock that clung to him. He was all she really had. All she'd ever really had. The only thing in the entire world that was irrevocably her own and she'd love him forever. When he raised his head, put his lips to her ear and whispered, "I did it," Claire felt her heart breaking. But she held him tight nonetheless.

Max Foley had encountered numerous stubborn, resistant forces in his medical career but none as perplexing as the combined assault of Victoria and Johanna Wolfchild. The women impressed him with their fortitude, and Foley was convinced they would have made excellent trauma unit nurses. They brooked no argument once a decision had been reached and they were committed as hell to the good of their patient. Joe Willie was going to require a lot of attention in the initial phase of his recovery, and despite Foley's protests the women assured him they could manage the work.

"We've picked that boy up after a lot of falls, Doctor," Victoria said. "We've got a practised hand at it by now."

"This isn't some schoolyard scrape," Foley said.

"No. It's not," Johanna said. "But when you're a mother you learn how to mother the fear that falling down and bleeding brings. Can you do that, Doctor? Are you that kind of specialist?"

Foley tried his best steely-eyed gaze, but the iron in Johanna's eyes was too stern and he looked away. He removed his glasses and polished them with the corner of his lab coat. "No," he said. "I've never trained in that kind of healing."

"Shame," Victoria said quietly. "It's likely the commonest disease around here."

"Fear," Foley said. "You have a cure for that? You'd be millionaires if you could bottle it."

Victoria laughed softly and reached out to place a hand on Foley's elbow. "No," she said, "there's no cure. It's one of those chronic conditions and the best you can do is learn how to live with it. Family is the best antidote, as far as I know. Joe Willie's better taking what we have to give in the long haul."

"Like I said, it's a lot to take on."

"That's why we'd like you to recommend a home care person," Johanna said. "Someone who can show him what to do to get himself around, how to get stronger, how to cope with the physical recovery."

"It'll cost you."

"It already has."

"He won't be receptive to it."

"He's not receptive to much."

"He'll resist it. I think you know that."

The look Johanna gave him made Foley feel ten years old and in it he could feel the staunch force of her motherhood. He knew it was the look Joe Willie had grown up in the light of, and Foley knew in that instant that hers was a medicine he had no hope of duplicating and he allowed himself a small measure of envy for the young cowboy. Foley put a hand to his face and rubbed his jaw contemplatively. Finally they crossed their arms and leaned against the wall and exchanged a private look, and in that moment Foley saw the scope of the territory the Wolfchild family had sprung from. What he knew of doctoring paled in the face of it.

"All right," he said, "but I'll want to be kept informed and you'll have to provide him with a physiotherapist for at least the next six months. I have one I can recommend. She's a tad flighty sometimes but she knows her stuff. You'll have to helicopter him home. Can you afford that?"

They looked at him wordlessly. Foley nodded and headed down the hallway to make arrangements.

The way Marcel Golec figured, it was all about concentration. He'd been a detective on the youth squad for a few years now and he'd about seen everything. The thing was, kids these days never learned how to concentrate, how to focus their attention on one thing for more than a couple minutes. Their music came at them in three-minute bursts. The movies they loved never stretched a scene beyond the same three-minute time frame. Hell, getting a kid to sit and read for an hour would take a court order most times, and except for computer time, the chat lines, action games, endless surfing and noodling about they did, they couldn't commit any time to anything. It wasn't their fault. No one took the time to show them the wonder of things anymore. Like music. Golec's kids went to the symphony with him and the missus every week. Their attention spans were incredible for their age. They could sit and listen to an entire symphony, and it showed in their appreciation of music in general. Sure, they still listened to the crap that was everywhere, but mixed in with the rap and hip-hop CDs were healthy dollops of Brahms, Dvořák and Elgar. They got scope that way, a way to measure, a means to compare, evaluate and choose. It seemed to Golec that most parents neglected their kids' attention spans far too frequently and the result was a reduced ability to choose. Hence the peer pressure bullshit, and hence kids like this Aiden Hartley sitting in his lock-up.

Golec had talked to him briefly when they brought him over from the courthouse. He hadn't said much, but what he had said he'd offered distantly but politely. No swagger. No gangbanger attitude. Just a kid who knew how to keep his mouth shut, and move quietly, resolutely. That was the word. This kid had steel in his spine. No need to act out to try to prove anything through display. Instead, he measured everything, calculated, reacted according to available information, and despite himself, Golec admired that. Those qualities were what good men were cut from. On the other hand they were also what created good criminals.

"What kinda tunes you into?" Golec had asked.

The kid looked at him. "Cole Porter," he said. "He rocks."

Now he just sat staring at the wall, waiting. It was all about the waiting. Before he moved to youth crime Golec had been in major crimes. He'd seen a lot of hard-asses and he knew that the difference between a solid crook and those who could be broken was how they handled the waiting. Some paced. Some rattled the bars. Some gathered allies from the others in the bullpen. But the sure ones, the toughest ones, just sat there, waiting, calm, patient as a viper. This kid had the makings of a viper. Sad too, because Golec discerned a brooding intelligence in the kid, some as yet unsponsored push that showed in the level way he looked at you.

"Hungry?" he asked.

"Is this the buddy-buddy part?"

"Nah. Wouldn't trouble you with it. Solid guy like you."

The kid brightened at the word. "Yeah," he said. "I could eat. Any Coke?"

"In the can, right?"

"All right."

"You'll settle, right?"

"Yeah. I'll settle."

"You know that other shit'll eat your brain," Golec said.

"Nah. It's food for thought."

"Cute," Golec said. "This an example of your best thinking? This five-star accommodation?"

The kid looked at him levelly again and Golec felt him pull away. "Can's fine. Maybe a sandwich."

"Gotcha," Golec said, giving him a thumbs-up. "Tuna okay?"

"Yeah. Thanks."

"You know, they'll move you pretty soon. Normally we like to get remanded inmates out to the juvenile lock-up right away. Your mom wants to know what you want her to bring you. You can call her if you like."

"No," he said flatly and looked away.

"No what?" Golec asked.

"No I don't need anything. No I don't want to call her."

"She could use it."

He looked up then and Golec saw the hardness in him. He'd seen it too often. Young men, all jut and edges and angles as their bodies filled out, lean with that elastic kid sort of energy, and it all faded when they stood here, all got transformed into something foreign and different as though they adopted the composure of the steel and the obdurate concrete and the dull flat of the paint around them. It aged them suddenly. It made them horrible caricatures of the men most of them would become. Aiden got up and walked slowly to the far wall and slapped a palm hard against the concrete before he turned and walked back to Golec. It was a practised walk. There was something in it that spoke of effort, and even though it was a good job of mimicry Golec understood that there was something other than the future gangster in the kid, something more than this story told. Aiden walked right up to the bars and looked at him.

"Don't wanna see her," he said.

"Excuse me?"

"I said I don't want to see her. Not in here. Not anymore. Not until it's over."

"That could be two years, kid."

"Don't call me kid."

"Sorry. Son."

Aiden almost sneered at the word, and Golec sensed a steeped and nurtured anger and the flicker of hope he held was nearly quashed under its weight.

"Don't call me that either," Aiden said.

"All right, Aiden," Golec said, and the two of them stood and looked at each other. "Your mom could use the call. That's all I meant to say."

"You make it."

"And tell her what?"

"Tell her I don't want to see her. That's it. That's all."

"That's pretty hard stuff. Mind if I ask why?"

Aiden bent his head down and moved the toe of his shoe around in a small circle, and Golec could see the kid in him then, and when he pursed his lips together and looked up at him again Golec could see the effort the hard line he was drawing cost him. "Easier this way," he said. "Better. She don't need to see me there."

"You don't need to be ashamed, Aiden. Lots of kids make mistakes. It doesn't have to be the end of the road if you can learn from it."

"Don't call me kid," he said, and the venom in his voice surprised Golec with its suddenness. "I'm not a kid. You figure I'm man enough to plan a score. You got me in here when you don't even know. But you figure I could. You figure I'm big enough, old enough for that. So don't call me a kid and don't tell me about my mother." He took a step away and then half turned, looking away down the long corridor of the cellblock. "She don't need this," he said.

"That your last word?"

He walked to the concrete ledge that served as a seat around the perimeter of the cell, sat and folded his hands and leaned forward with his elbows on his knees and stared at the floor. Golec watched him for a moment, then walked out of the range. He went to the security office and punched up the camera in Aiden's cell. The kid was sitting in the same position, and as Golec watched he never made another move, not for the longest time, and when he did it was to lace his fingers together and push his arms slowly above his head and twist his trunk at the waist one way and then the other before dropping his arms to his side and slowly bringing his hands clenched into fists together in front of his chest, pressing them hard into each other. There was a scowl on his face, deep and hard and bitter, and the grained texture of the video gave him the visage of a much older, much more hardened man. Then he cradled his hands in his lap, breathed deep and sat and waited. Patiently as a viper. Golec felt himself shiver.

It didn't surprise him. There was a consistency to his family that he'd leaned on his entire life, and when they came to announce that they would take him home and care for him he only nodded. There was an ache in him that lay beyond the throbbing shoulder and the dull pain in his leg. It was like a voice that hailed him, and the Indian in him recognized it as the call of the land, and the yearning felt miraculous and displacing as a lost thing that suddenly appears at your feet, stunning in the remembrance of its properties. Through the morphine he felt the chopper lift off, and the sensation of defying gravity, of being pushed upward, reminded him of the bull, and he clenched his teeth and squeezed the rail of the gurney hard with his good hand. As the chopper began its level flight he let himself imagine himself as an eagle soaring across the landscape, and the drug let him envision the changes in the land, and in his mind he saw the buildings relent to the flow of open territories so that eventually he calmed and the drug took him.

As they transferred him to an ambulance he turned his head and he could see townspeople watching and a few waved to him. He kept his eyes on them and he could see them shake their heads and rub their jaws, their lips pursed and a look of sadness on their faces. Beside him his mother walked purposefully, her head up, and the wind blew her long, straight hair around so that she assumed the look of a chieftain returning with her wounded. She took a lot of the looks away and he was grateful for that. He'd always been awed by his mother as others were, but he knew the strength of her, the grit of her, the sand that gave her beauty power, and he'd always wondered at its depth. Now, she walked proudly, determined to show her ability to transcend even this, and he craved a sliver of that staunch fortitude. She smiled at him when they slid him up into the ambulance.

"See you there," she said.

"Yeah."

"Welcome home."

"Not there yet."

"You will be."

Joe Willie got the feeling there was more to her words.

Once they'd arrived, he was introduced to Cheryl, his new physiotherapist, and they settled him into the spare room at the back of the main floor. From there he could see the hump of the mountains above the pastureland, the hazy grey-blue of them like a bruise he felt in the middle of him. He ached to ride them, to feel the balm and salve of their chill winds, the juniper, sage and pine sharp in his nose, and the trees in their thickness closing off the world behind his back, sealing him and the horse into a private chamber where only languid thought and a loose, ground-eating walk existed, carrying them deeper, higher, farther away from anything less. He craved it like a drug and he slapped a hand on the mattress, feeling the familiar air of home around him and angered at the immobility that bound him away from it.

When they left him he focused on the door frame, stared at it hard. Beyond it his focus was drowned in the opaque shadow of the hallway. The world, his room, ended there, and his world, the one he'd known forever, lay just beyond it, and he felt the imprisoning power of that shadow, felt taunted by it, and he closed his eyes and tried to push it down.

And saw the bear.

It rolled its head toward him from the edge of the pasture beyond his window. In the hard black pebbles of its eyes he felt drawn, called beyond the bed and the room. The bear ambled forward a few steps, the roll of its shoulders accentuating its strength, then it turned and looked at him again. He looked straight into the eyes. He felt known then, understood, and when the bear walked away toward the mountains he wanted to call to it, hail it, bring it closer to him one more time. But it walked on, and eventually the hard black dot of it melted into the trees at the foot of the climb and disappeared.

The crutches lay canted on an angle at the foot of the bed. He hooked one with his good foot and dragged it to him slowly, deliberately, until he could reach over and grab it with his right hand. He hefted it. The aluminum was cool to the touch, the lightness of it seemingly improbable for the chore he would ask it to perform. He closed his eyes like he always did when he asked his body for something, saw himself turn on his left hip, lift the bad leg with his right arm and spin slowly to the edge of the bed, drape his legs over the edge and ease the crutch under his right arm and push himself upward, taking all the weight on his left leg until he could right himself and try to move. He saw himself do it and when he opened his eyes he made it happen.

They didn't even look surprised when he humped into the kitchen doorway and stood looking at them with eyes afire in triumph.

Golec watched her face change. She'd agreed to meet him at a small café near the courthouse, and when she'd entered she'd looked purposeful, intent, and the set of her face gave it a harder, more beautiful line. But when he told her what the boy had said he watched that line alter. Led by the eyes the plane of it fell slowly, spiralling into something close to defeat but more akin to a deep and immovable sadness. She laced her fingers around her coffee cup and raised it, averting her eyes, fixing them on the tiny case of plastic flowers at the table's edge. She sipped slowly and her throat worked hard getting the fluid down past the welling of tears he knew was there. But she set the cup down gently in the saucer. She brought her hands down to her lap and looked at him, waiting.

"It's not strange to me," he said. "I've seen it before. Guys don't want their mothers anywhere near a jail. Protecting them, I guess."

"How can you reject and protect at the same time?"

"I don't know," he said. "All I know is, there's a lot going on inside them. Inside him. Maybe it's about shame. Maybe it's about anger, blame even. I don't know. But it's not uncommon for a guy once he's down to want to cut himself off from everything that's familiar and represents freedom. Never seen it in a young guy. Not a kid."

"He's not a kid," she said.

"Strange you should say so. It's exactly what he told me."

She looked at him and he could feel her reaching, down past the hurt, the rejection, the confusion and the shame into truth, and the effort of it gave the stoic edge back to her features. When she began to talk her voice was controlled and measured.

"He never had a father. Not really. He's had to grow up on his own for the most part. The men I was with never seemed to want to have much to do with him, and we moved around a lot." She took a sip of coffee. "It's never happened before. This," she said and touched her face.

"Never?"

"No," she said. "I wouldn't have allowed it."

"What's different now?"

She put her tongue against the inside of her cheek but the pain of the bruise made her wince. She put a hand to it and sat there a moment looking down at the table. "I don't know," she said. "Maybe I was just too tired. Maybe I held out too much hope that this one would be the *one*, you know. The one where all the little-girl dreams come true. The one where Aiden and I get to live the kind of life I thought we always deserved. But I don't know. I never thought I'd be in this position."

"Of what?" he asked.

"Of not having anything else to lose."

He drained the coffee in his cup. Then he sat back in his chair, scratching at the back of his head and looking out the window. Claire sat quietly while he thought.

"I have this friend of mine," he said. "He says that old-time Indians used to routinely give away everything they had in order to take on a new direction. He had an Indian word for it that I can't pronounce but it comes down to being disencumbered. According to him it freed you, allowed you to meet the world again square on, like how you got here, he said. And the act of it, the giving away of what everyone else regarded as important, returned you to the humility you were born in. That's how he said it. And that state, the state of being humble, was a spiritual thing, a powerful spiritual thing that made the new journey stronger, made you stronger."

"I'm not an Indian, Detective."

"Marcel," he said.

She looked at him and her eyes were clear of tears. She was luminous. He knew that a lot of men would gladly get themselves into a lot of trouble for a woman like her.

"I'm not an Indian, Marcel," she said.

"No," he said. "But you are humble."

"I am that," she said.

"So what do you want to do?"

"About Aiden?"

"That too."

She slid the cup back and forth in her saucer, then raised it to her lips and finished it in one long gulp.

"I don't understand a lot of things right now, Marcel. I don't understand how this could have happened to my son. I thought I was doing the best I could for him, for us, for everything. I don't understand how this could have happened to me. How I could be beaten like this, how I could have allowed it. I don't understand what Aiden is going through, what he feels for me, for life, for anything. I just don't understand. But you know what?"

"What?" he asked softly.

"I will."

"I believe you. Where do you want to start?"

"Eric."

"The guy."

"Yes."

"Well, the clearest way to go is, we pick him up for domestic assault, you get a judge's order that he doesn't live at home and can't go near the place actually. That gives you time to get something together for you and the boy and ride out the process."

She shook her head. "I know what that outcome is. A high-priced lawyer gets him a conditional sentence, probation even, and I'm on the street with nothing and still waiting for resolution."

"What, then? What's resolution to you?" Golec asked.

"Terror," she said.

"Terror? What do you mean?"

"I mean, it's terrifying to be the brunt of a beating from a man over twice your size. It's terrifying to have to lay there not knowing if he has enough control to stop himself, to pull the anger back, to wonder if you'll survive. It's terrifying to see your own blood sprayed across your furniture and to think that your son might have to come home and find your broken body. It's terrifying to not have an ounce of control. He needs a taste of that. He really needs a good fucking taste of that."

"And how do you propose to do that? Legally?"

"Rape."

"Rape?"

"Yes. He's been raping me for a while now. Taking me whenever he wanted. However he wanted. Forcing me to do things I didn't want to do but did anyway because I needed to keep things together for my boy." She looked at Golec, and there was a blaze in her eyes that was extinguished quickly and she averted her eyes and touched her face with the tips of her fingers.

"Hard to win in court."

"I don't have to win," she said, leaning forward in her chair. "He just needs to think I want to and that I'll do every possible thing in order to achieve it."

"Pardon me?" Golec asked.

"He just needs to think that I would charge him with the rape and the assault and bring his little kingdom to the ground. Publicity. Screaming headlines about the big rich white businessman and the poor black single mother. He needs to feel his reputation shredding, his image fading, his power leaving him, his business life and his money beginning to fall through his fingers. He just needs to think it's all at risk now, that because of what happened I have control of it, that I can take it all away."

Golec looked at her. "The threat of charges? How is that going to help?"

"I want out, Marcel. I want away. That's all I want. He'll pay me what I want to keep his face out of the papers and his ass out of court."

"What do you want, then? What's enough for this?"

"I want the car I drove down here in and I want ten thousand dollars to start my life over," she said simply.

"That's it?"

"That's enough."

"Really?"

"Yes. With the car I can get around to job interviews or training. The money will get us a nice place when I find work. Carry us for a while."

"That's all you want out of this. A fresh start."

"That's more than enough."

"Most people wouldn't think so."

"Most people haven't lived my life, Detective."

She'd said it so directly that Golec felt no need to press for details. He simply looked at her and saw the set of her. She sat there upright, focused, her hands folded on the table, and even with the effect of the beating there was a solemn regality to her. The discoloration lent her eyes depth, and the swell of her jawline accentuated its determined jut. This was no slouching, beaten woman bent by shame and humiliation. This woman was angry, but it wasn't an anger steeped in vitriol or a distorted need for vengeance. It was a quiet, determined, focused fury. She'd get what she wanted and she'd make it work for her. He saw that. He understood where the kid had come by his resolve.

"Okay," he told her. "We'll give it a shake and see what falls."

The pain under his left shoulder was too much. She showed him how to move around the house with one crutch, how to hitch-step, putting the weight forward firmly on the good left leg before swinging the crutch and his right leg up and ahead of it. It took some doing, but she was a good physiotherapist and a good teacher and he soon got the rhythm of it. Joe Willie resented being shown. She knew that, could read him, was used to the anger and resentment patients felt on the first steps of their recoveries. They didn't speak to each other beyond the necessary talk, and when she left him sitting on the edge of his bed he offered no parting words of appreciation. He just sat there staring into the mirror at himself.

Once he was sure she was gone he began to practise. He leaned the crutch against the wall and lay back on the bed, gathering himself, and then recreated the sliding move he'd done the first time and reached out to grab the crutch when he'd returned to the sitting position again. Then he placed it in his right armpit and pushed himself up with his good left leg. He did it over and over until he could feel the move become familiar, and when he'd done it the last time he swivelled on his crutch, wobbling some with the turn, and faced himself in the mirror. He hated how he looked. He hated the crutch stuck under his arm and the invalid look it gave him. The arm hung draped in a sling across his chest, and the thin lump of it looked like the bones of a bird's wing. It was ugly. *He* was ugly. He met his own eyes in the glass and he stared at himself, stared as deeply as he could and felt rage pooling in the depths of his chest, and he broke the look and sat down on the bed again. He clenched and unclenched his right fist and pounded it against the mattress. Then he stopped. He heaved a great breath and pushed himself up again and practised moving around the room, from the window to the dresser to the door. He did it again and again and again until the fatigue hit his muscles like a stick on the taut skin of a drum and the resonance made him stop.

He turned and looked at himself in the mirror again. His eyes were hard black pebbles like the bear's, and he grinned.

No one spoke to him at all. Aiden walked down the long line of the cellblock and felt the weight of the stares. Boys walked up to the bars to gaze at him or stopped the card games they were dealing at the green metal tables and there wasn't a word. It was noisy in other ranges, and the silence that hung over the corridor as he walked was heavy. But he kept his head up and his eyes straight ahead of him at the officer's back, making sure not to waver, not to trip or attract any unnecessary attention to himself. When he was shown to his cell he was glad of the slam of the steel closing behind him.

Only when the door closed did the level of sound outside his cell rise to drown out the noise of the neighbouring ranges. It was wild. He'd never heard anything like it. Shouting, swearing, catcalls, taunts and threats snapped across the air and filled it, so that the only place of quiet he could find was within himself. He crossed to the small metal sink-and-toilet combination in the corner, wet his face and looked at himself in the scratched and clouded polished plastic that served as a mirror. He stared into his own eyes. They were hard and black as pebbles and he practised making them flat, unreadable, cold, and the feeling that rose in his chest was hot and bitter and he found himself liking it, craving it. He practised raising his face to the mirror and letting his eyes go blank. He did it again and again, and when he was satisfied that he could do it on command he began to move around the tiny cell.

He took the lower of the two bunks. As he made it up he watched the boys cruising past his door out the side of his eyes. The population was like the neighbourhood he'd come from, a loose conglomeration of races, sizes and attitudes. The gangs would be here. That would make it tough. But when he finished making up his bunk and stood in the doorway watching, he knew he would cut it. He'd been in a lot of tough neighbourhoods and survived and he'd survive here. He felt the heat of the rage in his chest and it warmed him against the cool of the steel and the concrete and the empty gazes of the boys passing his door.

They came for him in the shower.

The water felt good after the long day of transfer. He closed his eyes and felt the water course over him, leaning one hand against the tiles and breathing deeply in the steam. He heard the splash of their feet and opened his eyes.

"Hey boy."

There were five of them. Black. They stood there with towels wrapped around their waists, leaning against the wall and looking at him balefully.

"You got smokes?" the largest one asked.

"Some," Aiden said.

"We'll be wanting them," he said.

"I can cut you in if you want."

"I don't think he heard you, Julius," another boy said.

The boy Julius looked along the line at his friends, bobbing his head in agreement. "P'haps we got to help him learn to hear," he said. "We'll be wanting them smokes. Boy. Any cutting in goes down around here gonna be a shiv in your ass."

"Café au lait lookin' motherfucker gonna cough up," another boy said, and they all laughed.

Aiden moved out from under the nozzle of the shower and into the middle of the floor, and the five of them side-stepped wider apart and they all stood in the steam and the hiss of the water on the tiles looking at each other. They were all lean and muscular and tattooed, and the steam rising around them gave the room the look of a jungle. Aiden wiped water from his forehead and shook his hand lightly to splatter it around. He looked directly at the big boy Julius and made his eyes go blank like he'd done in the mirror.

"Don't be giving me no jailhouse eyes," Julius said. "You got no wingers here, boy. You all alone here. You got no backup. You best come up with them smokes."

"And if I don't?"

"Then we got to beat on you till you do."

"And then?"

"Then we beat on you some more so's you keep the supply rollin' every time the moms drops off some coin."

"Bring it, then," Aiden said.

"Say what?"

Aiden felt the heat rising in him. It felt good. It roared in him and he wanted to run with it despite the danger. None of them was carrying a knife. This was going to be a beating and he was ready for it, looking forward to letting some of the heat in him dissipate in a flurry of violence. He wasn't afraid.

"I said bring it, then. If that's what's going to happen, let's get it done. Don't treat me like a goof. Just fucking do it. I'm going down but I'm making sure I take the first one with me."

"You fucking kidding me?" Julius said.

"Bring it," Aiden said again.

Julius laughed and looked at his friends. "This guy's got some balls."

"Yeah, but they shrinking," another said and they laughed.

"We gonna beat on you, nigger," Julius said. "Don't you hear that?"

"I hear it."

"You ain't worried?"

"Bring it, I said."

Aiden clenched his fists and moved back against the wall again so they could only come at him from the front. He looked directly at Julius and his eyes stayed flat and cold. The bigger boy studied him and Aiden sensed a shift in the energy. Julius smiled. He smiled and shook his head and looked at the other four and they all began to relax. Aiden kept his eyes on them nonetheless.

"Damn," Julius said. "That's some balls. You all right, kid."

"Don't call me kid."

"All right, all right. Don't get your panties all in a bunch. You all right though."

"So?" Aiden asked.

"So? So cover up them little raisins before they disappear up your belly," Julius said, and they all laughed. He raised a hand to the others and they all followed him to the shower-room door. He stopped and looked back at Aiden.

"We got room for a guy like you," he said, "if you need friends."

"I'll think about it," Aiden said.

"You do that."

"Julius?"

"Yeah?"

"Drop by my crib. I got some smokes you can have if you're short."

Julius grinned. "I ain't short," he said. "But I'll drop by."

Aiden could see the flatness in the other boy's eyes, an unwavering stare that spoke of tougher streets and harder encounters than this in a life that ranged further into darkness than he had ever travelled. He thought about Cort Lehane and the fat prick hitting his mother and he matched it and held it and Julius nodded after a moment and threw him a towel.

"Best cover those," he said. "You'll need them around here."

When Aiden walked back down the corridor to his cell the silent challenges from the doorways and the tables had stopped. He stepped into his cell and pulled the door shut behind him, threw the towel down in a lump on the floor and settled on his bunk and stared at a crack in the ceiling. It was deep and took him far away.

The thing about cowboys, Darlene had discovered, was that they were all pretty much the same guy. Once you got past the buckles and the blue jeans, the high-flying attitude and the down-home, folksy charm, they were all still little boys riding the rope barrel in the back yard. Dreamers. Not one of them could live a day in the real world without dreaming about the Big One, the big show, the big ride, the big payout, the big something that was going to make everything, well, bigger somehow. She'd seen them all. They'd amble into her parents' café all bowlegged and casual, slump into a chair, tuck their hats underneath it and watch her work, heads tilted, eyes aglitter and just a touch of a smirk at the corner of their mouth. They'd give her the "yes, ma'ams" and "thank yous" their mamas had raised them to say, but she always felt their appraisal. It was like being the filly in the paddock.

She'd discovered soon enough that they were a randy bunch. They certainly knew how to ride and she liked that.

She liked the sinewy toughness of them, the bandy-legged energy they brought to a bed, and she'd believed that she could just go on picking and choosing. But only the real cowboys. Nowadays kids from middle-class homes in big cities could get a college scholarship in bull riding. Kids who had never set foot on a ranch or a stirrup. Not them. Just cowboys, the ones from real working ranches. Cowboys had a thing about them. Cowboys were strong, resilient, hard and tough, but underneath that was a vein of gentleness, humour and honesty that got her every time. Every time. She adored the image of them bucking away on a barrel slung between ropes over a pad of straw in mama's back yard, dreaming big and dreaming hard and believing in those dreams. The bottom line was, she supposed, she was a sucker for a dreamer in a cowboy hat.

When Joe Willie came along it was like her world tilted. Suddenly there was a real cowboy. You could feel it in him, this bristling kind of energy that drew you forward. When she saw him ride she saw that energy ignite and explode, as raw and powerful and beautiful as she imagined perfection to be. God, he was gorgeous when he rode. He was tall and lean and hard, and even though Darlene had never had much time for Indians, this Indian was a cowboy and the best damn rider she had ever seen. She'd never heard anyone talked about in such tones before. It was like men lost the top end of their voices when they mentioned Joe Willie Wolfchild, a name reserved for the deep and low end, the murmuring just this side of jealousy. When she finally met him at Calgary he'd shaken her hand and she felt a thrum of energy like a tight rein on a wild horse. He looked at her with those deep, dark Indian eyes and she was thrown, flailing for purchase, bucked right off in seconds. A rodeo man. A cowboy.

She went out of her way to charm him, giving up the others she kept on a string and devoting herself to him. The others complained like the little boys they were, but once they got wind of who their competition was they settled into a begrudging silence. It was amazing the effect he had on people, and Darlene found that the most powerful aphrodisiac of all. One name could throw people like she'd been thrown, and to be the woman at the side of such a man was more than she had ever dreamed for herself and more than she was willing to lose. So when she gave herself to him she gave him the full routine, coaxing him, teasing him, leading him to an expression of the body that the cowboy struggled with at first but then caught the rhythm of and rode. Sex with Joe Willie was like the storm of rodeo itself. She made sure of that.

"You're a mustang, girl," he told her, after that first time, and she gave him the untamed, dangerous and free routine every time after. She let him explore her body in whatever way he chose, for however long he chose. And the truth was, he was a wild one himself, and Darlene loved the taut feel of his body, the sinewy, coiled strength of him, the harnessed violence he saved for bulls in the clutch and push and heave of him. He knew how to control his body better than any man she'd ever met, and even though that body was supposed to be broken up pretty badly, there wasn't a doubt in Darlene's mind that he'd walk out and mount up again. She'd make sure of that. She'd make damn sure of that. He'd ride and be a champion and she'd be the woman that made it all happen. Not his frigid bitch of a mother. Johanna had refused to let her visit him in the hospital. Family only, she'd been told, like the past four years hadn't existed, like she hadn't been a fixture on the family scene all that time. But she'd show her. Darlene would play it to the max. She'd show his mother how much she cared, how loyal she was, how loving, attentive, supportive and all the other sickly-sweet adjectives they could dream up for one hell of a woman. She'd be there with all the love and adoration and grit and gumption needed to coax that body back. She'd use the physical connection they had to cajole the muscle and sinew back onto a horse and they would continue their ride to the top of the world. Together. Joe Willie was the Big One and she intended to keep him.

"I invested way too much in this already," she said to herself as she turned onto the Wolfchild property. "Way, way too much."

The house was pretty much what Golec expected. From what Claire had told him, Eric Bennett kept up a good front. Big-shot account executive. Salesman really, but these days salesman needed the push of a fancier title. Golec's dad had sold cars all his life and he'd proudly called himself a salesman. Back then, an honest job with honest effort at maintaining it was all a man like his dad needed. Screw the title. Selling cars earned a good life for him and his family, and if the salesman turned out to be the owner of the largest dealership in the area, well, so much the better. Up until the day he'd retired, he'd called himself a salesman, and maybe it was that inherent humility that allowed him to remain grounded; simple, directed, a family man. They'd always had the best, but the salesman taught his children, Golec and his sister, that a simple need met was far more fulfilling than a grandiose desire purchased.

Golec smiled. His old man would never have stooped for this display, this architectural fawning for attention. The size of it far exceeded the needs of the three people who lived there,

and it sat on a corner lot like some bloated aristocrat demanding to be noticed. It was actually a fucking ugly house when
you got right down to it. Pastel. Golec hated pastel. The glee-
ful coral siding was the antithesis of the atmosphere inside. He
found himself growing angry at Eric Bennett. Claire Hartley
was a small woman and he'd beaten her like a rented mule. He
was a big man too from her description, and there was a part
of him that relished the private thought that maybe a quick
judgment in the alley would be far better punishment than the
rendering of a court. Yes, he thought, looking at the house and
waiting for the car bearing Claire Hartley and the social
worker, drag the lump outside by the hair and administer justice, fair and fast. It was entertaining to imagine, but he had far
too much respect for his position to do it. In fact, the whole
reason he was here was to let the asshole slip off the legal hook
if he would go for it. Golec knew he would. Any guy who lived
in a house like this would take the easy route. Golec was willing to bet on it.

Johanna had never much cared for soft women. It wasn't an
overt feminine softness that rankled her, because a girl couldn't
help but be a girl sometimes. What bothered her more was
women with elastic characters, the ones who had never found
a moral ground to stand on, never found a principled territory
to defend and consequently never found a woman to be.
Women like Darlene. She'd never liked Darlene. If the girl
would just allow herself to be beautiful, she would be. She had
all the attributes: tall, tanned, blonde, with a lean body and
dark brown eyes that gave her a perpetual little-girl look. But
Darlene was one of those people who absolutely needed the
esteem of others to feel it in herself. It meant she had the
potential to switch allegiances at any time, and it was this

more than anything that grated Johanna. Loyalty was a trait she took very seriously. You found it in yourself first, found the courage to stay true to yourself through anything, and then, only then, did you become able to stay true to the people in your life. She'd learned that lesson early, been encouraged to it by her people, and the Sioux were a people who lived in staunch loyalty. Darlene had none of that. The girl sought definition but she looked for it in others' eyes first. Her loyalty was to the belief that something outside herself could shape her world and herself. Johanna had always mistrusted her because of that.

"Darlene," she said amiably as the girl stepped from her pickup truck. "You're out and about early."

"Up with the chickens," Darlene said.

"Sensible."

"Yeah. That's me, though."

Johanna smirked. "Yes. That's always been my first thought."

"Where is he?"

"Darlene . . ."

"Look, Johanna," Darlene said, "I don't care what you think of me right now. I never really did. But I'm Joe Willie's woman. I been that for four years now and right now he needs me and I mean to see him."

"Why?"

"Why what?"

"Why does he need to see you?"

"Jesus," Darlene said disgustedly. "Because he's a man, that's why."

"That's your huge rationale?"

"Yeah," Darlene said. "He's a man and I'm a woman and I figure that's what he needs right now more than anything. A woman to make him feel like a man, not a little boy with a boo-boo on his knee."

"Darlene, Joe Willie's survived a major injury. He's lucky to be mobile at all."

"Yeah. I know that, because you told me. But you won't let me see for myself. Won't give me a chance to be there for him. But I'm here now and I will see him, I will be there for him now."

Johanna couldn't help but feel sorry for her. Not because her man was infirmed but more because Darlene had never grown beyond a girl's idea of womanhood. She played at being a woman like a girl with a dollhouse, every move imagined in the security of dreams and hopes and wishes. But life occurred beyond the cheerful placing of furniture and people, and a woman needed more than imaginings to shape a home and a family.

"Okay," Johanna said. "But let me tell you not to expect what you've come to expect from Joe Willie. The injury has changed him. A lot."

"I can deal with that," Darlene said.

"I hope so, Darlene. Because you and I and all of us are going to have to find a way to cut through the silence he's fallen into. We haven't yet. None of us. So I don't hold out a lot of hope in you getting much of a response."

"We've been together a different way."

"God," Johanna said. "Please don't tell me that you're going to rely on sweat and passion, or the memory of a real good time."

"It was more than that."

"Was it really?"

"Yes."

Johanna eyed her with a steely look, and Darlene shifted her feet under the weight of it. "I can't imagine," she said.

"No. You couldn't," Darlene said and flounced past her into the house.

"So you here because of a rat?" Julius asked.

"Yeah," Aiden said, studying the cards he'd been dealt.

"This rat got a name?"

"Cort Lehane." Aiden fairly spat the words.

"Kinda name is Cort?" one of the other boys asked.

"Name of the dead, motherfucker," Julius said.

Aiden looked up at him over his cards and Julius grinned. They were sitting at the middle table in the corridor. It was reserved for the big boys, the ones who ran things, the ones with the power in the cellblock. Julius studied him, and Aiden met his look casually.

"Kinda shit you down on, man?" Julius asked.

"Conspiracy," Aiden said.

"What the hell is that?"

"We were planning a score. A store. He went ahead and tried to pull it himself, got shot and spilled the beans, put it all on me."

"Shot, huh?"

"Yeah. I left the piece with him and he went all crazy and tried to do it himself. Guess he fired at the cops and they shot him."

"Damn. So he dimed you and you in here and he's walkin' around out there?"

"That's about it." Aiden threw his cards down on the table and lit himself a cigarette. Claire had sent money to him and he'd gotten what he'd needed. The others looked at him and he tossed the pack on the table. Everyone lit up.

"Lehane? White?" Julius asked.

"Yeah. Very."

They all laughed.

"Who he trip with?"

"Nobody. It's what I liked about him in the beginning."

Julius nodded. "How much time you lookin' at?"

"Maybe two years."

"Damn. And this Lehane? How much he get?"

"Who knows."

"But he'll go down for some. He'll come here before he gets shipped out to the main joint."

There was silence at the table as everyone focused on the words. "Yeah," Aiden said. "I suppose he'd have to."

"Then you know what you got to do."

"Even up," Aiden said.

"Damn right," Julius said. "Blood for blood."

"I didn't get shot, he did."

Julius smirked and shrugged his big shoulders. "Don't got to be no real blood. He cut you off from your own, your moms, your family, your blood. He took that away from you. You got to settle up."

Aiden nodded. He didn't care so much about the jail. He could handle that. But it was the taking away, the removal of freedom, the excising of his life for something that he'd only ever talked about that stung bitterly, and when he let himself feel it there were a hundred other cuts and bruises that seeped in until he sneered at the acidic taste of it. When he looked at Julius again there was an edge to his eyes that the other boy acknowledged with a firm nod and a raised fist to the chest.

"And if you don't settle it," Julius said, "if you don't put a beating on that rat, I'll put one on you. Word."

"Count on it," Aiden said.

"Don't got to," Julius said. "But you do."

Aiden looked around the table. The others all had the same level, matter-of-fact look. He felt worlds away from what he knew but at the same time felt connected to the vile brew in his belly, the patient, feral look of his new friends and the cold, dank, algae-coloured world of the cellblock. He looked around him and saw dozens of boys lounging along the bars on the upper tier, leaning on the doors of their cells or leaned in with their heads down huddled up close to the telephones, their shoulders hunched up around them like that space, that mere ten inches of world was all the privacy they had anymore. They were all cut off. They had all been bloodied in some fashion and they all bore the pain of those festering wounds here in the clang and crash of steel on steel. He fit here. He gathered the cards from the table in a long, sweeping grab, cradled them in his hands, packed them all in one firm, even lump and slapped them down on the table in front of the boy to his left, looked at all of them one more time with that flat, even stare.

"Deal," he said.

The first thing she saw was the empty sleeve. She stood in the doorway watching him examine himself in the mirror, catching him so totally immersed that he didn't see her standing there. Darlene barely breathed. Across the room Joe Willie sat at the edge of his bed running his right hand slowly across his torso, from his ribs, along the line of his chest, then upwards, left, toward the shoulder. Or where the shoulder used to be. Darlene stared hard at the slackness of the sleeve there. He'd always worn his shirts tight to the body as though he wanted to always feel the taut strength of himself, using the cloth like a second skin to gather muscle and sinew into a compact, coiled spring of force. This shirt hung in draped flaps of material off the left side of his neck. She watched as the hand moved across the ridge of collarbone, halting for a second while he scrunched his eyes tight together before inching slowly, spiderlike, to the flat of the shoulder. Joe Willie dropped his head to his chest. It hung like the head of a saint in penitence while the tips of his fingers moved along the shoulder, probing, pushing, pressing until at the cliff of the arm they stopped and she saw him grimace. He pushed downward with his palm. Darlene put a hand to her mouth when she saw the cloth compress flat to the touch. His shoulders trembled as his hand made the journey to the elbow, and she watched a hard scowl tear at the corners of his mouth. The fingers clenched about the elbow joint while his thumb traced a light line along the absent bicep before nestling into the crook of the joint. He grabbed it. Hard. She saw the force of him in the tendons of his right hand and the arm shook as he squeezed as though trying to move muscle from the good arm to the empty sleeve of the other by sheer force of will. Joe Willie's face was pressed together at every angle, and as she looked at him Darlene realized that she was looking at the face of rage stoked by an unbelievable sorrow. It scared her.

When Joe Willie slid the material of the shirt up along the narrow, withered arm, exposing it to the air and to her, Darlene was shocked. It was like the arms of kids in the starvation commercials, nothing but bone and skin and a sick jut of angles. There was no trace of the long ropes of muscle that had held her, lifted her, only a thin, withered, ugly stick. Ugly. Darlene saw Joe Willie's eyes open as he grabbed his left hand. He lifted the forearm and it rose slack and lifeless. As he turned it over so the palm faced up, Darlene saw hatred in his eyes, a look hard and cold and bitter all at one time. The arm was ugly and she couldn't stand the thought of touching it, or having it touch her. She backed slowly through the door. The movement alerted him and his eyes flicked up to the mirror. She could only stare.

"Darlene," he said, quickly rolling the sleeve back down.

"Joe Willie, I . . ."

"Where you been, darlin'?"

"Joe Willie, I gotta go. I gotta . . ."

He reached for the crutch beside him and slowly pushed himself to his feet, half smiling through the effort. It gave him the look of a crazy man. As he hitch-stepped along the side of the bed, the toe of the crutch slipped on the carpet. He lurched sideways and fell awkwardly against the side of the mattress. The crutch fell to the floor and he landed on one hip on the side of the bed. When he caught himself he looked up into the mirror again, and Darlene saw the face of an invalid: embarrassed, pitiful and scared.

"Sorry," he said quietly. "Don't exactly have the wheels yet."

"God."

"It's all right. Give me a second here." He reached for the crutch.

"No. Joe Willie, I gotta go. I gotta get back. I gotta . . ." Darlene fumbled for her keys.

"Hey, hey. Relax. It's me, darlin'."

He stood again awkwardly and turned to face her, leaning harder on the crutch this time. Darlene fought to control the muscles in her face. She wanted to cry, she wanted to scream. But more than anything she wanted out of that doorway and out of the house. She found herself staring at the empty sleeve despite herself, as though she could still see the wizened stick of an arm it contained. Joe Willie followed her line of sight and looked down at the arm dangling off the shoulder. When he raised his eyes to look at her again she could see the rage in him.

"Joe Willie, I . . ."

"Go," he said. "Just go."

She felt a tremor in her legs and she reached one hand up to her cheek. It shook. He stared at her. She couldn't meet his gaze and her eyes darted back and forth across the room until finally she pursed her lips, rubbed them with two fingers and a thumb, turned and walked quickly down the hallway. When she stepped out onto the veranda again she leaned hard against the wall, closing her eyes and heaving a deep, silent breath. She breathed out in a long, slow exhale. When she opened her eyes she saw Johanna watching her from the round pen where she was training a colt. The two women looked at each other across that space and it was like there was no space at all between them. Darlene felt herself leave long before she climbed into the cab of the truck and drove quickly down the driveway, disappearing in a long plume of dust toward town.

Johanna looked toward Joe Willie's window before turning to the colt again.

"No more Ken and Barbie world, I guess," she said to the colt and chucked at it to get it moving around the pen.

Eric moved slowly that morning. The hangover was severe and he'd called the office and let his girl know he'd be working at home. The girl was paid good money to say whatever he told her to say and because she was a good girl she'd do as she was told. Besides, the top-of-the-desk benefits he paid her after hours kept her tight-lipped. He smiled. Took a long time to find a girl who would go the extra distance for him and it had been worth the search.

The few extra hours at home allowed him time for the hair of the dog, and he'd had a couple to get the blood moving again. He'd been to the Gentlemen's Club. Claire had been away somewhere and he hated to miss a night's action, so he'd headed off for a massage and a high-priced piece of ass from a willing body, and he'd drunk a few too many of the complimentary beverages. He hated that. Sure, it was a good thing to be able to hump like crazy, move the bitch around wherever you wanted, get excited as hell, look down at her, watch himself give it to her good, but there was no release, the alcohol meant there was no delivery of the goods, no dumping into her or all over her like he enjoyed, and that pissed him off more than anything. Three hundred bucks for a hard-on and a hangover. That's pretty much what it had boiled down to.

Along with Claire's uppity attitude lately and having to bring her into line, things hadn't been going according to the script, and Eric Bennett believed in the script. He needed it. He worked hard to perfect it and find a woman to play the part he'd written. Claire had been that for the most part. But she'd told him no. Imagine. Uppity nigger. For all the good he was bringing to her world, the house, the car, the money, the opportunity to have a man like him, she would say no to his right. *His right.* Hitting her wasn't about punishment or even anger, really. It was about rightness. The rightness of his power and the rightness of his due. She'd see that when she got back from wherever it was she'd got to. God, she was a tight little thing. He loved fucking her. Fine black ass and it was all his. Bought and paid for. Earned. He thought about the compact lines of her and he felt himself get hard beneath the robe. When she got back he'd give it to her all romantically, slow the way women liked it, deliberately. He'd make her come and then fuck her dizzy like he'd wanted to the night before. Jesus. He was thinking about taking care of himself in the shower but the doorbell rang.

"Fuck sakes." He drained his glass and moved to the door.

The badge at the keyhole sobered him immediately. "What the hell?" he asked when the door was opened and he saw Claire standing with the cop alongside another neatly dressed woman.

"Detective Golec, Mr. Bennett. This is Lisa Keenan from Family Services and Miss Hartley you know."

"Is the kid okay? Did something happen?"

"We can get to that. Right now we need to talk to you about charges."

"What charges?"

"Like assault, Eric," Claire said, staring right at him.

"And rape," Lisa Keenan said.

"Rape? There was no rape. And there was no assault. We had a disagreement, that's all."

Golec pushed him into the house with the flat of his hand against the chest. Bennett stumbled backwards and righted himself against the foyer wall. Golec moved quickly and grabbed him roughly by the lapels of the robe. "Does that face look like it had a disagreement, Bennett? Does it?"

"You can't do this," Bennett said. "You can't come into my home and rough me up. It's my home."

"I can do whatever I want, pal. Beginning with maybe reading you your rights and hauling your sorry woman-beating ass downtown. Would you like that?" Golec asked, pulling harder on the robe.

"I didn't do anything," Bennett complained.

"I'll ask you again," Golec said. "Does that face look like it had a disagreement?"

"No," Bennett said.

"No. No, it doesn't. What it looks like and what it will look like in the photographs the judge and jury see, is a face that got the shit knocked out of it by some asshole. Sorry about the language, ladies."

"That's okay, Marcel," Lisa Keenan said. "Mr. Bennett, I think it will be better for everyone if we just sit and talk this out."

"Yes," Bennett muttered. "Yes. Certainly."

Golec let go of his grip and the four of them made their way to the dining room and sat around the table.

"What's this about, then?" Bennett asked.

Golec looked at him solemnly. "It's about a little word called no," he said.

"What do you mean?"

"He means that when a woman says no, it means no," Lisa Keenan said. "It means that if you continue a course of sexual action after she says no, it's rape. Claire said no to you, didn't she?"

"Well, yes, but not really," Bennett said.

Golec stared at him hard across the table.

"She was upset," Eric said.

"Why was she upset?" Keenan asked.

"You know. The usual stuff."

"Like having your dick shoved into me as soon as you got in the door without even a hello?" Claire asked. "Like being thrown on the sofa like a rag doll, talked dirty to and fucked like some whore? Like being forced to give you head because I didn't want you in me? That usual stuff, Eric? Is that the usual stuff you're talking about?"

"Hey, you never complained before. I thought you liked it a little rough."

Golec slammed his palm down on the table. "I can arrange a place where you can experience it a little rough, Bennett. Would you like that? Huh?"

"Let me spell this out for you, Mr. Bennett," Lisa Keenan said, "just so we don't have to waste anyone's time here. Spousal rape is a big issue. It wasn't long ago that it wasn't even on the books, but it's become so prevalent that we're charging men all the time now. You can't demand sex anymore. You can't come home and take a woman's body without her consent. It's rape. Plain and simple. The assault is self-evident, of course. Taken together, it's a very serious situation you've put yourself into. If we go to court, you will go to jail. Definitely. The press will have their way with this story, and I think you know what harm that will do to your business reputation. Then there's the NAACP, the women's groups, the community association, that sort of thing. You're looking at a long period of hell in your personal and business life, and that's after the court decision."

"You said if," Bennett said.

"That's right. What we're prepared to do is offer you a course of action that will preclude any of the eventualities I mentioned."

"Explain," Bennett said.

For the next few minutes she outlined the arrangement while Bennett sat quietly in his chair, one leg crossed over the other, and stared out the patio doors. When she finished he looked levelly at Claire. She held the look. Finally, Bennett smirked, nodded, rose and moved wordlessly into the small office he kept off the kitchen. He returned with a cheque and the car registration. He tossed them onto the table.

"How do I know she won't be back next month? How do I know I don't keep on getting screwed?" he asked.

Claire stood and looked across the table at him. "Because I'm not like you," she said.

"How's that?" he asked with a smirk.

"I don't take hostages."

"You ate up this life."

"This life ate me up, Eric."

"So your buyout is ten grand and a used car?"

"It's enough."

"Yeah, well, don't be ringing my doorbell when it comes up short."

"That will never happen."

"Right. Just get the hell out."

"Just as soon as she grabs some things," Golec said.

"Sure. But make it fast."

"It could never be fast enough," Claire said.

He tried to raise it. He looked at it in the mirror, then looked up. Joe Willie stared intently into his eyes and strained for control of his body, his arm. His girl had fled. Took one look at him and bolted. The same girl who'd welcomed him so warmly into her world, into her body when he'd been whole. Whole. No woman wanted a gimp. No woman wanted a cripple, half a man, a loser. He felt the anger rub against the inside of his ribs and he wanted that burn. Wanted to taste it in the blood when he bit down on the inside of his cheeks, his tongue, his lip. He wanted the salt of blood. He steeled himself, gathered all the resources and power of his will like he had in the chute all those years, forcing strength upward from the centre of himself, focussing it on the narrow bend of withered elbow. He moved it. Minutely. But it took all the concentration he had. The arm flopped down against his thigh and lay there, loose and rubbery. He arched his back and bent his head back as far as he could, feeling his spine compact and the muscles in his abdomen stretch, breathing quick, shallow breaths before lowering his head level to the mirror and staring at himself. He grimaced. Every ounce of energy was focussed on his left side, and he felt the strain in his back as he managed to pull the arm back from the elbow and the wrist slid along his thigh before lifting a fraction along his rib cage. It fell back to his thigh. With his eyes closed still, Joe Willie breathed, his right hand reaching over absently to cover the wrist of the left protectively. He arched his back again and felt the hot sear of anger in the tendons of his neck and the middle of his back. He clenched his teeth, scowled at the ceiling and tried to raise the arm again. Then he saw the bear.

There was a meadow: an alpine meadow with the sun shining on it and the blue push of mountains all around it. He knew where it was. He'd ridden there often when he needed to ride and think. The trail up to it wound back and forth along the face of Iron Mountain, and a horse and rider needed to be very careful and very good in order to make the journey. It was treacherous because of Iron Mountain's fast climb to the sky. It took a very deliberate horse and a determined rider to get there, but the payoff was the most spectacular view he'd ever seen. That panorama had never failed to settle him, and the meadow was one of those private pleasures he never shared with anyone. That was where the bear was. It sat on its haunches at the edge of the meadow at the lip of the west-facing precipice.

When it saw him the bear climbed to all fours and shambled closer, head swaying on its great neck, eyes focussed intently on him behind the tremendous snout and jaws. He watched it. The bear eased closer. Eventually it stopped swaying its head and instead lowered it, pushed it forward and down so the eyes of it were all he could see. The eyes stared at him intently, and he could see flecks of yellow in the dark hazel of them, the pupils set there as deep and mysterious as the mouths of caves, accentuated by the deep furrow of the brow.

It walked steadily toward him, neither threatening nor frightened, and the eyes stayed on him, studying him, watching him, reading him almost. Primal. That's the word that came to him. Ancient, primitive, untamed, strong, the eyes looked at him as the bear got closer and closer, the meadow receding, the mountains compacting, the sky closing off, until all that existed in the universe were the eyes of the great beast staring directly at him, closer and closer and closer. Joe Willie snapped his head down and found himself staring into his own eyes in the mirror. He shook his head to clear it. The image of the bear stayed with him, and when he looked into the mirror again the eyes drew him instantly. He stared into them, hard, insistently, looking for that primitive, feral edge he'd seen in the bear's eyes. Then he moved the arm again.

The Cadillac felt good. She'd never sunk herself into luxury before, and the street rolled beneath the wheels as smoothly as anything Claire had ever felt. There was no tremble in the steering wheel and no rattle and clunk like the ancient wagons and sedans she'd had in her time. This car was fine. In the rearview mirror she fussed with her hair and grinned at herself for her foolishness. It didn't take much for a girl to get the vanity back. Here she was all black and blue, hiding behind oversized sunglasses and still primping and preening as soon as she got the chance. All because of a fine car. All because of the ten thousand dollars headed for her bank account.

Ah well, she thought, she'd earned it. Call it survival benefits. Call it danger pay. Call it the high cost of loving. She liked that play on words. Except that love was never really a part of it. Not like she understood the word to mean. She hadn't really loved any of them. All of them, in their own particular ways, were skewed, lives out of kilter, so that loving them wasn't anything she could say absolutely that she'd done. No. She'd experienced them. She'd survived them. And it was curious to her, driving along that street, how she'd always managed to find another one. Despite the hunger she carried for a settled, predictable life with a reliable, loving man, she'd always wandered into the arms of the needy, the profane, the kinky, the emotionally unavailable, detached, controlling and now violent kind of man. All beautiful in their way. All fine physical examples of manhood. All cash rich, employed and driven. But beneath the skin and bone where the real man lived, the heart was always missing. Maybe that was it. Maybe she'd always been attracted to the vacuum, like a part of her was pulled relentlessly toward the empty emotional chamber like those poor sailors following the pull of the siren's voice in that myth. Her love life had always been a shipwreck. Boy, was that the truth.

But this car could take her beyond all that. This car and the money could move her into a whole new world. Celibate. She shook her head at the word. It sounded like a mental disorder, something they locked you away for, something socially unacceptable, whispered behind your back when you passed. Don't talk to her—she's celibate. Oh, poor Claire, she's just been diagnosed as celibate. Jesus. That kind of thinking really would drive you crazy.

"What are you thinking?" Lisa Keenan asked.

"Oh," Claire said, pulling herself back to reality, "I was just thinking about being celibate."

"Are things that bad?" Lisa asked.

"Frankly, yes."

"It's an extreme choice."

"It's been a kind of extreme life."

"I suppose," Lisa said. "I understand that Eric was likely the latest in a long line and that maybe your choices haven't always been the best when it comes to men, but you're talking about shutting your womanhood off."

"That's what I'm talking about," Claire said.

"Why?"

"In a word, Aiden. He's been through enough. Enough men, enough men's bullshit, enough instability, and I won't put him through that again. He's in jail and won't speak to me or see me. I only hope he reads my letters. My son needs me now. Me. The whole package. Not one that comes with a man included."

"I'd say that's a good call. But I'd also say that you can't displace yourself. You have to stay open to the possibility."

"What possibility?"

"The possibility of a good man appearing out of nowhere."

Claire laughed. "Lisa, I had a construction contractor with money falling out his ears. Big house he'd built himself, nice shiny life, great body, knew how to use it."

"Gay?"

"Bingo. Then there was the landscaper. A virtual artist with every bush but the one that counted."

"Gay?"

"No. Just never wanted sex. He only wanted a woman for show. It turned out that he could always take things in hand, if you get my drift."

"Porn?"

"Always. After that there was the cross-dresser, the alcoholic, then the drug addict, the womanizer and finally, Eric the batterer. So keeping myself open to the possibility of a good man appearing out of nowhere is a stretch right now."

"Well, I think you need to give yourself time to get your life in order, get settled somewhere, find a job, build your resources, live your life. You're still young, Claire, you're still beautiful. There's a man somewhere for you."

"I don't disagree with that. But until Mr. Wonderful explodes upon the scene, the gates to Playland are closed."

"Can you do that?"

"I can do that," Claire said. "I have to."

He sat at the kitchen table sipping coffee, watching the morning sun slant its way across the floor. She crossed his line of vision and he raised his eyes then to watch her work. It was her kitchen. The wranglers had their own quarters and cooked for themselves but she insisted on doing all the cooking for the family. Now, she busied herself with vegetables for the rich stew she knew he favoured, and he smiled as he looked at the line of her back. She was straight and strong. Her hands were steady and flexible as she whisked the edge of the peeler across the skin of the carrots and she watched the morning activities of the wranglers through the long wide window she'd wanted to run along the counter and the sink. She'd paced it off. It was a morning just like this and she'd paced off the perimeter of the house she wanted, hiking up the hem of her riding skirt and stepping assuredly through the tall, wet grass, talking to him, pointing, making sure he was hearing her. It was like she could already see it, and as he built it for her he became convinced that she had. She'd wanted a big kitchen, roomy, sunny, painted a warm yellow with lace curtains and a wide step-out porch facing south toward the barns and corrals. He sat in that very room and as he watched her looking southward out that window he loved her like he had when he was twenty-four and the adventure of their home life together was just beginning.

The house she had stepped off that morning hadn't changed in all those years but for the requisite paintings and reparations all houses needed as they aged. It amazed him because it had never needed to be more. Her vision had been complete way back then, and their home had emerged from the land as full and complete as a well-told tale and it had held the story of their time together easily, gracefully. He'd never questioned her vision. Not a lick in all that time. Victoria saw with her whole soul and her eyes were a bonus. Intuition, he supposed they called it in their highfalutin way, but he had no head for that kind of talk. Instead, he called it knowing. His wife had just known all her life what the next thing was. Hell, she even knew when the waltzes were coming at the country dances in town and she'd reach out to him as the chords of the last song faded, ready to pull him to his feet and into her arms. He only danced the slow ones and she always knew when it was her time. From the biggest thing to the smallest, Victoria had seen what was needed long before it was needed, and now, watching the straight, firm line of her working in her kitchen, he knew that whatever she was thinking had its answer built right in.

"Enjoying yourself sitting there watching a woman work, are you?" she asked without looking at him.

"Never more," he said.

"Well, I'm happy to provide your entertainment but we need to talk." She wiped her hands on the calico apron she'd sewn.

"Sure," he said, reaching under the chair for his hat. "Step out on the porch?"

"No," she said. She slipped her feet into the high rubber boots she kept at the door. "Let's walk. Out to your shed."

"My shed? When did you start smoking?"

"Funny. It's only you and Birch who forget that tobacco's supposed to be medicine."

"It is medicine," he said with a broad wink at her and a pinch at her fanny. "Calms me down. Just like the loving."

"Yes, well, at your age both of them could kill you."

"Man's got a right to die happy."

She smiled at him and put a hand on his cheek. "That's a fact," she said.

They stepped off the porch and walked across the lawn, through the gate and along the asphalt driveway a few yards before crossing into the main pasture at the front of the house. She locked the gate behind them and then stepped up to take his arm as they walked. The dog appeared out of nowhere and leapt around their feet awhile, happy to see them out and about that early. Eventually the dog moved out ahead of them, looking back now and again to make sure they hadn't changed their mind and headed back to the house. They walked without speaking, both content to gaze about at the freshness of the morning and the mountains around them enveloping the valley like the edges of a great wide bowl. When they got to the shed he opened the door of the old truck for her, and she stepped up on the running board and turned to look at him.

"Kinda like the first time, isn't it?" she asked.

"Every time," he said and tipped his hat to her before crossing to the other side.

He opened the heavy door and the dog snuck in quickly and settled on his haunches beside Victoria, looking straight ahead out the windshield and thumping his tail against the back of the seat. "Yeah, right," Lionel said with a grin, settling in behind the wheel. "Like this'll ever go anywhere again."

"It should," she said.

"Should what?"

"Go somewhere."

"No way," he said, assembling his makings on the dashboard. "She might not run anymore but this truck'll never see the dump, woman."

"I don't mean the dump," she said.

"What do you mean, then?"

"I mean, it's part of the family, it should go somewhere. It should run again."

"Yeah. Right. Running means parts, and parts for this old heap gotta be mighty hard to find. Besides, my bones ain't got the wherewithal anymore for the stooping and the bending and the gripping of the wrench."

"I don't mean you."

He looked at her steadily and knew where she was going. It hadn't occurred to him at all. In fact, as he'd sat there with the dog the night before he'd even thought of moving the old truck farther back into the shed and putting exercise gear there for Joe Willie to use. Moving it meant getting Birch and a few of the boys to push it back once the harnesses and tools and such were cleared away some. Actually getting the engine to turn over again wasn't even a glimmer in his eye, it was all about giving Joe Willie something, anything, to get him up and moving again. He could easily give up the evening smoke with the dog for his grandson's well-being.

She watched him rub the dashboard, small circles with the palm as if he were rubbing a favourite horse.

"Nineteen thirty-four Ford V8 pickup," he said. "One of the first years they made the V8. Gonna be the next big thing, the old man said when he give it to me."

"I recall," she said.

"Only girl ever rode in this front seat with me was you."

"I recall that too."

"We put a lot of miles on her them first years. Pendleton was the first show we got to in her, I recollect."

"Yes," she said. "It's still my favourite buckle."

He laughed and turned in the seat to face her, one arm slung across the seat back. "You and me and Pete the Pistol and Johnny Fines, the box piled up with our gear, singing crazy songs all across Wyoming with that buckle sitting right smack in the middle of the windshield. You wouldn't let me move it even when the sun shinin' off it nearly made me blind."

"There's a lot of stories in this old truck," she said. "Yours, mine, Birch's, Johanna's."

"Not to mention my daddy's."

"Shame to just let them sit here."

"Pure shame."

They looked at each other for a long time.

"Parts'll be hard," he said finally.

"You'll find them."

"Harder to get him out of the house."

"You'll figure that out."

"It ain't rodeo."

"You'll figure that out too."

"You're mighty certain about that."

"Never more," she said and squeezed his hand.

Administration Visiting was at the end of a long series of corridors near the front of the lock-up. Boys were summoned regularly to see social workers, psychiatrists, lawyers and case management workers after they were sentenced. When they came to get him Aiden was puzzled. The court-appointed lawyer wasn't scheduled to see him until the day before his court date, and there were no court-ordered appointments. He had no other business that he could think of, and as he walked along behind the two officers and looked at the jail he thought it was all probably a mistake.

Then he saw Golec. The policeman leaned against a wall and squeezed a rubber ball in his left hand. He nodded solemnly at Aiden, who was ushered past him and into a small room empty except for a table and two chairs. Golec waved the two officers away before pulling up a chair opposite Aiden. The boy looked at him blankly. Golec didn't speak right away, and the two of them studied each other. Whatever the kid was learning in here it couldn't be good because Golec could sense a deeper detachment than he'd seen before. There was nothing in the boy's demeanour to suggest either discomfort or anxiety, only a miles-away look that suggested either boredom or disinterest, and Golec realized how close he was to crossing the invisible line scratched into the hardscrabble surface of life. He'd seen it a lot. Men became as cold as the walls that held them eventually, their features as unadorned as the pocked and pitted concrete that framed their existence, and their emotions entombed like mummies in the deep recess. The boy sitting across from him was fast approaching the point where turnarounds became impossible. He squeezed the hard blue squash ball in his hand and watched the tendons flex.

"And I heard that cops had no balls," Aiden said. He spoke it without humour, and when Golec looked at him the placid cool of his face remained in place.

"Yeah, well, you hear a lot in here that's just guesswork."

"Gotta go with the evidence, I guess," Aiden said.

"Takes a lot of balls to find your way to this place, does it?"

"Takes a lot of balls to make it in here."

"And you? You're making it here, are you?"

"I'm making it."

"Shame."

"Why?"

"Because it seems to me that you have the stuff to make it just about anywhere you chose to. Doesn't have to be here."

"You come here for a pep talk? Is that why I'm here?"

"Not really. Just wanted to ask you a couple questions."

"I got nothing to say."

"It's not about your case."

Aiden allowed himself a puzzled look and he leaned forward in his chair and folded his hands in front of him. "What, then?" he asked.

"It's about your mother."

Aiden sneered. "Yeah, right," he said. "What do you need? Her favourite colour? Flowers? Perfume? You fucking guys are pitiful. What's your angle? I get you in good with the moms and you ease up on my beef?"

Golec squeezed the ball hard and held it, looking squarely at Aiden. Then he relaxed and changed hands with the ball. "Look, I'm sorry things went the way they have for your mother. She's a good woman and deserves a hell of a lot better than she got over the years, but don't throw me in the loop with other men."

"Why not?"

"Because I only want to help."

Aiden scoffed, then he smiled and shook his head. "They all only wanted to help. Help themselves, anyway."

Golec nodded. He rolled the ball slowly across the table. Aiden watched it roll, and when it eased against his knuckles he cupped it in one palm. "Squeeze it," Golec said. "It feels good. Releases tension."

"Who's tense?"

"You're not? I would be."

"You're not me."

"No, I'm not, but this place would make anyone tense."

"I'm not anyone."

"That's what they all say."

"That what this is about? They?"

"Look, Aiden," Golec said sharply. "I don't have to be here. I'm not here officially. I'm here because I want to help. You may not believe that, and frankly, it doesn't matter, but I'm here to help."

Aiden tossed the ball back lightly and eased back in his seat.

"Your mother. Has she ever been anywhere?"

"What do you mean?"

"You know, a vacation, a cruise, a trip. Anywhere."

"Are you kidding me? Guys wanted to go around the world with her all the time but no one ever took her anywhere, if you get my drift."

"She ever speak to you about someplace she wanted to go especially?"

"No."

"Would she like to get away somewhere?"

"What the hell is this about? You want to take my mother away on a dream vacation so you can make it with her? Is that it?"

Golec stood up and leaned on the table and looked down at Aiden. The boy didn't move a muscle. "Look, Aiden, it takes a hell of a lot to help someone. I know because I'm trying to help you and it's taking everything I have, believe me. So if you want to help your mother you better be prepared to drop the jailhouse bullshit and talk to me straight."

Aiden smirked. "All right. All right. No. I never heard her mention anything like that. Why?"

"Because I know a place you could both go."

"Now?"

"No. After your sentence, maybe during."

"During?"

"Yeah. I could maybe put in a word to the judge about doing the last part of your sentence somewhere other than the hoosegow."

"You want to send me and the moms on a vacation instead of the joint?"

Golec sat back down and leaned forward with his palms flat on the table. "It won't be a vacation. You'll be working your tail off. Your mom can just kid of relax there. Be with you. You could be with each other."

"Where?" There was a glint of interest in his eye and Golec could see the fifteen-year-old boy now.

"I have a friend who has a ranch in the west. In the mountains."

"A ranch? Like cowboys and yippee-cay-yay and all that?"

"Yeah. Yippee-cay-yay."

"You're crazy."

"Maybe. But it's out of the city, away from all the crap, lots of fresh air and hard work. It would do you good. It would do the both of you a lot of good."

"How you figure?"

"Because it's a change, Aiden. I can't help you in terms of what the court will throw at you. Obviously they're not terribly impressed by this whole routine or you wouldn't be sitting here right now. But I can make suggestions for sentencing, and if you finish up on the ranch there's a chance that maybe you can swing things another way for yourself. Change. A different look. That's all I'm suggesting."

Aiden reached for the cigarettes tucked in his shirt pocket and took his time lighting up. Golec watched him unwaveringly, and Aiden liked that. Somehow it made him feel valuable, like what he would have to say had girth and size and weight. Substance. Like a man.

"How long?" he asked finally.

"I don't know. It depends on the stretch you serve. The last third of it, likely."

"What do I do there?"

"Everything, I imagine. It's like a work placement. You do whatever they need you to do."

"How come you're offering me this?"

Golec looked at him hard. "Because you're on a freight train to nowhere. You're learning that tough and cool and wise talking can get you places. But it's nowhere. Your mother wants a life for you, a good life, and even though she might have made some poor choices along the way, it's always been in hopes of getting a good life for you. I just think the two of you need a break, a chance, a different roll of the dice."

"So this is all set?"

"If you tell me so, I'll make the arrangements with my friend and talk to your mother."

"If I say no?"

"Then you're on your own. It's all I can offer."

Aiden looked around the room and then returned his gaze to Golec. "Hmm. Concrete and barbed wire or pastures and barbed wire?"

"It's no joke, son."

"Don't call me that."

"Aiden."

They sat in silence. Aiden smoked while Golec waited, unmoving and mindful of the great moment they sat in, one of those defining moments when the universe gathers itself around you in expectation, the choice hovering in the air like lightning waiting to strike. Aiden sensed it too and he looked anxious for the first time, and when he spoke it was deliberate and measured and strong.

"I'll do it. I'll take it. But the same goes about my mother. I don't want her here or the main joint until it's all over. She don't need to see this. Only when I walk."

Golec nodded and stretched out a hand across the table. Aiden stared at it, then lifted his gaze to meet Golec's. They studied each other, and Golec felt the full measure of the boy's resolve. He took the proffered hand and shook it firmly and then stood up and went to rap on the door for the officers and then walked out without speaking again. Golec felt a part of him go with the boy into the darkness and dankness of the world he inhabited.

Birch looked at his father for a good long time, contemplating what he'd just heard. The truth was that he himself was at a loss as to what to do about his son. It cut him to see Joe Willie suffer, but Birch had been around rodeos and cowboys and hurt long enough to know that a man needed mighty big space when the bones let him down. Still, there was a pure need for a plan, and try as he might Birch hadn't been able to put a thing together that made a whit of sense. Given the circumstances, anyhow—and the circumstances were a cussed mess. He'd settled on just letting the boy get his feet under him on the ranch and taking it from there.

He pulled his tobacco makings from his pocket to give himself time to think. The old man hitched a thumb toward himself and Birch passed over the makings. For the next few minutes the two men busied themselves with building their smokes.

"Parts are gonna be a bitch, that's sure," Birch said finally, putting a foot on the bottom rail of the fence and leaning his elbows along the top rail. "The metal don't seem all that bad, so she might come up good with a scrape and paint, but that's the easy part."

"I hear ya," Lionel said.

"The boy ain't much for engines. Never was. Never seen much use beyond the usual. Rebuilding's a whole other tune."

"Go on," Lionel said.

"Well, the fact of the matter is, Daddy, that Joe Willie don't come across as being too partial to much right now. Mystifies the shit right outta me how you figure on getting him off the porch."

"I'm gonna tell him he can't."

"Can't?"

"Can't do it."

Birch smoked awhile and gave his father a sidelong glance. "You got a mighty peculiar way with motivation," he said.

"Maybe," Lionel said. "But think about it. Other than the back lot and the chutes, where does a cowboy spend most of his time?"

"On the road, I suppose."

"On the road in what?"

"In a truck."

"Exactly."

Birch nodded. "All right, but that still don't get the boy off the porch."

"Maybe not. But, son, if you couldn't have the whole deal, what would you want?"

"Well, sir, I reckon I'd want me a little of it."

"Exactly. I mean to give Joe Willie a little of it back. See, right now he's pining away for the whole deal because that's all he can see he's deprived of. Not being able to have it all hurts like a son of a bitch, and I figure the only way to ease that misery is by giving him a piece of it to hold on to. Trucks'n cowboys been one and the same for as long as there's been a highway to a short go, and that old truck carried the three of us to a lotta shows in its time. Recollect?"

"That I do," Birch said. "But she was a clunker when I had her. There's a lot of road under her. Maybe too much."

"Maybe. But I don't think so. The road and all them miles is the whole deal now."

"I don't follow."

Lionel smoked and looked across the ranch and valley toward the mountains. "When you hang 'em up finally, whether it's hurt or old age, you find out that all you have left is the stories. You got Yuma, Yakima, Laughlin River, all them grand old names, all the people you met when you were there. But you got the stories of getting there too. Damn, I still recollect nine of us all piled into that old girl. None of us did a lick at Abilene and we pooled whatever slim pickins we had for gas and growlies and headed up the line the only way we could. We took turns sleeping in the box with all the gear and riding and driving up front. You get hold of people in times like that, get hold of them firm, in ways that most people never get a chance to and wouldn't understand. The story of them times is what makes you who you finally become, and that old truck got a lot of stories in her. Not just yours or mine or my daddy's. That old girl got the taste of every tale that was ever told in her along whatever stretch of highway she ever drove. She carries the story of our lives, son. That's why I go and sit in her every night and it's why I wanna turn the boy loose on bringin' her back. She's the little part of rodeo he can have still."

"But you're gonna tell him he can't."

"That I am."

"Why?"

"What's the easiest way to get a cowboy to do something?" Lionel asked.

Birch laughed, took off his hat and slapped it on his thigh. "Tell him he can't," he said. "Tell him he surely can't."

"Cowpoke'll move mountains even when he don't know it's a mountain that he's moving," Lionel said.

Birch ground out his cigarette with his boot heel. "It's a mountain," he said quietly. "It sure enough is a mountain."

They found a small two-bedroom apartment in a neighbourhood where Claire had never lived. It was a working-class neighbourhood, and the sounds of daily busyness rose off the sidewalks like a melody hummed in a low register and the sounds of children playing eased upward from the small park across the street in small waves so that the area became the wash of pale sunlight that fell through her living-room window. Claire loved it immediately. Lisa Keenan arranged a reduced rent in exchange for painting, and Claire fell into the work with a fervour she hadn't experienced before. She chose a pale yellow for the kitchen and bath, a bluish green for the living room and bedrooms.

"It's the colour of sage in the mountains," she told Lisa. The social worker had been drawn to Claire and her story and now that she had reclaimed her independence Lisa had become a friend and an ally. "I want to wake up to that colour. It makes me happy."

The two of them painted the apartment, and while it dried they shopped for used furniture. By the time Claire had outfitted her new apartment with the essentials it was a bright, charming, casual home. When she stood in the middle of it and looked around, Claire felt proud, strong and resilient. For the first time in her adult life she had built a life, or at least the foundation of a life, on her own initiative and drive, and the feeling within her was as close to freedom as she imagined that feeling to be. She sat on the window ledge and looked out over the neighbourhood and felt a sense of being set down somewhere, placed intentionally like a precious thing, a keepsake perhaps, and she found herself shedding silent tears in the sunlight of that window.

"Don't be sad," Lisa said. "It's wonderful. You have a wonderful new home."

"I know," Claire said. "I've never had one all my own before."

"Never?"

"No. There was always a man."

"Well, there's just you now."

"That's what makes me sad. I wish my son were here."

"He will be. But use this time, Claire. This apartment gives you a base. From here you can find a job, get some training, maybe take some college courses. Anything. You can choose anything now. By the time Aiden comes home you'll be amazed how far you will have come."

"Really? It seems impossible."

Lisa sat on the window ledge beside her and took her hand. "You're a very strong woman. No one could live the life you've led without an incredible amount of strength. You're a survivor. And I know a place that's looking for a woman who knows how to survive."

"A job, you mean."

"Yes. It's a women's centre. They do a lot of peer counselling and I think you'd be perfect for it."

"I have no training," Claire said.

"Are you kidding me? You have a master's degree in survival, girl. Sometimes life gives you a better training, prepares you far better to reach people, touch them, affect them, than any other kind of schooling does. I'd trade my pieces of paper for half of what you know any day of the week. I've spoken to them already and they want to see you."

"No!"

"Yes. I've given you a strong recommendation. They owe me a few actually, and I think you'd be wonderful. It doesn't pay much. You wouldn't have a whole lot after the rent and food here but they pay for training, college, and the pay goes up the more training you get."

Claire laughed. "College? I barely made it out of high school and that was years ago."

"You'll do fine," Lisa said. "If you put yourself into this with half the grit you showed me at Eric's that morning, you'll sail, girl. Trust me."

"I do," Claire said.

"Then trust yourself."

The two women sat on the window ledge in the sunshine and held hands. Around them they could hear the sounds of the neighbourhood through the open window and it mingled with the smell of fresh paint and sawn wood from the new baseboards so that there was a keenness to the air, sharp, redolent with energy and what Claire believed was possibility. She closed her eyes and drank it all in, filled herself with it.

"I can do that," Claire said. She stood and faced Lisa. "Now, let's go and fill that refrigerator. I've got things that need doing."

Joe Willie moved to the front porch and settled himself on the swing seat. The easy back-and-forth motion took the feel of the weight of his leg away, and as he drifted into the sway it lulled the ache in his shoulder too. It was late morning and the brightness of the day irritated him. He clenched and unclenched his good hand and thought about all there was to do on a day like this. For a working ranch and a working cowboy there generally was never enough daylight to accomplish everything that needed tending to. But as he watched his mother work a colt in the round pen, the wranglers shifting stock from graze to corral and his father busy loading square bales into the barn, he knew there was nothing he could contribute. No one needed a hobbled-up, one-armed cowboy. Hell, he couldn't even sit a horse to bring in steers. All he was good for was sitting in an old man's porch swing watching life happen and waiting for someone to throw him a morsel of talk. Truth was, he didn't even want that. He had nothing to say. Nothing that would fill an empty sleeve or the gaping hole in the centre of him.

"Boy," his grandfather said from behind him in the house. "You busy?"

Joe Willie closed his eyes. "No," he said. "I'm not exactly what you'd call frantic right now."

"Good," Lionel said. "Let's take a walk."

"You're kidding, right?"

"I'm not kidding. It'll do you good."

"Where?"

"I want to show you something out to the equipment shed."

Joe Willie stared at him a moment, then shifted his gaze across the main pasture to where the shed sat a few hundred yards away. "You expect me to walk out there? With this?" he asked, pointing to the crutch.

"Sure do."

"You're crazy."

"Could be, but we're goin' nonetheless."

"What if I don't want to?"

Lionel crossed in front of where his grandson sat and leaned against the rail of the porch. He built a smoke and kept his eye on Joe Willie all the while. "Fact is, boy," he said, pausing to lick the paper, "I don't much care what you don't want. There's something that needs showing and there's something that needs saying. And it all takes place out to that equipment shed."

"You're telling me what to do?"

"I'm telling you. That's a fact."

"What if I can't make it?"

"Then I'll carry you."

"You can't do that."

"I can and I will. If it takes me all damn day, I'll get you there."

"Stubborn cuss, aren't you?"

"Gotta be," Lionel said, and they looked at each other silently.

Joe Willie saw his grandfather against the pale blue and green of the mountains to the west. He looked like one of those western portraits, as seamlessly part of that backdrop as the treeline on the mountains themselves. As he bent his head to light the cigarette, Joe Willie saw the wrinkles in his face etched sharply against the harsh flare of the match. He trusted the old man, had always depended on his guidance, his opinion, his experience in everything. Now was no different. Despite the aggravation he felt over the intrusion, he struggled to his feet and waved away the hand Lionel offered. "It's that blasted important to you?" he asked.

"Surely," Lionel said.

"Well, let's go, then," he said, and they moved slowly off the porch.

It wasn't easy. He hadn't tried to walk across anything but floor and pavement, and the uneven ground pitched him off balance, but when Lionel offered a steadying hand Joe Willie ignored it and humped along harder. Even the dog seemed to understand the necessity for focus and padded patiently ahead a few yards, then turned and waited for them to catch up before skipping off again. Joe Willie hitch-stepped awkwardly, yard by yard, and by the time they were three-quarters of the way he was covered in sweat. Neither of them spoke. They stopped so Joe Willie could gather his breath, and when he looked at his grandfather Lionel could see fire in his eyes. The same fire he'd seen in the chute just before he would nod hard to the rope men at the gate, slapping his hat hard to his head, the tendons in his neck stretched to their limit in a deep, hard scowl of concentration and his eyes burning, already seeing the horse or the bull rocketing out of the chute, the energy of him focussed on one tiny pinprick of time. Joe Willie stared at the next fifty yards of ground, heaving deep breaths, then looked at Lionel and nodded. They covered the distance in about fifteen minutes.

Joe Willie hadn't been in the shed since he was maybe thirteen or fourteen, and as he gazed at the mayhem of artifacts and curios it amazed him that nothing had been moved in all that time. The truck still sat where it had always sat. The dog gave a yip and ran ahead to the driver's door, where he thumped his tail against the oil-and-grease-stained ground and waited for Lionel to open the door.

"We're sitting in that?" Joe Willie asked.

"Only place out here," Lionel said.

"Sure it won't fall apart with our weight? The three of us?" Joe Willie asked, jutting his chin toward the dog.

"She'll hold up." Lionel opened the door for him and Joe Willie leaned his good hand on the old man's shoulder to get up on the running board. He sidled in and settled himself, then handed the crutch to his grandfather, who leaned it against the front fender.

"I ever tell you about the Ping-Pong Pawnee?" Lionel asked as he stepped around the front and made his way to the driver's side.

"Don't recollect it," Joe Willie said.

Lionel opened the door and the dog sprang in, licking at Joe Willie's neck as he took his place in the middle of the seat and stared out the windshield. "Your great-grandfather told it," Lionel said as he pulled the door closed. "Around 1908 it was. Daddy'd been with Pawnee Bill's Wild West show. He was one of them wild red Indians getting shot off his pony in the big finale."

"I heard this," Joe Willie said.

"Not everything," Lionel said. "Daddy'd been about everywhere he could have imagined with that show, Chicago, New York, Paris even. Thought he'd seen everything there was. But one day as he was crossing the lot to get his horse ready for the show, he saw something that changed his life—and mine, your daddy's and yours."

"What was that?" Joe Willie asked, absently rubbing the dog behind the ears and staring out the windshield.

"Well, there were some war chiefs in that show. Real warriors who'd fought the cavalry at the end of it all in the late 1800s. Great chiefs. Great men. Daddy said he was always proud to be around those men because he could feel the history in them. Said it made him feel more Indian. One of them was a great Pawnee chief. Pawnees were tough sumbitches. Fearsome fighters. Daddy said when you looked at that man, even then, even all painted up and wearing a headdress of painted turkey feathers and galloping a shod horse across an arena, you got a sense of all of it, how it had been one time, how powerful it was, the life our people led.

"But as he walked across that lot that day he saw that great war chief all decked out in his regalia holding a ping-pong paddle and batting that ball back and forth with another chief while people laughed and pointed and someone took a picture. It changed it all for him. That scene. That image."

"Changed what?" Joe Willie asked.

Lionel began to build another smoke. "Changed how he looked at himself, I guess. He couldn't stomach being a cartoon Injun anymore. He walked out on old Pawnee Bill that day and rode his first rodeo a week later. Made the short go with the broncs and a fistful of cash and that was the start of it all for us. If Daddy hadn't seen the Ping-Pong Pawnee none of us would've rodeo'd. Who knows what we mighta been."

Lionel finished twisting his cigarette and held out the makings to his grandson. When Joe Willie nodded he began building one for him too.

"Coulda told me on the porch," Joe Willie said.

"Coulda," Lionel said. "But I wanted you to see the truck."

"I seen her before."

"I know. But I never told you how she come to be."

"Still coulda told me on the porch."

Lionel handed Joe Willie the finished cigarette. He lit both for them and they sat there awhile, smoking.

"Well?" Joe Willie said finally.

"In them days it wasn't easy for us. Big-money rodeo was a white man's game. The idea of an Indian cowboy seemed as off centre to them as it did to us. Daddy was one of the first to make a dent in it. When I come along all I knew was rodeo.

Grew up with it. Got my schoolin' in it. There was nothing else for me when I got to be old enough to choose and Daddy understood that—that it was my blood. I got to be a regular at the pay window and it was starting to look like I was on my way to the top. Course then there was no jetting or airplane riding around from show to show, a cowboy had to drive, and I had no wheels. Been bumming rides all along but that was mighty unpredictable at the best of times, and Daddy wanted to see me make it, wanted to see me be a champion. Only way was to have your own ride. This'd be the middle of '41, the year I met your grandmother.

"Anyhow, Daddy'd been saving up money for years and keeping it on the sly. One day he just drives this old girl up and hands me the keys. She was a beat-up and sorry-looking mess. Rancher'd used her for pretty much everything and she was covered in mud, dented up from wrangling steers, busted-off tailpipe so there was smoke curling up around both sides of the box and the inside smelling like old horseshit and wet cow dog. But she drove good.

"I stood there with my eyes bugged out and he hands me the keys and says, 'Well, she ain't exactly dream wheels like the young bucks say, but she'll get you where you wanna go.' And she did. I fixed her up with winnings and we drove the hell out of her for two full seasons. When I got busted in Mesquite your grandmother and I drove here in her. She built this ranch. Everything that's part of what you see was hauled here in this old girl, and when Birch went pro he took her on the road with him. She's been to every place with a name that rings in a cowboy's heart and she's been sung in, puked in, slept in, cried in, celebrated in and likely or not had some damn good lovin' made in her too."

"She's butt ugly," Joe Willie said.

"She deserves to be. She earned it."

"And you wanted me to see her why?"

"Because she's still dream wheels, boy. She can still take you where you want to go."

"I don't want to go anywhere and besides, this old heap'd never turn over even if there was a place I wanted going to."

"She's your history," Lionel said.

"She's a piece of shit."

"History don't necessarily gotta be pretty for it to be your own."

"It'd help," Joe Willie said, and the two of them laughed.

"Course, it'd be way too much for you," Lionel said.

"What?"

"The truck."

"Whaddaya mean?"

"I mean she's yours now. Long as you don't mind me'n the pooch still coming out to sit in her and smoke and watch the sun go down."

"I don't want this heap," Joe Willie said. "What would I do with it?"

"Rebuild her, I was figuring," Lionel said.

"You're crazy."

"You're right."

"What?"

"You're right, I'm crazy. It's the years, I guess. Don't rightly know what I was thinking. It took you almost twenty minutes just to get out here and you needed my shoulder to get up into her. No way you could find your way around her well enough to find a way to fix her up."

"Damn straight," Joe Willie said.

"Shame, though."

"What's that?"

"Shame to see the line get broke. My daddy, me, Birch. All of us got a stake in this old truck. Got our blood in it, our gumption, our grit. Got rodeo in her, all over her. Shame to see her sit and crumble. Still, she's yours now," Lionel said and tossed the keys on the seat beside him.

Joe Willie didn't make a move to pick them up. He sat and stared at them. Finally, he shook his head slowly and gave an exasperated little breath.

"I know you can't fix her, boy," Lionel said. "Sorry for even thinking that. It'd take a hell of a lot of work and there's purely no way you'd be able to do it. But she's your history. She's rodeo. She's the Wolfchild story. That's why I kept her here pointed at those mountains all these years. Kinda hoping I guess that she'd pull another load some day, haul another of us toward wherever it was we wanted to go. Dreaming, though, I guess. Only dreaming. Just a part of being old myself."

Lionel opened the door and got out. The dog jumped out after him and he walked around the front of the truck and opened the door. Joe Willie just sat there.

"Coming?" Lionel asked.

"No," he said, flatly. "You go on."

"You want me to get the pickup and come back for you?"

"No. I'll get there."

"You're sure? No trouble."

"I'm sure. You go on."

Lionel studied him for a moment. Joe Willie sat straight in the seat, his eyes looking out toward the mountains, and Lionel recognized the quiet he'd slipped into. It was like the quiet after a competition and the noise, when the road stretched out in front of a man like a whispered promise.

"Okay," he said and closed the door gently. "Call if you need me."

Joe Willie looked at him briefly, nodded and drifted back into his silence.

"Watch this," Julius said.

"What?" Aiden asked.

"The corridor. Right now."

They stepped out of Aiden's cell and leaned against the bars. Julius nodded toward a line of five boys walking insolently down the corridor. When they got to the front of a particular cell the last two boys in line took up positions on either side of the door and the other three stepped quickly inside. There was a short yelp of surprise and then the solid thwack of punches and the lower, softer thud of kicks to the body and the rattle of metal and the grim silence of the cellblock as boys raised their heads from card games or rested their elbows on railings to listen to the sounds of the beating. It was over quickly. The three boys emerged from the cell and the five of them ambled off in different directions, losing themselves at tables or in other cells within seconds. There was only silence from the cell they'd been in.

"What the fuck was that?" Aiden asked.

"Justice," Julius said. "It's called the blanket treatment."

"What's that?"

"You throw a blanket over the rat's head so he don't know who you are, then you square the fucking deal. This boy got lucky."

"That's lucky?"

"Yeah. He didn't get shivved. Only took a beating. Most rats get a blade in the belly, but he'll remember this. Fuckin' rats. I hate 'em. That's what's gotta happen with your rat when he gets here."

"Knife him?" Aiden asked.

"Knife him, pipe him, beat on him, I don't give a damn either way it goes down. Just so long as it does," Julius said.

"Why should it matter to you?" Aiden asked.

Julius stood up to his full height and looked down at Aiden. "It's my world, man. All things gotta be right in my world. If it ain't then things go all to hell. Your world too now. You got to keep it right. You got to maintain the respect. Rat got no respect so he gotta pay, pay large. If you don't square it means you got no respect either and you gotta go down too. That's just the way it is, man. It's a fucking jungle an' you gotta be Tarzan."

Aiden thought of Cort Lehane, and that thought led him to other thoughts, of his mother, of the fat prick beating on her, of all the rooms in all the houses he'd occupied, all the bullshit men, all the new starts with all the same old endings and how now, this cold, grey, opaque world was all he was left with, all he had to frame a life with, and he squeezed the bars in his fists until he could feel the tendons start to strain, then he turned wordlessly and left Julius standing at the front of his cell.

For Golec home was a feeling you carried inside you. It had always seemed to him that he'd found that feeling first and then the wheel of life had brought him Karen, then the job, then the kids and lastly the brick building on the cul-de-sac where he'd laid everything out like unpacking luggage, ordered it, stored it and learned its rhythms through the soles of his stocking feet. Before all that, before he'd found the force and the calling he still felt after all these years, he'd been a rambler and seen his share of menial work in diverse places. It's how he'd met Birch Wolfchild. He'd been pulling fence in Wyoming for a rancher who favoured whiskey over work and was rich enough to hire out everything when it became necessary. Golec had been there a week when the old man asked for a ride to Gillette for the rodeo. He'd put them both up in a good hotel, paid for Golec's ticket to the show and given him day money over and above his wages in return for driving him around town to wherever there was a party to be had. He hadn't minded the rodeo, but driving a half-drunk old man around Gillette all hours of the night grated on his sensibilities. He'd been sitting in an all-night café waiting for the club to close, drinking coffee and planning his next move once he'd been paid off for the fencing.

A cowboy had come in and slumped down casually on the next stool. Before he knew it Golec was telling him everything about his life and the cowboy had ordered them food and sat and listened and asked questions. It still surprised him after all these years that Birch had so easily got him to talking. Effortlessly. There was something in the languid motion of the man that told Golec that he could be trusted and that there wasn't a whole lot in the world that might disturb him. They talked for a couple hours, and when Birch asked him to accompany him to the back lot the next night he'd agreed.

"She looks different back there" was all he said. "For me the real rodeo's always been back there, out of sight, there's a feel for it there you can't get in the seats."

So he'd sat on the railing with Birch and the other cowboys and seen the world of rodeo up close. It had been the start of a great friendship. Golec had eventually met the entire Wolfchild family and visited the ranch whenever he got a chance. When Karen came along Birch and Johanna travelled to his wedding, and whenever Joe Willie had ridden anywhere remotely close through the years the Golecs and the Wolfchilds always met for a reunion. It was a relationship built on the easy flow of language and talk. Birch could always get him going effortlessly, and through the years had reciprocated in kind so that Golec knew for a fact that there was a man in his corner that he could trust absolutely.

"Are you sure?" Claire asked. "Why would they do this for a complete stranger? Why would they open their home up to a boy getting out of jail?"

Golec looked around at Claire's new apartment. It was cheerful, and there were tasteful pictures on the wall and a selection of books and music that told him that this woman had refinement built into her, and he was glad to see that she was getting the chance to find it in herself and express it. Golec smiled. "Because he's a cowboy and because he's an Indian."

"What's that got to do with it?"

"The ranch is his world. Everything has got to be right in his world. For Birch it means respecting everything, nurturing it, making it grow. If he doesn't do that he's not being respectful, and cowboys and Indians pay a heap of attention to being respectful. He'll help Aiden because I asked. They all will."

"Just like that?"

"Just like that."

"Amazing," Claire said, and she felt the warmth of a profound gratitude seep through her and tears slid down her face, and Golec put an arm around her and she let him, lay her head against his shoulder.

"Thank you," she said softly.

She'd sunk on her springs after all the years of sitting there, and when he shifted his weight around he could feel her sway. Even the cracked-leather seats in the cab were sunken. He could see the depressed imprint of the driver in a perfect horseshoe shape, and as he gazed along the bench seat he saw the dips where tired legs had rested, and beneath him he could feel the same used and tired hollow against his thighs and buttocks. She'd had her share of passengers, that was sure. And she had the familiar, particular smell of rodeo in her, that pervasive funk of liniment, tobacco, rope, straw, leather, sweat and beer that brought a sudden grin to his face. He rubbed a circle of dust from the dashboard and felt the slight, hard ridges where cigarettes had burned down while cowboys slept before the driver or another passenger had reached over to pick them up and smoke them off. He felt small cuts and abrasions, nicks from the rowel of spurs tossed onto it, and here and there as he looked at the patch he'd cleared, he saw the stain of tobacco juice, wiped hurriedly but not completely after a cowboy's burst of laughter at a real good one, told as the old truck chased the white line toward another show somewhere down the road. There was history in her, that was sure.

The front end of her curved deeply, diving sharply downward to gather in the twin grilleworks on either side of her nose. She was a pale red, more orange now than the vivid scarlet he imagined her to have been when she was new. The metal of the hood had oxidation marks, the natural wear of age, but she looked solid enough. The shed had kept her safe from snow and rain, and even the west wind that blew through the open door had been gentle to her. Joe Willie closed his eyes to imagine how the rounded nose of her must have looked arrowing down the road, and when he did he saw his mother and his father, young and fresh and vital, laughing as they drove, Birch with one arm flung around her shoulders like he always did and Johanna resting her head on his shoulder, her right hand helping him to steer, singing. Then Lionel and Victoria, tired, worn from the road, sitting stalwart on the seat, themselves young and strong, heading north into the mountains toward the valley where they'd build a ranch, a home, a future. They were beauti-ful. All of them. Joe Willie saw it like a vision, like the ceremo-nial gift his grandmother told him that some young men were given when they sacrificed. It came from somewhere at the back of his eyes as crystal clear as a scene from a movie and it rattled him some with its intensity. He kept his eyes closed to see more of it, to recapture some of the lives before his own, to see his-tory, the line of him begun almost a century before.

Then he saw the bear. It moved slowly out of the draw, the great hump of its shoulders easing over the lip of the rise. It stood there then, stood there against the great blue-grey and green of the mountains, looking at him. Looking and not mov-ing, the feral gaze locking him in the seat of that old truck, watching him, studying him. And then it stood on its back legs, its great front claws draped in front of its chest, its snout rising, pointing into the breeze, and Joe Willie could hear the huff of it like a bellows across the gap of pasture that separated them. Then it dropped to all fours and walked slowly toward him. Thirteen steps. He counted them. Sat there in the truck and consciously counted the steps the bear took with his eyes closed, the scene bright and sharp. Then it stopped, its head lowered to look at him, the eyes more hazel than deep brown, before it turned and began to walk away. Thirteen steps. Then it rose again on its hind legs and walked to the lip of the draw, where it stopped and looked back at him again. It wasn't a bear's face. It was the face of the woman, and she gazed right into him with knowing hazel eyes before dropping to the ground in bear shape again and disappearing into the draw toward the mountains.

Joe Willie gasped and opened his eyes. He smelled the rich old smell of the truck, rubbed a hand along the dashboard again, exhaled deeply through puffed-out cheeks and pushed the door open. There was something here. He knew that for certain. He didn't know what but he knew that he'd come back to get more of it. Maybe it was nothing, maybe it was all the product of hurt and loss and anger, but it was something, and it was his. He grabbed the crutch and struggled out of the cab. When he got to the door he turned to look at the old truck again. Dream wheels. The damnedest thing. There might be something to it after all.

book three

THE CHALLENGE

e could still remember the feel of the pipe in his hand. It was a mop bucket handle and he'd wrapped it in a towel and stuck it down his pants and walked down the corridor behind Julius and another boy toward the cell where they'd put Cort. It felt solid, the heft of it assuring him of the rightness of things, the necessity to order things in his world where he'd been sentenced to spend the next two years. Cort had drawn six months. He'd written a blistering statement about how Aiden had forced him into the crime through threats against his family. It played so well that even Claire had looked over at him speculatively and he'd squeezed the railing of the prisoner's box hard to avoid screaming. Like he'd squeezed the pipe. They'd walked down the corridor and all around him he could hear the deadening of sound, the strange half-muted drawing in of breath and conversation that happened when something was about to go down in the joint, when the population intuited energy transferred into fists or blades or pipes and waited for the release, the solid pop of wills broken or proclaimed and the silent thrill of blood. The tiny hairs had stood up on his arms and he felt his throat constrict and dry.

Julius and the other boy had taken positions outside the door and he just walked into the cell and up to Cort, who was sitting at the small metal desk with his back to the door. The first blow felt justified. The thwack of it sent a jolt up his arm. The towel cushioned the shock and there was blood only after his head slammed down on the desk and he tumbled to the floor and split his chin. The second, third and fourth blows were just for effect and he avoided the head, settling for the ribs and arms before dropping to one knee and cradling Cort's head in his hand and looking straight into his drooping eyes.

"Rat," he'd said and then laid the boy's head down on the cold concrete floor. He wondered why he hadn't just let it fall.

They'd made him for it. Even though Cort in his heightened state of fear refused to say anything, the fact that they were co-accused made Aiden the logical fall guy. So he'd drawn Southwood, the maximum-security joint for youths with management problems. He'd laughed at that. The only management problem he'd had up until then had been in trusting someone other than himself. He wouldn't make that mistake again. He was rightly pissed to have to go down on someone else's stupidity and weakness, and the act of vengeance, of putting things right, had gotten around quickly. So he'd walked into Southwood as a kind of celebrity. First because the word *conspiracy* lifted him over the break-and-enter, car theft, assault, possession of stolen property and small-time drug beefs other guys walked in with. It gave him status. It smacked of style. It made him a *criminal*. Plus, getting even with the rat meant he was solid, he stood by the inmate code and he took no bullshit.

Julius had people there, so he was known before he even walked in, and he'd had no problem getting accepted and drawn into the best clique in the joint.

They were called Johnny's Crew. Johnny Calder was an old Navy mechanic who'd worked in corrections for about twenty years. He was a bowlegged stump of a man, every line of him rounded by muscle, and his face bore the scars of a lifetime of wild brawls. Calder only liked tough guys around him, and the auto shop was where the solidest of the solid worked. No one without status had a chance to get in there. Calder handpicked his crew. He read the sheets of every boy coming into Southwood and he could be seen at the edges of the athletic fields and the classrooms, watching, gauging, reading. When he rolled into your cell to add you to his list you knew you'd made the best grade in the joint.

"Way I figure it is, we're all doing time here," Johnny would say. "Might as well shake it with good people."

He had a small ring set up at the back of the shop and it was where management disputes got settled. There'd been a huge farm boy named Jurgens once, a monster in strength and rage who'd made the mistake of trying to run Johnny's shop. The fight between them was a piece of prison legend and Jurgens had been dispatched so quickly, so efficiently that no one was willing to make that choice again. Instead, they drank coffee all day, smoked, listened to good music and learned engines and boxing.

He drove them hard. But he did it man to man and Aiden appreciated his no-bullshit attitude, and when the old guy bent over an engine to show him how to adjust or replace something, Aiden felt as though he wasn't so much teaching him something new as reminding him of something he'd just forgotten. It was the same in the ring. Calder liked Aiden's natural athleticism and he taught him very deliberately, making him throw two hundred jabs at a time with each fist and skipping rope endlessly. He showed him the feints and the footwork and combinations, made him repeat them over and over before he ever allowed him into the ring.

"Life ain't fair, Hartley," he said. "Truth is, it ain't about being fair. You got to be ready for the fight before it ever happens."

It was the same with the cars. No one stayed in the auto shop if he couldn't figure his way around an engine. Aiden found that he could lose himself in the tinkering under the hood, and spending time in the shop made time disappear altogether. After a year had passed he could pretty much determine what a car needed by the sound of it. When the assault on Cort sabatoged his early release and his deal with Golec, it was Calder who channelled his anger, put him in the body shop where he could spend less time in population and more time working on the staff cars and joint vehicles.

There was a life force to automobiles that Aiden could feel, and he knew what they needed by running his palms along the fenders, hoods and side panels. Once he'd tuned the engines he'd focus on the bodywork. He'd concentrate. He'd close his eyes and try to envision the finished project, see himself doing what needed to be done, watch himself bring that life force back, and he would. Slowly but surely he would, and the solitary pursuits of mechanical work and workouts on the heavy bag made time disappear. Aiden sometimes missed entire days that way, and eighteen months were over before he knew it and he was finally released. He was almost seventeen.

He'd done his time like a man, never backing down from trouble or looking to incite it. He'd learned to move in a calculated quietness, his face emotionless, barely speaking to anyone, and the force of that solitude gained him an edge, a hint of danger that made drawing himself inward easier, and distance became his greatest ally.

"You're a tough monkey, Hartley," Johnny told him his last day in the shop. "Hang on to it. Learn how to use it. Don't let it use you or you'll wind up in a place like this that won't be so con-fucking-vivial."

Then he'd simply slapped him on the shoulder and wished him luck.

But he could still remember the feel of the pipe in his hand. It had been powerful, solid, the measure of him, and walking with it down that corridor had been both an opening and a closing. It slammed shut on the need of anything or anyone but himself and it had swung open on the knowledge that he had what it took to handle anything. When they came to get him he stood at the door of his cell with the small bag of belongings at his feet holding the bars with both hands. He squeezed them. Hard. He wanted to remember how unyielding and cold and immovable they were. He wouldn't make a criminal mistake again. He was sure of it. Instead, somehow, he'd do what Johnny said and learn to curb his toughness, make it work for him, use the silence he moved into in the joint to keep people off him until he decided they were solid, loyal, trustworthy. If no one measured up in the end, so be it, he figured. He flexed his shoulders like shrugging off rain and walked out of the cell and down the corridor without speaking to anyone.

Golec was waiting for him in the parking lot.

Turning the wrench was like lighting a fire in his wrist and forearm. Still, Joe Willie gritted his teeth and pushed from the elbow and the shoulder. He felt the nut slip some. The hand shook and he had to use his right hand to guide the wrench into place. His grip was okay, but the muscles along the length of the arm had shrunk and there was nothing left around the shoulder to aid in lifting or turning. But he did all the work on the truck left-handed. That was a decision he'd made when he first came out to the shed.

It started with the driver's side mirror. It bothered him the way it threatened to fall off each time the door was opened or closed. He'd sit in the cab relishing the privacy and the mirror would distract him. Eventually, it had driven him nearly crazy and he'd rummaged about and found a toolbox. It seemed like an easy enough procedure to snug the bolt, and with his right hand it would have taken no time at all. But he found himself wondering if he could turn the bolt with the arm. That's how he referred to it. The arm. Life with the arm. The arm was a curse. Things would be fine if it weren't for the arm. So he'd taken the cold metal in his left hand and lifted the arm into place with his right. Snugging the bolt took hours, and the burn in his shoulder as bone turned on bone was incredible, but he eventually twisted it tight. With every push, every twist he felt the anger surge out of him. He'd done the passenger-side mirror the next day. After that he'd made it his place. No one but his grandfather was allowed to go out there, and if the old man began leaving tools, manuals, oil, grease and bit parts lying around in the cab after he and the dog had paid their nightly visit, he'd pretend not to notice and not a word was ever said about it.

Instead they let him be and he silently appreciated that. Words had become foreign things. There was no way Joe Willie could figure to say what churned in him most days. It was a heady mix. Days went by when he just flatlined. Zeroed. He moved about the shed like a zombie those days, focussed only on the chore at hand. Other days the rage would seize him and he'd curse while he struggled with tools and the rusted-on arrogance of metal. Still others he'd feel the lostness the desertion of Darlene had struck him with. She'd never called after that day and she and Smith, the contractor, were the new big thing in town. Smith, after all, had two arms. Joe Willie's sense of manliness had walked out the door that day and he might have learned to adjust to that if it weren't for the fact that there was always a mirror, always a reflective surface somewhere to display him to himself and to the world. When he looked at those reflections the first thing Joe Willie saw was the arm. The lack. The deformity. The wrongness. The inadequacy. He hated it. He covered it with long-sleeved shirts whenever people were around. When he had to present himself he took great pains to only be seen from the right side. The left hand was always tucked in a pocket or covered with the right. The hardest thing to cope with was the look the arm always garnered. The look was an irritating mix of pity, sorrow and accusation. Cripple. Gimp. Deformed. Handicapped. He hated every one of those words and every time he passed a mirror they seemed to jump out at him. His dresser mirror had disappeared the same day Darlene had. But there were others everywhere and the shed was his only refuge. He only allowed himself the truck. He'd grown to like sitting in her and he usually ended his day in the shed by having a smoke in her. He smoked more now. It calmed him. The feel of smoke in his lungs made it easier to get past the churning he carried in his gut. It was the ranch. Being so close to the stuff of rodeo without actually being able to live it was the worst kind of torture and only the closing of the shed doors behind him and the flare of a smoke in the darkness could calm him. The shed had become his world, and his surly protection of it kept everyone away. Now, flat on his back on a thin mat beneath her he stopped to rub the arm. No one was allowed to see him work. No one was allowed to see the fumbles, drops, shakes and general immobility of the arm. It angered him and no one was allowed to see the anger either. Instead, he walked in a calculated quietness, his face emotionless, barely speaking to anyone, and the force of that solitude gave him an edge, a hint of danger that made drawing himself inward easier, and distance had become his greatest ally.

The arm was a wreck and so was the old truck. That seemed appropriate somehow. He'd sit awhile in the cab and have a smoke and meditate on the moves he wanted to make, tried to see himself doing it like spurring a bronc on the mark out from the chute. Then he'd settle himself with the tools and try to make it happen. He took all of the pent-up heat in him and put it into the effort. He swore. He cursed. He damned the arm out loud, but he never quit. The pain was the closest thing he could get to the challenge of a bull, and he rode the pain as determinedly as he'd once fought for eight. It was the closest thing he could get to the pain of Darlene's rejection of him, and the sweat that stung his eyes burned the tears of rage away and he wiped them with a taut, coiled fist. No one could see that. No one could witness his torture. He was ashamed and he was angry and he faced it alone. Only when he'd settled again, calmed himself with a cigarette and a few minutes of relaxing in the seat of the old truck, could he walk across the pasture again and be in that other world.

He could walk strongly now, quickly, and he was gravely intent on making sure to move the arm, swing it into the regular rhythm of walking. He concentrated on that. It made him feel normal. Two arms in motion gave him the semblance of wholeness, and if the stiffened elbow of the left arm coupled with the swivelled swinging step of the right leg gave him a weird rolling motion through the offset leg and shoulder, he pretended not to care. But his body remembered the lean, sinewy toughness of motion before the ride. That was the tough part, the body memory. He wouldn't speak of it. He pulled it tight around him and stared outwardly from it, sullenly. He lived alone, drawn inward by anger and his shame and only allowing the truck to let him breathe.

Now he leaned into the turning of the nut again. The clench of his teeth met the rusted hold of the metal, and for a moment there was contest until finally, gradually, the nut slipped and he exhaled and began turning it freely off and into his palm.

"What the hell are you doing here?" Aiden asked.

"We had a deal," Golec said.

"Yeah, well, unless you hadn't noticed that deal got fucked when they wouldn't let me out."

"That deal got fucked when you beat that poor boy."

"That poor boy was a fucking rat and he deserved what he got."

"No one deserves that, Aiden."

"Maybe not in your shining world, Golec, but it's a grimmer place back there." Aiden hooked a thumb back toward the jail.

"Maybe so. Maybe what you did was about honour. Some strange sense of honour. Maybe I can accept it that way, knowing that you had to show honour in order to survive in there. But you know what?"

"What?" Aiden looked around the parking lot, wondering where his mother might be.

"You have to have honour out here too."

"So?"

"So we have a deal."

"Fuck that, Golec. I did my time. I got no need for your giddy-up bullshit now. In fact, you got no need to even be talking to me."

"True enough. Except we have a deal and your mother's expecting you to honour it."

"She is?"

"Yes. She is."

"Why?"

"I don't know. I told her myself that you didn't have to follow through, that you did your time and you have all the right in the world to just walk away and disregard it. But she seemed to think you'd agree. She seemed to think that you'd be man enough to do it anyway. For her. For yourself. Especially for her."

The man leaned against the fender of his car with his arms folded, and Aiden recognized the insouciant grace of the tough guy in his manner. At that moment Golec reminded him of Johnny Calder, and it was that more than anything that kept him in the conversation. "Why?" he asked again.

"I told you before. She's all you got, Aiden. You might come walking out of that joint with the attitude that you can handle it all now, you been in max and survived. Hell, from what I hear, you were one of the big boys. That might lend you the thought that you don't need anybody. But we all need people, Aiden. Even you."

"Nice speech. But I don't think so."

"Don't think what? That you don't need anybody?"

"Don't think I need the Roy and Trigger routine. I ain't no cowboy. I can get me a job right around here."

"Can you? You're an ex-con now. You got a sheet. Maybe a short go on the ranch'll give you a reference, get you a foot in the door when you want to apply for a job. Maybe other than a few weeks in the fresh air and sunshine and some hard work you'll come away with the bricks to build a new foundation for yourself. Unless you don't give a shit and want this grimmer life."

Aiden lit a cigarette and looked back at the jail. He was silent a long time while he smoked. He knew he had no plan. When he'd considered his life after he walked out, he'd settled on the fact that he'd have to make things happen for himself. No one was going to walk up and offer him anything, and he was sensible enough to know that it was going to take a lot of hard work to stay straight, to avoid this place and others like it, and that he'd need a break or two, that he'd need to reach for them when they presented themselves. Johnny Calder had told him one day while they were working on footwork that a good fighter never waited for a guy to give him an opening. Instead, a good fighter used the ring and all he knew to create an opening for himself and then drove into it with everything he had. That's how you won a fight, he'd told him and showed him how to make a man move where he wanted him to move.

"I'll go for cash. And a reference when it's over," he said finally.

Golec studied him. "And your mother?"

"Her too," Aiden said and ground out the smoke with his heel.

"I'll see what I can do," Golec said and reached for his cellphone.

"You do that, cop," Aiden said.

They were herding a dozen steers down out of the high pasture. The steers were on their way to a rodeo, and they wanted to give them a day or so in the pens to increase their feed and get them ready for the show. They rode casually, and every now and then Lionel would whistle sharply and the dog would yap a few times, sneak in and nip at the heels of a slower steer and keep them moving down the trail. It wasn't hard work. Both the steers and the horses knew their way down, and the two men spent a lot of time looking through the trees for glimpses of the valley. They never tired of the view.

"Got a new wrangler coming," Birch said.

"How's that?" Lionel asked.

"Remember the kid I told you about a while back? The one Marcel called about?"

"The convict?" Lionel looked at him over the cigarette he was rolling while he rode.

"Yeah. He's coming. Him and his mother. Marce wants us to give him a leg up getting started again. Kid doesn't have to come. He's a free man now but he's coming anyway."

"What'd he do anyhow?"

"Marce says nothing."

"Mighty peculiar to do a bunch of time for nothing." Lionel lit the cigarette and then chucked to the horse, who kicked a little at the smoke.

"Yessir, it is. The way Marce tells it, the boy had a plan for a heist, even got a gun to do it but his partner pulled it without him, got himself shot and put all the blame on this boy."

"Still don't seem worth a stretch out of a young guy's life. Mother know?"

"She knows. She's getting Joe Willie's old room upstairs ready and the extra."

"The kid's a handful, is he?"

"Marce says he's a pretty good kid. Tough, though. Hard to reach."

"Reckon we got a handle on how to deal with that."

"I reckon," Birch said. They rode on silently awhile and then Birch looked over at his father. "Why you figure Joe Willie never says anything about anything?"

"There's words in Joe Willie," Lionel said. He looked at the cigarette with dissatisfaction and ground it out against the chest pocket of his jacket. "There's words and plenty he means to say but he hasn't been able to fight through to them yet. Everything's discombobulated. Nothing's the same as it was, and the way he feels, it never will be. So it's gotta be hard. Hard enough fighting back from a big hurt to get everything back to normal, but knowing there's no normal to get back to anymore has got to give the fighting a mighty bitter taste. Hard to talk through that taste, I imagine."

Birch nodded. "Kills me to not hear him sometimes."

"Kills me too."

"You reckon this new boy's gonna be about the same deal?"

"Never been to jail myself," Lionel said. "Never seen much percentage in it. But it seems to me that when you lock a man up you lock up the whole deal. Turnin' his body loose is only halfway to freedom. Takes a while for the insides to catch up."

"Meaning?"

"Meaning we only got the one truck."

Birch looked at him silently and pushed the hat back on his head and scratched at his ear before resetting the hat, kicking the horse up to a canter and moving to head off a steer aiming for the freedom of the trees. Sometimes his father was just too damn deep.

Claire watched the light break across the skyline. Her eye followed the jut of buildings across the expanse of park, and it seemed to her then that the angles of the city were harsh, severe, and she found herself craving roundness, the poke of angles reduced to slow rolling humps of land and the strict rectangle of city grid eroded into undulating swatches of meadow, brush and trees. She was a city girl, had been all her life, and it was only in daydream she'd experienced the open land. Now, though, as she prepared to leave for the west, to meet her son at the ranch where Marcel's friends would host them for three weeks, the land emerged fully realized in her mind. She hadn't seen Aiden in eighteen months. He wrote to her, sent Polaroid pictures of him with cars and told her some of what he was doing, but Claire sensed that she wasn't getting the whole story. Golec told her about the assault on Cort. That had scared her. Now, as she awaited her cab to the airport, she wondered how this great stretch of time had affected him.

"He's harder," Golec had said, a few weeks ealier. "There's more push to him now."

"Push?"

"Push back. You can't approach him so easily anymore."

"God."

"He's a kid, Claire," Golec had said. "He's coming out of there looking like a man, but inside he's still the fifteen-year-old kid that got swallowed up."

"And you're sure going to this ranch will help?"

"Yes."

"How?"

"I worked on a ranch when I was younger. It's hard work. It might look all romantic and casual in the movies but it's a hard life. You need an extra gumption gene to be any good at it. It's like prison that way."

"I don't follow."

"Living in a jailhouse situation, even if it's a kids' joint, takes a lot of nerve. If a boy's going to make it in there he needs an extra serving of grit on his plate. Aiden made it. He reached down inside himself and found the grit and gumption to do what it took to survive. It takes a hard man to do that.

"The Wolfchilds are rodeo people, have been all their lives, and when he's out there with them he's going to see that life. He's going to see one-hundred-and-seventy-pound men getting up on the backs of two-thousand-pound animals. It takes a hard man to do that. Aiden's going to want to take that challenge."

"Why would he want to do that? He has no idea about rodeo," Claire said.

"No. But he has an idea of challenge."

"What do you mean?"

Claire watched him think. The men she'd known had all been slick thinkers, the answers at the ready, the talk glib and casual, and she felt uncomfortable at the depth of thought Golec put into his response.

"What I mean," Golec said finally, "is that from what you've told me, everything has presented itself as a challenge to Aiden. New schools, new neighbourhoods, new friends and a parade of new men at home. Hell, and I don't mean this as any sort of put-down to you, Claire, but home itself has been a challenge for him. You said as much yourself. So all he knows is how to step up and greet something head on. It takes a whole lot of nerve to even think about doing what he'd planned with that robbery.

"It tells me that there's a whole lot to him. A whole lot that even he doesn't know. Now you could spend a ton of energy trying to bring him into line, but to my mind it just wouldn't take. Or you could introduce him to something that will challenge him more than he's ever been before."

"The ranch?" Claire asked.

"Yes. I know the Wolfchilds and I know their world. I know that it's their world that makes them what they are. Good people, steady. Aiden would do well to be in that world awhile. So would you."

"You're sure."

"Never more."

And that had been it. Now, she stood in the middle of the room and wondered why they called it a living room. When you were alone there wasn't a great deal of living going on. She glanced around at the accumulation of stuff, the small gathering of things that sat on the shelves, hung on the walls and graced the windows. None of it worked. None of it performed a function beyond the filling of space. None of it held any special properties, any attractant energy that could pull life together. None of it mattered in the end. What mattered was the energy of people. People made a living room live. History didn't lie within the things you kept. History lay within the people who filled the rooms. History was what her family needed now, and she reached down and grabbed her bags and stepped toward the beginning of her history with her son.

Against the sky the trees looked like fingers stretched upward in something that looked like praise. Joe Willie shook his head. Sometimes a man thought the most amazing thoughts alone on the land. When he used to ride the trails above the ranch he'd find himself drifting from thought to thought like a kid leaping stone to stone across a stream. It was the part of riding he enjoyed the most, the long, uninterrupted musing on horseback that made him feel joined to it, hooked up to the same energy he could feel in the things around him. Kinship. He remembered his grandmother calling it that and telling him how the old people regarded the land as a relative. Nin-din-away-mah-john-ee-dog. That was the Ojibway word. All my relations. He never used the language, only recalled snippets of it now and then when the conversation prompted it, but the word sat on his tongue as he walked. He whispered it. Then, as he got comfortable with the pitch of it he said it louder. It gave him a cool feeling in his head, as if it emptied somehow and there was nothing there but space and time and a rich blankness that he savoured. It's why he came here. Evenings when there was no one about. It freed him to disappear without questions and he'd taken to walking up the long, steep trail he used to ride, up Iron Mountain.

He'd never made it all the way. The leg generally gave out long before he arrived at the final upward push, and he'd sit in the trees resting before easing back down as the night fell around him. More than anything, Joe Willie wanted to make that journey, wanted to stand in the meadow that faced that sheer face of rock. He knew it took a horse to do it, that walking it was one of the toughest hikes even a two-legged man could attempt, that his pinned and shrunken right thigh would surrender somewhere far below the meadow, but he came anyway. A foot. A yard. Every trip he tried to make it farther, leaning a rock against a tree to mark his distance. He wanted to see that peak again. There wasn't a reason in his head, nothing he could point to as motivation, only something in him understood that to face the spire of Iron Mountain again under his own power meant something big. Important. More than just the fact that he'd made it there. He'd do it even if it killed him. He'd do it if it took him years, if he had to crawl the last hundred yards. But there was something more there. Something he felt in that rich blankness in his head that came with that old Ojibway word. He wouldn't give it a name. To name it, to shape it by reason and language might dispel its particular magic and leave him morose at the foot of the mountain, cleared of the feel of the word on his tongue and the taste of the air, the pine, juniper, and the warm, moist fungal smell of the land. That's what he came for. His senses felt sharper, keener, more attuned. His insides moved out here and he found himself cherishing that and protecting it, stashing it away because its foreign softness felt stolen somehow. He'd never been a spiritual man. Rather, Joe Willie believed that life was about clenching the teeth and making things happen, will bent to power, action spurred by desire. But here he felt pause. Nin-din-away-mah-john-ee-dog.

The shadows were deeper now and he could tell by the light through the top of the trees that he had about a half an hour before he'd have to turn back. He took a sip of water from the bottle at his belt and looked through the trees. Then he switched his gaze to the bend in the trail ahead of him, focussed on it, measured its slope and pushed off with the good leg, swinging the left around assuredly, feeling the pressure when it planted and gritting his teeth to push off again.

He'd never seen anything like it. Golec punched him lightly on the thigh and he raised his head and looked out the windshield. The land was rich in dozens of shades of green. The mountains hard against the clear blue sky scalloped the length of the valley, and the variant colours of the rock, the long, V-shaped funnelling of slides, the poked peninsulas of trees and the undulating suggestion of lesser, rounded humps of peaks before them gave it a wild kinetic energy, an intensity humming in the stillness as though all of it, the mountains, the valley, the sky, was vibrating with the effort of holding itself in. To his eyes, used to the dullness of concrete and steel, it was a feast, and Aiden sat straighter, watching it unroll before them. He could feel the openness work against his insides. As his eyes reached farther down the length of the valley he felt smaller and larger at the same time. As the car ate up the distance, he felt less like he was moving through it as he was moving with it, becoming a part of the sage and pasture and draw and the severe slope of the valley, and the feeling crested and broke against his ribs and he exhaled long and slow.

"Something, isn't it?" Golec said in a way that wasn't a question.

"Yeah," Aiden said. "It is."

They watched the land in silence until Golec slowed and turned into a long, curved driveway. The ranch sat sprawled in the sunlight like a lazy old dog and there was a contentedness about it that made Golec smile. Aiden drummed his fingers against his thigh. As they neared the main buildings people began to stroll out toward where the driveway spilled into the large rectangle of the yard. Aiden stared straight ahead and Golec felt his intensity, a pushing out, a distancing, a cool barricade of sullen nonchalance that started in the jaw, and Golec could feel him downshifting his face into neutral as they parked. It was a look Golec was familiar with, the look of stern, obdurate men planting their feet in defiance, as cool and unbreakable as the concrete that had forged it.

"Let's meet the folks," Golec said and opened the door.

Aiden watched as Golec was swept up in welcome. There was an exuberance to it all that seemed false to him, as though they were play acting for his benefit and hadn't learned the script well enough to play it any better so that you could read the holes in it. No one greeted people like that.

A tall older man walked around the front of the car to Aiden who stood with the door open, one foot resting on the bottom panel and leaning an elbow on the roof watching them. "Aiden," Lionel said, reaching out a hand. "Lionel Wolfchild."

Aiden regarded the old man before finally stretching his hand out to shake. "You're an Indian," he said.

"Last time I checked," Lionel said. "And as long as we're noticing, you're a black fella."

"Yeah. I am."

"Met a lotta great black cowboys in my time. You could be another one."

"Yeah, well, I'll watch. I'm just here for the work."

"Watching's good and you're welcome to do all of that you want and this is definitely a working ranch, son," Lionel said.

"I'm not your son," Aiden said.

"No, you're not," another tall, lean man said. "But around here you'll be treated like family, so get used to it. Birch Wolfchild. This is my wife, Johanna."

Aiden stood rigidly looking at the two of them.

"Son," Birch said, "it's customary around here to recognize people when they greet you."

Aiden reached his hand out. "You're all Indians," he said.

Birch laughed. It was a great bursting guffaw and his face exploded into a thousand wrinkles and furrows and gullies of pleasure. "As a matter of fact, we are," Birch said finally. "Indian cowboys."

"I didn't know there was such a thing," Aiden said.

"Son, Indian cowboys have been around a good long time and we got a lot of champions come from our stock. You'll meet a few while you're here. When you pitch in you'll get a chance to work side by side with real professional cowboys."

"Pitch in how?"

"Well, there's more to the business than just riding. A real cowboy does it all, from mucking out the stalls to feeding to moving stock to pulling fence to tending to the tack. It's pretty much a sun-up-to-sunset proposition."

"I'm not afraid of work," Aiden said.

"Well, now that's the funny thing," Johanna said. "It all sounds like work when you're standing here thinking about it. But when you start into it, let it sink into you, all the smells, all the motion, all the sounds, it doesn't feel like work at all. It feels like something you've done all your life. I'm Johanna."

She was the most exotic woman he'd ever seen. He held her hand momentarily once they'd shaken and stared at her. "Okay," he said.

"Good," Johanna said. "Have you ridden before?"

"No," Aiden said.

"It's not so hard. Once you're settled in we can take you to the corral and introduce you to some of them. Tonight you'll ride."

"Tonight?"

"Yup. Marcel says you agreed to come for three weeks. You don't want to be wasting any time, do you?"

"No. Well, yes. I mean, no," Aiden stammered.

"Good. We'll start in the round pen until you're both used to it—you and your mom when she gets here. We'll have you feeling like old-timers in no time at all."

"My wife has taught a powerful lot of people how to ride," Birch said. "Used to be one fine barrel racer and she knows horses. People too."

The front door opened and Joe Willie stepped out onto the porch. He let his eyes settle on Aiden. The boy felt his measure taken and he stood taller, pressing his shoulders back some, and when he looked back at the man on the porch the look was held and the eyes shone dully, flatly, with a look Aiden recognized immediately. They regarded each other for a long moment, then Joe Willie put on his hat and pulled the brim low down over his eyes. He put his head down and walked slowly off the porch and detoured around the opposite side of the car. He never said a word. They all watched him walk in the direction of the equipment shed.

"That's Joe Willie. My grandson," Victoria said, stepping up beside Aiden.

"He's crippled?" Aiden asked.

When there wasn't a reply Aiden looked around him. "What?" he said. "He *looks* crippled."

"My grandson was the best rider anyone ever saw at one time," Victoria said. "He was a champion from the time he was a boy. There wasn't anything he couldn't ride. We don't think of him as crippled."

"So what happened?" Aiden asked.

"He lost a half a second," Victoria said. She looked directly at Aiden. "It happens to the best of them. But I'd appreciate it if you didn't bring it up to him and I'd appreciate it if you didn't use that word again."

"Crippled?"

"That's right. My grandson's still a champion to me, always will be. I'll never see him as any less."

"Champion what?" Aiden asked.

"Champion of the world," Birch said. "My boy was seconds away from being World Champion All-Round Cowboy. That means he was the best at riding saddle broncs, bareback broncs and bulls. Especially bulls."

"Is that what happened to him? A bull got him?"

There was another long silence.

"We don't know yet," Victoria said finally.

She had to stop the car every few miles. Claire had rented a sporty convertible, and with the top down and the sun shining out of a hard electric-blue sky the land was invigorating. She pulled over to the shoulder and stepped out and allowed it to envelope her. It felt like it had hands. The breeze that blew across it brought the scent of juniper, pine and sage and animal smells that only served to heighten the sense of open space, so that standing there Claire felt the soul and the spirit of it all and she almost cried. There was a private place inside her that recognized it, and she allowed herself to breathe deeply and fully of it before driving on until the next vista beckoned and she stopped again. There was a song in it. She was sure of that. It was an ancient refrain that resided within everything, and she closed her eyes and let the breeze play across her face and tried to catch it, snare it with all her senses, reaching out even with her skin, so that when she hummed, a low, throaty note that was more moan than melody, it felt right and good and old as the land itself. She let it rise out of her. She stretched out her hands wide at her sides with her eyes closed and her head tilted back and let the note escape her, ragged and bruised and raw, and as it slid into the air she felt the land refill her, nestle into the spot where the note had lived and slake a thirst she never knew she carried.

She drove casually after that. The little car had pep and she let herself enjoy the thrill of it, the feel of speed on an open stretch of highway another song she felt within her. By the time she made the turn through town toward Wolf Creek she felt ready to greet her son again.

The ranch pleased her. Nothing ostentatious, merely a comfortable, settled place with two huge weeping willow trees in the front yard that framed a view of the valley that was as breathtaking as anything she ever imagined possible. Golec was the first to greet her and introduced her to the Wolfchilds. They seemed a very open family, and even though Claire had never had anything to do with Indians before, she felt an instant ease with them. Lionel and Birch were gangly and good-natured, with a shy side that had them scratching at their hat brims at times or simply pursing their lips and nodding toward the ground while they listened to the talk. But the women were amazing. Victoria was a matriarch. Claire could tell that from the bearing she had, walking straight backed and purposefully, speaking directly to her, engagingly, and holding her with her eyes so that Claire felt present and understood. Johanna was spectacular. She was quite likely the most regal-looking woman Claire had ever seen. Johanna was taller so Claire had to look up to meet her look. At that moment Johanna Wolfchild seemed iridescent, shining with a light that seemed pulled out of the valley itself so that when she smiled at her, Claire felt drawn in to everything, made welcome and included and important in one rush of energy. She reached out to shake her hand and the skin was warm and smooth and strong, and Johanna smiled at her again, then pulled her into a deep, full hug and held her a moment before letting her go. Claire felt honoured. Johanna looked at her and she felt known, stripped bare and understood and accepted.

"Good to see you, sister," Johanna said.

"Thank you," Claire said, and for a moment they all stood in silence looking at each other.

"They boy's in the main barn," Victoria said. "He's a mite ruffled by all this but those feathers will smooth now that you're here."

Claire looked at her. The old woman bore the same light as Johanna. "I wish I could be so sure."

"Go to him," Victoria said. "I've heard it's been a long time."

"It has," Claire said.

"Time shrinks all on its own, girl. Go on now."

"I'll go with you," Johanna said. "Might be good to have another mother around."

Claire smiled at her. "Yes. Thank you."

The two women stepped away from the others and crossed the rectangle of yard toward the barn. Johanna placed a hand at the small of Claire's back and walked beside her. There was depth to the small gesture and Claire wondered how much the Wolfchilds knew about her and Aiden's history, how much detail Golec had shared with them. "You know about our troubles?" she asked her.

"Not much," Johanna said. "Enough to know that a mother and a son need time and a place to mend their lives. I'm honoured to be able to give that."

"Why?"

Johanna stopped and Claire turned to face her. "I have a son I haven't talked to in a long time too," she said. "Only my son lives right here, an arm's length away from me. So I know how hard words are to find sometimes. I know how life can destroy language."

"Yes," Claire said. "What happened with your boy?"

"We'll talk about that in time. Right now you have to go to yours. Victoria's got him mucking out a stall before dinner."

"I imagine he's happy about that."

They found him at the far end of the barn. He was having trouble getting his footing in the wet straw, and as they watched him, he cursed quietly when his feet slid sideways as he tried to punch the pitchfork into the muck of the stall. Claire barely recognized him. He'd grown taller. His hair was longer and he'd filled out a lot. She was amazed at the lean muscle he'd developed and the strength he showed driving the tool downward and pitching the load into the wheelbarrow at the stall gate. His face was stern, flushed with the

effort of the work, and there was a driven look to his eyes she
hadn't seen before.

When he looked up and saw them through the slats of
the stall he stopped and she watched his face register her presence. It was like watching a high cloud in the wind, the features
dissipating, the way his face lost the intensity of the work and
the anger and smoothed mysteriously into a placid, stoic mask,
the eyes becoming obsidian, distant. He placed the fork against
the wall and the dull thunk of it echoed in the silence. He
wiped his forearm across his face. When he stepped awkwardly through the muck and out of the stall she saw no ves-
tige of the narrow-shouldered, thin boy who'd stood in the
prisoner's box so long ago. A piece of straw clung to his shoulder, and she stepped up and reached out to remove it. He
flinched but caught himself and settled and watched her hand
take the straw and flick it onto the floor.

"Hey," she said.

"Hey yourself," he said.

"Looks like a big job."

"Yeah. From one shithole right into another."

"I'm sorry."

"For what? This current shithole or the other one?"

"Both, I guess."

"Yeah, well, save it."

"Save it?"

"Yeah. I don't need to hear it."

"Hear what?"

He looked at Johanna. "Any slippery words of woe," he
said.

"Yes, well, I'm just glad it's over."

"It's not over. It's a long way from being fucking over."

"You're out, Aiden. You're free."

He laughed, hard and ironical, and Claire could feel his bitterness washing like a wave through the air between them. "You call this free? You and the cop set it up so I would come here. You and the cop and those bullshit words about honour. Well, I'll do this stretch too just like I did the other one. It's the second stretch I do because of you."

"Aiden, I didn't put you into prison."

"You don't think so?" he asked. "Think again. You built the situation."

"What situation?"

"My fucking life, mother. You never once thought about what I might want. It was always you, always what you wanted, always another man down on the muffin. You know why I wanted to stick up that joint? So I could start buying my way away from you. Away from you and your self-centred little jelly roll."

"That's no way to talk to your mother, son," Johanna said sternly.

Claire saw Aiden's eyes flare.

"I'm not your son. I'm not anyone's son. Don't call me that, and you can tell your bullshit old man to stop calling me that too."

Johanna stepped forward and stood directly in front of Aiden, who met her gaze steadily. She brushed a long strand of hair off her face, then folded her arms across her chest. "You can start using warrior words around this ranch when you start acting like a warrior," she said.

"I am a warrior," he said and punched his chest.

"No, you're not. You're a hurt little boy who wants his mother. Well, your mother's right here, right now, and you'd do well to try reaching out to her instead of pushing her back."

"Yeah, well, what do you know?"

"I'm a mother too and I have my own wounded son."

"The cripple?"

Johanna dropped her hands to her sides and spread her feet a little wider. She looked at Aiden calmly. "I'll stop using your word if you stop using mine," she said.

Aiden held her gaze. Then he nodded. "All right," he said.

"Okay," Johanna said. "Now talk to your mother."

She walked away and the two of them stood a scant yard apart, and Claire could feel each second as it ticked away. It struck her then that language is built of silences, the real words tucked away inside the wide gulf of the silences people fall into between the words. She wondered how long she and her son had struggled for talk, how many years had been built more of gulf than coastline, and she hungered for him to say something, anything so this wave of anxiety could crest and break and allow them air. As she looked at him she could see the boy beneath the visage of the man and she trembled a little in recollection of him, the wide-eyed, beaming boy she'd struggled to raise, and she wondered if he could recall him too. He only looked at her mutely, the eyes narrowed by caution and the beaming radiance of him lost in the stoic jut of jaw. She stepped forward and put a hand up slowly to that jaw and he recoiled in a small way before he caught himself and let her touch him. His skin was coarse with stubble and Claire felt like crying. She traced his cheek with her fingertips and when they got to the mouth she kept them there, the pads meeting the moist fullness of his lips and feeling the warmth of his breath. She raised the other hand and cradled his face lightly with her fingers and brushed both hands across his mouth again and then put them to her own face, her own mouth, and kissed them lightly and closed her eyes and let the first tear roll down her face. He put one big knuckle up and caught it. He held the hand in front of him and looked down at it before slowly rubbing the tear into the skin with his other hand.

"Thank you," she said, and he nodded and turned and went back to the work of mucking out the stall.

He didn't like guests. Guests disrupted the flow of things, the order, the predictability, the routine. In the last year or so he'd come to depend on things being what they were day in and day out. It steadied him. He had no need for expectation and there was only the work on the old girl and the vague idea he had come to develop about getting her up and on the road again. Time wasn't anything he counted or measured anymore. There was just the matter-of-fact satisfaction of the job. It was all he needed and all he cared to claim as his own. Guests, however long they arrived for, altered the pitch of things, and he resented the effect they had on his routine. He was preparing to lie out and examine his work on the undercarriage when there was a knock at the door before it slid open and the old man poked his head in.

"Okay to come in, boy?" Lionel asked.

Joe Willie heaved a sigh and put the flashlight down on the workbench. "Yeah," he said.

"Don't mean to bother you."

"Why do it, then?"

"Call it cussedness, I guess. I just wanted a word with you."

"About?"

"About our company."

"Your company."

"Yes," Lionel said and put a foot up on the running board of the old truck. "Our company. The kid is kinda gonna need a hand getting straightened out."

Joe Willie snorted. "Probably coulda used a hand a lot earlier. Right square on the backside. Wouldn't have needed any straightening out now."

"Can't say," Lionel said. "Don't know the whole story."

"No need. Convicts ain't peaches. They don't just grow."

"Well, he's a guest. He's welcome."

"Not around me he's not. Don't like convicts no matter what their story."

"Seems to me you aren't exactly partial to most folks," Lionel said.

Joe Willie picked up the flashlight and turned toward the old truck. "Long as they leave me be," he said. "I'm partial to that."

Lionel watched him bend and roll onto his back and push himself under the truck. There was the sound of metal scratching against metal and his boots never moved at all, and eventually the old man tired of waiting for words and walked out of the shed and back to the main house. Once he'd gone Joe Willie climbed back out and up into the cab. She didn't complain so much anymore when there was weight presented to her. He grinned at that and flexed his left hand. The bolts on the undercarriage were changed and tight now. It had taken all that time but the old girl felt solid or at least as solid as her age allowed her to be. He thumbed open the engine-repair manual and began to read, nodding and dog-earing important pages. The springs were next and then the engine, the guts of her: the growl, the moan, the promise of the road. It surprised him how much he wanted to hear that.

"In the round pen there's nowhere for the horse to go," Johanna explained. "You don't have to worry about them bolting and can just concentrate on sitting. Sit the horse. Feel its motion."

"There's no saddle," Aiden said flatly.

"I want you to learn to feel the horse," Johanna said. "I want you to feel it with your legs. How a walk feels, a trot. Riding's all about partnership, and feeling with your legs is the best way to start to form that."

"Injun style," Aiden said.

Johanna looked at him levelly. "You can call it that," she said. "It's how we rode in the purely tribal days but it's just bareback, that's all. It's all about rhythm, Aiden. A horse has got it and so do we. The trick is matching them up, making them work together."

"Can't be all that hard, then."

"Why don't you hop on up and we'll see," Johanna said.

"No, thanks. My mom's the one who wants this."

"Scared?"

"Me?"

"Yes, you."

"No."

"Well, then?" Johanna held the reins out to him.

He looked at her, and for a moment she thought she'd pushed too hard. He looked over his shoulder at the others, who were laughing at some shared joke. When he turned to her again his jaw was set grimly.

"All right. What do I do?"

Johanna led him to the mounting block. She showed him how to stand on it and ease himself up onto the horse. She could see him gather himself, a steady pulling inward of focus. It was a look she recognized completely. When he moved it was a lithe, deliberate motion and he was on the horse smoothly, without the usual slithering about and nervous hitching and kicking of green riders.

"Good," she said. "You did that very well. Always try to be

that smooth, that fluid when you move around a horse. No herky-jerky."

"Got it," he said.

"Now, I'm going to get him to move around the pen and lead him with the training lead. When he starts to walk, try to feel the rhythm. Feel it with your legs and in your seat."

"My butt?"

"Yes. Keep your back as straight as you can and drop your heels so they're in a straight line with your shoulders. Relax."

Aiden settled into the position and stared straight ahead.

"Don't squeeze the reins so hard," Johanna said. "Let them sit in your hand. Nothing is supposed to be tight up there. You'll feel the rhythm better if you're loose. Just sit, relax and feel the motion. Remember, there's nowhere for the horse to go in here and I've got him on the lead."

She chucked the horse into a walk, and the others watched as Aiden worked at adjusting to the slow roll of movement.

"Good," Johanna said. "Good. Can you feel that on the inside of your legs?"

"Yes," Aiden said and kept his gaze centred straight ahead.

"Good. That's a good seat you have. Good seat."

The boy held the posture and gradually, as they circled, his shoulders dropped into their natural position. By the time they'd done a half-dozen loops around the pen he was settled.

"Stay relaxed just like that," Johanna said. "We're going up a notch now into a trot. It'll feel strange but concentrate on getting the flow with your legs and butt. Try to see it in your head."

The boy was still except for the motion of the walk and he continued to keep his eyes fixed on a point somewhere just beyond the horse's ears. He nodded but didn't say a word.

When she coaxed the horse into the trot there was a struggle for balance and Aiden's seat came up and bumped the horse's back a few times, but he reclaimed his equilibrium with the same deliberate set to his face. Within three laps he had the rhythm and his position was perfect. They continued to circle and Johanna watched him adjust, seeing the concentration in his face and the focus settle into his hips, thighs and seat. He didn't fight the rhythm with the usual desperation of green riders and he seemed to ease himself downward into the gait as though he could intuit the movement and placement of the horse's feet.

Without saying anything Johanna urged the horse up to a canter, and again there was a battle for balance but Aiden reclaimed it quickly. He kept his seat and everyone watched him circle the pen perfectly in time with the gait. Johanna watched his hands. He held the reins comfortably, draped along his palms, and his wrists bounced lightly against the inside top of his thighs. When she brought the horse down to the trot again and then into the walk without telling him, the boy adjusted perfectly. When he stepped off the mounting block with a pinch-lipped grin, she could see a familiar fire.

"Perfect," she said. "You've never ridden before?"

"No," he said. "You're a good teacher."

"Takes a good student to make a good teacher," Johanna said. "Now, I want you to take the reins and lead him back to the stall. Walk right beside him, talk to him, thank him for the ride, stroke him and lead him right into the stall. One of the boys will show you how to brush him out and get him watered. Can you do that?"

"I can do that," he said. "But when can I get back up there again?"

She laughed and rubbed between his shoulder blades. "Soon," she said. "We'll trail ride a bit before sunset. Introduce you to a saddle."

Aiden walked off toward the barn, talking quietly to the horse, who swished his tail and perked up his ears at the talk. Johanna crossed the pen.

"Did you see that?" she asked the others.

"Kinda reminded me of someone I saw once before," Lionel said. He chewed on a piece of straw as he watched Aiden lead the horse to the barn.

Claire struggled. It was difficult for her to get into rhythm with the horse like Aiden had. Walking was fine. She could relax and sit the tiny mare they gave her, but once the gait changed, rhythm went right out the window. She felt panic, and she concentrated more on not falling off than on riding. She made it awkwardly around a dozen or so times before Johanna got her off.

"We'll work with the saddle," she said. "Don't worry. Not everyone takes to bareback right away. Most people prefer the security of a stirrup, and besides, you've been up already. How'd it feel for a first time?"

"Scary," Claire said. "But I really loved it."

"Good," Lionel said and draped an arm around her shoulder. "This old girl will know that, and the more you ride her, get to know her, the more she'll adjust to you."

"Horses adjust?" Claire asked.

"Sure do," Lionel said. "I had my old boy for fifteen years now and it's like he knew before I did what I could handle at my age."

"Amazing," Claire said. "I've always wanted to ride. From the time I was a little girl."

"Well, then, our mission is to get you comfortable and let you do it every day you're here," Birch said. "Why don't you lead her in, give her some water and groom her. We'll tack up and head out on the trail soon."

Claire led the mare into the barn and into the stall beside Aiden, who was busy brushing his horse. He nodded to her, and Claire busied herself following the wrangler's instructions and getting used to being around the horse in the stall. She loved the smell. The horse odour, dusty, oily, old, seemed to lead her nose deeper, further into the world of the stable, into the tang and sharpness of liniment, the grassy dryness of hay, the mouldy wet of straw, the flat, papery husk of rope, the warm invitation of leather, and beneath it all the sour pungency of manure and urine. It pleased her. Claire believed it was the first real smell she'd ever experienced, so full and true and alive. She brushed the mare and talked to her in low tones, praising her for the work she'd done and telling her how she was looking forward to the adventure of the saddle trip to come.

"Ankle deep in horse shit and you look like you're loving it," Aiden said.

Claire saw him peering through the slats in the stall. "I am," she said. "It's like everything I ever imagined and nothing like it at all, all at the same time."

"Good for you."

"And how are you doing?"

He stepped across the stall and dropped his brush onto the small shelf with the curry comb. He stopped to rub the horse along the neck and when he turned to her his eyes told her nothing.

"I'm fucking glad to be out, I know that. But it's like I could be anywhere and feel the same. Everything just feels weird, that's all. I don't feel like I belong anywhere. I don't feel seventeen, I feel fucking eighty. Except for maybe being on that horse."

"Thank god for horses, then."

He nodded solemnly. "Yeah. I can handle more of that riding."

"I hope I do better with the saddle," Claire said. "Maybe they can just tie my feet to the stirrups and my hands to the big knob thing."

"The big knob thing?" He laughed. "Spoken like a true cowgirl."

They gathered in the yard as Golec prepared to leave. To Claire he seemed like a different person out here and she wondered if the same held true for her. She hoped so. The city had the power to reduce people to a frenzied sameness, and as she had become more and more locked into her job and the concern for establishing a good, clean, predictable home for Aiden on his release, she'd felt herself slipping more and more into the main stream of city life and it bothered her. It struck her that people didn't reach out of themselves very often. Not like here. Out here it seemed as though the country gave people an openness like the land itself, and although it was foreign to her, she craved it like an exile craves the language of her homeland. She watched the Wolfchilds express their affection and regard for Golec, and the envy she felt was accompanied by a note of regret that her life lacked the same generosity of spirit. Aiden stood beside her and watched, awkwardly moving one foot back and forth in the dirt.

"Claire," Golec said.

"Marcel, I don't know how to thank you."

"There's no need. You just enjoy this, that's all I need."

"Well, it's hard not to enjoy. It's fabulous."

"You earned it," he said. "You worked hard. I'm proud of how you handled everything."

"You got it started."

"No, that's not right. You got it started. You got out. I was only around for leverage."

"Well, thanks for the leverage."

"Anytime. I mean that."

"Thank you." She hugged him.

"Aiden," Golec said and stepped away from Claire.

"Cop," Aiden said.

"You did a good thing coming here."

"Did I?"

"Yes."

"How so?"

"You gave yourself a chance for something better. And you gave your mother the same."

"Forking shit's a better chance?"

"In the long run."

They stood and looked at each other a moment. Golec reached his hand out toward him and Aiden stared at it. He eased his hands out of his pockets and dropped them to his sides and tilted his head back up to look at Golec again. "Thanks for helping the moms," he said.

Golec nodded. "Anytime," he said.

"Yeah."

"See you."

"I doubt it," Aiden said and turned away.

Golec made his way toward the car again, and the Wolfchilds followed him, leaving Claire and Aiden to stand a few yards away. They were chatting by the open driver's door when Lionel looked up and away toward the pasture across the driveway. "I think there's someone else wants to say goodbye," he said, and they all turned to watch Joe Willie stumping his way across the pasture.

"Who's that?" Claire whispered to Aiden.

"The cripple," he said.

Joe Willie made his way quickly across the expanse of grass and when he stepped through the gate and across the driveway there was a thin sheen of sweat on his face. He took a handkerchief from his back pocket and mopped it roughly before adjusting his hat and stepping up to Golec, who smiled to see him.

"Marce," Joe Willie said.

"Joe Willie."

"Bit off your beat, wouldn't you say?" He cast a look at Aiden, and Claire could see the same sullen wariness she saw in Aiden's face.

"Long arm of the law, you know," Golec said.

"Yeah. Well. Wanted to see you off."

"I appreciate that."

The two men looked at each other, and from the distance she stood Claire could sense the weight of words on the backs of their tongues, held in place by a hard unknowing, an uncertainty borne on the back of pain, and the silence sat between them like a wiped-off space on a chalkboard, the sentences halted in their path, broken, awaiting a hand to connect them again, give them flow. "Well, you take care now," Joe Willie said finally.

"I will. You too."

They stood there awkwardly until Golec reached out his hand. Joe Willie took it and shook it once, firmly. Then he turned, pushed his hat lower on his head and headed back toward the pasture and the equipment shed. As he reached the gate and unlatched it Victoria called to him.

"Joe Willie. We have guests," she said.

He stopped with his hand on the top rail of the gate and stared upward and away toward the mountains, then traced the line of them back across the long V of the valley until he turned to look back at Claire and Aiden. He thumbed his hat brim up and leaned on the gate with one forearm. The look he gave her was blank and she wondered if he even saw her. But when his eyes met Aiden's his face became pinched and severe and she looked across at her son. He held the stare with a hard expression of his own and for a long moment the two of them held it, the air between filled with tension. Joe Willie broke it first, nodding his head slowly and tugging his hat back down.

"Good for you," he said and made his way through the gate.

Lanny and Jess Hairston were the new wranglers at the ranch, brothers who'd never fared well in competitive rodeo but made able and knowing hands for a working ranch. They'd been raised in the life, and if they were rough and coarse as men they were calm and deliberate as cowboys and ranch hands. They'd only been with the Wolfchilds a little more than a week, and after getting their feet under them with their new bosses they'd become their usual tough-talking selves. As Aiden busied himself with preparing for the evening ride, the wranglers were in adjoining stalls grooming and tacking. There was much laughter as they wrestled with latigos and stirrup lengths.

"How about that Johanna?" Lanny said, hiking a look over the top of the stall to be sure he wasn't overheard by any of the Wolfchilds. "How'd ya like to mount that?"

"Be wild," his brother said. "Little old maybe, but prime anyhow. What do you figure there, Mundell?"

"She's very attractive. A real lady," the other wrangler said.

"Yeah, yeah. But what about the old loose and wild Injun style?" Jess asked.

"Pardon me?"

"Jesus, Earl. Would you jump her?"

Earl cleared his throat. "I suppose," he said quietly.

"Suppose? I'd take me some of that brown meat anytime," Jess said.

Aiden walked by their stalls to find another blanket for his horse. He'd heard this kind of talk for a year and a half inside and it tired him. He stared straight ahead and went about his business.

"Hey, Slick," Lanny said as he passed. "Pretty good ride out there. You figure you could handle that redskin without a saddle?"

The two men laughed. Aiden kept walking in stony silence. The two brothers were nearly forty but they spoke like teenagers, and Aiden held no respect for that.

"Come on, we're just joking with you," Jess called. "Guy stuff, you know. We're all in this together. Might as well have a little fun."

Aiden swapped blankets in the tack room and made his way back down the barn. He kept his eyes focussed on the door to the round pen and never looked at any of the men as he passed. The Hairstons regarded him coolly.

"Seems the brother's not the talkative sort," Jess said and spat behind Aiden's boots.

"Uppity," Lanny said. "Hey, kid. You mind if I tell a coloured joke?"

Aiden lay the horse blanket along the top of the stall. When he looked at Hairston it was neutral but steady.

"Do ya? It's all in fun," Lanny said.

"Only if you let me tell one first," Aiden said.

"You're gonna tell a coloured joke? Sure. Go ahead. Should be good."

"What's black and blue and floats down the river?"

"Damn. I don't know," Lanny said. "What is black and blue and floats down the river, Jess?"

"Not sure I know. Tell us, kid."

Aiden held the level look. "The last guy who told a coloured joke. But it's all in fun, right?" He smirked and turned into the stall.

"Son of a bitch," Lanny said. "I don't think he likes us much, Jess."

"Don't sound like it. But he don't have to. I have nothing to say to him really, but I wouldn't mind taking a shot at that mother of his."

"Yeah. That's some fine black ass," Lanny said.

"Damn right. I'd take her over the Injun. Especially after she gets finished rubbing up against that pommel awhile."

Aiden laid the blanket across the horse's shoulders softly, and gently pulled it into place for the saddle. Then he stepped out into the corridor.

"That's my mother you're talking about," he said.

"Catches on quick, don't he," Jess said, taking a step forward.

"Nothing slow about him," Lanny said.

Aiden could see Lionel and Birch and a couple other wranglers enter the barn from the opposite end and begin making their way toward them. The Hairstons stood oblivious, rocking slowly on the balls of their feet and glaring at him.

"Well?" Jess asked.

"You just need to shut up about my mother, that's all," Aiden said.

"Don't diss his mama, Jess," Lanny said.

"Wouldn't dream of it. Not while I'm fucking her any-way," Jess said.

He hit them so fast and so hard that it took a moment for the action to register with the Wolfchilds and their men. One sliding step forward with the left foot and a driving, twist-ing punch to Lanny's jaw followed immediately by a twisting elbow smash backward to the nose of his brother. They both fell to the floor.

"Lord," Birch said and ran forward.

Aiden looked down at them calmly, then returned to saddling his horse. Lionel and Birch watched him move quietly around the horse, no emotion, no reaction to the scene that had just transpired, murmuring reassurances to the animal and gently rubbing it.

"Lord," Birch said quietly again. "Lord, Lord."

"It's not his fault. Not really," Claire said. "You know that he just got out of jail. He's angry. He's hurting."

The trail ride had gone smoothly. Claire had gained a sense of rhythm with the horse. The stirrups helped. They lent her an assurance of balance, of staying put, and by the time they'd reached the turnaround point beyond the creek she'd been comfortable enough to adopt a casual lean in the saddle. Now, she sat on the veranda with the Wolfchilds and another one of the wranglers who'd seen the scuffle.

"They pushed him to it," Earl Mundell said.

"How?" Birch asked.

"They were talking about women," Mundell said. "Dirty talk."

"Which women?" Birch asked.

"Does it matter?"

He looked at the wrangler carefully. "No. It doesn't."

"They wouldn't let it go," Mundell said. "Wouldn't stop. When he told them to leave certain people out of it they kept right on. Worse. Personal. So he clobbered them. Mighty well too."

"Damn straight," Lionel said. "The boy fights like a man. But coming from where he comes from I guess he'd have to. Sorry to hear about your trouble, Claire."

"If you want us to go, I understand," she said.

"Go?" Victoria asked. "Why would we want you to go?"

"Well, I guess because angry, violent young men aren't exactly the kind of guests you want."

"Honey, the rodeo world is full of angry, violent men. It's nothing we haven't seen a thousand times and will see again as long as we're connected to that world. Your boy just needs somewhere to release."

"Yes. He's so quiet at times," Claire said. "Like he burrows himself in some dark place I don't know how to get to. And other times I can look at him and see that he's just a kid, just my Aiden. The anger scares me, though."

"You never want to keep a bull too long in the chute," Birch said.

"Pardon me?"

"In rodeo the stock handlers make sure the bulls get into place fast. They don't keep them waiting in the chute. They get anxious, edgy, all boxed in. They wait too long and they go beyond being aggravated. They get mean. I'm not saying your boy is mean, I'm saying all his energy's been shut up too for a long time. Now the chute's open and he's got nowhere to put it all."

"Powerful lot of energy too," Lionel said.

"Put him on a steer tomorrow," Victoria said. "The way I

see it, the boy's just like you two were at his age. All spit and yowl like a wet tomcat. Put him on a steer and see how he likes that."

"Birch?" Lionel asked, thumbing back his hat.

Birch looked out toward the equipment shed. He was quiet a long time. Then he rolled a smoke carefully. "Things sit in a man sometimes," he said. "Sit all dark and heavy in a place he can't see. Makes it hard to figure. Most men get rankled at it, take it out on the ones close by, or they just grow dark and heavy themselves. I figure the second kind's the hardest to watch.

"When you can't get at it, it starts to drive you crazy. When it's a big hurt or a loss you can sort them out eventually and move past it. But sometimes it's just the way life went and that can muddle the smartest of us, like finding yourself somewhere you don't recall heading for. It takes something special to show you the way back."

"What are you saying, Birch?" Johanna asked.

He reached out and squeezed her hand. "Deal I made with Marce was to work him, show him how hard a guy has to work to make it in the real world, get him ready for his life when he gets back to the city, make him sweat out some of that hardness he found in himself. But I figure putting him on the rope barrel and chucking him in the hay often enough to piss him off should do the trick too. Then we send him out on the rankest little steer we have. From what I seen today he'll like the tussle."

"Is it dangerous?" Claire asked.

"Just enough," Birch said.

"For what?"

"To rearrange the muddle," Lionel said. "Maybe into something he can figure out. Give him a challenge. A hard one.

It's something we've been trying out around here for a while now. Seems to work as far as we can see."

Aiden watched Joe Willie emerge from the trail. He'd climbed into the hayloft and found the gantry door where the bales were loaded in. He stood there looking out across the ranch and the valley wondering if the crap was ever going to stop. The Hairston brothers were stupid men. He hated stupid men. In fact, he didn't much like men at all, and except for Johnny Calder none of them had ever given him any kind of template he wanted to use to frame his life. Now, standing in the dark barn, he felt lonely, lonelier than he ever had in stir. It was crazy. He was free. It was over. But he felt a deep, heavy pang for something he couldn't define, something he couldn't recognize, something somehow beyond his reach. Standing in the dark watching the night settle on the valley made him feel less like crying.

He watched Joe Willie stump his way across the pasture. The man drove the bad leg forward with each step and in the fading light it gave the impression of a boxer driving the same punch into the air over and over again. As he got closer Aiden began to make out features. There was a hard, downturned scowl on Joe Willie's face and a faint coating of sweat that gave an odd phosphorescent sheen in the darkness. When he passed directly beneath the gantry door Aiden could hear him breathing, hard and deep and angered, muttering something. He could hear the man below him fumbling around in the darkness. There was just enough light left in the hayloft for Aiden to find his way back to the ladder and down to the main floor of the barn.

There was light coming from a small room at the back, and he walked toward it as quietly as he could. As he got to the door he heard the sound of water sloshing in a pail, and as he got to the door he saw Joe Willie dousing himself, rinsing the sweat from his upper body. He was lean, sinewy like a cat, and the muscles on his right side were sharply defined and delineated, taut, bulging, rivers down the length of him. But when he turned to grab a towel from a gym bag on the floor Aiden was shocked. The left arm was bone with a slack sag at the shoulder, the joint there jutting like a skeleton's, and except for surgical scars he might have believed it was fake. He watched Joe Willie reach up to towel his hair, and the difference between the right and left sides of his torso was pronounced. There was no padding around the left shoulder at all. He could see the shoulder bone like a tiny paddle, and when Joe Willie reached the arm up he saw the socket and ball of it separate, grind against each other under the skin, and he grimaced. It was ugly. As sorry as he felt for the deformed man in the room it was still an ugly sight. He turned to go, and as he did his foot connected with pitchfork tines and it tumbled to the floor. Joe Willie spun around and looked at him, quickly draping the towel over his shoulders and covering the arm. He stepped to the doorway, and even in the blocked light Aiden could see the rage in his face.

"What the hell do you want?" Joe Willie asked.

"Nothing," Aiden said.

"Then what the hell are you doing here?"

"Nothing," Aiden repeated. "Just walking, that's all."

"Well then, keep right on walking."

Joe Willie took another step forward and Aiden could feel the tension of him. He'd felt it before. There were guys in maximum who gave off the same air-shrinking force, who told you with their eyes that territory was being defined for you and you were trespassing. You respected that and moved on.

The look on Joe Willie's face was harder than any he'd seen before. But he'd also learned that you didn't just shrink in the face of this, you didn't leave the perception of fear, you didn't leave the power in the other guy's court. So he stayed where he was and looked calmly back at him, his own face betraying nothing. Joe Willie moved another step closer. They stood mere feet apart.

"What are you looking at?" Joe Willie growled.

"Your arm," Aiden said.

"Yeah? Well, it ain't going anywhere. But you are."

"Where?"

"Anywhere but here, kid." They continued to face each other. "Go on," he said. "Get along. Guests shouldn't be around the barn after dark. Someone might get hurt."

Aiden nodded. "Someone might," he said.

They broke together. Both of them took a step back and turned at the same time. Aiden walked slowly out of the barn.

They rode together up through the draw and out into the flat of the pasture. Claire could see the shadowed face of Iron Mountain with the sun arching over it and she let her gaze trail down its slope and onto the valley floor. Beside her, Aiden leaned forward casually on the pommel and watched her. When she caught him watching her he shrugged and nudged the horse with his heels to get him walking again. They'd woken early, and after a brief talk with Victoria, who was already busy in the kitchen, had saddled up and headed out for a short ride. A couple of wranglers stood nearby as they tacked up, and Claire had needed only a few hints to get ready. Aiden mentioned nothing about the fracas the night before and Claire didn't push him to explain. Instead, they rode quietly, each of them experimenting with their seat, trying to put into practice what Johanna had told them the first day. Claire liked the feel of the saddle, and as she moved with the horse's gait she could feel it lulling her, the roll of it familiar somehow, and she felt no anxiety. Aiden just rode. He'd kicked his horse into a trot and a canter a couple of times, and Claire was amazed at his ease. She'd trotted a hundred yards or so but found it too difficult to feel the horse and she'd stopped, content to walk and look about her at the land. Now, as they approached the main buildings again, they saw Birch and Lionel waving them toward one of the corrals.

"Good morning," Lionel said. "Glad to see you making yourselves to home. Good ride?"

"Wonderful," Claire said. "Aiden trotted some but I wasn't ready for it. It was nice though."

"Good. Claire, why don't you walk the horses in and get one of the boys to put them up. Then come join us over behind the Quonset."

"What am I doing?" Aiden asked. "I'll tell you right now I ain't shovelling no horseshit without breakfast first."

"No, nothing like that," Birch said. "There's a critter over there we'd like to introduce you to."

"Critter?"

"Yessir. Mean little spud, but you'll like him."

They dismounted and Aiden handed the reins to Claire. She watched the three of them walk away and hurried to get the horses in so she could get back to watch. The Wolfchilds were laughing and Aiden looked back and forth between them. From where she stood he looked like a ranch hand in his jeans and hat, and she smiled.

The men circled the corral and walked behind the Quonset. Aiden saw a small structure with only four corner beams and a roof. Ropes were tied to each of the beams, and in the middle of their stretch hung an oil barrel with hay and mattresses spread beneath it. Four of the wranglers sat around waiting.

"That's the critter," Lionel said. "It's called a rope barrel."

"For?"

"For riding. Well, more like, for trying to ride."

"Me?"

"You bet," Lionel said.

They walked up to the shed and Aiden studied the setup. There was a length of rope slung about the barrel's girth with a small loop on the top for a hand hold. The barrel moved slightly in the breeze.

"Doesn't look so bad," he said.

"Bradley, why don't you get on up on that thing and show the boy how it's done," Birch said.

"Sure thing, boss man," the wrangler said and pulled a pair of leather gloves from his back pocket. Aiden watched as he slung his long legs over the barrel and wrapped his gloved hand in the loop of the hand hold. The other hand he held to the side, up and away from his body like making a stop signal. The barrel bobbed on the ropes.

"That's it?" Aiden asked.

"Not quite," Birch said. "Boys?"

Birch and the other three wranglers took up positions at each of the ropes holding the barrel. Bradley settled himself on the barrel, took a few deep breaths, then nodded to Birch. As soon as he did, the four men on the ropes began yanking violently. The barrel exploded into motion, and the wrangler struggled to maintain his seat. Aiden was fascinated. There was no rhythm at all to the motion of the barrel, and even though the wrangler did a good job of hanging on, the men on the ropes were able to throw him off. He landed on the hay and mattresses with a thud.

"Well?" Birch asked.

"Wild," Aiden said. "Anybody ever ride that thing?"

"Some," Lionel said.

"Gimme that cuss," another wrangler said and stepped up to the barrel. Once again the rope men worked together to create mayhem with the barrel, and the wrangler landed in the padding. Claire walked up and put a hand on Aiden's shoulder.

"What's going on?" she asked him.

"This is crazy," he said. They watched while the third wrangler took a turn. He held out a little longer than the previous two but the result was still the same.

"Well," Lionel said. "Ready to give it a try?"

"Me?" Aiden asked.

"Didn't bring you out here to watch," Birch said.

"I'm here to work, not ride this dumb thing. Besides, it doesn't prove anything."

"Proves you got the stones to try."

"I already know that."

"Then mount up, hardcase," Bradley said from his position at one of the corner ropes.

Aiden looked around at the men. They stood lazily, slouched against the beams or on one out-thrust hip, casually examining him. His steadiest gaze earned him nothing back, and in the deflection of energy he found a grudging respect for them. These were harder men than he'd met before. They had no need for a pretense of toughness, he could see it in their casual way with danger, the striding up to it, the unquestioning acceptance of the challenge and the same slouching, matter-of-fact dusting off after they hit the dirt, ready for another ride.

"All right," he said.

He walked right up to the barrel as confidently as they had, but there was a spear of anxiety in him. It excited him. He felt charged like he had when he'd thought of pulling a gun on someone during a heist. Only this was far more immediate. This was a one-on-one deal where there were only two ways off, in the dirt or standing tall. He knew which one he wanted.

Birch explained how the barrel was set up to mimic the unpredictable nature of a bucking bull or a bronc and how the cowboy used it to learn technique. He showed him how to settle himself behind the rigging, how to use his back and shoulders to centre his butt, how to keep his free arm up and away from the barrel and how to reach out with his legs.

"There's only one thing I can't tell you."

"What's that?" Aiden asked.

"How to land. You pretty much gotta try and figure that out in the air."

"Thanks. That's comforting."

Birch smiled and gave him a friendly slap on the shoulder. "Get on, then. Remember what I told you. Keep that free arm up and away."

Aiden settled himself on the barrel. Even slung between the ropes it shimmied and wavered weirdly. The slightest motion of his body made it wobble, and he clutched with his knees and thighs to find purchase. When it settled to a slight tremble he gritted his teeth, raised his left arm high to the side, clutched hard with his right against the rigging and nodded. The men on the ropes began their sawing motions, holding back in respect for the green rider, but the barrel still exploded in ripples of motion. Aiden held on for three or four seconds, then flopped to the side and landed in the hay. The men laughed good-naturedly while Aiden stood up and dusted himself off. He turned sharply and glared at Birch.

"Again," he said. "Only this time don't treat me like a fucking kid. Make it buck like you did for them."

"They're experienced riders, son," Birch said. "You gotta start slow."

"I can handle it if they can," Aiden said.

Lionel and Birch looked at each other. Birch reached up and scratched his eyebrow with one finger and studied Aiden, who stood beside the barrel, unwilling to take a step away.

"Make it buck," Aiden said.

"Boys," Birch said, stepping over and relieving one of the wranglers on the rope, "I believe we got a rider here. Not full out, not right now, but let's give him a ride."

"Full out," Aiden said.

"You gotta earn full out, son. But we can sure give you a step or two above casual."

"I'll earn it. Just make it buck," Aiden said. There was a look in his eye that Claire didn't recognize, and when he mounted the barrel again and steadied himself on it he became a stranger. This was a man, intent and deliberate. Every shred of the seventeen-year-old was left in the bootprints in the hay below the rope barrel. She was aware of Victoria and Johanna walking up and standing beside her, and behind them, the Hairstons and Mundell.

When he was ready Aiden nodded sharply and the barrel exploded beneath him. Two maybe three seconds later he was thrown and landed squarely on his back. But he stood almost immediately, gave Birch a fierce-eyed look and said simply, "Again."

"Son," Birch started to say.

"Again." Aiden mounted the barrel.

He rode five more times. Each time he was thrown and each time he stood, glared at Birch and said "Again" before slinging his leg around the barrel and finding his seat. The wranglers shook their heads in admiration and complied. The last time he landed Aiden was clearly winded and lay in the hay longer than he had the previous times.

"Okay," Victoria said firmly. "That's enough carrying on without breakfast. Everyone up to the house."

"One more," Aiden said.

She looked at him evenly, tilted her head to one side and nodded. "You got fire in you, boy. But fire's gotta be stoked, and right now you're eating breakfast. Everyone's eating breakfast. Now."

Birch and Lionel grinned. "Best listen," Lionel said to Aiden. "Only way I survived so long with her's on accounta I learned to listen right off the hop. We'll come back later."

Aiden nodded. He looked at the barrel. "Sumbitch," he said quietly and turned to join the others.

There was a world contained on the living-room wall. Photographs, dozens of them. Aiden and Claire studied each picture with rapt curiosity. From the grainy quality and scalloped edges of the older ones to the gloss of the newer shots, the photographs bridged the breadth of time from the 1920s right up to the present. The faces in the grainy shots were unfamiliar but eventually Lionel could be picked out, Victoria, then Birch, Johanna and Joe Willie. They were rodeo shots for the most part, bucking bulls and horses, Johanna on her barrel horse and others filled with cowboys, cowgirls, rodeo clowns. Banners in the background had names like Abilene, Cheyenne, Yuma, and Madison Square Garden. Here and there were faces of famous people, actors, musicians, newsmakers, all seemingly overjoyed to be with their hosts. The world captured there fascinated Aiden and Claire. It led them right up to Joe Willie. The photographs of him seemed able to jump right off the wall. There was a wildness to the shots of him spurring a kicking bronc, an explosive energy to the mid-air splay of bull with his free arm in perfect form.

"The cripple," Aiden said quietly.

"Appreciate it if you wouldn't use that word," Birch said from behind them. "Even if you think none of us can hear you."

"He didn't mean anything by it," Claire said. "But what happened to him?"

"Your son can tell you," Birch said. He came and stood beside them as they looked at the pictures. "Can't you, Aiden?"

"Guess," Aiden said, not taking his eyes off the photographs.

"What does he do now?" Claire asked. "He disappears all the time."

"He's healing."

"What hurts?" Aiden asked.

Birch gave the boy a long look before he answered. When he did he spoke slowly, solemnly. "Most of us have a dream of what we want to be. In truth, most of us never come close to it. All my boy ever wanted was to cowboy and he cowboyed better'n anybody. So now, to be surrounded by it every day and not be able to touch it, to live it anymore, well, that's a bitter thing. Hard to swallow that, and he's trying to learn how to live with it."

"Why doesn't he just leave?" Aiden asked.

"We never raised a quitter. He's a dust-me-off, mount-me-up, hit-it-again cowboy. He's also an Indian, a Sioux-Ojibway warrior, and that kinda blood doesn't have quit in it," Birch said.

Aiden thought about the sweat-drenched man he'd seen stomping across the pasture the night before. The seething man who'd stood toe to toe with him in the barn hadn't struck him as the back-down kind. He had a hardness and a coldness Aiden knew well and respected.

"He was the best?" Aiden asked.

"The best," Birch replied.

"Wish I could have seen him ride."

"You can. Anytime you want," Birch said.

"How?"

"The magic of video. We got a ton of stuff we shot right here in training and there's the Pro Rodeo videos, stuff from television, lots of it."

"Really?"

"Yessir. Anytime you want. Right under the TV back in the rec room."

Aiden looked at Claire, and for a brief second she saw the little boy in him again.

"How's it going, son?" Birch asked. Joe Willie was sitting on the veranda drinking a coffee. His father shunted him over on the swing seat and began making himself a cigarette.

"Passable," Joe Willie said.

"Passable's good."

"Yep."

"Got some interesting visitors."

"Good for you."

Birch eyed him. Joe Willie stared out across the valley, and when Birch nudged him with his elbow and handed him the makings he took them silently and kept his eyes averted. "You'd like the woman. Claire. She's got some fire. Like your mother, I think."

"I doubt that," Joe Willie said.

"Well, yeah. Ain't many like your mother, I agree with you there, but she's got some steel in her. Pretty little thing too."

Joe Willie gave him a flick of the eyes and handed the makings back. He lit his cigarette and took a long draw, exhaled, and chased it with a good belt of the coffee. "And the kid?" he asked.

"Just a kid. Seventeen. Full of beans. You know, I think he might make a rider."

Joe Willie snorted. "What makes you think that?"

"I don't know. Just a feeling. He rode the rope barrel."

"I done that at three."

"Yeah, but he showed some real fire. Didn't want to stop."

"Must like it flat on his ass." Joe Willie ground the smoke out against his boot heel and tucked it in his vest pocket. He stood up and adjusted his hat.

"Well, the boy did eat some dirt but he showed a lot of toughness there. I mean, I knew he had it in him after I seen the fight." Birch watched Joe Willie's back straighten.

"What fight?" he asked without turning around.

"Well, it wasn't really a fight. Not like some of the ones we seen on the circuit. This one was over fast. Boom boom. The kid knocked down Jess and Lanny. Just like that. We seen it. Hell of a punch the kid's got."

"Convict," Joe Willie said.

"Mundell says the boys were talking dirty about your mother and Claire. Guess he didn't appreciate that much."

Joe Willie turned and looked at him. He stared at him for a long moment and Joe Willie flexed the fingers of both hands and squeezed them together into loose fists.

"Can't say I wouldn't have done the same if I'da heard it," Birch said. "Still ain't decided what to do about them boys."

"Kick 'em out," Joe Willie said.

"Ah, boys'll be boys, you know that. I'll just have a talk with them about respecting the women."

"And the kid?"

"The kid's gonna ride a steer today."

"That'll be a sight."

"Should be. You could come watch."

Joe Willie moved down the first two steps. "I ain't got time for no Little Britches rodeo. You play all you want. Kid's a city kid, a convict, only thing he'll ever ride is his own ass back to prison. Sounds like nothing but a heap of trouble to me."

The three of them walked the horses quietly into the trees. A thin trail meandered up toward the ridge behind the ranch, and they allowed the horses their heads and sat easily to enjoy the lurch and sway of the climb. The smell of horse was thick in the air, and as she breathed it in with the mix of pine gum and moss Claire felt herself transported. This was the landscape of the dream she'd carried. The trees threw angles of light in soft beams everywhere and there was a dappled quality to it that made her feel like she rode through a painting. Swaying easily in the saddle, she closed her eyes briefly and allowed herself to feel the ambience and the texture of her being in this place. She sighed.

"Getting our money's worth, are we?" Victoria asked.

She opened her eyes and smiled. "When I was a girl I dreamed of this. There never was much hope of it being realized the way we lived, but I held on to this as tightly as I could through everything."

Victoria half turned in the saddle. "How did you live? What did your parents do?"

"My mother was a junkie," Claire said. "Chronic. For as long as I knew her she fought it. She went through periods when she didn't use and we'd think that maybe the monkey had crawled off her back for good. But there was always another run. She'd work some in the clean times but we mostly lived off welfare. She never could hold on to a job for long, really.

"So our life was rooming house to rooming house. They were never anything more than one-room mansions, but it was the best that she could do for us. We moved a lot. I don't think I ever got a chance to settle anywhere when I was a kid and it probably would have been a lot more terrible except that my mother could be magical. She was grim when she was straight, like it was punishment, but when she used she laughed and pretended everything was all right in our world. I actually liked her loaded better than I liked her straight. Isn't that terrible? But we were like sisters then. We'd play with makeup, get dressed outlandishly and parade down the street, all lit up in big bursts of colour. But she'd use again and all the colour went out of our world, seeped out slowly, faded just like her. She died of an overdose when I was pregnant with Aiden. He never knew her. Her name was Angela. It's Greek. It means heavenly messenger. I don't know if she even knew that."

They rode on in silence for a time and then Claire said, "We'd sit up late sometimes and tell each other stories. We'd laugh and we'd tell each other our dreams."

"What kind of dreams?" Johanna asked.

Claire laughed. "The craziest kind of dreams. She'd dream about walking down the street one day and suddenly being lifted up and out of our life and plopped down into a big, bright, shining one with a mansion and money and servants and no monkeys lurking in the shadows. But there was the one dream in particular that my mother held on to tighter than any other."

"What dream was that?" Johanna asked, reining in her horse and allowing Claire's to move up beside it.

"That one day a prince would solve it all with a kiss," Claire said. "Men flummoxed her. She was pretty, nice body despite her addiction, and men were attracted to her. The wildness, I guess. She kept on hoping that the one magic man would emerge one day, sweep her off her feet and change everything. She passed that on to me unfortunately, and I'm afraid I led Aiden down the same merry trail."

"Ah," Victoria said, nodding firmly. "That's the bones of it. Good girl. You hang right on to all that shame. Hang on to it good and tight and don't ever let it go. It does you so much good. You can blame yourself for everything then, the prison, the anger in the boy, the fact you two aren't talking. Lay claim to all of it and give it to yourself good."

"I'm sorry?"

Victoria chucked her horse over to a stand of small pines and dismounted. Johanna and Claire followed her and the older woman led them off the trail to a thrust of boulders over-looking the valley. She motioned for them to sit with her and for the next while the three of them gazed quietly over Wolf Creek Ranch and the incredible valley it sat in.

"The people used to come here in the old days," Victoria said. "It was a gathering place. A special place. Over where that equipment shed sits just at the lip of the draw was where they'd set up the big circle of lodges. Teaching lodges. Every summer they'd come and there would be a hundred teepees, maybe more. People would gather the sage for ceremony and there was always sweetgrass in the low places too. Sweat lodges were built right beside the creek down there. It was beautiful. A huge gathering of people unlike anything we ever see anymore.

"And in those teaching lodges men and women would get taught principles. Spiritual principles meant to allow them to enjoy the life they led. It was a hard life. Forty below zero sometimes, with the wind howling and nothing but the thin skin of a teepee for protection. Only a spiritual way of being will get you through that, and the Old Ones gave them what they could.

"Anyhow, what they gave them was choice. In the end, it's all we ever have. We can have all the head knowing in the world, be all proper educated and smart, but life is about choices, and that was the big spiritual secret that got handed down in them teaching lodges. Nothing huge, nothing complicated, because they knew that the last thing smart people need is more smarts. But we all need simple truth. Something that cuts through the fat of things."

"What truth is that?" Claire asked.

Victoria looked at her, and for some reason Claire felt like crying.

"That choice is our superhuman power. It allows us to change everything all at once," Victoria said. "It lets us see what's possible, then make it happen in our life. Every ceremony, every ritual, every symbol points us toward the energy of choice. We choose what to believe, how to behave, how to think. We choose how we live our lives. Us. No one else. Our choice. You look at things the way they are, and if you don't like it you choose to change it."

"How?" Claire asked.

"That's what everyone asks," Victoria said and squeezed her hand. "But the better question is why?"

"Why, then?" Claire asked.

"That's your question to yourself," Johanna said, standing. "Indians never actually went around asking how. They walked around asking why."

Claire looked at the two women. She felt safe here, accepted, and there was something in the talk she sensed was given to her to unwrap through consideration.

"It must have been beautiful. That gathering," she said, standing beside Johanna and looking out across the valley.

"Yes," Johanna said. "But Victoria, you never told me that before. How long have you known about this?"

Victoria struggled to her feet. She smiled. "About three minutes," she said and walked back toward the horses.

Johanna laughed, loudly and raucously.

"Sumbitch," Aiden said and dusted himself off with his hat. He slung his leg over the barrel and glared at the wranglers at the corners. They shook their heads in admiration and reached out to grab ropes again. It was his sixth attempt and the result had been the same the first five times. He sprawled in the straw in a billowed cloud of dust but sprang back to his feet quickly. Birch and Lionel sat back on some hay bales and watched. Now, as he prepared to tackle it again, they rose together and approached. Birch raised a hand, and the wranglers backed off the ropes. Aiden looked up at them hard eyed.

"I ain't quittin'," Aiden said.

"Nobody's asking you to quit, boy," Lionel said. "We just want to give you some advice, that's all."

"That's right, son," Birch said. "What you've been doing is good. But you been focussing on holding on."

"What the hell am I supposed to do? Focus on falling off?"

"Well, in a word, yeah," Birch said, tilting his hat back on his head.

"What?"

"First thing you gotta learn how to do in order to ride well is learn how to fall. Seems to me you've about got the lesson," Lionel said with a chuckle.

The wranglers laughed, and Aiden's face reddened. He stepped off the barrel and stood face to face with the Wolfchilds.

"What are you saying? That you've been making a fool out of me on this thing?"

"No, son, that's not what we're saying. We're saying you're ready for the real deal now," Lionel said. "You're ready to ride a steer."

"A steer?"

"Yep," Birch said. "Got a few of the randiest little buggers you ever seen just waiting for you. If you're not too sore from falling to try."

Aiden nodded grimly at him, and Birch clapped a hand on his shoulder and led him out of the rope barrel area and toward the main corral.

"Coulda told me right away," Aiden said bitterly.

"Coulda," Birch said and laughed like hell.

Motors were built by the devil. For the life of him Joe Willie couldn't figure how they ever got the idea of horsepower for a lump of steel like this. Horses were easy to figure. This tangle of wires, plugs and casings was impossible. Somewhere in this flathead V8 was the power of ninety-five horses. He understood the horse reference well enough but the technical stuff was gobbledygook. As he read and then looked up the words in a dictionary, he came to understand that this engine was different.

It was a flathead first and foremost. They were called flatheads because the usual collection of valves were in the back beside the pistons instead of over them. There were no valve heads showing, and it resulted in a flatter visible top. That much was easy. Then there was the weird placement of the camshaft. It wasn't centred over the crankshaft, and the crankshaft in turn wasn't centred on the cylinders. That's where he began to get dizzy. He had no head for compression ratio or bore and stroke measurements. In fact, the exploded-view drawings only served to show him a world he'd never entered before.

Sure, like every other road cowboy he'd learned to change a flat, tinker with an oil pump, a starter, the spark plugs, adjust timing and the ordinary roadside stuff of life, but he'd never seen the guts of a vehicle. The drawings worried him. They pointed to a lot of time spent hunched over the old girl's motor. And that was after he figured out how to get the block out of the chassis. The first thing was to find the mounting bolts and get them off. Then, it was likely going to take an A-frame, a chain and a block and tackle. That might require help unless they made such a thing as a push-button block and tackle these days.

He'd be damned if he was going to ask anyone for help. *Help* was erased from his dictionary. This was his arena now. He'd come this far on his own and he wanted to see it through the same way. The arm was strong enough to handle the extra twisting and fine adjusting to come, and despite the occasional shiver and tremble it held up pretty good. He could still not get used to the strange feeling of lightness on his left side, and having to reach across his body with his right hand to do something ordinary, two-hand ordinary, pissed him off as purely as pity. There wasn't a day when he didn't have to stop, crawl out from beneath the old girl and cuss and swear and kick at something. He'd hung an old punching bag off the rafters in the rear of the shed and he'd walk over and punch and punch and punch until gradually he felt the cloud lift and he could think again.

He saw the bear in those moments. It always floated up out of somewhere behind his clenched eyelids and stared at him, coaxed him to feel the fire in his belly, and he'd rock the bag until he was greasy with sweat and tears, the anger too tiring to chase anymore. Then he'd sit in her and smoke. He'd rub the tiny spot in front of the windshield that was scarred by a cigarette and see the gnarled knuckles placing it there as the undulating roll of Nebraska, Wyoming or Colorado hummed beneath the wheels of her and someone's transistor radio strapped to the visor wailed some lonesome Jimmie Rogers train song and the family croaked along valiantly through the night while sore muscles were soothed by the soft rocking of the old truck and the whine of the tires became a song itself that made the night less lonesome, less cold, the miles halved by the vagabond togetherness of rodeo and the promise of another stab at glory in a chute somewhere beyond the next sweeping bend. He'd sit in her and see all that, feel all that, and become calm enough to crawl back under her with the solid earth of home at his back and work again, deliberately, steadily, focussed on that same sweeping bend and a ragged chorus of notes in the night. "Get up, girl," he'd say and lose himself in the work.

"Keep your feet on the rails until you're ready to settle," Lionel said to him. "Otherwise the little spud might crush your legs against the sides."

Aiden listened intently, his lips pressed tight and his hands clenching and unclenching quickly.

"He's gonna go out crazy," Lionel said. "All he wants is out of here and you off his back. And it won't feel like the rope barrel. We give it to you good out there, pretty much full out, but he ain't gonna feel like that. He'll go out flat at first. Running full bore. Then sometime after the first few yards he'll start to kicking. Hold on tight and try to feel him with your legs. Don't press 'em in. Get you a good seat and try and feel with them."

When he felt ready, Aiden lowered himself down onto the steer's back. He looked down at its brown shoulders and found his place behind them like Birch had advised him. The pocket. All the power the steer would generate came from the rear, from behind the pocket. Aiden shrugged his shoulders quickly and felt the steer react to the motion. Then he reached one hand down to the rope rigging.

"Two hands, son," Birch said from the front of the chute.

"No way," Aiden said through gritted teeth.

"Two hands or nothing," Birch said, firmer.

"No way," Aiden said again.

"Stubborn cuss."

"Damn straight."

"Pap?" Birch asked, looking up at Lionel.

The old man stepped down onto a lower rail and cleared his throat to get Aiden's attention. "Keep it up away from you. Can't let it touch you or the steer. When you feel yourself start to fall press it out flat away from you, don't let it bend. Less break that way."

Aiden nodded in small, tense shivers.

"Ready?"

"Give 'er," Aiden said tightly.

"Nod when you're ready."

"Go."

Aiden felt Lionel's hand press flat against his chest, steadying him, and the weight of it was comforting. He nodded hard.

The steer pushed hard into the sudden flare of open, and Aiden felt the first loss of contact with the earth. He leaned back, pushed his feet forward in front of the steer's shoulders, pressed his free arm up and away and gripped hard with his rigging hand. The steer bolted twenty feet into the corral then popped off a series of kicks and bucks, still running as hard as it could. Aiden felt the pocket in his groin, the press of shoulder bone against the cup of the athletic supporter and leaned backward slightly more. The steer thrashed mightily. He could feel its force with the inside of his legs and he caught a flare of blue as the sky flashed above him, then the swirling halo of whitewashed rails and the awkward tilting horizon of barn and mountain and sky again. From somewhere far away he heard Birch yell "Time!"

He felt the steer in running, thumping, jolting kicks that rattled him crazily and when he got the timing he threw his left leg over top of the critter and landed running, off balance and stumbling until he raised his head and saw the fast-approaching rails of the corral that he reached his gloved hands out to like a baby to its mother. He fell into the rails but caught himself with his arms and pulled himself straight.

The wranglers were whooping it up along the length of the corral. As he regained his breathing and felt along his ribs for hurt he stared straight at Birch and Lionel and said, "Again."

"You must have missed him incredibly," Johanna said as she and Claire worked putting up the horses in their stalls.

"More than I ever believed possible," Claire said.

"I don't think I could have done it."

"There was no choice. He didn't want me to see him there. Too much going on inside him, too much to handle on his own without seeing my pain too. I understand that now. I didn't then, not for the longest while."

"Still. I know how it feels."

"You do?"

"There's different kinds of prisons, Claire. But I can see my son in his."

"How do you cope?"

Johanna finished brushing her horse, untied the halter lead and removed it, patted the horse gently on the withers and stepped out of the stall into the corridor. "I guess if loyalty wasn't so tough it wouldn't be a virtue," she said.

"What do you mean?" Claire asked, finishing with her horse and stepping out to join Johanna in the corridor. Johanna nodded in the direction of another stall and the two women started to put up Victoria's horse as well.

"I suppose I mean that what Victoria said is true. That choice is our superhuman power. We can bend things to suit us, just by choosing."

"How?" Claire said. "I mean, why?"

Johanna grinned. "The natural thing would be to worry, fret over him, try to make things easy for him, coddle him. But that wouldn't solve anything. In the end it would only hurt him more. So I have to choose to let him walk the path he wants to walk. Choose to be confident that I raised him with the principles that will save him. Choose to believe in him. And ultimately choose to not worry—the ultimate unnatural act for a mother."

"Faith," Claire said.

"Courage," Johanna said. "Faith is what we earn when we have enough courage to face what's in front of us."

"Is that an Indian teaching?"

"It is now," Johanna said.

"He rode the hell out of that steer," Birch said.

"That's a fact," Lionel said. "One-handed all the way."

"Steer's a steer," Joe Willie said. "Ten-year-olds ride steers."

"Six times?" Birch asked.

Joe Willie looked up quickly. "He rode clean six times?"

"Thing is he woulda rode a dozen," Lionel said. "The boy's stoked up. He'd rode until we ran out of stock."

"Clean?"

"Clean as I ever seen," Birch said. "He got better with every ride, but it was the first time that really opened my eyes."

"Same here," Lionel said. He leaned on the veranda rail and faced Birch and Joe Willie. "All six were prime. Not a blooper or a crow hopper in the bunch. All arm jerkers and he never bailed out. Competition he'da covered on every ride."

"Bullshit," Joe Wille said. "Too tall. Too old. Too big. Steer's a steer."

"You should have seen it," Birch said.

"I don't want to see it. The two of you jacked up over a fluke is enough."

"Wasn't no fluke," Lionel said. "The boy's a rider. We're trying him on the bull machine tomorrow."

"You got to be kidding me," Joe Willie said and stood up. "City kid, green as grass, nothing but attitude, and you're thinking you want to put him on a brindle? Is that it?"

"Maybe not," Birch said. "But he wants to try the machine."

"So what's Cowboy Copas up to now?" Joe Willie asked, stepping down onto the veranda steps.

"The boys are showing him the rigging," Birch said.

"Jesus H.," Joe Willie said. "Marce must have paid you a whack of money to get you to act this foolish."

"Not about money," Lionel said.

"What's it about, then? Hungry for excitement?"

"Not a hair," Birch said. "I only ever seen one pure natural in my life. Only ever got me close to perfection one time." He looked squarely at his son, who tilted his head to the side and eyeballed him right back. "And the fact is, son, it's a rare thing. You can't learn harmony like that. It's put in you, plain and simple. And Creator in her wisdom puts it in some mighty strange places sometimes and all you can do is wonder. Wonder and let it play out."

"Why?" Joe Willie asked.

"Because it's the only way to find out what's in it for you. Why the lesson come wrapped the way she's wrapped."

"Yeah, well, take the shortcut, I say."

"And what's that, son?"

"Put the sumbitch on four. If he holds on to that you might have something to talk about. If he face-plants like I figure, it don't rightly matter how she's wrapped."

He eased his hat lower on his head and made his way toward the barn to prepare for his evening hike up Iron Mountain. As he passed the wranglers in the corral showing Aiden how to rosin the bull rope, he shook his head and spat on the ground. The boy looked up and the two of them stared at each other. Joe Willie stopped in his tracks. Aiden held the look. The wranglers looked back and forth at the two of them, waiting. Finally, Joe Willie shook his head and moved on toward the barn.

"Kid's got stones," he muttered.

Played out in slow motion the ride took on a ghostly quality. There was an eerie dreaminess about the way the violent bucking and twisting of the bull and the extension of the arms and legs of the rider came together then flowed apart. Slowed down to a few inches of tape per second, eight seconds of ride lasted more than a minute, longer with rewinds and freeze-frame. It was all about explosion. He could see that from the way the bull burst from the chute into the wildly gyrating spins, four-legged leaps and explosive kicks that all appeared in slowed-down time like a giant horned accordion, collapsing, unfolding, collapsing again. There was an impossible elasticity that stretched out magically in the way the bull's head and shoulders could twist one way while his trunk and rear went opposite while lashing out with his back hooves all at the same time. Then came the jaw-dropping breaches of gravity. Nothing that large and heavy should be able to leap that high. Not without thirty yards of running room to build speed. Not even then. Yet there it was. Elevated straight up from a force of propulsion that could only come from rage, a powerful wave of flesh rising unbelievably in slow motion with the rider on its back resembling a surfer far out to sea, reduced to flotsam, shrunk by the sheer tide of the bull cresting beneath the bull rope, building more and more momentum, waiting to crash him onto the hard-packed coast of the corral. It hung in the air, head thrown back then lowered, bawling, horns thrust fiercely side to side, globs of snot flung from its nose, the great shoulders hunched then stretched and the wide girth of it levitated suddenly over five feet of daylight beneath the dangling clatter of the clank belt. He felt the power of it. Awesome. Terrifying. Thrilling. Over and over he played the ride. Then others. Each time it was the same, the same cataclysmic release of energy, brief sometimes, brutal, punishing, and longer other times, the eight seconds an eternity, the inferno of it captivating, horrifying. He couldn't get enough of it. Everything about the bulls called to him, called to a primal something he could feel in the gut, like the feeling he got just before a fight in the joint, a gathering of will, power and strength steeped in a vitriolic stew of fear, anxiety and sheer excitement. Played out in slow motion, the ride became magnetic.

Eventually, he turned his focus to the rider. He leaned closer to the television, the remote pressed to his chest, and watched the lean power of Joe Willie Wolfchild. In slow motion the man rode like a ribbon flowing outward and inward, looped and straightened with every motion of the bull. There was an ancient, barbarian quality to the deep scowl on his face and a warrior-like intensity to the plant of him in the pocket, the spot behind the shoulders of the bull becoming sacred ground to be defended, protected and occupied relentlessly. Aiden paid rapt attention to the thrust of his legs, the spurring at the neck as though coaxing the bull even further into rage. He watched closely the small adjustments the camera caught, the tiny lateral moves to regain the pocket or the desperate hauls back into place when the bull forced him dangerously over the shoulders or backwards closer to the seat of the tornado. Every move became a battle. Every second a private struggle. All of it, everything, titanic, colossal, insane. He watched until his eyes burned and the tiredness forced him to normal speed. The thrashing Joe Willlie endured was purely violent. Nothing in his experience prepared him for the brutality of those moments, and as he watched the rides he began to see the links, the seamless unity between Joe Willie and the bulls forged in a quality of courage he'd never experienced either. He watched every ride. He watched the man walk toward the camera after, hat thrown off, hair askew, the hard grimace slackening visibly into a great easy grin, the elastic strength of him impressive in its easy stroll toward the camera. In the background the flash of bull fighters chasing the monster back to his lair. The man, oblivious now, at ease and pointing to someone in the crowd, grinning, waving, safe back home on earth again to await the next challenge.

Claire wrestled with the martingale. Victoria told her to tack up the same horse she'd ridden the night before. She could be a spooky sort at times and needed the extra rein to keep her from throwing her head around during the ride. The trouble was, Claire couldn't figure top from bottom now. She'd done it with Johanna's help, and obviously there was a way to hook it to the bridle, but try as she might she couldn't discern it. The length of leather lay in her hands and she willed herself to stare it down long enough to figure it out.

"You lost there, ma'am?" someone said behind her.

She turned. Joe Willie stood there with a length of rope coiled around one shoulder. He stared at her placidly and she found herself struggling for words.

"Well, yes," she said. "I've got the rest figured but this has me bamboozled." She held the martingale out toward him, and Joe Willie nodded.

"Here," he said and shrugged the rope off his shoulder. He took the rein and stepped into the stall beside her. The horse nickered, threw its head about and stamped its back feet. Joe Willie moved calmly, chucked at it and rubbed the underside of its neck. The horse settled and he called to Claire. "You want to turn it over like this, then snap it here and here," he said.

"Thanks," Claire said. "Pretty dumb, huh?"

He looked at her in the same placid way. "No," he said. "Dumb woulda been to ride off without it."

"Yes. I wasn't about to do that."

"Not dumb then."

"I guess not." She held out her hand. "I'm Claire."

Joe Willie wiped his hand on the back of his jeans. "Joe Willie," he said.

"I know."

He nodded. He pulled the left arm up from where it hung at his side and put the hand in the pocket of his jeans and shifted his feet a little like a shy little boy. Claire saw slackness of the fabric along his arm and the birdlike boniness of the wrist. Joe Willie caught her look. He bent to retrieve the coil of rope. Despite herself Claire dropped down to grab it for him and they almost collided at the depth of the crouch. Their hands were on the rope.

"I got it," he said tersely.

"I'm sorry," Claire said. "I just thought . . ."

"I got it," he said again.

They stood up at the same time and faced each other, mere inches apart. She had to look up to make eye contact, and he looked out over her head at first, gazing side to side. She took a step back.

"Thanks," she said.

"Welcome," he said.

"Would you like to come?" she blurted out.

"I don't ride," he said.

"What a shame," she said and instantly regretted it.

He hitched the rope around his shoulder and stepped around her to make his way down the corridor. "Ma'am," he said as he passed, touching the brim of his hat with two fingers.

She watched him limp out of the stable. He was tall and lean and young looking but there was a hardness to him, something she likened to Aiden in the way he drew himself in, closed up and went away to some private place.

"That could have gone a whole lot better," she muttered to the horse.

"Trick is the grip," Lionel told him.

"It's your hold and your release all at the same time," Birch added. He handed Aiden a thick leather glove. He showed him how to use the rosin to make it sticky, tacky, like flypaper, and to wrap it tight to his hand.

Aiden flexed it, and the palm crackled. Raising it to his face and looking at it, he felt stronger, more capable, the glove in its oversized thickness giving his fingers a talon-like curl when he flexed them.

The bucking machine sat in the middle of a veritable sea of thick blue padding. When Aiden put a foot to it and pushed, it offered little give, not at all like the feathery give of the hay and mattresses under the rope barrel. The machine itself was eerie. It was cut to look like the trunk of a bull. There was even a rubber head and horns mounted to the front end. The rectangular riding block was covered in hide and the bull hair was coarse, wiry. It sat at a steep angle, the rear of it kicked up sharply. In his mind Aiden tried to imagine what the rest of the bull might have looked like in that pose, rear legs thrown back and high, the head cast to one side trying to hook the rider's legs with the horns. He squeezed his fingers together and the crackle of the rosined leather exhilarated him. He walked around the machine, his feet sinking into the blue padding, and tried to imagine himself whirling around and up and down at the same time, reversing direction on the rise, the strain at the wrist eased some by the rapid kicking out of his legs and feet. There was a tornado coming, and he felt the electric tickle of its approach on his skin. He gave the machine a final firm slap.

"Anything else I should know?" he asked Birch.

Birch pointed to a hay bale set on its narrow side. "Ride that first," he said.

"You're kidding me," Aiden said.

"No, I'm not. Get you a seat on that bale and I'm gonna show you how to use your arms."

Birch showed him how to throw his legs out, how to keep the free arm up and away at the same time. It seemed silly at first, like a child's game, but when he sat on the bale and went through the motions Aiden got the first glimpse of how hard this would be. The legs and the arm had to work together. When they did he could feel the weight of his body centre on one small area of his butt, one remarkably tiny area that was keyed to fit the same fragment of the bull's body, the pocket right behind the shoulders. The flinging outward of the legs coupled with the raised arm centred him in the pocket, and as he went through the spurring motion he saw in his head the images of Joe Willie's rides and tried to mimic them.

"Ready?" Lionel asked Aiden.

Aiden looked at the machine. It sat idle but seemed filled with ominous intent, like a bad-mannered dog. "No," he said. "Let them go first."

The Hairstons cackled.

"Chicken, huh?" Jess said.

Aiden just looked at him passively and moved to sit beside Mundell, who drank slowly from a coffee mug.

"Nervous?" Mundell asked.

"Some," Aiden said. "I want to watch it first."

"Good thinking. See what you're in for."

"Yeah. Something like that."

Jess got up onto the machine and settled himself into the grip Birch showed him. When he nodded, the wrangler at the controls flipped the switch and the machine began rising and falling, turning slow circles at the same time. Aiden watched carefully. Hairston managed to make his way awkwardly through a minute of the action before Lionel held up a hand and the wrangler stopped the machine. Jess leaped off the machine and sprawled into the padding. His face was red when he stood up and high-fived his brother, who mounted up for his ride. Lanny fared as well as his brother, and when his ride was over the Hairstons celebrated, whooped wildly. Aiden never once took his eyes off the machine.

"Ready now?" Birch asked.

Still staring at the bucking machine, he walked to it wordlessly and tightened the glove as he approached. He leaped up onto the machine, he watched as Birch instructed him on the rigging. He felt the elevation from the floor. He felt the rough texture of the rigging and flexed his grip a couple of times before he looked at Birch expressionlessly.

"Give 'er," he said. He locked eyes with the wrangler at the controls, unblinking and aware of every muscle in his body. Slowly he raised his free arm up and away, setting his jaw firmly and forcing himself to concentrate. Then he nodded.

It was like being pushed upward and forward by an invisible hand directly under his hips. When he felt the force he raised his arm a little higher and pushed his legs outward. He immediately felt the pressure in a rectangle of space at his tailbone. He concentrated on that. As the bucking machine whirled around and tilted he willed himself to copy the moves he'd watched Joe Willie make and he felt elastic, strong and in sync with the machine. Then the dips and pushes came quicker. They were giving him more. He set his jaw tighter and focussed. The circles seemed tighter, but he held his seat. He felt more power surge through the machine and he was aware of a sudden loss of contact with horizontal and vertical. The only thing that existed was the cyclone. His only focal point became the pocket, and he spurred outward and raised his free arm to maintain it. When even more power came he felt the hard junction of his wrist and rope. He held it. There was a high whine in his ears as the machine worked harder, accompanied by creaks of leather and the throaty sound of voices raised in excitement. He was juiced. The adrenaline forced his mouth open and he closed it again, gritted his teeth and spurred and pressed outward with his free arm, feeling the thrum of the motor against the inside of his thighs and the air cool and moist against the sweat of his face. He felt a power in him that was electrifying and freeing and primitive, and when the machine began to slow he gathered all of it, all the joyous, rapturous, hair-raising thrill of it and kicked away from the machine with one leg, twisting his torso hard the same way and felt the separation and the sweet empty of the air before he landed on his feet in the thick blue padding.

"How high did you turn it?" he asked, dry throated.

Birch raised five fingers.

"Again?" he asked, swallowing hard.

"You bet your ass, again," Birch said.

Damn. There was no way past it. He was going to need help. While the beam across the roof of the equipment shed was strong enough to bear the weight of pulling the engine block up and out of the truck, there was no way Joe Willie was going to be able to haul it himself. He tried, but the weight and the motion required two strong arms, maybe more. For a while he toyed with the notion of buying a hoist and frame from town, but there was something about the feel of the old girl that told him that she'd prefer old-fashioned sweat and gumption. Besides, there was a small thrill in being able to say that he'd done the work up to this point with his own power, and he was determined to see it through with the pure strength of hands and arms. Arms. Funny. He had a burgeoning faith in the left to lift and twist when he needed it. Sure, there were things he couldn't do with it, normal things, everyday things that pissed him off to think about, but it had come a fair way with his effort. He still hated to look at it. He still sought to hide it when anyone was around and though he much preferred solitude over visibility the damn thing was stronger, less prone to tremble, moved more easily in the destroyed shoulder socket. But it was still ugly. That wasn't going to change. Ever. He rubbed it now as he considered asking for help. He could almost curl his thumb and fingers around it. Damn. The muscles had atrophied so badly that when he turned it over so the palm of his hand was upwards the boniness of it made his hand look like a small paddle, meatless, and flat.

He hated to ask for help. It meant he was incapable. Invalid. He rubbed the arm and sat in the cab of the truck. This was his arena. This was his challenge. It was how he'd learned to fight. Alone in a saddle or tied in the rigging, there was no need for anyone else. Ever. A man found his own way up there, relied on nothing but his own instinct and know-how, trusted only the power of his own body, the strength of his own mind and the grit of his own gumption. Help was something you accepted from the pickup riders and the bull fighters once the fight was finished. This fight was far from finished, but clearly there was no way past it. He smoked.

"Damn," he said.

They were standing around the main corral watching the wranglers load bulls in the chutes. He walked up purposefully. Lionel caught his approach out of the corner of his eye and nudged Birch.

"Need some help," he said.

"That a fact?" Lionel said.

Joe Willie rubbed the stubble on his chin and toed the dirt with his boot. "Yeah," he said. "That's a fact."

"What kind of help, son?" Birch asked.

"The old girl," he said. "I gotta haul the engine out of her."

The wranglers edged closer to catch the conversation. The Hairston brothers were owl-eyed and slack-jawed in that awed way of rodeo fans, and it irritated Joe Willie. The convict kid just leaned one elbow on the fence and looked at him with an unruffled air. That irritated him even more.

"How you figure on doing that?" Lionel asked.

"Rope," he said.

"Chain'd be a mite safer," Lionel said.

"Rope," Joe Willie said shortly. "I got a rope."

"Okay. We'll do it with a rope then. Pulley?"

"What?"

"Figure maybe drive a pulley into the main beam and haul her out that way. Easier," Lionel said. "A few more hands and we can guide her to wherever you wanna put her."

Joe Willie nodded. He hadn't considered that. "All right," he said.

Birch explained what needed doing, and the Hairstons and Mundell agreed heartily. Aiden held his position on the fence looking calmly at Joe Willie and his father. Finally, he nodded and moved to join the others.

"Mr. Wolfchild," Jess said to Joe Willie, "we ain't had a chance to talk to you since we been here. My brother and me been fans an awful long time. Maybe you could watch us ride this afternoon and give us a few pointers."

Joe Willie turned and started walking toward the equipment shed. The others began to follow.

"Fuckin' prima donna," Jess whispered to his brother.

Aiden smiled and kept walking.

Johanna moved around horses as though she was one of them. There was a regal quality to the way she threaded herself between them, leaned into a flank, used her body weight to edge a horse a step or two to the side or look it square on while she approached with a halter. As she watched her bring horses in from the corral, Claire was envious. She wanted that for herself, that sense of kinship, that ethereal connection to wild. The horses related to Johanna. She could see that. They were unafraid and compliant, and when Johanna moved to control one there were no signs of resistance, only a casual acceptance of things as they stood, a will given over to will, a knowing that was shared between animal and human. Leading them into the barn and on over to the round pen, Johanna spoke to them, a conversation rather than a trite bubbling of syllables, and the horses pricked their ears attentively, seeming to enjoy, even hear and comprehend, the words and phrases.

"Why do you do that?" Claire asked, walking beside Johanna on the side away from the horse. "Talk to them like that."

"Like how?"

"Like they're human."

Johanna gave her an easy grin. "I guess because I never really saw a difference. I guess because they've always been friends to me and I took the time to get to know them as friends, not animals, not stock, not anything. Just friends."

"It makes them happy," Claire said.

"Yes, it does. They want to be recognized. Just like us."

"Affirmed, you mean?"

"Yes. Good word. When I was a girl I was taught very carefully about horses. About all creatures, really, but horses mostly."

"By your people?"

Johanna laughed lightly. "Yes. By my people. The Sioux are horse people. You might even say that the whole flow of our culture stemmed from our relationship with horses. It certainly was how we rode into the history books."

"A tradition."

"Yes."

"I can't identify a tradition in my life. Mama wasn't big on ceremony and we never observed a ritual of any kind. We kind of floated around waiting for someone or something to explain us, define us, give us shape. Men mostly."

"Sounds familiar," Johanna said, leading the horse into the pen and grabbing a long lead that was slung over the rails. Claire climbed up on the top rail to watch Johanna work the horse. Johanna led the mare into the very centre of the pen and talked to her calmly, stroking her, easing her into the idea of work while she connected the lead. When she was ready she backed away in long, measured steps until she was at the end of the lead. She continued talking to the horse and began a series of hand signals that the horse picked up on and stepped backwards and forward on command. The lead hung slack between them, and only as the horse stepped closer did Johanna pay any attention to it at all, gathering it in as the distance between them narrowed. They worked that way for a while until Johanna was satisfied. She motioned to Claire.

"You do it," she said.

"Me? I don't know how."

"Sure you do. You've watched me do it all morning. I'll stand right here. Give her the signals and then trot her a bit."

Claire took the long lead and turned to face the mare, and began talking in the low, soothing tones Johanna used. The horse focussed on her attentively. She gave the hand signal to approach and the horse stepped forward. There was a small thrill in her spleen, and when the horse backed up on the hand command Claire was elated. She gave a light flick on the lead and guided the mare into a circular walk around the end of the lead before easing it up to a trot. She spoke to it all the

while and the mare responded beautifully. Johanna touched
her on the shoulder and Claire brought the mare back in.

"Wonderful," Johanna said. "Simple, wasn't it?"

"Exhilarating," Claire said.

"Can you do it again the same way?"

"I believe I can."

"Good. That's how you build a tradition." Johanna smiled.

Even with a large pulley attached to the main beam it took six
of them to ease the engine out of the chassis. The frame creaked
as the weight was lifted and the truck rose some on its springs
when the engine was finally airborne. They'd cleared a heavy
wooden table of the assortment of crap and clutter that filled it.
They'd had to use a second rope to guide the engine over, and
as it settled on the old wood it offered up a tired creak.

Aiden had never seen anything like it. Every engine he'd
worked on had been relatively new, and the vintage block held
mysteries he felt keen to explore. The old truck needed a lot of
work, but when he pounded the fender skirt some it was
amazingly sound. The men gathered around the engine and
stared at it wordlessly. Joe Willie was clearly anxious and
whenever any one of them reached out to touch part of it,
Aiden saw him flinch. Nothing you could call a reaction, just
a small tightening around the corner of the mouth. Aiden
looked at the arm. At a casual glance you couldn't really tell
there was anything different about it. There was a slackening
of material along the entire length of it, and the way the fabric
draped off the nub of bone that was the shoulder joint gave it
a peculiar hang, but clothed in a long-sleeve shirt and standing
the way he did, slumped to the right with his hands on his
hips, hid the damage the bull had done. Still, Aiden couldn't
fathom how someone would adjust to that, the sudden ripping

away of a dream and the shrinking of a world. It had to hurt. His eyes flicked back and forth between the right arm and the left as he tried to picture the man he'd watched riding monstrous bulls, an incredibly strong, whole man, a man clumping along in fringed chaps, flinging his hat into the crowd, bristling with life, the dust of the arena like a halo around him and the feel of a behemoth conquered fresh in his chest. He couldn't see that man here.

When their eyes met Aiden froze but held the look. He felt Joe Willie look right into him, and in the unwavering intensity of that gaze he saw the bull rider.

"What?" Joe Willie asked sullenly.

"Nothing," Aiden said.

He watched Joe Willie breathe, the slight flare of nostril the only sign that there was life beyond the hard, unyielding force of that gaze.

"You've really got to see this kid go," Birch told Joe Willie after everyone had left the shed.

"Why?" Joe Willie busied himself with the engine.

"When he rides he's all business. It's amazing, really."

"It's a machine, Daddy."

"He took it to eight."

"Seen ten-year-olds do eight seconds on a machine."

"Level eight."

Joe Willie slowly set the wrench down on the table. He turned to look at his father. "Green kid took it to eight? Didn't bail?"

"Didn't bail. He spurred it too."

"Why?"

"Don't know. We only showed him how to hold on. Figured to throw in the legwork after."

"Jesus."

"That's what I said."

"Still, it's just a machine. Don't mean nothing. Not really."

"Not really," Birch said. "Anyone can fluke level eight four times."

Joe Willie looked at him as hard as any man had ever looked at him. "What are you gonna do?"

"Got no choice," Birch said. "We gotta rig him up."

"When?"

"No need of waiting."

Joe Willie scratched at his head beneath his hat and looked up at the rafters of the shed. "Then I guess I'd better see this thing. Let me know when it's time."

Aiden found Claire picking the hooves of a gelding in the stable. He watched her go about the chore and talking to the horse, telling it about her girlhood dream of riding in the dappled sunlight of the mountains on a horse just like him. The horse seemed to enjoy the talk, and when Claire changed to another hoof, scuffing around the animal's body easily and familiarly, he lifted it at the touch of her palm. Aiden smiled. She looked at home around the horse and as he watched her move he wondered at the strange power of time to offer things, choices mostly, that you wouldn't make in a normal situation, like this journey to a ranch, this way of life so different from the one he knew, the anonymity of the city. She looked nothing like the woman he remembered before the joint. This woman was vital and natural, and he could see her natural grace in the way she scraped away with a hoof pick in a shadowy stall. It was worth it to see this. Worth every second in that place. Worth every lonesome minute of refusal, his sparing her the sight of him in coarse denim surrounded by ghostly concrete painted a subdued green like the fading memory of grass and lawns and meadows. She caught him looking.

"Chores get done faster by doing," she said.

"Yeah, well, I'm better at the other end."

She laughed. "Really? You want to muck out this stall, then?"

"No. I meant the top end."

"Yeah? How's it going?"

"I'm going up."

"Up where?"

"On a bull."

Claire stood up quickly and the horse shied some. She spoke to it soothingly and stroked its withers. "I don't know if that's a good idea," she said to Aiden. "Isn't it dangerous?"

"Getting sent to the joint wasn't a good idea and it's plenty dangerous there. I'll take a bull over two hundred angry dudes any time."

She looked at him leaning casually against the stall. There was a quietness about him now, not the angry, sullen silence she'd seen before, but more the laconic, bowled-over kind of quiet that settled over men at births and deaths and surprising twists of fate. Awe, almost. But easing closer to respect. He grinned at her and she felt her heart compress.

"Okay," she said, putting the hoof pick in its place. "But let's do something first."

"What?"

"Let's go blast around in that little convertible. We'll put the top down and you can drive and we'll race down the highway and see the sights. What do you think?"

"You want me to drive?"

"Yes."

"I've only driven for short jaunts. Parking. Backing up. Moving cars around."

"You'll get the hang of it fast. You get the hang of every-thing fast."

"When?"

"No time like the present," she said and walked out of the stall. Aiden looked at her with surprise and then followed her out of the barn.

He understood what it meant. He understood it fully. There was a charge in the blood that he could feel even now. Even now after these long months of working on the truck and feel-ing as removed from rodeo as a worn-out bronc put out to pasture, he could feel the heat of it. It had burned in him all his life, and if the kid was as good as they said, then the fire would be in him too. God, he missed fanning those flames. Joe Willie had studied gymnastics for years in order to learn how to control his body in the air. He'd taken judo to learn how to fall and land correctly, absorbing impact in a directed roll of the body. He'd taken yoga for elasticity and breathing during stress and he'd even taken dance classes in order to learn rhythm, timing and control of motion. And he'd learned how to shrug off the pain of impact. It took all of that just to prepare, just to make yourself ready to compete. To stoke the fire that burned relentlessly in the gut. He'd spent hours on the rope barrel and the bucking machine adjusting to the pitch of wild bucking and that eerie sensation in the head when there's no focal point for balance, when the world and all you knew of it spun and twisted and gyrated wildly and relief was most often found spread-eagled on the hardpack. He'd done all of it out of a pure and unencumbered love. That's what it took. As he worked his way across the pasture he felt the incredible ache of absence. He'd never felt it for a person in his life and he wondered if that felt anything near as bad as the longing he carried within him for the arena, the action, the sight and sound and smell of rodeo.

He sneered to see the boy and the woman head into the house. The kid was a fluke. It couldn't be anything more, some weird combination of balance and timing that grace had given him. He'd rig up on one of the ranch bulls and probably scare himself right back to the city, right back to whatever sad and sorry life had landed him in prison and likely right back into it. Snot nose. If he had some guts and some sand it was because of the same generous hand of grace that gave him the balance and the timing. He'd go. He'd go and watch the kid slam into the dirt, clamber up with a hand to his lower back, limp to the rail and lean there with his head on his forearms, crying at the shock, the brutality, the loss of himself as he flew through the air and the realization that he'd been beaten, good and solid and final. He wouldn't wish it on him. But he knew it was the only sure end to the fantasy his father and grandfather had. Natural. The kid was no natural, but the ending sure would be.

Aiden drove with a small grin on his face. Beside him, Claire lounged with a map unfolded on her lap, pressing it down against the wind with one hand and brushing at her hair with the other. He'd unlocked the confounding combination of clutch, shift and gas almost immediately and he drove with control. He kept the car at a steady, purring clip, only passing when it mattered, never risking, never taking chances. How he could do that with so little time behind the wheel she didn't know. There was so much she didn't know now, so much she wanted to learn about him, and as she stared at the highway ahead of her she was glad of the car.

He twirled the dial of the radio until the car was filled

with a country two-step replete with fiddle and pedal steel guitar.

"There," he shouted over the wind and the radio. "Mood music."

She laughed. "I know this song," she yelled back.

"Sure you do," he said.

"No, really," she said and leaned across the console so he could hear her. "When I was a girl we lived in this building with our window facing the apartment across the alley. It was only about ten feet. We never had a radio or a TV, but the man who lived across the alley loved country music. I could hear it through his window. So I sat on the ledge of our window at night when Mom was gone and listened to music.

"He saw me one night and he walked toward the window. I thought he was going to close it but instead he leaned out, grinned at me, turned the music louder, snapped his fingers and did a little dance step. He'd turn the music up whenever he saw me at the window. We never spoke. I never knew his name. But I sure learned to love that music."

He drove and they listened to the song until it faded into the next one. It was a different kind of silence. Claire could feel that. Aiden stared ahead at the road but his thoughts were far away, and when he spoke to her again it was in a voice that had a curious overtone, the sound of a boy, a boy's sense of wonder spoken in the rumbling voice of a man.

"There was this kid in the joint," he said, "had a guitar. Everyone laughed at him because he only played this kind of stuff. Hillbilly, that's what we called him. But I used to lay on my bunk and read and listen to him play. He wasn't bad. Some of those songs would reach out and touch me when he sang them. Real. You know?"

"Yes," she said. "It's what got me too."

"So I'd lay there and pretend not to notice. Made me feel kinda lonesome when I needed to feel lonesome and quiet when I needed that. I never told him. Never thanked him for it."

"What happened to him?"

"He got out," Aiden said and lit a cigarette from the lighter and stared harder at the road, smoking. "But he was back in less than a month on a murder beef, coming down off morphine and crack real hard, skinny, all fucked up. Didn't have the guitar anymore."

The song ended and Aiden turned down the volume on the commercial that followed. They drove on in the quiet.

"Did you meet a lot of kids like that?"

"Not really. Kept to myself. It was better that way."

"Yes."

"But I sure missed that music."

He turned the radio back up. Out here the land rolled outward, languid as a dream, unfurling itself into gullies, ridges, plains and occasional sweeps of open territory that made a solitary tree magical, fantastic, like something unseen before, and as it opened itself to the sky, Claire could feel the land begin to lull her, easing time and forgetting into something small at her centre, coiled, eased, wrapped about itself, slumbered and gentle to carry. She looked at her son. He drove with the wrist of one hand bent over the arc of the steering wheel, at ease, comfortable with the car, the road, the feel of the land. As he powered the car around a wide, sweeping curve, he reached over and squeezed her hand. Once. Quickly, then released. Wordlessly. Claire felt as though he had spoken volumes.

For Victoria it was always the same. Once the bull fever set into them there was nothing else for her to do but follow along and wait it out. They'd forget routine things like meals and chores and time itself. Bad enough with the saddle broncs and bareback broncs, but the bulls carried their own mystique, and it was like the air around them became electrified, and the men shimmered around them like iron filings, shaped and defined by energy. She'd seen it forever. It was the same for Birch as it had been for Lionel, and when Joe Willie came along, bull riding was as natural a thing in a day as grits and grease. It was good to see again, though. All of them got that look in the eyes, eager like a pup, hungry and excited all at the same time, and it always made her laugh.

She laughed now as she headed for the main corral. Lionel had stumped through the kitchen on his way to their room and stumped back through again with a pair of his chaps hung over a shoulder and winked at her broadly. She'd known then and she quickly made up sandwiches, gathered some fruit and chocolate, filled a water jug and headed out to where her men, her boys, were getting ready to play their favourite game. The wranglers had shunted a dozen bulls into the back pens and three more were waiting to be pushed up into the bucking chutes while everyone prepared. She set the snacks and water in the shade of the bleachers and sat with Claire and Mundell and the Hairstons.

"Exciting, isn't it?" she asked.

"Did you ever worry?" Claire asked.

"Always," she said. "Didn't matter though."

She pointed to Birch and Lionel and the wranglers busy near the chutes, laughing and teasing. "See that? How could anything matter seeing something like that? Seeing men as boys. Seeing them alive as alive can be. They never worried. Worry'd take them right out of it, right out of the one place in the whole world they really want to be."

"Still," Mundell said, "it's dangerous."

"So's walking. But you never think about it. It's just something you do."

"But your grandson?" Mundell asked.

Victoria could see Claire watching her carefully. "Well," she said, "everyone thinks it takes courage to get on a bull. That a man's gotta be crazy or stout-hearted or both. But the truth is that it takes a lot more courage to decide to ride a bull than it takes to get up on one. Takes gumption to choose that. And when you're a mother you want that sort of grit in your kids— the pluck to face the hard stuff head on. That's what you work for. That's your job.

"So when they choose it outright like Joe Willie did, you stand by that. Because that's your job too. And when they're hurt, even as bad as my grandson got hurt, you stand by that too, because you're the one that put that heart there, that courage, those guts, and it's your job to believe that they'll connect to it again, to show them that faith, even if it hurts to watch that journey unfold.

"The courage is in the decision to be brave."

Claire looked away across the corral. The iron filings gathered themselves around the attractant.

Joe Willie sat on the top rail of a holding chute and watched. He could have done it in his sleep, this ritual of preparation, but as he saw his grandfather and his father coaching the kid through the elaborate mechanics of readiness, it took him back to his own early days. The days when the thrill of the ride lay right here, in the sunlight and the dust behind the corral, in the smell of rope, leather, rosin, bull dung and in the high, arching push of nerves that felt like they were drawn across the surface of the skin, itching, raw, pulsing. Nothing changed. There was no room for change here. Instead it was predictable, a hushed, anxious, deliberate, matter-of-fact preparation, a gathering of energy that allowed a cowboy a gradual release of tension in the small acts of ritual. He watched Aiden rosining the gloves, then the bull rope, yanking downward on it hard with the gloves to burn the stickiness into every fibre, then testing it for tackiness and grip. He watched him strip and climb into the large athletic supporter and the knee pads before pulling up his jeans. He nodded solemnly as Aiden pulled the Kevlar vest around his ribs that would protect him from the raking of horns when he was on the ground. When Aiden closed his eyes and pushed his head back against the thick roll of padding around his neck, Joe Willie found himself breathing harder, deeper. Then the pantomime. Lionel acted it out first, then Birch, then Aiden: standing with legs spread wide, the rigging hand down at the groin, the free hand held up and away from the body, each of them mimed the upper action of the body that would happen after the bull erupted out of the chute, their talk pointed, sharp, eager. It was a bizarre dance, strange and baffling to the eye but necessary as a warm-up and a reminder of what was to come. When he watched Birch lead Aiden through the stretches, the impact-specific twists and rockings that got his whole body ready, Joe Willie felt all of it. Then, finally, the clank belt. They inspected the heavy length of rope that girdled the bull with the brass cowbell attached, the clunk-and-clatter device that drove the bulls wild. Satisfied that it was sound, they gave the kid a solid slap on the shoulder and led him to the chute. None of them looked up. None of them had the time. None of them could spare the focus. He understood that.

He heard the thwack and rattle of the boards when the bull thumped into the chute. It bawled wildly, and the solid thunk of its horns on the sides of the chute was as fresh to Joe Willie's ears as if it were yesterday. The men moved more deliberately now. The wrangler at the back end of the bull pushed harder, spoke to it with a voice high with tension, cussing, commanding it, edged it up tighter to the head of the chute. Birch clambered over and began fixing the pull rope to the front of the chute, his eyes widened with excitement, flicking them up at Aiden, who was straddling the chute on the top rails. Beside him on the scaffolding behind the chute, Lionel coached him downward rail by rail until he settled for the first time on the broad, muscled back of the bull. It reared, its great snout tossed upward, and the boy scrambled up against the rails again. The men around the chute snapped at each other, hard directions, all verbs, all business. When it calmed, Lionel directed Aiden back down onto the bull's back. He slapped it firmly, let it know he was there, then began hauling on the bull rope. Lionel showed him how to wrap it over the palm of his hand. Joe Willie watched, unblinking. Lionel leaned in closer, whispering last instructions to the boy, who sat still, his face tight across the cheekbones, a fierce look in his eyes, breathing through clenched teeth. When they were ready Lionel reached one hand over his shoulder and pressed against his chest to steady him, reassure him, and the kid pushed the hat down low on his head, grimacing now, the cords in his neck standing out in red relief as he nodded vigorously to Birch, who yanked hard on the rope and backpedalled quickly to open the chute.

At first it seemed like the bull wouldn't move. Then it kicked out of the chute madly, driving into the open with its rear legs, launching into a running series of bucks before spinning to the left away from Aiden's grip. The boy spurred it, his free hand moving in sync with the kicking-out motion of his legs. The bull spun quicker, kicking furiously. Around and around it spun in a tight circle, and Joe Willie could see the kid leaned out, back, flat to the spin, his knees kicked up, driving his feet to the bull's shoulders, the free hand clear of the bull and himself. The spin slowed but the bull bucked harder, higher, running a few short sharp steps then bucking again, and at the last it leaped high with all four legs, the back hooves kicked out hard into an arabesque, the violent ballet of bulls, and landed again and kicked itself wildly counterclockwise, sending clods of dirt flying hard into the bleachers so the onlookers had to duck them and Aiden spurred it and lifted that free arm high and wide and free and Joe Willie held his breath to see it and he could see every move like a slowed-down tape and he recalled all of it, all the aching glory, all the pain, the anxiety, the violence, the release, and he remembered how he loved it so and then Birch yelled "Time!" and he felt himself breathe. The pickup riders moved in swiftly, hemming the bull in on each side, and it ran, the bucks subsiding until finally Aiden could reach out with one arm and haul himself off. The pickup man made sure the bull was clear before he dropped Aiden carefully to the ground. The bull trotted into the chute leading out of the corral. It was over before Joe Willie realized the hard clench had cramped his hands on the rail. He loosed them, rubbed them to ease the cramp, climbed down from his perch and began walking away toward the quiet of the equipment shed, his heart beating hard against his ribs.

His whole body ached. That was the first thing he noticed. Then he noticed that the smile wouldn't disappear from his face. Try as he might he couldn't stop himself from breaking into a giggle, then a full smile and a laugh. God, it was good. As Aiden towelled himself off after the shower he couldn't believe the feeling that coursed through him. It was electric but purer than that, keener if that were possible. Sharper than anything he'd ever felt. There was bruising at the inside of his thighs and on his butt and a gathering tightness in his neck and shoulders, but they were little more than minor bothers to him now. He felt alive. It was like there was an open chamber in his chest, filled with the cleanest air he'd ever breathed and all the light he could imagine. He wiped a circle of condensation from the mirror and peered at himself. He looked the same but he felt like a whole new person. He could see himself in the hard sunlight of the corral, the bull spinning like a dervish, dust billowing around them, the taste of it glasslike in his mouth, whirls of image at the corners of his eyes, clouds, sky, ground, sky again, and the sharp grunts of the bull beneath him, its coarse hide against his legs, the feel of it, monstrous, colossal, hard as wood and then the push of it like a fist against his tailbone, rattling the entire length of him, the jarring as it landed grinding tooth against tooth in his mouth, the vaguely metallic taste of blood, the stretch of back muscle, the brutal wrench at the shoulder of his free arm, the strain of rosined rope against his upturned palm like being branded by the rigging, then the crazy, impossible release of gravity as the bull jumped at the last, all rules of earthbound existence exempted in one final burst of challenge and the sound of language in his ears jangling and strange before the pickup rider helped haul him off. He wiped sweat from his brow and smiled again. God, it was good.

Claire leaned against Johanna and cried. They sat in the shade of the main barn away from everyone and she cried. Leaned in against the other woman's chest, her arms looped around her shoulders.

"I know," Johanna said softly, "I know."

"I was so scared," Claire said.

"Yes."

"I couldn't breathe."

"I know."

"But that's not why I'm crying now." Claire looked up at Johanna.

"I know that too," she said.

"He looked so free," Claire said. "So free that he didn't need me anymore."

"I know," Johanna said again and hugged her close. "We all know."

"What do you think, Pap?" Birch asked.

"About the kid?"

"Yessir."

"I think he's got some go," Lionel said. "Learns fast. Good athlete."

They were resting on the veranda, the four of them, drinking tea and eating fresh-baked cookies Victoria had made.

"Scary good, I figure," Birch said.

"What's scary?" Victoria asked.

"He's good, Mama," Birch said. "Flat-out good."

"So?" Johanna asked, prompting him. She understood that Birch often put things together aloud the first time.

"Well," he said, giving his head a scratch, "born naturals can be a stubborn bunch. That's why they only ever come along once in a long while. Gives the rest of us time to consider."

"Consider what?" Johanna asked.

"Consider how much it means to us."

"Rodeo?"

"I guess, but anything, really."

"Come on, son," Lionel said. "Get to the meat of it."

Birch stood up and stretched. He tilted his hat back on his head and rubbed his face with one hand. He settled against the veranda rail finally and began to twist a smoke. "It gets to be the life of us, rodeo. It's how we live, the measure of our days. We breathe it like air. But breathin's so natural we never think about it. Leastways until something comes along that makes us catch our breath. Then we gotta think to start it up again.

"We breathe different after that. Like we're sucking in a different kind of air. They show us what Creator can do, them naturals. Plop down a heaping helping of talent in the most unlikely places and ask us to watch. Put it in Joe Willie and we were all fascinated, right from the get-go. Made our world brighter, that boy, made rodeo brighter for all of us."

He stopped to light the smoke and take a few draws. He was a thoughtful man and thoughts uncoiled in him as languidly as a practice tossed lasso.

"And the fact is, that it's in that boy, in Aiden, and I'm plain flummoxed to tell you why. Shouldn't be. Should be in a cowboy, someone born to it, raised in it, breathed their first lungful of it. But it's not. It's in a green-as-grass city kid with problems. I seen the way he rode that bull today and it scared me. Scared me on account of now I gotta give him that world. I gotta give him rodeo. What I know of it, how I feel about it, what I dream of it. The whole shebang. Because it isn't just a ride anymore. Not just a thrill. It's a calling for him. I think you all seen that.

"I gotta give him his way in it. Show him what it means beyond the riding. Offer him up the straight goods so he can learn to honour it his own self. Coach him, be a guide. So I sure as hell better know what it means to me, why it moves me, how it works in my gut, how it makes me wonder—because that's what he's gotta know, that's what he's gotta build a ride on. Nothing less."

"You're talking about tradition," Johanna said.

"Hell yes, tradition," he said.

They sat in silence and watched the sun work its way behind the mountains to the west. The valley seemed to absorb the falling light, the shapes and colours of things beginning to disregard their daylight boundaries and melt into each other, everything becoming purple easing into blue-grey. As they watched it they saw Joe Willie walk out from behind the main barn and head out toward the trailhead at the foot of Iron Mountain. He walked confidently, purposefully, and it gave them each a small joy to see it.

"Maybe it's not yours to do," Victoria said.

Birch exhaled the last of the smoke and pinched it out against the railing. "Never considered it, Mama, but maybe it's not."

He pushed against the mountain. He bent into each step and drove himself hard up the face of it. The muscles in his repaired thigh ached but he wanted to feel their burn, needed it, craved it. The image of that ride and the memory it triggered angered him more than anything he could recollect besides his own last five seconds on a bull. He saw himself in that kid. That was the thing of it. He saw freedom there. Freedom. The whole huge, aching depth of it, and he knew how it felt in the lungs, the head, the bruises, the bone-deep soreness, and in the soft, warm pool of the heart, how it sat there beating, calling you, relentless, insistent, endless, a part of you forever. He recalled how that felt and he drove himself harder against the face of the mountain. Damn kid. Cocky, smartassed, city-bred ex-con. He had no logical reason to be such a natural. No sane explanation for the way he stuck to that critter. There was nothing in his raising and nothing in his experience to qualify him to ride the way he rode. Free. Free and reckless and wild as any sumbuck that Joe Willie ever saw. Except himself.

He drove the right leg into the next few steps and kept his eyes glued to the rocky, gravelly, pine-needle-strewn bed of the trail. He knew how it felt. He remembered the exhilaration of finding the ground again that first time, stumping wide-legged in the chaps across the infield, the sunlight hard against the white rails of the corral, the dust caked on the teeth and the air feeling like it blew clean through him, the sky suddenly endless and open, like if he closed his eyes he could drift up into it, the sound of the clump of the retreating hooves a dull counterpoint to the breath of him, measured, deep and hard. Yes. Freedom had a feel. Like having silk inside. Like everything was glassine, smooth and cool. Like there were no edges anymore. That's what the kid felt. That's how he would react—and he didn't deserve the joy. He wasn't a cowboy. He was a city kid, lacking any connection to this at all, something to talk about on the street corner, a thump-on-the-bar-for-a-beer story he'd tell in his fat old age to others as fat and old and as removed from the life as he was. That's what pissed him off the most. The waste of it all. Bull riding was more than a simple spill in the dirt. It was an honour. It was pure privilege. It was the ultimate tribute to courage for the rider and the bull, a contest of will, respect and dignity. Not for the light-hearted, not for piss-ant city boys. It was the grand heritage of rodeo and everything it entailed. He drove hard against the mountain, eager for the strain and the sweat and the ache of it.

He heard it before he saw it. A huff of breath and a low growl.

Joe Willie stopped and raised his head slowly. The bear sat on its haunches in a berry patch a few yards ahead and above the trail, staring at him. Joe Willie's arms felt leaden at his sides and his legs quivered from the effort of climbing. He willed them to stop. He stared straight at the bear and directed his will to stop the tremor in his thighs. He didn't want it misread as fear, though fear tickled at his gut. The bear lowered its head and looked at him across the broad expanse of its snout, tilted its head like a curious dog, then clambered up to all fours. Joe Willie stood stock-still, the quiver gone from his legs.

The two of them stood locked together by the eyes, and Joe Willie felt the bear reading him, judging him, measuring him. When it stood slowly, majestically, up on its hind feet, its huge front paws and claws tucked in front of the huge cliff of its chest, rolling its head side to side before raising its snout to sniff at the air, Joe Willie kept his stance, the sweat cool on his face now. The bear growled once and dropped back to all fours. It lowered its head and looked at him awhile, then turned and made its way up the side of the mountain, easing finally through a cleft of boulders.

Mukwa Manitou. Bear Spirit in his father's language. The bear was a protector, and its medicine power was the power of the warrior and the warrior way. It had been coming to him in his visions to prepare him for the fight, to remind him that he already carried all the arrows he would need, that the power to heal himself lay within himself and that the anger, the rage, were the spurs he needed to coax himself into action. The clarity of those visions had shocked him, awed him some at their intensity and their mystery, but this face-to-face confrontation was harder, less clear. It could mean so many things. He'd need his mother and his grandmother for a proper interpretation. He'd need his father and grandfather to put it into a man's perspective. Joe Willie exhaled slowly, looking at the spot where the bear disappeared. When he turned back down the trail he felt silk inside and he smiled.

When he'd asked her out for a walk, Claire had no idea he meant to here. They'd strolled through the stables, visiting the horses and looking at the other rough stock in their pens, and eventually skirted the far side of the main pasture where the land dipped away into the draw. Aiden hadn't said anything through the course of it and she'd surreptitiously studied him. There was nothing to suggest anything but calmness in him, a satisfaction of sorts, and she was glad to see that in him. When they stood looking westward across the draw toward the mountains, he'd taken her hand silently.

"What scared me the most in there was the crying," he said. He poked some dirt around with the toe of his boot and looked toward the sunset. "You heard guys cry all the time. Not out in the open. Not for everyone to see. But at night, when the lights were out, nights I couldn't sleep, you'd hear it. Muffled kinda by pillows but big sobs, big moans. Guys who could take endless amounts of shit without saying anything, gang guys, cold guys, broken down in the night. That scared me, the fact that there was something bigger in the world. Something bigger than tough and hard and violent. Something you couldn't see but that would come and get you anyway in unguarded moments. That scared me more than anything."

She put a hand to his cheek. He closed his eyes tight and there was a tremor, brief and hard, and then he looked at her again.

"You could have told me," she said.

"No. I couldn't."

"Then why tell me now?"

"Guess I owed it to you."

"You don't owe me anything."

"Figure I do," he said.

Now they sat in the darkening equipment shed behind a table with a partially disassembled engine lying on it. The truck was a lumpen shape in front of them.

"What are we doing here?" she asked in a whisper.

"Wait" was all he said.

They didn't need to wait for long. She heard the door roll open with a creak and the shed was bathed in the dim spray of sunset, everything awash in a pale red light. Joe Willie stepped through the door and eased it half closed behind him. He removed a water bottle from his belt and wiped his brow under his hat with a towel before turning to the truck. She watched him place a palm on the fender and walk toward the front of it, sliding it along, feeling the line of the truck. He stopped to wipe at a spot above the front grillework, then crossed to the driver's side and hopped up into the cab. For the next while he sat quietly, smoking, looking out the door across the draw and up toward the mountains. He was far calmer than she'd ever seen him, settled, at ease here, and she felt guilty at her silent intrusion. Joe Willie reached his right hand out and rubbed a small circle on the seat beside him, humming. Claire strained to hear. It was an old song, one she recognized from the open kitchen window across the alley. "The Yellow Rose of Texas." He hummed it slowly, like a hymn, and when he finished he looked up at the mountains again and heaved a deep sigh, then stepped out of the truck. The angular cut of his cheekbones in that fading light was striking.

"Watch," Aiden whispered.

Joe Willie moved deliberately. He lit an old hurricane lamp and set it on the table beside the engine, then walked to the other side of the truck and lit another one. The soft, old-fashioned glow was comforting even in a garage, and Claire saw the old truck differently. It pulled the light to it like an embrace, and she was charmed by the wide roll of its fenders, the running board and the scarred and battered bed of it. The truck sat in the light like a proud old woman. Joe Willie saw her that way too. She could tell. He walked around her slowly, admiringly, and Claire saw a softer look on his face, like pride but deeper, more profound. She struggled to name it.

Once he'd made his way around her Joe Willie removed his shirt and prepared to work on the engine. When Claire saw the arm she put a hand to her mouth. She watched as he chose a tool with the arm, lifted it, turned it in his palm, willed the arm to motion. But it was his face that compelled her. As he raised the tool to the engine his features were sharpened by the shadows thrown by the old lamps. It gave him the look of a painter at work in his garret, studious, grim, determined, but hedged with a softness like love that eased all the lines into a seamless portrait of someone bathed in all of it, the work, the light, the encroaching darkness, the hope, the possibility, the timeless energy of art. The arm became unimportant.

He struggled. He scowled and even then she was swept up in it. Wordlessly, he worked, gritting his teeth with impatience, steadying the arm with the right now and then and studying a manual opened up on the table beside him. Joe Willie never once used his good right hand and arm to do the work. He willed the left arm to work and move. He made it beautiful with the effort.

When Aiden spoke it shocked her.

"That's not how you do it," he said and stood up.

Joe Willie straightened abruptly and peered into the shadow behind the worktable. He was different immediately, charged with anger. Aiden stepped into the light. The two of them stood looking at each other, their features a matched set of grim detachment.

"What the hell are you doing here?" Joe Willie asked.

"Watching somebody screw up a truck engine," Aiden said.

"Yeah? Well, what would you know, convict?"

"Convict?" Aiden laughed, short and sharp like a bark. He looked to the side, tongue pressed to his cheek, and shook his head. "I'm a branded man," he said.

"What?" Joe Willie asked.

"Branded man. You oughta know that. It's a country song. About convicts."

"I heard it a time or two," Joe Willie said. "Doesn't tell me what the hell you're doing here."

"I told you. Watching someone screw up a truck engine."

"And how the hell would you know?"

"It's what they taught me."

"Who?"

"In the joint."

Joe Willie snorted. "Give you a certificate, did they? Send you out with a licence? Made an honest man out of you?"

Aiden stepped closer to the table. "They didn't make me anything," he said.

"That shows."

"Hey, fuck you."

Claire stepped out into the light and she saw Joe Willie flare. He grabbed his shirt and threw it on.

"Sorry, ma'am," Joe Willie said, fumbling with the buttons. "Caught me by surprise is all. No one comes here. Not supposed to, anyway."

"It's us who should apologize," Claire said. "Sorry to intrude. And it's not ma'am. It's Claire, and this is my son, Aiden."

They looked at each other, neither one making a move. But she'd opened the door to propriety and they struggled with it, something in both of them recognizing the need to behave with a woman present. As she looked back and forth between them Claire could feel the force of them, the will strong in the air, electric. It began with a nod. One small low-ering of the jaw from Aiden followed by the same measured dip from Joe Willie, and the two of them reached out to shake hands, firmly, twice, never once taking their eyes off each other.

"Convict," Joe Willie said.

"Hack," Aiden said.

"I'm sorry," Claire said. "We really shouldn't be here. It's your private space. We'll be moving along now."

"How long you think it'll be before you realize you can't do this job?" Aiden asked.

"I done it this far," Joe Willie replied.

"What? Got the engine out with help. Maybe done a lit-tle work on the undercarriage. A convict could do that."

"What can't I do?"

"Can't do what you're thinking of doing."

"And what would that be?"

"Well, you're tinkering with the carburetor. But they don't make that kind anymore. Even if you could score a part from some specialty place you'd have to replace the rest of the innards too. It's too old. It's sat too long. Rust. Not to mention the block you want to put them all in is shot."

"And how the hell would you know that?"

"Shit, even in this light you can see the cylinders are cracked."

"So? I'll weld 'em."

Aiden laughed. "Weld? You can't weld smooth enough. You'd have to fix them with a sleeve."

Joe Willie looked at him with narrowed eyes. "You sure?" he asked.

"Word," Aiden said.

Joe Willie nodded, bit down on his lower lip and turned to lean on the table. Aiden moved with the break and leaned against the fender of the truck. "Okay to smoke?" he asked.

When Joe Willie nodded, Aiden pulled a cigarette from the pack and tossed it to him. The two of them busied themselves with lighting their cigarettes.

Joe Willie tossed back the cigarettes. "You know how to do that job? The sleeves?"

"Maybe," Aiden said.

"Maybe what?"

"Maybe if we make a deal," Aiden said.

"Aiden, I don't think—" Claire started to say.

"No, no. Let him finish," Joe Willie said.

"I figure we could trade," Aiden said. "I can show you how to get this truck up and on the road and you could show me something."

"What exactly?" Joe Willie asked.

"How to ride a bull."

Joe Willie smiled, shook his head, took a haul on his smoke and looked up at a point on the ceiling. "Ride a bull? What makes you think you can do that job?"

"I done it this far," Aiden said.

Joe Willie laughed again. "You rode a machine, boy. Then you rode a tame bull. You rode a bull that's as shot as this engine. You rode a bull that anyone could ride. A spinner. That's all he did was spin, few bucks, one leap, that's all he had in him. There's a world of difference between a ranch bull and a rodeo bull. Trust me."

"There's a world of difference between a truck that runs and one that doesn't. Trust me."

"You got lucky, kid. Pure lucky. You need to face that, swallow it, learn to live with it."

"I rode the damn thing," Aiden said. "No matter what you say, I rode it."

"All right. You rode it. Be happy. Call it value for your dollar. Go home and make it a memory, a story you tell sometime."

"It's bigger than that," Aiden said.

"How?" Joe Willie asked.

"I don't know. Ever since all the shit came down in my life I've been looking for something to make it all matter. Like it led to something. That it wasn't wasted time. At first, tinkering round with engines and cars made it go away and I felt good. But not like this. Not like I feel when I ride."

Joe Willie was looking at him now. "Go on," he said.

"Up there it was like everything that ever happened, everything I went through, everything that ever mattered one way or another came down to one tiny single point in my belly. One tiny pinprick. Like fire. A point of fire in my gut. And when I sat there and I gathered myself, it all coiled around that point, collected there, and I could feel it in my breathing, at the sides of my head, in my eyes, in every muscle in my body. Everything went away then. Everything. All that was left was that point. That's where I lived—and when that bull came out of the gate I exploded along with him. Boom. I never felt as free as that. Free of everything. *Everything*. I wanted it to last forever."

"I hear that," Joe Willie said.

"That's why you gotta show me what you know," Aiden said. "Because you gave me that much already."

"What?"

"I watched you. I watched the videos of your rides. I played them all back in slow motion and I did what you did. You got me this far. But I can go further. I know it. I don't know how I know it but I do."

Joe Willie turned to Claire. He ground the smoke out on the side of the table and exhaled the last draw. "There's a lot more to this than guts, kid. Any fool can screw up enough nerve to try it, but it takes a precision not many have. You gotta straddle the border beyond common sense and crazy every moment. You gotta not only deal with pain, you have to accept it like breakfast. You have to push yourself harder than any- one's called to do because there's a ton of crazy waiting for you all horns and hoofs and cussedness. It ain't easy to watch. It's harder to do."

"I can do it."

"Can you?"

"Yes."

"What makes you so sure?"

"I don't know. I just feel it."

"Feelin's not doin'."

In the flicker of the lamps Claire could see the matched intensity of their faces. She walked to the open door of the shed and gazed across the blackness to the mountains that sat like a serrated edge to the world and she felt them watching her. She'd worked for a moment like this. Everything she'd done for the last two years had been in preparation for a moment of choosing. She'd just never expected it to be wrapped in cowhide. She looked directly at Joe Willie.

"I came here to answer a dream, Mr. Wolfchild," she said. "Right up until now I thought it was mine. I thought coming here would bring me and my son together again after everything that happened. I thought it would get the glue back between us, make us stick again. But it's not my dream that's important. It's my son's. I've never given him the chance to find one before—and now he has and I'm telling you, I'll see he gets the chance. Here or somewhere like it. I'll see to that. I will."

"Gonna take longer than the time you got."

"I'll see to that too."

She seemed taller suddenly. There was a grit in her like Johanna's and he grinned in recognition. "I imagine you would," he said. "Thing is, kid, that dreams get busted up too. Gotta be tough enough to handle that."

"Are you?" Aiden asked.

Joe Willie lifted the arm and flexed it at the elbow. He huffed out his breath. "I'm getting there," he said.

"Deal, then?" Aiden asked.

"You gotta do everything I tell you. No questions, no attitude, no games."

"Same."

"Are you kidding me?"

"No. I know trucks, you know bulls. Deal's a deal."

"Not quite," Joe Willie said.

"What's left?"

"You," Joe Willie said, pointing to Claire.

"Me? Me what?" she asked.

"You have to know everything too. Every trick, every choice, every move, every danger. Just like my mother knew. Like my grandmother knew. You're in on everything or we don't do anything. When he lands he's gotta land with you. You gotta be there. Regardless."

"I can handle that."

"I believe you can. And, kid, if you got half what she's got inside you, you might make a rider."

Aiden stepped away from the truck and Joe Willie stepped away from the table to meet him. They stood facing each other again but the silence was easier this time. Joe Willie reached out a hand. Aiden took it and gave it a firm shake. Behind them the truck sat solemnly in the dark, waiting it seemed, and when she moved to stand beside the two of them, Claire could almost swear she heard it settle a little deeper on its springs like an old woman sinking into her favourite chair.

book four

DREAM WHEELS

he walked into the kitchen and turned on the light. It was too harsh for morning and he turned the knob that lowered it until he found a level he could deal with. Outside the land was purple, greyed in the dimness. There was a thick scud of cloud that hugged the ragged line of mountain, and he could see the rain at the end of the valley. Leaning into the window screen he smelled it. He'd never tried to smell the rain before. It was how he imagined mercury must taste, and as he hauled the moist coolness into him he smiled to think of it. The bulls were in the field. There were seven of them. From here they looked like he imagined buffalo would look, all humped like boulders against the grass and sky. The light made the small moves they made look solemn, and he believed he could see the hard coal of their eyes glint across the space between them, making the air electric in their sight of him.

He stepped through the door onto the veranda. In the cool air his breath plumed and he could see them breathing too. They turned to face the narrow end of the valley as if they wanted the mercurial taste of the rain in their lungs, and he could see the swish of their tails as they stepped slowly away from the house and him. They rolled as they walked. The weight of them pressed into the earth with each cloven hoof, and he could feel the power of them, the severity of their girth. He stepped out onto the steps, and some of them turned their heads as though they sensed him. He crossed the stretch of grass and across the driveway, the pop of gravel from his boot heels turning them toward him. When he got to the fence he leaned on a post and smoked, watching them. In that faint light their eyes glimmered like mirrors and he imagined how they held him in place, laid him out against this charcoal world, fitted him into the backdrop of ranch, valley and mountain and wondered if there were too many jagged edges to him to place him there securely, if the city and the joint had excised whole chunks of him, made fitting anywhere a gamble, or whether the hard fact of his blackness made entering this seemingly white world possible at all. He pinched out the smoke against the top of the fence post and felt the need for coffee. When he turned toward the house again he saw him curled under a blanket on the veranda swing, staring at him flat and expressionless as a bull. He hadn't a hat on, and from where he stood the blanket gave him the look of an old-time Indian, history etched into the crevices and lines of him so that when he spoke, Aiden was surprised it wasn't guttural, savage, the ancient tongue leaning clumsily into English.

"Early for you, ain't it?"

"I guess."

Joe Willie's hands appeared from under the blanket. He lit a cigarette, then waved the pack toward him. Aiden took it and leaned against the railing while he lit up. When he'd taken the first draw he tossed the pack lightly into Joe Willie's lap.

"There's coffee," Joe Willie said.

"I'll get to it. The smoke's good for now."

"You anxious?"

"About what?"

"Bulls."

"Not from here."

They laughed.

"We start today," Joe Willie said.

"Good."

"Nervous?"

"I guess."

"It won't be what you think."

"What do you mean?"

"You'll see. You'll need to coffee up. And eat. It's a long day."

Aiden took a long haul on the smoke and turned to look at the bulls again. They'd drifted farther into the pasture and the distance made them look softer, amiable almost. "All right," he said.

Joe Willie nodded. "All right," he said.

The thing about bulls, Birch figured, was that they never learned the difference between horizontal and vertical. It was all the same direction to them. Once you got up on them there wasn't any consideration of gravity or the general restraints of physics. They were plumb mayhem. It made reading them impossible. Even the ones you drew before, the ones you rode a handful of times, could surprise you with a new twist, spin or crazy elevation. They could learn. That was the amazing thing. He'd seen a bull change from one ride to another. When you drew a bull a few times it sometimes felt like he knew you before you slid down onto his back. Like he recognized your weight, the pressure of your legs, the feel of your knuckles through the back of your gloved hand or the bony point of your arse. A cowboy could feel that knowing, sense it in the calm wait of the bull in the chute. No bawling, horn tossing, showing off or the leaning in they sometimes did to crush your legs against the rails or stomping the feet and shimmying the loose folds of their skin to unsettle you. Nope. At a time like that a bull was stone and you could slap him all you wanted with your free hand and you couldn't get him to stir. That's when you knew you were in trouble. Stone-cold bull. Well read and dangerous. When a bull had a read on a man there was only ever going to be one winner. Unless the cowboy up on him was special or just plain dumb lucky.

He leaned on the corral watching the stock mill about and waiting for the kid and Lionel to appear. He hadn't been on a bull for years. Still, it was something you held on to, something irreplaceable, world-changing and mysterious as discovering you could lie. It took a powerful heap of doing to rig up on a bull. Birch had always had the heart for it, but that particular magic that makes champions didn't exist in him. He only carried the love of it. The bruises and breaks were a rite of passage to a world most people never got the chance to feel or even comprehend: a brutal, unpredictable world inhabited by laconic, drawling men who spit courage as easily as tobacco chaw. Birch could never really leave it, and bringing someone to it, introducing them to the spectacular nature of it, seeing them move from awe to admiration, never failed to make him smile.

"Mite relaxed for a working man," Lionel said.

Birch turned to greet his father. "Where's the kid?"

"Don't know. Said he'd be here."

"Likely nervous."

"Likely. He rode some good yesterday, though."

They leaned against the rail to study the bulls together. "Pick out four, I imagine," Lionel said. "Ought to be enough for one day."

"There won't be any bull riding today."

They turned to see Joe Willie stumping toward them. Aiden and Claire were with him.

"What's that you say, son?" Birch asked.

"I said there won't be any riding today. Not for him."

Birch and Lionel exchanged looks. "Young fella wants to learn to ride a bull," Lionel said.

"Then that's what he'll get. But he'll earn it first."

"What are you talking about, son?" Birch asked.

"I'm training him."

"Training him?"

"That's right. And there won't be any rigging up today."

"Wait a minute," Aiden said. "We agreed. We made a deal."

"Deal we made was truck for bulls," Joe Willie said.

"Yeah. So why aren't I riding?"

"You'll ride when you're ready to ride."

"I'm afraid I'm a little lost here, boy," Lionel said. "What's going on?"

"Turns out Pretty Boy Floyd here's a mechanical genius," Joe Willie said. "Figures he can get the old girl on the road again. So we made a deal. I teach him not to kill himself and he teaches me how to fix up the truck."

"So how come there's no riding today?" Birch asked.

"He ain't ready to ride."

"What are you talking about?" Aiden said. "You saw me ride that bull."

"I saw you ride a tame bull that a toddler could ride. I saw you stretch dumb luck out for eight seconds."

"Dumb luck?" Aiden stepped up close to Joe Willie.

Joe Willie took the same measured step toward him and they stood face to face while the others watched. "Dumb luck," Joe Willie said slowly.

"Bullshit."

"A handful of videos and a jailhouse attitude won't make a rider out of you, kid."

"Did so far. Got you to make this deal."

"What got me to make this deal was the truck. That's all I care about."

"You'll get your truck, but I want to ride."

"When you're ready."

"When's that?"

"When I say."

"You said it starts today."

"I said it won't be what you think."

"What the hell does that mean?"

Joe Willie held the hard look but stepped back, then turned to the corral and pointed to the bulls milling about as though sensing the tension in the air. He hooked one boot heel on the bottom rail. "It means you need cowboy muscle to do a cowboy job. You're gonna need a stronger back and shoulders and arms and legs than you ever believed. Mucking out stalls is good for that. So is tossing bales, stacking oat stacks and pulling fence. Cowboy work. That's what'll get you ready."

"That wasn't part of our deal."

"I'm afraid it was."

"How so?"

"You do everything I say. No questions, no attitude. That was our deal."

Aiden looked at Claire.

"Don't look at her," Joe Willie said. "You want to be a cowboy, be a cowboy. Mama can't help you with that. There's no
shortcuts, kid, and from right now you're a working cowboy."

"Is this really the best way?" Claire asked. "Shouldn't he
train specifically?"

"He is," Joe Willie said. "Riding bulls is a tradition. It
came from all this. Everything you see around you. This life.
When you cowboy, your focus comes from there, from the
sense of that tradition, that heritage. The best cowboys, the
best riders have that focus. But you gotta live it to get it."

"So he's going to train by doing ranch work?" Claire
asked.

"You cowboy from the ground up."

"What do you mean?" Aiden asked.

"I mean it's the land. The dirt," Joe Willie said. "You get
you a feel for that and it never leaves you. It gets in your lungs,
your nose, in the creases of your hands, the lines on your face.
When you ride bulls it gets in the seat of your pants, the flat
of your back, or sometimes you face-plant hard, right into it.
But you come to love that dirt because you work in it every day.
It's how you breathe. Good cowboy's gotta have that in him.
Only way to get it is by getting down in the dirt and learning
how to love it. Marce brought you here to work. That's what
you're gonna do."

"When do I ride?"

"When you cowboy up."

"When's that?"

Joe Willie gave him a level look. "You'll know," he said.
"We'll all know."

Ranches exist beyond the stretch of ordinary time. Even Wolf
Creek was prone to the same casual slouch. There were

seasons for everything and time had a slippery quality, a
greasy-in-the-hands feel that lent itself to an unfolding of
events that surprised a person with the easy suddenness of
their return. Ranch people stayed busy through the tide of a
year, and the markers that announced time passing were as
familiar as old friends on a country road, something to wave at,
smile and maintain direction. So changes in routine were
shocking. Time slid to a stop in a spray of dust like the hooves
of a roped steer. Victoria considered that as she watched her
men heading out onto the flat plain of the ranch. Behind her
Johanna rattled dishes as she collected them off the table,
busying herself, giving herself a distraction to arrange thoughts
around. When she brought them over to the sink the two
women stood looking quietly out the window.

"Worried?" Johanna asked.

"No," Victoria said. "Awed some but not worried."

"Me neither."

"I wonder about her, though."

"Claire?"

"Yes. I wonder what there is for her in all this. Something
beyond the way a mother's supposed to feel when her young
find a way to fly."

"That's not enough?"

"Generally. But she found us for a reason. A reason
beyond the boy, beyond a dream of horses, and I'm perplexed.
It's all so clear. Everything but that."

Johanna arranged the dishes in the sink for washing later.
She ran the water until the last edge of porcelain bobbed
under, then eddied it with her finger, watching the bubbles stir,
break and disappear. "When you talk to her she drinks everything in. Like she's open," she said. "And that could fool you
some, make you think she's got all the blocks arranged. Like

she's formed and you're only adding to the foundation. But there's a hole there."

Victoria nodded. "Shame. She's so beautiful. Strong, smart, independent. Like a horse. But she's hobbled somehow. You can see it."

"She has a way with them, the horses, a gentleness you can't teach, as though she understands a bit between the teeth."

"That's it," Victoria said, snapping her fingers. "It's what I never recognized."

"What?" Johanna asked.

"I never seen a horse put the bit on itself."

"What do you mean?"

"I mean she hasn't let herself run for some time now. Free, all out, natural. She's the one who hobbled herself. For the boy. Everything's been for the boy. She drinks everything in because she's thirsty, she wants it to fill her like you said."

"Fill her with what, Mother?"

Victoria smiled and laid a hand on Johanna's wrist. "Recollection. The remembering of what it's like to be a woman—free, all out, natural. Generally, women are my age when they get to that, and it's just age that eases things away. Young ones like her make a choice not to celebrate themselves."

The two women continued to look out the window, and when Claire entered the kitchen they turned together and greeted her warmly, knowingly.

He'd spent the morning mucking out stalls and the afternoon whitewashing the rails on the back corral while his mother enjoyed a long ride up the ridge behind the ranch. Now, as late afternoon came, he was tossing hay bales into the stock pens. The two-handed motion made the muscles in his back and shoulders ache. They felt bruised. The forking, shovelling and painting hadn't seemed like much in the beginning, but he could feel the effects now with even the smallest movement. The ache itself angered him, and he worked harder, faster, determined to show his resilience. Joe Willie had appeared every now and then throughout the day to watch him work, and it galled Aiden to see the smug satisfaction on the cowboy's face as he sweated through the chores. Now he could see him approaching from the main barn with his mother, who was leading a horse.

"You want to talk to them when you do that," Joe Willie told him.

"Why?"

"They like it."

"I'm supposed to rap to a steer because he'll like it?"

"Strange but true, greenhorn."

Aiden mumbled something about figuring slavery had ended a long time back while he pitched the next bale over the rail. Amazingly the steers bawled back. Or at least it sounded like they did. He shook his head and hurried to finish.

"So what's chow tonight?" he asked. "I'm so hungry I could eat one of these buggers raw."

"We'll find that out when we get there. Grandma's gonna keep it warm for us," Joe Willie said.

Aiden turned from the corral and stared at him. Then he shifted his gaze to Claire, who stood quietly with her hand on the horse's neck. "Why am I not liking the sound of this?" he asked. "What are we doing if we're not having supper?"

"Going for a walk."

"What's the horse for?"

"I'm carrying water," Claire said. "I don't know where we're going."

"See that peak up there?" Joe Willie pointed to a sheer rock cliff facing west.

"Yeah," Aiden said carefully.

"We're walking up to that peak."

"You don't walk up a mountain."

"We do."

"Why?"

"Because you only worked the top part of you today. Now we're gonna work your legs and your lungs. Walking up that mountain's the best thing for them," Joe Willie said.

"There's gotta be something illegal about that kind of cruelty," Aiden said. "Look at that thing. It's almost straight up."

"That's why I have the horse," Claire said.

"Three of us can't ride that horse," Aiden said.

"Only her," Joe Willie said. "I wouldn't ask a woman to try to walk up that sumbitch. It's not polite."

"But asking me to is real mannerly?" Aiden asked.

"You can't train for bulls like anything else, kid. You can't lift weights for strength. What you need is long, wiry muscle built for endurance but tough as steel. Walking up that mountain will build those legs up."

"I'm not climbing that thing."

"Scared?"

"No. Sensible."

Joe Willie nodded. "Scared."

"Look, I'm not scared. It's just crazy."

"You calling me crazy?"

"No."

"That's good, because I do it every night. As much as I can stand, anyway. But you're right, it's probably too much for you. You wouldn't be able to handle it. I'll think of something else a little easier for you."

"I could do it," Aiden said. "I could do that easy."

"Nah. You don't have the focus. You're a city kid, a greenhorn. Forget it," Joe Willie said. He turned to Claire. "Do you mind riding along behind me tonight while I do it?"

"No. It's probably really nice on horseback," she said with a smile.

"It is. It's really a horse trail. A trail like that is only meant for horses. Way too steep and the footing's too loose for two-leggeds. It goes up awhile then sweeps back down then up again so that we'll have to stop and recinch that saddle for you. The inclines pull your weight either forward or back and she'll get loose real quick. Kinda dangerous riding. You got yourself an endurance saddle there. Lighter. Easier on the horse in that kinda terrain. Generally only horses and mountain goats get up there, but it's beautiful. Especially when you get to the cliff."

"You made it that far?" Aiden asked.

Joe Willie rubbed his bad leg and grimaced slightly. "Not yet. But I will. It's in my head to do it and I'll get there. And it's how *you* start earning the right to rig up on a bull."

"The tests of Hercules?" Aiden asked.

"Something like that."

"Well if you can do it, then I sure can."

"You think so?"

"I know so."

"Let's do it, then," Joe Willie said.

"Damn straight," Aiden said.

The trail, if it could even be called that, was a rounded, twisting, gravelly seam that climbed up through the trees and boulders. The angles were severe in places and the footing was hazardous, the clumps of rock and sand made every placing of a foot a challenge, and Aiden often found himself reaching for shrubs, overhanging branches or the trunks of trees for anchor.

He could hear the rattle and grate of sliding detritus behind him every time he pushed upward another step. It was a mountain-goat trek as far as Aiden could determine, and pushing up it was an agony of the sort he'd never encountered. Each step called for a push with the thighs and the butt, and now and then he had to straddle his legs out wide to find the purchase to keep climbing. He felt the strain on muscles he'd never known he had. His lower back ached from being hunched over, and each reaching back with the elbows pulled severely at his shoulders. Breathing became a challenge. Only the horse seemed able to navigate without any discomfort, and Claire rode cautiously but steadily in the saddle.

After a few hundred yards the trail levelled out some into a shady stretch of rock bits and pine needles, and they eased up the pace. The trail continued to climb but it was lazier here, easier walking.

Joe Willie signalled to Claire and she handed down a pair of canteens. The two of them leaned on trees to drink and douse their heads. The sun flooded the slope with rose and orange hues. Somewhere birds twittered and the sound of the wind against the brush and bramble was like a hushed whispering. Looking out to the west they could see the ranch below them, the outbuildings given a hard glow by the intensity of the setting sun.

"It shines," Claire said.

"It's mighty pretty," Joe Willie answered.

"Is this your favourite view?" she asked.

"No. Up there," he said, hooking a thumb up at the cliff that towered over them. "Can see it all from there. There's a meadow I used to ride to all the time to watch the sun go down. It's like a balcony overlooking the world."

"Will we see it tonight?"

"No," Joe Willie said. "It's a hell of a climb."

"You saying I'm not up to it?" Aiden asked.

"What I'm saying is that it's a hell of a climb. What you just experienced is only the first push. There's more like it. Harder, even. I been trying for a while now and I ain't walked up it yet."

"But I have two legs," Aiden said.

Joe Willie straightened and looked up at the peak. When he turned to Aiden his features were hard and set, chilling in their dangerous aloofness. Despite himself Aiden looked down.

"This mountain will teach you a lot if you let it," Joe Willie said. "Mostly it'll teach you that in the bigger scheme of things, you ain't shit. This mountain can beat you all on its own. Add a little rain, some wind, fog, cold and you're screwed. Screwed outright.

"But for you, kid, tonight and the nights to follow, it's gonna teach you that it's not your legs that'll carry you up this mountain. Only your heart can get you there. Only the strength of it, the sheer will of it to win. Your legs will push you up, but it's your heart that'll carry you—and I got one of those."

"I didn't mean . . ." Aiden began.

"I know what you meant," Joe Willie said harshly.

"Sometimes Aiden doesn't think before he says things," Claire said. "I'm sorry."

"Nothing to be sorry for."

"Still."

"Still nothing."

They stood in awkward silence. Aiden watched Joe Willie as he took small, measured sips from the canteen, then a handful he wiped across his brow and around his face and up through his hair. He did it with the left. He flexed his fingers when he finished. Then he straightened his back and stretched, both arms pressed high above his head, twisting at the waist then bending to touch his toes. Aiden copied him. When he stood, Joe Willie was looking right at him, measuring him.

"What?" he asked.

"Ready for more?"

"Bring it."

Joe Willie allowed himself a small grin. They handed the canteens up to Claire, and while she tied them to the saddle the two of them looked up along the snake of the trail. The sun was lower suddenly and the shadows deepened in the trees. There was a profound calm and a moist quality to the air that spoke of coming rain. The horse nickered at it, and somewhere in the trees off the trail a branch snapped as some animal passed. The wildness of it all sent a thrill through each of them but none of them acknowledged it to the others. Instead, Joe Willie nodded once, short and sharp, huffed out a breath and pushed up along the trail. Aiden followed one step behind. Claire watched them go. She sat on the horse and looked around her at the sepulchral majesty of tree and rock and sky and breathed, pulling all of it deeply into her, feeling the swell of it pushing against her ribs, pressing her diaphragm like a hand. She closed her eyes, tried to see all of it with her mind's eye, sealing it within her being, and moaned luxuriantly. Then she nudged the horse lightly with her heels and moved up the mountain after the shadowed figures of her son and the cowboy.

He poked the last of the wrangler's fire with a long stick of alder, stoking the embers until they glowed hot orange again. Then he added wood shavings, chips and chunks thrown from the axe and watched the lazy lick of flame work its way upward. When he'd gotten it going good he sat back on one of the long, peeled cedar logs they'd dragged in for benches. The leg throbbed where it was pinned but he welcomed it with a certain satisfaction. The boy had done better than Joe Willie had expected. He'd figured the city muscle to play out quickly, maybe even have to double him up on the horse with his mother on the way back, but the kid had showed grit and pushed himself a good long ways. Still, the mountain had asserted itself finally, and they stopped in a hump of boulders near where he'd seen the bear. When he'd looked at him the kid was breathing hard but expectant as a pup waiting for command. They'd had a good long drink and allowed the horse to lead them back through the gathering dark. He'd showered, sat in the old girl awhile and then, feeling tired but exhilarated, he'd come to the fire once he'd heard the boys head off for the bunkhouse.

It was late and the sky in the sheen of the quarter moon was sprayed with stars. Against the horizon the mountains ran southward in a long, undulating line, all edges removed by the hand of the darkness so that they seemed to him less precipitous, less daunting and more like a series of low, rolling hills seen from a narrow band of coast. He shook his head. Such images came infrequently to him, and he was always charmed and spooked by them at the same time. He'd never had a head for poetry beyond the usual rhyming scheme of a country song or the rowdy cowboy ballads he'd heard around fires just like this one in his life on the road. But he found himself gazing contentedly at the smudge of mountain against the purple stain of night.

"Do you mind some company?"

Claire stood at the edge of the light, a blanket about her shoulders. He stood awkwardly and removed his hat.

"No," he said. "Just sitting here thinking is all."

"Thanks," she said and seated herself on the log opposite him. She held her hands out toward the flames. Her teeth glowed white against the backdrop of dark pasture and mountain, and her eyes sparkled in the light of the fire. "I couldn't sleep and I saw the fire out my window. It's nice. So far away from the city."

He struggled for something to say to that and when he couldn't find it he settled for poking at the fire and sending tiny comets of spark up into the night. She watched him until he set the stick down beside him.

"Thank you," she said quietly.

"For what?"

"For helping my boy."

"Don't really figure I helped any yet. In fact, he's probably cussing me pretty good right now after that hike up the hill."

"He loved it. He won't say so but I know."

"Powerful peculiar way of having fun."

She laughed. The glint of flame highlighted the laugh lines around her mouth and eyes, giving her a softness that flickered out with the turn of her head. "He passed out right after his shower. I haven't seen him sleep like that for years. You wore him out."

"Sorry."

"No. Don't be. I meant it in a good way."

"Oh."

They sat looking into the flames together.

"I'm really sorry if he offended you. What he said about two legs."

He picked up the stick again and stood it on its end beside his knee, then laid it across his thighs and rolled it slowly back and forth with his palms. "It's all right," he said. "I pushed, he pushed back."

"I don't think anyone's ever pushed him before. Or asked him to push himself."

"No pap?" he asked.

She shook her head slowly. "His father left while I was pregnant. There've been men after, of course, but they never really cared about him except in how they could use him to get to me. He raised himself, mostly."

"Gramps?"

"No. My mother never even told me his name. I don't know anything about him except what I've made up in my mind, and that's not a whole lot, really. I don't think my mother was very proud of her life, except for maybe me. She never spoke of it, never offered much but a handful of colourful stories. She was a junkie. She died of it before Aiden was born. It's always just been Aiden and me."

"Tough go," he said.

"Yes. I never knew how tough until he went to jail."

He stared into the fire again. "I grew up here. Lucky. Never knew how it was not to have family around."

"They're incredible," she said.

He poked at the fire with the stick, then stood to place another log on it. He settled and looked up at the stars. "Yeah, they are. I haven't exactly been a joy to behold the last while. They're always there, though. No matter what."

"They believe in you."

She could see the fire reflected in his eyes. They glimmered crazily, and against the angles of his face he looked mystical, like an old shaman by his fire.

"Why would you say that?"

She smiled and looked into the fire. She sat there for a long spell until Joe Willie thought she must have missed his question and he shifted restlessly on the log.

"The way they look at you when you don't see. When you're busy with your own thoughts or moving toward something you need tending to, they look at you. And it's like there's a story in their eyes, you know? The story of you. Like they can see all of you in that moment. Where you've been, what you've done, all your dreams, your wishes, everything. That look is so strong it's like they push you with their eyes, push you toward whatever it is you want, push you toward whatever you might choose, or toward what they might choose for you, wish for you, dream for you. I've never been on the receiving end of a look like that. I can only hope that it's in mine when I look at my boy." She looked at him and smiled.

"You talk like Gram. Or my mother," he said.

"Now that is a compliment."

"Truth," he said.

They looked at each other across the fire. The night had deepened and the flames spread an orange halo across everything they touched. The only sound was the crackle of flame and the solid snap of knots in the wood surrendering sparks into the night.

"Can I ask you something?"

He stared down at the fire. "I guess," he said.

"Does it hurt?"

There was a sudden yip of coyotes across the draw. They both raised their heads to listen, craning their necks like animals themselves as though that primordial action could sharpen their senses. When they looked down again he met her gaze.

"It hurts," he said. "But not like you'd think. There's no ache in the bones anymore like there was and I move better now, easier, stronger, can do more things. But when that bull busted my body he didn't break my heart. Now, today, I can't do the things I lived to do but I still got the heart for it . . . and that's what hurts."

"Thank you," she said quietly.

The coyotes began a chorus, and they looked up to see the moon hovering over the mountains to the east, full and fat and silver, pockmarked with ancient collisions, the spray of them like wrinkles on an old man's face. The wild was in the air. A horse nickered in the corral and they could hear the basso thud of bulls stamping restless hooves in their pens. There was a breeze suddenly and the flames flickered higher so that when they looked across at each other it was like their faces were in motion, flowing between age and youth, mask and reality, upward into the breeze and across the draw to join the coyote chorus sailing to the moon.

"You're welcome," he said.

When he bent down under the chassis of the old truck Aiden could feel the muscles in the back of his legs cramp and tighten. He'd never known that the muscles there ran all the way up to the curve of his butt. It felt more like they stretched all the way to his armpits. Every move was agony. He didn't want to show it, though. He'd wheel-barrowed manure all morning and helped the wranglers pull fencing in the early afternoon and he'd never even grimaced. Now it was mid-afternoon and he'd agreed to meet Joe Willie in the equipment shed. The cowboy was his usual taciturn self, merely nodding to him as he entered and fiddling with the old carburetor. Aiden walked as strongly as he could to the workbench to watch the work Joe Willie was doing, and then strode over to the truck to examine it more closely than he had on his previous visit. As he hunched over the rear wheel well, the muscles in his thighs felt like they would rip right down their length.

He pressed a hand to them, squeezed them a few times, then arched his back and stood up slowly. Joe Willie was watching him and grinning.

"Sore?"

"No," Aiden said. "You ready for work?"

"Always," Joe Willie said.

"Good, because it's payback time."

"How do you figure?"

Aiden leaned against the truck. "You got me forking horseshit, stomping all over hell's half acre with Goober and Gomer, painting posts and pulling wire and then walking up mountains. Now it's time for the other half of our deal to kick in."

"And that would be what?"

"That would be you doing the work I show you on this old pig."

"Old pig?"

"Yeah. I never saw anything in this sorry kind of shape."

"You don't know where she's been."

"Looks like she's been down a few too many country roads. What did you do? Haul cows and shit in her?"

"Something like that," Joe Willie said. "She was part of the life."

"What life?" Aiden asked, fishing in his pocket for a smoke.

"Rodeo. My family's life."

"Yeah? So?"

"So she's more than just a truck."

"Looks like a truck to me. What is she, then, if she's more than that?"

"Tradition," Joe Willie said.

"Tradition?"

"Yeah. You don't know what tradition is?"

"Sure. Like Christmas, I guess." Aiden shifted his weight against the side of the truck. He flicked a look at Joe Willie and then stared at the ground.

Joe Willie walked over to the truck and trailed his hand along the side of it. He walked right around it and when he got back to where Aiden stood he pulled his cigarettes from his jacket pocket and took his time lighting up before passing the lighter to Aiden. They stood there smoking in silence for a moment. "It's a record of where you been," he said finally. "Keeping it alive is what makes it important. People do it with ceremonies sometimes, like Christmas like you said, but lots of times it's stuff like this old girl here. You got any traditions?"

Aiden took a long draw on the cigarette. "Never bothered."

"Never bothered?"

"No," he said sharply, "I never bothered, all right? Can we do this now?"

"Do what?"

"Do the damn work here."

"What work?"

"Jesus. Changing the truck."

"Whoa, no one said anything about changing."

"Are you kidding me?" Aiden asked. "Look at the way she sits all low and awkward. She's begging for a new suspension."

"I been under her. I tightened everything."

"Tightened? There's a lot more to this than just tightening a few bolts. If you want her to move anywhere out of this shed she's gonna need a whole overhaul. We're gonna have to change a lot."

"Bull crap. We get her back to the way she was. That's the deal."

"The way she was won't work," Aiden said. "A lot of the parts we're going to need they don't even make anymore. The more work we do, the more you're going to see how much we have to change. Like tossing that old carburetor, for one thing. The engine we drop in will need a four-barrel, anyway."

"You ain't changing her."

"No, I ain't. You are. I'm showing you what needs to be done. You're doing the work."

The two of them lapsed into silence, staring at each other. Joe Willie scowled. Aiden tilted his head and gave him a baleful look in return. They both crossed their arms and rocked lightly on the balls of their feet.

"Damned if I am," Joe Willie said.

"Why? Because tradition can't change?"

"No."

"Why?"

"Because it's tradition."

"Then there's no deal," Aiden replied.

"You won't be a bull rider."

"That's okay. I wasn't when I got here and I did all right."

"Being a convict's all right?"

"Yeah," Aiden said, pulling himself straighter. "It is. Because it's over."

"You think?"

"Yeah."

"Then why carry the attitude?"

"What attitude?"

"The one where you figure you don't need anybody. The one where you figure you're tough enough to handle every-thing yourself."

"Bullshit."

"Think I don't know that look, kid? I practically invented it."

"Don't call me kid."

"Then quit acting like it."

They stared at each other. Beyond the door they could hear the faint sounds of the ranch.

"You don't know me," Aiden said finally. "You don't know where I've been. You don't know anything about me."

"Same," Joe Willie said.

"I know enough," Aiden said.

"Like?"

"Like you always had this place. Always had your family. Always had a place to come back to no matter how long you'd been gone. You never lost anything. You never lost your freedom. You don't know how that feels."

Joe Willie smoked. He put one foot up on the running board and smoked deliberately. When he finished he pinched out the butt against the button of his jacket and stashed it in the pocket before turning to look at Aiden. "They never put me away anywhere, kid. They never locked me up. But when I lost my arm and my leg got crushed, well, they might just about as well have. When I rode? That was my freedom. So you figure I don't know how it feels to have that plucked away? Bullshit. I know it harder than you."

"That's supposed to make me feel bad?"

Joe Willie pushed his hat back on his head. "It's not supposed to make you feel anything."

"Good. Because I don't."

"Sure you do."

"Sure I don't."

"You feel pissed, kid. I know that. Hell, I been out here in this shed boiling over just like you for a year and a half. Only thing is I let myself be pissed. You hold on to it like rigging. Like you're scared it'll throw you and you don't know where you'll land."

"Right."

"Damn straight, right," Joe Willie said. "You gotta learn to go halfway before you can go all the way, kid."

"What the hell does that mean?"

"Ask your mother. She knows."

"Leave my mother out of this."

"Sure," Joe Willie said slowly. "Might as well. You do."

Aiden stepped up to Joe Willie, put his face a few inches away. Joe Willie lowered his hat on his head and put his hands in the back pockets of his jeans and held the look. Aiden put everything he had into the force of the look and balled his hands into fists, flexing them a few times while Joe Willie arched his eyebrows and looked back at him, waiting.

"Go on," he said.

"You're a loser," Aiden said, breaking the look and stepping back. "You couldn't teach me anything anyhow. Except maybe how to lose."

Joe Willie grinned at him. "Well, you know what they say."

"Who's they?"

"The wise ones. Those who been there in life."

"And what do they say?"

"It's better to rig up and get thrown than to not have the guts to try."

"Try and fix your truck, then."

"I will. I have."

"Don't look like it."

"Does to me."

"Screw you. I don't need this. I can walk right away from here. I'm a free man now."

"Sure you are, kid. Sure you are."

Aiden gritted his teeth and flexed his hands a few more times. He shopped for something to offer back and when he came up empty he just looked around the shed and at the old truck. He rubbed the fender skirt with one hand and looked sullenly at Joe Willie again before walking out of the shed and out into the pasture toward the house. Joe Willie put a hand to the truck's cool metal himself, then he went back to the workbench and fiddled with the old carburetor again.

"Spirit Dogs," Johanna said.

"Pardon me?" Claire said from the other side of the stall. She was wrestling with latching a rein to a cross tie so they could wash a small mare.

"Spirit Dogs. It's the name my people have for horses. Well, the old Sioux way of referring to horse anyway."

"I love that. It's so romantic and mysterious and all."

Johanna stepped under the horse's head and into the corridor, where she retrieved a bucket with sponges and fly repellant. Then she watched as Claire adjusted the flow of water from the hose and gauged the temperature with her palm before spraying the horse's flank. The horse whinnied, made a couple of light steps, swished its tail and settled under Claire's gentle rubbing of its nose.

"We didn't always have the horse. Before they came we had dogs," Johanna said. "The dogs were our constant companions, our sentries at night and our game pointers. They even hauled things around in the travois we later used with horses. Sometimes, in lean times, dogs even sacrificed themselves to feed us. It was a special relationship—all built on loyalty, trust and community.

"When horses ran away from the Spanish they ran straight to us. The old people saw that they were just like dogs. They had the same unqualified desire to serve us, to be loyal, to teach us things. But they were special because they brought freedom with them, and only spirit beings could do that. So they became Spirit Dogs."

Claire smiled. "That's beautiful. They *are* just like that. Even when they have a roll in the dirt, all twisting around and joyful like puppies."

"Yes, and they always need a good wash. Start with her legs, then move up to her belly. Spray lightly with the hose, evenly, and rub with your hands." Johanna handed Claire one of the big sponges.

For the next while the women worked quietly, humming, speaking softly to the mare, who lifted one back hoof and leaned, enjoying the feel of the water and the gentle hands on her. Eventually Johanna stepped back and allowed Claire to work on her own. She marvelled at the way the city-born woman had adjusted to working with the horses. Claire moved almost elegantly around them. Her step was assured and graceful, and she showed no fear or anxiety when a horse reared some, flattened it ears or nipped at her. She always laughed her throaty, almost man-like laugh, teased them a little, offered a rub of reassurance and continued with her work. She was a natural.

"Everything in your people's way is about relationships in one way or another, isn't it?" Claire said.

Johanna smiled at her. "Everyone's way is about relationships."

"I don't think so for me."

"We all started out as tribal people. For all of us, if we look back far enough, there was a fire in the night where we gathered together for shelter, security, companionship, community. It's what we all have in common. It's what pulls us toward each other, that latent gene that tells us that we all started out around a fire in the night, huddled together against the darkness. We need each other. All of us. So everyone's way is about relationships."

"I never thought of it that way," Claire said.

Johanna took the hose from her hand and adjusted the spray to a fine mist and began washing the horse's face. When she was finished she looked around for Claire and saw her sitting on a bale across the corridor from the stall. Johanna shut off the water and settled on the bale beside her. "What is it?" she asked.

Claire gave her a sad smile. "I don't know. I guess being here, watching all of you, seeing you operate as a family makes me sad somehow. We never had that. Either of us. Aiden or I. We only had each other and it was always a struggle, always a challenge to adjust one way or another. We could never settle somewhere and just be."

"You had each other."

"Yes, but sometimes I feel like I managed to screw that up too. Always chasing after some man like he was going to change everything, like he was going to make me a better woman."

"And now?"

Claire laughed. "Now it's just the two of us again. Or at least I hope it is. There's no man. The man was never the answer. Hell, the man was never even the question. Took me way too long to learn that."

"So what do you do?"

"Do?"

"About men?"

She laughed again and stared out the open door at the end of the corridor. "I do nothing. Not for a couple of years. I won't live that way again. I won't give it all up. I won't surrender myself anymore. Everything I've done since Aiden was put away has been to work at making a home available, our home, his home. Finally."

"Celibate," Johanna said.

"As all hell," Claire said, and they laughed.

"Well then, we'd better get you on a horse mighty quick, girl," Johanna said. "On a saddle with a high pommel over rough terrain in a hot trot. You gotta put that woman spirit somewhere."

"Do I?" Claire asked seriously.

"Sometime, somewhere, yes," Johanna said and gave her a small hug. "It's what we do."

"Indians?"

"Them too," Johanna said, and they laughed.

He leaned a foot on the bottom rail of the corral and watched the stock mill absently about. There was a taste to dust and he'd always favoured it. Now, it kicked up in small clouds that held the sunlight and he could smell it. When he closed his eyes it was like his whole life could be summed up around that smell, every significant event and memory was dusted with the rich brown tan of the corral. The kid would never get that. There was no hook for him. The ranch and the atmosphere of it was nothing because he hadn't anchored himself to it and he could likely head off back to whatever kind of life he had in the city and not miss it. Bull rider. Joe Willie spat in the dust.

A smallish ranch bull stood alone in the middle of the herd, same one Aiden had ridden. When he looked at it Joe Willie could see the shape of See Four in miniature. That was the thing. These bulls were antsy enough and they could give a novice rider a hell of a thrill, but they were nothing compared to pure rodeo stock bred for bucking. That's what the point of all the grunt work was. It took a stern will to rig up up on a mountain of mayhem, and the only place that will was born was in the tough, sinewy work of ranch life. That was the tradition. Real cowboys, real, genuine working cowboys showing off the skill they'd acquired. Even some fluky city kid with great balance and a handful of nerve could get there, but there were dues to be paid. Joe Willie had paid them and so had every cowboy he'd met on the circuit. The kid needed to pay his and he wasn't going to. That was fine by him. The truck would get done. He'd see to that. He'd see to it even if he had to pay a mechanic to come out and guide him through it. She'd sit straight on her pins again and hold the tradition.

That was the thing of it. The kid had no head for tradition. Everything was all guts and glory to him. All he wanted was the thrill. For Joe Willie the thrill, the eight seconds of glory that you earned the right to, was only the culmination of the life you lived leading up to it every time. He rode as an expression of himself, a real working cowboy, and the kid, to his way of seeing, had nothing to express beyond attitude and recklessness. Well, he'd seen many broken, busted men who'd tried to forge a career on unruly posturing, and it wasn't a pretty sight. The kid was better off heading back to the city life he knew and leaving the bull riding to men who were bred to it.

His grandfather stepped up alongside him and set a foot on the bottom rail and leaned his elbows on the top. After a moment he pushed his hat back on his head and lit a smoke, then offered the pack to Joe Willie. They smoked awhile and watched the stock.

"Mighty deep well you're in," Lionel said.

"Mighty."

"Everything okay?"

"I suppose. If right is okay."

"What do you mean?"

"The deal's off. The kid won't follow through."

"Really? Seemed full of gumption to me."

"Yeah, well, gumption's only half the thing, ain't it?"

"I reckon. He was awful fired up, though."

Joe Willie smirked. "Aw, he's just a kid with a head full of dreams. Rode that ragged-ass bull over there and figures he's world champ. But he don't wanna pay the price to get there."

"What do you want?" Lionel asked.

"Pardon me?"

"What do you want? Seems to me there's two parts to a deal, and if she breaks there's generally a pair of reasons for it."

"He won't do the truck."

They smoked, and Joe Willie could feel the weight of his grandfather's scrutiny. Finally, the old man pinched out his cigarette against the top rail. "Well, the boy's in a tough place."

"Meaning?"

"Meaning you got reins on all of it. Rodeo and bull riding's your world. So's the old girl. You get to call the shots and he's got to follow. He's got no room to negotiate. Tough place to deal from, really."

"What are you saying exactly?"

"I'm not saying anything. I'm just looking at it and seeing that Aiden's got no wiggle room. In the end, whatever you say goes."

"You're saying that's not fair? He made the deal."

"I'm not saying anything. Well, other than it's too bad. Seemed like he had a good head for trucks and he woulda made a good rider with the right direction."

"Yeah, well," Joe Willie said.

"Suppose they'll be heading off, then?"

"I suppose."

"Shame," Lionel said.

"Yeah. Real shame," Joe Willie said. He stared at the stock and didn't hear his grandfather walk away.

Claire found him in the rec room watching television. He sat on the couch with his fist pressed to his jaw staring dull-eyed at the screen. He made no notice of her presence although she knew he'd seen her come in. There was a rodeo program on and she glanced at. When he made no effort to communicate she went to the couch and sat at the other end. She studied him closely. He looked like a typical bored teenager and she smiled to herself.

"Look at him," he said quietly.

"Pardon me?"

"Look at him. When he comes out of the chute."

"Who?"

"The bull. See Four. The bull that wrecked Joe Willie."

"Oh. Yes." Claire turned her attention to the screen.

The bull blasted out of the chute and it seemed to Claire that it was impossible for a huge body to behave that way. There was a paroxysm of twists, bucks and humps all at the same time, and the cowboy was flung high and wide, landing on the flat of his back in a matter of seconds.

"Wow," she said.

"Wow is right. That bull is awesome."

"Did Joe Willie tell you to come watch this?"

"Joe Willie didn't tell me anything. Won't listen to anything either," Aiden said. He began to rewind the tape. "The deal's off. I'm just watching this because I'll never get the chance to see him again."

"Joe Willie?"

"The bull. He's fantastic. He's beautiful."

"He's huge," Claire said. "And why is the deal off?"

"Because the bulls aren't the only stubborn things around here."

"What happened?"

"He won't listen to me. He doesn't want to do what's necessary for the truck. Only wants things his way. He won't even try to think another way."

"So what's next?"

"Nothing. It's over. I'm watching this tape and we're going home. That's it," Aiden said, sending the image of the bull and rider cascading across the screen again.

"I'm sorry," Claire said.

"Yeah, well, screw it. We had a word in the joint for guys who wouldn't keep their word, wouldn't stand up for themselves. Goof. That's what we called them."

"You're not in the joint now. Those rules don't work out here."

"They work everywhere. A goof's a goof no matter where he's walking."

"I think you're wrong."

"Really?" He laughed derisively and turned off the TV. "Everyone always wants to tell me how wrong I am. Like I'm a kid. Now you. Is this the heartfelt-mom routine? Pull the kid into line? I'm not a kid. I keep telling people that."

"Aiden," she said softly.

"What?"

She could see the depth of disappointment beneath the anger. The image of him as he rode the bull came to her and she knew how it must have felt to him to lose that sense of freedom. He crossed his arms and sat back deeper on the couch. Claire reached out and put a hand on his knee. When he offered no reaction, she let him sit with his hurt and disappointment. She left the room and went looking for Victoria and Johanna.

The bonfire was crackling loudly. After talking to Claire about the cancellation of the deal, Johanna and Victoria had suggested everyone gather for a farewell fire and had brought out thermoses of tea, soft drinks and snacks, blankets and the old guitar Birch seldom played anymore except on nights like this. Aiden and Joe Willie sat across the fire from each other, glum and silent, watching the flames and sipping idly at drinks. While Lionel poked at the fire to stoke it, Birch fumbled through a few chords, tuning the guitar methodically, and when his father eventually settled he launched into the opening chords of a song.

"Oh, that's lovely," Claire said, and for the next few minutes she sang in a clear, steady voice while Birch accompanied her. When she'd finished they applauded. "God, I haven't sung that in years," she said. "I used to hear it all the time when I was a girl."

"'The Yellow Rose of Texas'?" Victoria asked. "Doesn't seem much like a big-city song."

"It's not," Claire said. "Maybe that's why I came to love it so much. Because it could take me way from the city."

She went on to tell them the story of the open kitchen window and the music rolling freely between tenement buildings. The Wolfchilds stared into the fire, nodding solemnly, knowingly. They could hear coyotes in the background and the sounds of the stock in the corrals. The dog slunk in from the darkness and curled itself in a ball at Lionel's feet. He reached down and scratched its ears. When she'd finished Claire walked around the fire and poured herself some tea from the thermos. "Good to sing that song again," she said.

"Never heard it talked about quite that way before," Birch

said. "But it fits. There's a powerful bit of yearning in it. Seems to me that yearning ain't strictly a cowboy thing."

"Amen to that," Johanna said and smiled at Claire.

"You come from that?" Joe Willie asked. "Poor like that? When you were a kid?"

"Yes," Claire said. "I never knew it as being poor, though. It just was what it was. Nowadays I like to think it made me tougher somehow. Not tough enough to prevent me from recreating it when I became a parent, but tough anyway."

"Him too?" Joe Willie asked, tilting his chin in Aiden's direction.

"Yes," Claire said, looking at Aiden. "We never had much. Not of our own, at least. Occasionally we did okay. Didn't we, Aiden?"

He gave her a neutral look and kicked at the dirt with his heel. "I guess. But what's that got to do with anything?"

"We're just talking here, son," Birch said.

Aiden looked at Birch. "Talk," he said. "Talking never accomplished anything."

"Talk's talk," Birch said. "Better to fill the air with something other than a whole lot of empty."

"Empty suits me fine," Aiden said. "At least there's no lies in empty."

Joe Willie looked up and glared across the fire at him. "You don't want to be calling me a liar, kid."

"You can stop calling me kid any time now."

"It's what you are."

Aiden leaned forward. "I did time like a man. That qualifies me for something other than kid."

"When I say kid I mean someone younger than me, a lot younger. Too young to know that, that's all I mean by it," Joe Willie said.

"Sure. And all this crap about cowboy muscles? It's just so you can put me down. Just so you can laugh at me forking cowshit. It never had anything to do with me wanting to learn how to ride. It was all about you and how you could make yourself feel better by dishing out all the crap on me."

"I ain't asked you to do anything I wouldn't do myself," Joe Willie said, standing and looking across the fire at Aiden. "Nothing I ain't never done to get ready."

"Yeah, right," Aiden said, slowly standing too. "Tell me another one."

"That's the trouble with you, convict. You think everyone's out to get you. You can't get it through your head that maybe, just maybe, some folks just plain don't give a shit."

"You can quit calling me convict too."

They glared at each other. In the light of the fire their faces were hard, set.

"All right," Joe Willie said finally. "I'm sorry. I won't call you that again."

Aiden nodded and slowly sat back down. After a moment Joe Willie turned and took a step in the direction of the main barn.

"Joe Willie," Victoria said. "Wait. There's things that need saying around this fire."

"Like what?" he asked.

"Like you owe Aiden an explanation."

"About what?"

"About the truck."

"What about the truck?"

"Everything. Everything you think about it. If the two of you are going to scuttle a deal then you owe it to each other to tell each other why."

"It won't make any difference. He's leaving."

"That may be, but at least give him the dignity of leaving knowing why."

"Still won't make any difference."

"You don't know that."

Joe Willie stepped over the log toward the darkness. He took a few steps, then stopped and turned slowly back to face them again. "All he sees is a truck," he said. "Can't see nothing other than that. To him she's just a bucket of bolts." He stepped back over the log and sat down. "There's a little depression you can feel with your fingertips on the panel by the passenger side window," he said. "You wouldn't even know it's there unless you ran your hand along the length. But when you feel it, it's like it talks to you. It says, 'This is where your grandmother drummed her fingers in time to the songs your grandfather sang.' Or it says, 'This is where your mother rested her fingers while she held you in the other arm on dark nights between go-rounds a long, long time ago.'

"Then there's the burn mark on the ledge by the steering wheel. It says, 'This is where your daddy rested a smoke while he drove with both hands and peered through the windshield during a spring whiteout in Nebraska.' Or the pinholes in the roof above the windshield. They say, 'This is where Mama hung the maps so they could find their way to those small rodeos off the main circuit, going there to ride because the riding was bigger than the purse.' There's nicks and bumps and scars all over that old girl. They all got her a story in them, a story about rodeo, about the west, about my family. Changing it means the stories disappear—and I don't want that."

The fire crackled and hissed and the small breeze coaxed the flames into a lively orange dance. Nothing was said for a good long time.

Finally, Johanna leaned in from her seat on the log and took the stick from Lionel's hand. She poked up sparks and watched them scuttle upward to disappear in the dark. She spoke quietly.

"You could take an ember from this fire, wrap it in damp moss, put it in a sack, carry it somewhere else and start a whole new flame. That's how fire travelled in the old days. The fire-keeper would wrap it and protect it from the wind, carry it long distances until the people stopped. Then he'd bring it out in this new place and start another fire. But it was really the same flame," she said. "And as another night moved in around them the people told stories to bring them closer around that flame. Closer like family. Closer like a tribe. That same flame burned and the stories it generated and the stories it held for the people went with them too."

"You're talking about a dream wheel, aren't you?" Victoria said.

Johanna looked at the old woman and smiled. "Yes, I suppose I am."

"Mama?" Birch asked. "What the dickens are you talking about?"

"I'm talking about us, son. I'm talking about the stories of the lives of a people. Doesn't have to be a nation. Can be a family or a town, a valley like this or a broken-down old truck like that old girl out there," she said. "A dream wheel is the sum total of a peoples' story. All its dreams, all its visions, all its experiences gathered together. Looped together. Woven together in a big wheel of dreaming."

"I don't follow," Aiden said.

Victoria stood and placed another two logs on the fire, then took the poker from Johanna's hand and stirred the flames, sending arching sprites of spark into the night. "The fire was the keeper of the dream wheel. When people gathered around it, the stories came. Even way back when, people were charmed by fire, stared into it like you are now, somehow feeling like it could conjure something, take them somewhere—and truth is, it could. When the stories started they were transported, lifted up and out of their lives and their fears of the night and taken on dream journeys."

"To where?" Aiden asked.

"Anywhere, but mostly to themselves," Victoria said. "To every place their people had ever been. To every strange and wonderful event that had ever happened and to every strange and wonderful event they ever dreamed had happened. Legends. Myths. Trickster tales. The whole great wheel of themselves, their lives, their peoples' lives.

"Wherever they went, the stories went with them. Even when the time of firekeepers had passed there was always a keeper of the dream wheel. There was always someone or something that held the stories, protected them, kept them safe, held them for sharing on nights like this, around another fire in a new time, in a new place, a new world."

"The old girl," Joe Willie said.

"Yes," Victoria said. "That's what I believe."

"But what does it mean?" Aiden asked.

"It means we got to keep her on the road," Joe Willie said.

"We?" Aiden asked.

"Yeah. We. You're a snot-nosed little son of a bitch and you got a pile of attitude I don't really need, but you know how to get this done. Or at least you talk like you do. Maybe it's time to prove it."

The others watched, waiting. Joe Willie stared evenly across the fire, his face betraying no emotion, and in that light he looked strong, warriorlike, timeless. Aiden gave the same unshrinking look in return.

"Maybe you got some proving to do too," he said.

"Like what?"

"Like proving that you're not so strong and tough that you don't need anybody's help, nobody else's way of seeing things. Like proving that you can teach me about bulls instead of running me up hills and keeping me knee deep in horseshit."

"That's part of the training, kid."

"Oh, cut the crap," Aiden said, standing. "It isn't part of the training. It's you trying to find out how much I can handle. Whether I'm worthy of you. You think I can't see that? You think I'm just some dummy? Teach me. Teach me what you know without the bullshit and I'll get your truck on the road for you. Square and simple."

"If I push you it's because what you want to do is the hardest thing in the world."

"Yeah, well, the same with me."

Joe Willie barked a laugh. "Fixing a truck's not near as dangerous as riding a bull."

"I'm not talking about danger," Aiden said. "I want to ride bulls because I feel like if I do I can be more than I ever was, more than I ever hoped to dream I could be. You gotta want to work on that truck for the same reason."

Joe Willie nodded his head slowly. "Still gotta do the work," he said.

"Fine. Just don't snow-job me about it."

"What's first, then?"

"You gotta dig a pit so we can get under her to see what needs doing."

"What?"

"You heard me. We need a pit about six feet deep and ten feet long," Aiden said.

"That's a lot of shovelling."

"Yeah, well, welcome to the fucking club."

They laughed.

"These dream wheels," Joe Willie said, looking at his grandmother. "They're ours, right? Ojibway? The Sioux?"

"In the way we're talking, yes, but every people has one, or something like it if they look hard enough," Victoria said.

"And it's important?"

"As important as it gets."

"Why?"

She smiled at him across the fire and when she did her eyes glittered magically. "Because we forget," she said. "Everyone forgets. Forget how a simple thing like coming together around a fire makes all the worrisome things less so. Forget how the simple act of being together is the most important thing."

Joe Willie looked over the fire toward the shadowed mountains and scratched his head under the brim of his hat. "I'd best get busy, then," he said.

"I'll help you," Aiden said.

Joe Willie crossed his arms on his chest and stared across the fire at him. The two of them measured each other, unblinking.

"If you like," Joe Willie said.

Aiden reached down and gave Claire's shoulder a squeeze and followed Joe Willie, who had already started in the direction of the shed.

They made it a half mile farther the next night. When they passed the flag Joe Willie had dropped by the boulders to mark their progress, they looked at each other grimly, then pushed on up the trail, wordless and determined. The trail became more talus and the footing was less predictable. The scree of gravel and rock chunk around a bend slowed them, and their breathing was ragged in their chest. Only Claire on the horse behind them was offered the security of an assured footing. She rode confidently, trusting the horse entirely to navigate the severe slope, and found herself enjoying the climb and the view it provided. Above them the solemn cliff of Iron Mountain seemed to float forward with the tendril of cloud pushed above it by the wind they could not feel on the trail below. The trail wound into trees again and Joe Willie signalled a stop. They leaned against logs and drank greedily from the canteens.

"Done?" he asked Aiden.

"No way. You?"

"Not hardly if you ain't."

"Not hardly."

So they pushed on again. Despite the lazy roll the shadows gave it, the trail still climbed, but they gave in to the illusion and climbed harder, faster, side by side now and staring down at their feet, arms swinging high behind them. Their steps cracked branches on the trail, and the staccato snap of them echoed off the wall of rock around them, giving them an off-tempo beat to pace to, and they stepped quick and lively, surrendering now and then to the compulsion to peek over at the other, measure him and push upward harder still.

They arrived at a small clearing that offered a view to the west, and this time Aiden signalled the stop.

"All right," he said.

They drank. In that mauve light of near dark there was no clear defining line between distance and closeness so that the face of the mountains to the west across the valley seemed touchable, the valley below it hidden by the height. The sun was a smear of orange along the tops of the trees. Claire dismounted, handed fruit and water to them, and together they stood looking out from the clearing. When their breathing slowed they ate the fruit and rested on logs while the horse grazed lightly on the scrub grass. No one spoke. The land lulled them, and when the shadow became thicker Joe Willie nodded to them and they began preparing for the walk back down the mountain.

He moved to help lift Claire into the saddle and she smiled. She put a hand on his shoulder for balance while she reached for the stirrup with her lead foot. They glanced at each other before Claire swung herself up to find her seat, and it was only then that Joe Willie noticed that it had been his left shoulder she'd cupped with her palm for balance. He rubbed it lightly.

"Thanks," she said quietly.

"Ma'am," he said, touching the brim of his hat and grinning.

She laughed. "Oh god. Doomed to ma'am already."

"Claire," he said, nodding.

"Joe Willie."

Aiden came and handed the canteen back to his mother. "I could use a wash," he said. "And some grub."

Joe Willie motioned Claire to let the horse lead the way again. She nudged it forward, and they fell in a few steps behind.

"Helluva spot," Aiden said.

"Yeah," Joe Willie said. "Ain't it?"

"How did you know?" Birch asked. They were standing together in the fading evening light watching the land as it changed shape and substance in the lengthening shadow.

"About what?" Victoria asked back.

"About the fire. About the two of them hashing it out like that."

"I don't know. Women's intuition, maybe."

He laughed and pulled at the brim of his hat. "Come on, Ma. What's the deal here?"

She laughed too. "It's a fundamental thing, fire. Got its own particular kind of magic. Just like everything else we take so much for granted. Water, air, the land. They all heal us in their way. If you learn to trust the fundamental things they'll always bring you to where you need to be, help you find out what you need to find out about yourself."

"That's not an Indian teaching," he said.

"Not especially. Everyone who has a tie to the land and the wide openness of it all carries that kind of knowing. Trouble is, the world changed and a lot of people changed with it, left the land and its teachings behind them. I always held that reclaiming that part of ourselves would show us better how to heal ourselves."

"Which part is that?"

"The part that lets the land fill us. Everyone finds it, or, at least, rediscovers a small part of it now and then. People come here and stand on that veranda and look around at the valley and heave big, deep breaths into themselves and think that they're just struck by the wonder of it all, the beauty."

"They aren't?"

"Yes. Certainly. But there's the deeper calling going on. The voice in them that says, 'I remember this.' They forgot how to respond to that voice."

He chuckled and began to roll a smoke. "It's beyond me," he said. "All this talk of voices and remembering. I get where you're going with it but it's still beyond me."

"That's what everyone thinks, son. That it's too late now. But we're all tribal people. Every last one of us living and breathing right now started out as the same kind of people. People who lived in community and together on the land. All the things we call Indian were the same for everybody at one time. The reason we get so far away from each other is because we've learned to think we're different. But we're not. Take anybody and put them in the middle of something as beautiful as that alpine lake up in the pass over there and they're going to be touched by it, feel something move inside themselves. Hear that old voice that tells them they remember. It takes time and commitment to remember how to really hear it, but anyone can do it."

"So sitting around the fire was gonna let Joe Willie and the kid remember how to hear that voice."

"Not necessarily. But it was gonna make it easier for them to talk to each other, make it easier for them to hear that much, anyway."

"And that's not an Indian thing?"

She gave him a firm hug and then let him go. "If you're an Indian and it makes you feel better, then I guess it's an Indian thing."

He finished rolling the smoke and lit up and took a few draws and watched the steers moving in the field and then pinched it out on the top of the fence rail and looked at her. "You and my wife got the market cornered on how to bamboozle a man. But I hear it. That's the strange thing. Indian or not."

"I think you're getting it," she said, and they both laughed.

Mornings were a small glory. Claire liked the feeling of standing at the edge of the veranda facing the mountains to the west. In the burgeoning early light they seemed magnified, closer somehow, like if she reached out a hand she could touch them, trace their rippled, jagged outline against the sky, maybe even poke a hand right through them into the cool mystery of their other side, sense the lives there, enchanted and beguiling as the secret lives of dolls. She'd breathe then. Close her eyes, stretch out her arms to their full length, splay her fingers as wide as they would go, then bring them forward slowly like an embrace, inhaling slowly, pulling it all into her until, when her arms encircled her finally, she could feel it enter her, fill her, become her.

She'd taken to rising early as soon as they'd arrived at Wolf Creek, and it had become habit. But more than that. More like a ritual, a small ceremony she practised alone.

Aiden slept later. The work and the fresh air were doing wonderful things for him. She could see it in the glow of him. Excitement. Focus. Joy, almost. She tried to think of when that last shred of imprisonment had dropped from him, that thick, unyielding silence he'd fall into at first, but it wasn't clear. Mostly it had been a process. Each day had offered him something more, something far removed from the reality of jail life or any of the realities he'd lived up until then. It was the men. Men and bulls. Funny, she thought, but before she came here she likely would have lumped the two together—unpredictable, dangerous, wild, driven by urge. But these men were different. As different as this morning hovered over mountains was unlike a metropolitan morning. Birch and Lionel were laconic and unruffled, a sagacious pair of bookends hewn from the land they occupied. Tough and wiry, they were no-nonsense when it came to the life they'd chosen or the women they'd chosen to live it with. The loyalty amazed her. It wasn't announced or put on grandiose display. Rather, it lived in the quiet way they moved. They saved their bashing about for the pens and corrals of their livelihood, and when they moved in the presence of their women they became almost elegant, refined, and pliant. Pliant. She'd met a lot of obdurate men in her time and pliant, bendable, compromising was a quality that was foreign to her. It spoke of respect, and she admired the two grizzled rodeo men for that.

Joe Willie came from the same stock. You could see it. The surliness seldom surfaced around his grandmother and mother. When it did he clamped it down and went off somewhere else with it. Behind the aloof shield he put up in front of himself, Claire sensed the ripples of Birch and Lionel shimmering just beyond it. It showed in the way he treated horses, quiet, tender. It was a beguiling combination of strength and gentleness she saw in him, in all of them. In Joe Willie it was stunning in its intensity, like he reined in both at the same time, as though he didn't fully trust either. As though they needed to be saddle broke before he'd let himself relax with them. He was good for Aiden, she could see that. There was enough of the wild in both of them to call to each other and enough of the Indian cowboy sensibility to calm them when they collided. *Indian cowboy.* She shook her head amusedly. Never in a million years would she have believed that her son carried a cowboy gene, but she was glad he did. If he came away with a shred of what these men carried she would be forever grateful.

"You look as though you almost wanted to laugh."

Johanna sat on the porch swing wrapped in a blanket.

"Have you been there all this time?" Claire asked.

"Yes. But you looked so entranced I didn't want to bother you."

"Good word, entranced. I guess I was. I always am."

"It's a powerful valley."

"Yes. It must be wonderful to call it home."

Johanna shuffled over on the swing and motioned for Claire to join her, and she spread the blanket out and draped it over the both of them. They sat in the swing and looked out over the valley in silence.

"Did you know? That night? Did you know that they'd break through it and get back to the work?" Claire asked.

"No. It was just important to let him know what they were working with."

"Joe Willie?"

"Him too."

"But the truck. How did you come to identify the truck that way? As a dream wheel?"

"Things carry stories, Claire. It's why we keep things. Because the histories they bear make them precious. There's no big Indian magic in that, we all know it or feel it. But like Victoria said—we forget. We forget how vital those histories are to us and we get lost in the price of things instead, their worldly value, their cost. That's what we consider if we lose it."

A hawk peeled a line across the sky. They watched it as it circled, riding the thermals, dipping and climbing without moving its wings.

"If your life's been a constant process of losing and starting over, again and again and again, and all the things you ever had are always getting lost, where's the history in that? What is there to hang on to?" Claire asked. "I'm asking for Aiden."

"The dream itself," Johanna said.

"What dream?"

"The one we all carry. Home, belonging, community, stories around a fire."

"Sounds too easy."

"Try it."

Claire looked at her. Johanna sat calmly with the blanket draped over her, like an old woman in her shawl, comfortable in her years, confident in their lessons. "Okay," she said.

The hawk flew closer and closer to the mountains until it dipped below the edge of the draw, disappeared as quietly as a lost thought. Claire let herself sink deeper into the morning, allowed it to seep into her, find its hollow and gather, pool quietly and follow the hawk into the stark warm breast of the mountains.

They'd pushed the truck forward one length so that the nose of her was stuck out the front of the shed. Then they'd dug the pit. By the end of that afternoon they'd stabilized the sides with boards and timbers so that they could stand in it and reach up with their forearms clearing the edge of it. It was hard work, but they fed off each other, neither one wanting to show any tiredness or discomfort, so that heaving the shovels of dirt and rock up over their heads and clear of the rim of the hole became a contest of silent power. They'd taken turns wheel-barrowing the detritus over to the lip of the draw and tilting it over, making sure the trips and loads were equal. When they pushed the truck back into the shed it nestled perfectly beneath the shed's main beams.

The next day Birch and Lionel devised a plan for block and tackle using the beams for leverage, and when they lifted her the first time the beams held and the old truck swayed slightly as though she loved the new medium of the air and wanted to test it for speed and traction.

Aiden showed the Wolfchilds the weak points in her structure, the wear of age, the tiny fractures that would split and grow and cause more aggravation if left to carry weight again.

"We strip her to the chassis. The body can stay up while we sandblast it, repaint, and redo the axles," Aiden said, lost in his study of the truck and not paying attention to the looks the Wolfchilds were giving him. "First thing to take care of really is the leaf springs. Either replace them or take them to a shop to weld. After that we can work on the axles and start thinking about what kind of motor we want to drop in. Dropping in a newer engine will make the work faster. No need to sandblast parts. The body will be easiest. She's in such good shape we can sandblast and paint pretty fast. Not here, though. Shop in town, I guess. Same with the upholstery. Unless you wanna do it yourself, which in that case will add a hell of a lot of time."

"Whoa, boy," Birch said, laying a hand on his shoulder. "A little at a time now."

"You sure know your way around a vehicle, Aiden," Lionel said. "Never would have seen any of this myself."

"Well, there was an old guy who ran the shop in the joint. Old Navy guy who knew engines and trucks inside out. Taught me a lot."

"Wasn't easy, was it?" Lionel asked.

Aiden looked up at the underside of the truck. "You don't do time, you lose it. You spend all of it remembering, recollecting or dreaming of how you want it. You're never in the moment you're in. You lose all those."

"I hear that," Joe Willie said.

"Still, you learned something, didn't you?" Lionel asked.

"Engines," Aiden said. "That, and that I won't go back again."

"Powerful education, then," Birch said. "Never been to jail myself. Never seemed a likely choice for success. But you come out okay."

"Yeah?" Aiden asked.

"Mistakes are like bulls that throw you," Lionel said. "You can never ride 'em different. You just learn from how you fell and climb back up there."

"If you can," Joe Willie said. "If you're damned lucky you can climb back up again. Some mistakes change everything."

"Some do," Lionel said. "I guess the only thing you got control over is how you handle the change."

"Yeah. Right," Joe Willie said. "Now are we gonna actually do some work on this truck or are we going to talk about it all day?"

Claire was working on tack when she noticed Joe Willie leaning in the door of the tack room.

"Has he ever been hit? Hit hard?" Joe Willie asked.

"Aiden?" she asked, setting down the rag.

"Yeah. Like boxing. Or in a real fight. A mean one. One where he got pasted good?"

"I don't know. I wouldn't want to think so. And I don't think he's ever boxed. Why?"

"I need to ask you if I can put him in a ring."

"What on earth for? He wants to ride a bull. Call me a city girl, Joe Willie, but I don't think bulls wear boxing gloves."

"They don't. But they hit awful hard and he needs to know how to react when he gets clobbered."

He stepped into the room and sat on a sawhorse they draped saddles on. When he looked at her she could sense the seriousness of his question. "When a man gets hit, square and flush and hard, there's a fraction of a second of fear. Real deep, hard fear. In that fraction of a second the old flight-or-fight thing comes screaming to the surface. Most try to backpedal, run off, get out of the way of the next one because getting smacked hard isn't an everyday thing. It takes some severe gumption to shake it off and stand up to it. He's gotta learn to take a good solid shot without backing off. In eight seconds he'll get clobbered like no man's capable of hitting him and there's no time for wanting off, for running. He needs to learn that. You gotta say it's okay."

"He's big enough and old enough to choose," she said.

"Sure. But this is your deal too. You're the one that needs to be standing there when he lands. You gotta get used to seeing him take a lick. Gotta know you endorsed it."

"It's a tough business, isn't it?"

"The toughest. Tougher than any jailhouse fight he ever had. These ones you gotta choose to take on. There's one other thing."

"God. You just asked me to okay my son taking a beating. There's more?"

He grinned. "Nothing so tough. I want him to work with a gymnastics coach."

"Well, that sounds a little more peaceful, something I could get used to watching. But it seems like a strange combination."

"Not really. He needs to learn how to move. How to always be in balance. How to control his body in the air. How to be graceful."

"You're kidding me."

He looked at her seriously. "No. I'm dead serious. You look at a bull blowing out of the chute and you think it's all mayhem, all violence and spur-of-the-moment action. But there wasn't a bull I ever rode that didn't think about what he was gonna do once he left the chute. Spin, blow or kick out. They choose that, and you never know coming out what to expect, how you're gonna get hit. You need balance, you need rhythm and you need grace. Especially when you get thrown.

You gotta be able to find your balance in the air, and nothing'll teach you that like gymnastics."

"Grace?"

"Grace."

She looked at him and he met it evenly. There was a hardness to him, a toughness, but just under that was a pool of compassion, a gentleness that tempered it, eased it and made him manly. She could trust that kind of man with her son. "I don't think I could ever equate riding a bull with being graceful. It seems more like you'd need to be strong and supple, slightly crazy too, I suppose. Not graceful."

"Come with me. I'll show you."

He led her to the house, into the rec room, and knelt in front of the television leafing through a collection of videocassettes. He slid one into the player and sat on the sofa beside her. He thumbed the remote and the screen soon filled with a bull and rider exploding into an arena. He fast-forwarded, then stopped the tape at a point where the camera was focussed on the chute. Claire could see a rider poised for action behind it and the rope men bent strangely by the free frame in front. "Watch," he said.

The tape started, and instead of the blur of action she expected Joe Willie had it set to slow motion. What she saw amazed her. A gigantic bull flowed out of the chute. It rose majestically, like a tidal wave, and launched itself into the light of the open space. On its back a cowboy flowed with it, the small of his back tucked in above his hip bone and tight behind the bull's shoulder, his free arm rising like a flag with the motion. She could see each bunch of muscle in the bull's hindquarters gather, compact, compress like huge fists and then the explosion of them opening in a wild thrust upwards, the height of the jump magnified by the slow, surreal timing of the tape. She felt her jaw drop. Beside her Joe Willie leaned forward and cupped his chin in his palms. The cowboy on the bull's back stretched out incredibly, elastically, each tucking in of his knees accentuated by a long unfolding of the free arm above him and then the outward surge of his legs toward the bull's shoulders followed by a pulling down of the arm. The tension was all gather and release, gather and release, and Claire began to see the poetry in it, the rhythm, the grace he spoke of and the pure, unadulterated thrill of wild captured and slowed to a snail's pace. When he thumbed the remote and the streaming quality of the ride dissipated into the chaos of real time she found it hard to breathe.

"Oh my god," she said. "Aiden."

"He'll be all right," Joe Willie said. "But he's gotta learn to feel that rhythm you just saw. Gotta know without a doubt that it lives there. Gotta know where it lives in him so he can match it up."

"That was magical. I would never have believed it if you'd just told me. How incredibly devastating. How beautiful," she said.

"Yes," he said. "I haven't watched that ride for a long time."

"Who was that cowboy?"

"It was me," he said, handing her the remote and walking quickly from the room.

At first it came easy. The trainer Joe Willie brought in reminded him of Johnny Calder and he liked his rough-and-tumble, no-nonsense approach to things. He listened closely and watched as the old boxer bobbed and wove and shadow-boxed around the ring. When it was his turn he took to it naturally, the athlete in him responding to the challenge to his timing, his balance, his ability to move. In the joint he'd only learned how to throw a punch, how to throw the combinations and move around the heavy bag. Calder had never allowed them to actually fight each other. So this new approach intrigued him, and he wanted to learn. He put himself into it and found an easy familiarity with the skill. The old pug tousled his hair, called him champ, and he liked it. Then the gymnastics coach turned out to be a pretty, fit little blonde, and he gave her all of his attention. She taught him how to stretch, and they worked on floor mats. At first the movements she showed him made him feel awkward, too big for his body, slow and tight, but gradually he limbered, and again his athleticism allowed him a measure of confidence and he responded well. At the end of that first day he felt enthused, capable and interested in learning more.

When the first punch landed everything changed. The old boxer was lightning quick and Aiden barely saw his hands move. When the jabs hit him they rocked his head back, and even with the thickly padded helmet he felt like he'd been pounded with a hammer. He pedalled backwards, trying to find a neutral space to gather himself, but the old fighter kept coming for him. His arms suddenly weighed a ton, and it was nearly impossible to think with the explosions of white in his head that followed the punches. There was an anger that came with being hit and it was this more than anything that enabled his body to remember the footwork he'd been shown. As the trainer bore in on him again he shuffled, left then right then back, bending at the waist like he'd been shown, and he felt the breeze of punches sailing past their mark. He felt elated. But then the old pro keyed on his rhythm and he got plowed again and again. After what seemed an eternity Joe Willie called time, and he collapsed on a hay bale in the corner of the ring. His head felt swollen and cottony.

After that the trampoline was nearly impossible. His body ached from taking blows to the chest, belly and shoulders and he was stiffening rapidly. But he didn't want to appear weak and he stretched out hard with the coach and she showed him the basics of bouncing. He liked the feel of flying through the air. There was a freedom in it and he watched closely when she showed him how to find his balance in the air. She worked him through a simple routine and kept him at it for fifteen minutes. His legs ached. His arms got stiff again and he found it difficult to maintain his posture in the air. When he began to travel off centre she yelled at him, reminding him, and he struggled.

And then the mountain. After the training Joe Willie and his mother came with the horse and they set out on the trail again. In the beginning the peak they aimed for had seemed reachable, but after a full day's work on the ranch and then the boxing and gymnastics it was all he could do to keep up with Joe Willie. It felt steeper, the footing harder, more elusive, and he seemed to sweat more. But the cowboy kept going and Aiden was unable to find any quit in himself. They climbed, and on the third night Joe Willie halted at a bend in the trail just beyond where the line of trees began to thin.

"Almost," he said.

"Almost what?" Aiden gasped.

"Almost there. Up around this bend there's one final push, one last hard climb and we're at the meadow. The cliff face is around this bend."

"Now?" Claire asked, looking around at the darkening sky.

"No. Too late now. Tomorrow. Tomorrow we'll start earlier. Get there so we can watch the sun set. Bring tents, food, so we can camp."

"Sounds good to me," Aiden said. "Do I ride after that?"

"No," Joe Willie said. "Not until you're ready."

"Jesus. When's that?"

"Don't know."

"You don't know? Who the hell knows, then?"

"You do." Joe Willie signalled for Claire to hand a canteen down, and he drank slowly, watching Aiden. "You'll show me when you're ready."

The boy scowled at him, then took the canteen he offered. He drank slowly like Joe Willie had, small sips over the course of a couple of minutes, then splashed a handful of water on his face and mopped it with his neckerchief. He walked away to the edge of the trail and stood watching the sky. Claire and Joe Willie saw his shoulders slump, then his head dropped. He cupped his face in his hands, bent forward at the waist, then knelt slowly on the ground with one knee. Claire made a motion in the saddle to dismount and go to him, but Joe Willie stopped her with a palm on her leg. They watched him for a long time. Finally, he rubbed his brow with the fingers and thumb of one hand and they heard him moan, one long, deep, ragged moan, before he rose and turned to them.

"Best be some good fucking camping then," he said.

Lionel showed him how to load the tarpaulins for balance and then helped Aiden tie them onto the packhorse. It was only an overnight stay and the gear didn't amount to a big load, but the old man took his time and taught the boy exactly. He showed him how to work around the horse so it stayed calm, the reassurances he gave it in a low, soothing voice. Aiden listened carefully, biting down on his lower lip and watching intently as Lionel showed him the knots a second time. When they were finished the old man gave him a big clap on the shoulder.

"That's your responsibility now," Lionel said. "You got her?"

"I got her," Aiden said and shook his hand.

"Good man," Lionel said, and Aiden smiled.

The other Wolfchilds walked in as Claire finished saddling her horse. She'd chosen a fractious little half-Arabian mare she'd ridden three or four times. The horse was a handful, its Arabian blood giving it a wildness that had scared Claire at first but which she enjoyed tremendously when the horse settled and pranced its way around the round pen or galloped across the main pasture. She wanted to challenge herself by navigating the flighty little mare up the mountain just as Joe Willie and Aiden would do on foot scaling upward all the way to the peak. Handling the Arabian through the unpredictable footing would give both of them the necessary confidence for the long mountain trail ride Claire was planning for herself.

"This is the night you figure to beat it?" Birch asked.

Joe Willie nodded grimly. "We should," he said.

"Long climb," Birch said to Aiden.

"We trained for it. We're good," Aiden said.

"You're looking at three hours," Birch said.

Joe Willie and Aiden exchanged a look. "We know," they said in unison.

Birch slapped both of them on the back. "Take a mighty good pair of legs to get you up. Not to mention walking back down tomorrow. Different muscles. Different kind of tough."

"We got the legs," Aiden said, and Joe Willie arched an eyebrow at him.

They walked the horses through the corral and out the gate. They stood about looking up at Iron Mountain. It stood stolidly in the bright afternoon sun, proud and ancient, an old warrior watching the sun arc its path across the sky. Johanna and Victoria hugged Claire tightly before she mounted up.

"You watch over my men now," Victoria said.

"I will," Claire said.

"Something for your trip," Johanna said and handed up a small hide bag on a thong.

"What's this?" Claire asked.

"Medicine bag," Johanna said. "Wear it under your shirt, right next to your heart. It's got good medicine in it. It'll keep you balanced."

"On the horse?"

"That too," Johanna said.

"You need us for anything you light a smoky fire, hear?" Birch said to Aiden.

"Me?"

"Yeah, you. You're the scout on this trip. It's a big honour. Ojibways figure the scout is the bravest one. The one who goes first, takes on the danger first."

"What danger?"

"Figure of speech," Birch said.

Aiden and Joe Willie stretched some and then moved off wordlessly toward the trailhead. Claire kicked the horse up and tugged lightly on the rein for the packhorse to follow them. The Wolfchilds stood at the corral and watched them go. When they got to the trees they didn't break stride to stop and wave. They disappeared into the trees.

"Big mountain," Lionel said.

"Big mountain," Birch said.

"Figure of speech," Victoria said, and they turned to head back to the house.

It was hot. When the sun broke through the trees it flared against their bare backs in a splash of heat and they both broke sweat early. They pushed up the trail side by side. Behind them, Claire was bowled over at the casual way Joe Willie had thrown off his shirt and tucked it into the back of his jeans. It was like second nature, something he did unthinkingly, and she was touched at the display of trust it contained. Now, watching them drive their way up the steep incline of the trail, she didn't see the narrow thrust of the arm as anything other than another part of this muscular, proud assault on the trail, on the challenge. It pistoned up and back in time with the other arm, and if he thought about it at all Joe Willie didn't show it with his body. He and Aiden matched strides and their heads were down, eyes focussed on the trail in front of them, the pebbly, twig-scrabbled path that must have seemed mere inches from their faces. The bad leg didn't seem bad at all. Instead, Joe Willie set the pace, a gritty, driving pace that put them ahead of the schedule they'd been on previously. She worried a little about dehydration but she knew the cowboy in Joe Willie wouldn't let them go too far without a water stop. For them and the horses.

When they did stop the two of them were bathed in sweat. Their breathing was so hard and ragged that they were reduced to the tiniest sips from the canteen. "Pap says three hours," Joe Willie said. "We can do her in two."

"You figure?" Aiden asked, leaning over with his hands on his knees.

"It'll take a helluva push, but yeah. You good?"

"Never better."

"Good. You lead, then. Set your pace. Your call for the next water stop."

Aiden huffed out his breath. "Okay. Ready?"

"Go."

Claire sat a moment longer, drinking in the view as she sipped from the canteen. It was fabulous. It was like the trail in her girlhood dream. The little Arabian nickered and kicked out a tad, and Claire eased it into a walk, watching closely as it shook its head about. The horse settled into the climb and Claire let herself relax, the motion of the walk comforting and familiar now, the need to press up slightly in the stirrups now and then something that she did without thinking. Ahead of her Aiden pressed on at the same tempo Joe Willie had set initially, and they climbed the slope side by side, silent, not looking at each other. Claire nudged the Arabian and they ate up the distance easily.

Aiden strode right past the previous markers. They took the next section of trail quickly, and when they passed the little clearing where'd they'd stopped before Claire was amazed at how far they'd come so fast. Neither of them looked tired. Instead, they burned with the challenge. Now and then they allowed themselves a small glance at the other, a brief check, a search for flagging resolve, but they didn't find it, and it began to look to Claire like they'd do the whole climb before stopping again.

Finally, Aiden stopped at their last marker, and the two of them looked at each other a moment, then up toward the bend in the trail that curved into the approach to the peak. They signalled for water and splashed some over their heads and backs before drinking. The sun was still high in the sky, the slanted light of evening slinking toward them from somewhere behind the peak they could see poking above the trees.

"Final hump," Aiden said.

Joe Willie wiped his face. "She's a killer."

"Yeah?"

"Yeah. Generally takes a goat from here."

"Far?"

"No so much. Just plumb steep and rocky."

They pushed off again, handed up the canteens without looking at Claire, their eyes focussed on the wide bend of the trail as it disappeared into the last treacherous climb to the meadow at the base of the cliff. The horses seemed to sense the end of the ride and stepped eagerly into the walk. When they rounded the bend and cleared the last of the trees, Claire was stunned. The last of the trail was a series of switchbacks, snaking upward in a long coil of rocky, narrow trail that was more a suggestion than a real pathway. The Arabian reared. Claire leaned in toward its head and whispered encouragement. The horse shifted its hooves nervously but moved out onto the narrow ledge of walkway. Claire remembered to maintain a steady pressure on the drop-off side, a constant press of the foot to keep the horse moving along the inside of the trail. Ahead of them Joe Willie and Aiden had slowed, the pace reduced to hard compressions of muscle made more difficult by footslides on the loose rock. Even the horse struggled, and Claire was forced to use every shred of skill she'd learned from Johanna to keep them moving. She could feel the keen electric burn of fear in her belly, the fine hairs on the back of her neck stiff, and the dry, unblinking focus of her eyes. Her skin felt moist and she shivered. She could hear the two of them huffing hard, groaning, straining into the mountain. She wanted to yell something but worried about spooking the horses. Instead, she reached a hand up and clutched the medicine bag inside her shirt, feeling the lump of it and calming some. The Arabian sensed it and moved less skittishly. Behind her the packhorse whinnied.

When she looked up, Claire felt reduced, ant-like beneath the huge tower of Iron Mountain that stood over the last press of the trail like a protector, a sentinel, its granite face obdurate, omniscient, ancient and wise. She squeezed the medicine bag and turned her head to scan the face of the peak. It was magnificent. Joe Willie and Aiden spoke to each other but the words were unintelligible. They were pressing their hands on their thighs as they pushed and she could see the break above them on the last turn of the path, the flattened line that marked the start of the meadow. They saw it too and she heard excitement in their voices, the thrill of energy pushed to its limit, the idea of rest, completion, burning hotter than the muscles in their legs. Aiden slipped and Joe Willie gripped him by the belt and kept pushing. Their feet kicked small rocks loose and they were forced to turn their toes outward, angled against the steepness of the climb. Aiden reached a hand back and grabbed Joe Willie's belt and the two of them rocked upward in turn, pulling the other along after each step.

Finally they crested, and when Claire eased the horses off the narrow belt of pathway the meadow revealed itself to her yard by yard and she saw the two of them resting on a log of fallen cedar, arms around each other, heaving air and looking around at the meadow. She walked the horses up and dismounted, dangled the canteens in front of their sweaty faces. They drank slowly, wiping handfuls of water across their brows before pouring it over their heads. It took a while before any of them could speak, Claire struck speechless by the sheer beauty of the place and the two of them still reclaiming breath.

"Iron Peak," Joe Willie panted, pointing to the rock face at the far end of the meadow.

"We ain't gonna climb that, are we?" Aiden asked.

They laughed like hell through struggling breath.

The great bear raised herself to the full measure of her height and sniffed the air with her block of a snout. There were man sounds coming from the far end of the meadow. The distance was too far for her to discern shape and form, but she could hear man and horses. The wind carried their scent to her and she huffed once and dropped to all fours again. She padded to the front of the small waterfall that sluiced out of a crack in the rock face. It would cover the sounds of her in the brush and tangle. The man beings would need to carry food and she was hungry. The summer in the high country had been hot and dry and the berry patches had been skimpy and far between. After her cubs had been killed in a rockslide she'd lost the urge to eat and settled for a loose rambling across her territory and that of other grizzlies so that now, healed some and easing away from the weight of the great sadness in her belly, she felt the high pangs of hunger again. Her skin hung slack from her sides and she was weak, light-headed sometimes from climbing the high country. She would eat. The wind was changing. She used the sound of the water to hide her travel along the stream to where she could emerge downwind of them, the horses quick to pick up her scent if she stayed where she was. The man beings were no longer travelling. Instead she could hear the sound of them, high pitched and shrill, still gathered at the lip of the meadow. She growled, walking carefully among the boulders and strewn windfall of trees.

She kept the man sounds at her shoulder as she circled. Men were drawn to water too and she knew they would travel to the end of the meadow near the rock face to rest, eat and erect the small hide dens they slept in. They would have fire. But her hunger was so great she did not fear flame. If she could not avail herself of ready-made food, pillage the sacks and boxes they left about, she was prepared to take a horse. She'd eaten horse before. The mustangs that still ran free in the upper plateaus provided a rare meal and she'd taken the old and slow before. She preferred berries, mice and smaller game to the sinewy stink of horse, but she was hungry and there would be no chase, the man beings tying them in place whenever they stopped at night.

The wind brought their smell to her again. She stopped. Carefully she rose to her full height again and waddled awkwardly about to sniff. There was something more in the air. Something beyond the foul man smell. Something old. Something ancient that she felt in the blood. A call. Like a challenge but of a higher order than that. She sniffed again, drew the smell into her and growled. She dropped to all fours and padded carefully along the stream's edge, and when she crossed it she felt the call in her blood, fully formed now, the smell of it driving her into the trees far away from the man beings to lie down in a thicket, wait for the darkness, for the time, for the response to the ancient order of things.

"Watch," Joe Willie said.

"What?" Aiden asked.

"The cliff."

"Why?"

"Just watch."

The three of them turned to face the cliff. They'd sat in the icy water under the waterfall, the three of them, Aiden and Joe Willie to assuage their tortured muscles and Claire for the pure electric thrill of it. After the heat of the climb the water felt sharp, like a knife that cut into their very centres, and they'd laughed like children in a sprinkler, shocked by the sudden chill of it. After, they'd made camp, and as the sun began to slide behind the mountains to the west across the great chasm of the valley, he'd asked them to walk with him, leading them to the lip of the meadow before pointing to the spire of rock. It sat hard against the sky, and as the sun slipped lower they saw it begin to change. It wasn't anything immediately obvious, but the longer they looked the more they saw the barely perceptible shifts of it, the motion like a gauze curtain in a small breeze absorbing the colours of the setting sun, holding it briefly then curling into yet another subtle hue. They watched as it eased from high orange to a red that revealed the iron in its face, into pink and onward, deeper, into blue-grey. When it became dark enough for the rock to reassert its stern countenance they began walking back toward the camp.

"That was awesome," Claire said. "Thank you."

"My favourite place," Joe Willie said. "I used to come here if I'd been bashed about to lay in the crick and let it heal me and then watch that rock change colour like it done there. Always made me feel right again."

"And now?" she asked.

"Now," he said, watching the cliff as he walked. "Now I been bashed about some."

"Did it help?"

"Yeah. It did."

They walked the rest of the way in silence. The sharp scent of juniper and pine added a fragrant undertone to the chill edge of the breeze, and the crunch of grass and root and stone at their feet filled the encroaching darkness with echoes off the wall of rock behind the trees. A bat flapped wildly by and they could hear the yip of coyotes from somewhere far below them. The meadow had slid through a hundred darker shades of green into a grey that intoned a long purple evening around a fire, and they stepped quicker to get it started before complete darkness fell.

While Joe Willie and Aiden scavenged kindling from the brush, Claire dug the makings of supper from the bags that

Lionel had stowed in the tarpaulins. She hummed to herself contentedly while the sound of an axe cleaving dry timber thunked in the gloaming. The two men spoke quietly and the sound of their voices was calming, the way she imagined voices had sounded forever while fires were being lit and people gathered after the events of a day. When the first flames licked upward she walked an armful of food to the log near the fire.

Aiden sat with a long stick of green alder between his knees and he squinted up at the sky and the rippled edge of rock high against it. The flames lent his face a mystic quality, and Claire smiled to see it.

"Like it?" she asked.

"It's nothing I ever saw. Or even imagined I'd see."

"It's an old place," she said.

"Yeah," he whispered, nodding. "Yeah. It's got that deep quiet about it like it's got its breath held in. Like it might explode with secrets if it spoke."

She laughed. "Yes. Like a sly old man who's seen everything."

"Grandmother," Joe Willie said, stepping into the light of the fire. "It always kinda felt like an old woman place to me. Don't know why."

"Old nonetheless," Claire said.

"Amen," he said.

They sat and Claire handed out sandwiches and fruit and placed a pot of tea near the flames that had stoked nicely. They ate quietly, each of them content to look around at the night, the sky, and the reflection of the fire off the rock in the near distance. Deep shadows behind the talus boulders danced about with the lick of the flame against the night. There was a sudden snap of branch from the far end of the meadow.

"What was that?" Aiden asked.

"Nothing," Joe Willie said. "Anything that was anything wouldn't make a sound. Sometimes a rock'll roll off the cliff and hit something. Make a noise."

"How's your leg?" Claire asked.

He looked at her, and the fire gave the sober look an intensity like a picture of a Renaissance saint. He rubbed it. "You know, it's not that bad. Hurts some but no deep-in-the-bone ache. I been tryin' this hill a long time."

"Could you ride?" Aiden asked.

Joe Willie stared into the fire and chewed awhile. He took a drink from the thermos and wiped at his mouth before he set it back down at his feet. "Maybe," he said. "But never like before."

"What was it like?" Aiden asked, quietly.

"Like the wind," Joe Willie said. He closed his eyes and leaned his head back. He drew the night air deep into his lungs and exhaled it long and slow. He slumped with it, sat upright and gazed into the fire. "Never the same way twice," he said. "Like when you step outside on a frosty morning and you feel it on your face, all full of winter and the taste of snow.

"Then you step outside again and it's summer. There's a warm to it that's all sage and cows and growing things. Or it's autumn and it's like it's full of smoke but there's nothing burning. Every time there's something in it that you make your own. Every time there's another feel to it, another story, another way of being in the world that you carry around in you forever.

"To ride is like that. Every time is different. Every time there's something more. Something more that fills you up, makes you live. Something you carry around like luggage everywhere you go. And when you lay it out you remember all of it, not just a piece, but all of it because it's what kept you living, gave you breath. Like the wind."

"You miss it," Aiden said, poking at the fire.

"Only when the wind blows," he said.

He got up and placed another log on the fire. They watched the flame gather itself around the base, lick at it appreciatively and then begin to alter it, heat it, burn it, render it into yellow, orange, blue, purple, red. Sparks flew off the blistering bark and spiralled crazily into the dark, snapping and popping. The smoke funnelled in the wind, climbing with the drafts of whirling air.

The bear stirred. She rolled her massive shoulders slowly and clambered up onto all fours. It was deep night now. She sniffed the air and caught the smell of fire in the distance. There was smoke to it and she could tell that the man beings had let it dwindle when they tired and that by now they were asleep in their hide dens. She began to move. Against the night her massive bulk was shadow, and she slipped between rock and tree easily, treading patiently, carefully, the ground beneath her compressed, surrendered to the sheer weight of her. Soundless. She worked her way to the edge of the meadow and then stood on her hind legs to sniff about. Mixed with the fire was the scent of food. Fruit. Berries. Her hunger was an ache she felt keenly, and she arched her head around to ascertain correctly what she would face at the man camp. Three. Two horses. She sniffed harder for the smell of dog but none came and she lowered herself to the ground and prowled closer.

Halfway across the meadow she froze. Stock-still against the darkness she lifted her snout and breathed. It was there— the high, piercing, primordial presence, like blood in the breeze. A growl rumbled lowly in her chest and she stepped cautiously forward. The horses hadn't got a whiff of her and they stood with their heads lowered, sleeping. She wanted fruit. That and anything else they may have left about. The horses didn't interest her. As she moved closer she could see the white sack hung from a branch beyond the fire and dens of the sleeping man beings. But each step brought the old scent closer, as though the measured walk to the camp was a procession to a spectacle, the sharp odour of it becoming more feeling than scent, a ragged anxiety in the gut of her, gnawing, growing more intense. She hadn't felt anything quite like it and it excited her.

She circled now, moving beyond the horses, arcing slowly toward the tree where the white sack hung. She could feel the edge, the weight of moment deep within her, and she kept a close eye on the man dens, knowing the danger of thunder sticks and wanting none of their explosive threat. A horse nickered. She stopped. Long moments went by before she walked again, and in the breeze the food sack swayed slightly. When she got to it she scanned the area once again before launching herself to her full height and stretching out her great claws toward the promise hung in the tree. They hadn't anticipated the size of her. She snapped the branch off along with the sack, and the loud crack of it sent the horses into paroxysms of panic, her scent reaching their flared nostrils. The night exploded around her and the ancient smell was high in the air.

Two men burst from their dens and the horses in full fear broke free of the rope that tied them in place. They galloped crazily across the meadow. A third, smaller being, a female, struggled out of her den and there was shouting, the man voices quick, hard and filled with the shock of fear.

She swatted at the sack and her claws shredded the sides of it, spilling the contents on the ground in front of her. There was the sweet smell of berries and she licked at a spot of liquid,

her tongue rewarded with the slick, gummy wash of fruit. The
men edged closer together and she looked out the tops of her
eyes as she licked at the stain of fruit. One of them separated
and approached, something clutched in his hands. It was their
chopping tool. He held it up, yelling, and it glinted severely in
the light of the half moon. She growled, loud and long. The
man being stopped and she raised herself up on her back legs
again to show her girth, her power. She bellowed, a terrible roar
that rattled off the sides of the cliff and sent the man being
backward a step or two. When he stepped forward again the
other male moved with him, this one clutching a smaller,
shinier thing and walking purposefully toward her. She roared
again and dropped to her four legs, swivelling her head in
response to their brazen approach. They used their throats to
call at each other, high, shrill notes that angered her. The blood
drummed in her ears, and as she clawed at the ground in front
of her the ancient smell asserted itself like a cloud around her
and she stood once again to declare her dominance over the two
smaller beings walking slowly, crouching, toward her. She
roared, dropped down to all fours, and as she did the female ran
up beside the two males, all of them now, screaming, waving
their arms in the air, stepping forward, jumping up and down
making a horrible noise in the night. It was the noise of fear, but
riding its crest, balanced there, was the smell of the challenge.
The bear welcomed it.

She bashed away at the ground, sending sprays of dirt
and grass to each side of her. The men stopped. She swivelled
her head and growled, then bellowed again, a great air-splitting
roar meant to dissuade any further advance. But one stepped
forward. One of them calmly walked closer, one arm raised,
clutching the chopping tool in his hand, out and away from his
body. The great bear shuddered. Its fur rippled, making it look

bigger. The other two stepped to the side, arms raised, calling out to the one who approached her. The bear sniffed the air and the call pierced her nostrils, burning like an ember from the fire that lay in a weak orange lump near the man dens. She growled and stepped closer.

The man stopped. She growled again but he did not retreat. He stood there, and as she stepped closer he raised his hands. She swung her head back and forth in front of him, telling him the moment had arrived, that this was the point the call had brought them to.

He called to her.

The bear stopped. Unsure of what was happening, she held herself still to concentrate on the man. The man talk rolled smoothly into the night and he stood there in front of her, crushable, breakable, letting the flow of the talk meld with the high presence of the ancient beckoning. She growled, lower this time, slowly. The man being stepped closer. She let him. She could not smell fear on him. Instead he was calm, stepping closer with his arms outstretched, raising them higher like the wings of the great eagle. The bear shifted her weight from paw to paw. When she raised herself up on her back legs again it was to show respect for this bravery, this surrendering to might, to power, to fate. The other two man beings stepped up beside the brave one and the bear roared, twisting its tremendous snout back and forth, spittle spraying from its jaws. They stood together in front of her and she let them have the moment.

She dropped to all fours and turned halfway around. The man beings held their place. She walked away a few steps, then looked back over her shoulder. Still they stood watching her. She walked another few steps and looked over her shoulder again. She kept doing this until she reached the edge of the meadow. The man beings stood staunchly in their place. There was a whiff of the ancient smell, and when she reached the trees she stood and bear-walked toward them and bellowed a triumphant roar for the courage of the man beings before dropping to all fours and disappearing into the trees.

The call drifted away on the wind.

They held each other. They encircled themselves with their arms and bent their heads close together, breathing in a collective relief. Claire wept quietly and her shoulders shook. Aiden fought to get his breath back. It felt as though he'd held it so long his brain had forgotten the rhythm of breathing. It took some doing to breathe normally again. Joe Willie felt a chill from the sweat he'd broken and he shivered tightly, his head clear of all thought. They stood like that for a long while until they felt security return, the sounds of the night resolving into thick alpine quiet. Finally, they broke and walked to the fire that Joe Willie stirred to life, and after he added wood and allowed the flames to climb higher into the night, each of them heaved a ragged breath, staring out into the mysteries of the dark.

"I can't stop shaking," Claire said. Aiden wrapped a blanket around her shoulders and hugged warmth into her. "I've never been so scared."

"Me neither," Joe Willie said.

"What? You walked right up to it," Aiden said. "You talked to it."

"Don't mean I wasn't scared," Joe Willie said. "And what the hell were you two doing walking up there?"

"I don't know," Claire said. "It was a reaction."

"Mighty strange reaction."

"When I saw what you were doing, I thought me with the knife was better than you out there all alone with that axe,"

Aiden said. "If I was only gonna get one poke it was gonna be a good one."

"Thank god it didn't come to that," Claire said.

"Did you feel it?" Joe Willie asked.

There was a silence. They looked at each other in the flicker of firelight and sat down on the log beside each other. They stared into the flames, and only when Aiden added another log to it was there room to speak again. "It felt like time stopped," he said, poking the embers under the new wood. "Like there was nothing else. Like there was nowhere else. Just us. Just us and the bear."

"It was like existing without breathing," Claire said. "Like air didn't exist. Only energy. Like I breathed energy through my skin."

"It felt old," Joe Willie said slowly. "Like you said before about this place. Like I'd done it before. But there was something else, something swimming underneath all that. Something strange but familiar too. Did you feel that?"

"Like fog," Aiden said. "Like fog inside."

"The oddest thing," Joe Willie said. "I knew what to do. Knew that I needed to walk up to her, look at her head on and say something."

"How do you know it was a she?" Aiden asked.

"Because I've seen her before."

"Up here?" Claire asked.

"Yes. But in dreams mostly."

"Dreams?" Aiden said.

"It was always so clear," Joe Willie said. "Like life. Like real. After the ride, in the hospital, I saw her for the first time. I thought it was the drugs, but she kept coming back. Even here. And she never felt threatening. I never felt in danger, and that's how I knew what to do tonight."

For the next while he told them about the dreams of the bear. They drank tea, smoked, and Joe Willie talked. He told them about the ride. There were details he recalled for the first time and he described See Four, how magnificent he was in his brutal strength and how he felt slipping into the rigging that night. Eight seconds. He spoke about the eight seconds that separated him from cowboy legend and the feeling of that in his chest, how it lived in every motion of preparation and cracked like lightning when the rope man pulled the chute. He talked about the pocket disappearing and the helplessness of being latched to a thousand pounds of enraged bull. Then he talked about waking in the hospital, the rage he felt, the black hole he fell into, and how the bear had come. When he spoke about the arm he reached out with his right hand and rubbed the shoulder, letting his fingertips slip into the trench where the joint had been. He told them what a cold thing rage could be and how it took forever to be able to discern warmth again, how the bear had walked him straight into the heart of his wrath and allowed him to feel it, inhabit it, and then to crave emergence like a hunger in the belly. It took rage itself to climb out, and he told them how that had confused him and how climbing the mountain had become his release, how the trail allowed him to leave bits of it, shards of it, at each turnaround point, how the bear when she had appeared at the edge of the trail had shown him that.

"So what did you say to her?" Aiden asked.

"Nin-din-away-mah-john-ee-dog," Joe Willie said.

"What's that?"

"My father's talk. Ojibway."

"Bear talk?"

"Yeah. I guess it is."

"What does it mean?" Claire asked.

Joe Willie looked away from the fire in the direction the bear had gone. "It means . . . all my relations."

"I'd have said something a lot stronger," Claire said.

"There is nothing stronger," Joe Willie said "It's an honouring phrase. It means that you see everything the way it's supposed to be. Clear of illusion. You see the relationship you have to everything, how you're tied to it, how it's all a part of you."

"And you're a part of it," she said quietly.

"Yes."

"But there was more," Aiden said. "You said a lot more than that."

"Yeah. I did," Joe Willie said.

"What?"

Joe Willie stood up and stretched. He took the long alder stick and knelt to poke at the fire, his face sombre. "It was Sioux," he said. "My mother's talk. I didn't know I remembered. But it came back to me clear as a bell. I haven't spoken it for years."

"Another honouring thing? A warrior kind of thing?" Aiden asked.

"'Twinkle, Twinkle, Little Star' actually," Joe Willie said. "It was all I could remember."

Their laughter rolled out across the meadow. The guffaws and knee slapping spilled outward from the fire like a spark, its energy careening wildly in its sudden freedom. Tears rolled freely down their faces, and in the light of that fire, their eyes shone when they looked at each other, a tribal glint, an ancient light culled from the depths of the shadows of the night and stoked by the light of a common fire. High up in the darkness, the bear heard their celebration, huffed her breath and moved deeper into the backcountry.

Aiden had gone off to sleep. There was a trace of indigo light at the edge of Iron Peak and the bird sounds told them it was approaching morning. Claire and Joe Willie sat by the fire, its light dwindling, more smoke than flame now, and flakes of ash floated up and away to land in the meadow grass yards away. They watched them float downward, drank tepid tea and watched the world shrug itself into wakefulness again.

"Why did you say what you said to the bear?" Claire asked.

He looked up at the peak before he spoke. "I spent every morning of my life as long as I can recall walking out onto the veranda. I'd sit there and look out over everything and feel like the colours of things seeped into me, like the land entered me. Like I breathed it in.

"But when I got busted up I lost it. I could go there once I got home but it was hollow, like there was a note missing, and I couldn't figure how to get it back. Then Grandpa give me that truck, and sitting in her, I could feel the stories she carried, the stories of my family, my people, and it was like the note was there, shimmering in it, in all of it, but I didn't know how to coax them out. Then the bear came. She walked toward me, looking at me out the tops of her eyes, and it was like she was telling me something. It took a long while to hear it."

"What was it?" Claire asked.

"She told me to go ahead and growl."

"You're kidding me."

"No," he said. "It was like she gave me permission to be pissed off. Pissed off about all of it. Not just being busted up but everything that came with it. My girl. My girl I was with for four years come to see me, got one look at my arm and took off. Never seen her since. She never called. Nothing. Guess she couldn't bear the thought of being seen with a cripple. I hated it for that. The arm, I mean. Hated it for its ugliness. Hated it for its useless weight. Hated it for how it made me look to people. Powerless. Useless. Helpless. Like I wasn't a man anymore. I wanted to rip it off. Tear it right off and be without it. Like if I was only gonna have one arm then I just might as well only have one arm. Just looking at it filled me with anger.

"But seeing that bear told me that the only way I was gonna hear the stories that old truck held was to walk through the rage. Growl and spit and swear. So I did. I did everything left-handed. I made that arm work. Took all the spit and venom I had inside me and put it to work. Took a long time to walk through it. To get to what the bear meant."

"What did the bear mean?" she asked.

He stood and watched the clouds slip over the edge of the peak and the faded blue sky of morning ease higher, wider where night had been. "In rodeo you always have to qualify for the big round. To prove your worth. She meant that life isn't rodeo. That I qualify. That I'm a part of things regardless. Guess I forgot that. Or never learned it in the first place."

"I know what she meant," Claire said.

"Yeah?" He went back and sat down on the log beside her. When she didn't speak right away he picked up the fire stick and poked around at the embers until a tiny lick of flame climbed up and caught the logs again. They watched the fire grow.

"Yeah," she said in a faraway voice. "The last man I was with beat me. Beat me bad. Before that he used me. Used my body. It was like I wasn't a person, I was a device, a toy. He didn't care about me or about Aiden. All he wanted was the sexy black woman. His fantasy. His reward. When he punched me it was like an indictment, a judgment for every man I'd ever served it up for. Because he wasn't the first. Sure, he was the first one to hit me but he was far from the first I ever gave it all up for. All of me, I mean.

"I swore I wouldn't let myself do that again. I wouldn't be a body. I swore I wouldn't let a man touch me. I set out to become independent, and I did. When Aiden got sent to jail it was the perfect opportunity for me to lose myself in my chase for liberty. I buried myself in work and achievement. I thought about men, found myself craving that heat, but I let it pass.

"But your mother and your grandmother taught me something. They taught me that there's a big difference between being free and being independent."

"What's that?" Joe Willie asked.

She looked up at the peak and smiled. "You can share freedom. Independence you hang on to like you hang on to a bull—alone, with all you got."

"Yes."

"That was the bravest thing I ever saw," she said, looking at him directly.

"The bear? No choice, really. Not a lot of room for bravery when you got no choice."

"I don't mean the bear. I mean telling me what you just told me."

"It ain't the bravest thing," he said.

"What is, then?"

"Choosing to tell you."

Even as they emerged from the trailhead the women could tell they were different. Claire lounged in the saddle like a trail boss, no longer obsessively vigilant about posture, balance, the placement of the heel in the stirrup. Instead, she moved in the horse's rhythm, casual, easy, letting the sway itself find her seat. Joe Willie and Aiden walked on either side of the packhorse, and they could see them talking animatedly back and forth to each other, their hands creating a parallel language in the air. Now and then Claire turned in the saddle to join in, and when she faced forward again they could see the whiteness of her smile, the head-thrown-back insouciance of her laugh.

Johanna and Victoria walked slowly across to the main barn to greet them, waving to summon the men, who were busy unloading a truck by the equipment shed. The four of them angled toward the back paddock and then leaned on the rails watching the adventurers cross the pasture. When they got closer the Wolfchilds stepped through the rails to greet them.

"Good trip?" Victoria asked.

"Amazing," Claire said, hugging them all in turn.

The men's voices were higher suddenly, and everyone listened intently as Joe Willie described the encounter with the bear. He talked while they walked the horses into the barn, where a couple of the wranglers appeared to put them up in their stalls.

"So she stood up at the edge of the meadow again then dropped down and disappeared," Joe Willie said. "We sat up until daybreak and she never showed again."

"The three of you yelling and making a lot of noise was probably the best thing you could have done," Birch said.

"It was the lullaby that calmed her down," Aiden said. When the Wolfchilds looked at him, he told them about Joe Willie's conversation, and they all laughed.

Johanna seemed unsurprised. "You two weren't strangers," she said to Joe Willie.

"No," he said. "Not hardly."

He told them about the bear, and for the first time the men were quieted, intent on his descriptions of the dreams. When he finished they nodded, then looked to the women for words.

"The bear is a protector," Johanna said. "She carries medicine meant to heal. She told you that in the hospital and she kept coming back to you to help you through because this healing would be the hardest thing you ever did."

Joe Willie nodded. "That's a fact," he said.

"But the most important thing is the thirteen steps she took in her last visit. That was the biggest healing sign she left you," Johanna said.

"Why's that?" Joe Willie asked, leaning forward to catch his mother's words.

"Thirteen is a spiritual number. There's thirteen poles in a teepee. There's thirteen principle stones in a medicine wheel. A turtle's shell has thirteen segments in its middle. Each of them has a principle attached to it that tells us how to live in community."

"So?" he asked.

"So," Johanna said, "she took thirteen steps and you counted them. The bear was telling you that you could only heal yourself through community, only come back by letting other people into your lodge, let them join you in your journey."

"What do the thirteen mean?" he asked.

"Things like loyalty, trust, honesty. Things you already know. What we taught you or tried to teach you all your life. Things you forgot because of your pain."

"Love especially," Victoria said.

"Pardon?" He looked at her.

"It's the hardest principle when you hurt like that. Letting yourself be loved through it," his grandmother said.

"You had to make that journey back to it on your own. The bear was telling you to be strong, that you had it in you to make it back."

"Did I?"

"You tell me."

"I made it to the peak," he said.

"And?"

"It was beautiful. Like always."

"Amen to that," she said and smiled.

It was a 1982 Cadillac engine. Aiden had found it in a hot-rod magazine, and after explaining the subtleties of a 249-cubic-inch V6 to Joe Willie, they'd ordered it. They stood staring at it in the hoist three days later. It gleamed, swaying slightly in the air as though eager to be churning, and Joe Willie reached up a hand to it and felt the cool, hard promise of it.

"Tell me again," he said.

"Jesus," Aiden grumbled good-naturedly. "Digital fuel injection with 190 foot-pounds of torque in 249 cubic inches."

"It'll go?"

"Like stink."

"Aiden," Claire said sharply.

"Cowboy talk, Mom."

"Is that what it is?"

"Yes'm," he said, nodding and touching the brim of his hat with two fingers.

She laughed. "What have I created?" she asked of the ceiling.

"A bull rider," Joe Willie said.

Aiden looked at him. "What are you saying?"

"I'm saying we need to get to work now."

"Bulls?"

"Damn straight, bulls."

"No more gymnastics and getting socked in the face?"

"Oh yeah, you still gotta do that. And I need you running every day and lifting weights too. But we can rig you up now," Joe Willie said, walking to the door of the shed. "And I mean now."

"Well, let's go! Let's pick out a couple of those bulls over there and get at it," Aiden said, hurrying after him. "I'll go wrangle them myself."

"Oh, no," Joe Willie said. "You're not riding them bulls there."

"Which bulls, then?"

"Them bulls," Joe Willie said, hooking a thumb toward the stock truck that was making the turn into the Wolfchilds' driveway.

They were the most frightening things Claire had ever seen. She stood next to Aiden watching the bulls thunder down the ramp and into the corral. Joe Willie was standing with his father and grandfather talking with the two men from the truck. The wranglers herded the bulls out of the truck yelling and whistling loudly, repeatedly, so that the whole process took on an air of urgency, volatility, danger. As they thudded by her Claire could feel the weight of them. Immense. Colossal. Dangerous. They shook the ground as they trotted malevolently into the corral and they took up her whole field of vision beyond the rails. She stepped back. As tall as a man at their shoulders, with heads as wide and thick and heavy as a car bumper. Some of them had nubs of horn like clenched fists and others bore a broad hook of horn at each side of their head. Each of them was covered with great clumps and slabs of muscle, and their hooves were heavy, devilish blocks of granite.

Joe Willie came and stood on the other side of Aiden.

"Brahmas," Aiden said with awe.

"Not exactly," Joe Willie said. "Brafords. Brahma and Hereford cross."

"Rodeo bulls," Claire said.

"Real ones," Aiden said, staring.

"The Brahma blood makes them good athletes, good jumpers, buckers, spinners. They'll kick like sumbucks. The Hereford in them makes them muscular. It gives them gumption too."

"Mean, you mean?" Claire asked.

"I mean gumption."

She looked at him. There was a no-nonsense look on his face that was neither devious nor condescending. Instead, it bore the weight of simple, direct truth and Claire trusted him. Trusted him with Aiden.

"If he can ride these he can ride anything," Joe Willie said.

"Are they dangerous?"

"Not if you leave them alone."

"God," Aiden said. "You see them on TV and they look big enough, but when you stand right beside them they're like tanks. Nothing like the bulls here."

"Our bulls are greenhorn bulls," Joe Willie said. "These are the real deal. Pure no-detour bred-to-buck rodeo stock. Chaos with hooves, horns and attitude."

He clapped an arm around Aiden's shoulders. Together they leaned on the rails and peered through at the bulls milling around the water trough kicking up tufts and puffs of dust like schoolyard bullies. Claire laid her arm across Joe Willie's, the warmth of him comforting, assuring, the feel of her son vital as breath. The bulls clomped about, their eyes flat, baleful, rimmed with white so that when their gaze caught her Claire felt studied. Some of them shook their heads so that their horns jabbed the air like pitchforks and they scraped at the ground anxiously.

"There's thirteen of them," Aiden said quietly.

"Amen to that," Joe Willie said.

Aiden stood up then and turned to face him. Joe Willie rose slowly and the two of them stood face to face, a foot apart, wordlessly.

"You can change your mind," Joe Willie said. "No shame in that."

"Rig me up," Aiden said.

They turned and walked toward Birch and Lionel, who were waiting with the truck wrangler. As they got to the front of the truck Aiden stopped and turned. He looked at Claire intently a moment, then slowly raised one arm and held it out to her, reaching for her with an open hand. She walked to her son.

The ritual of bull riding began. Joe Willie was a patient and methodical teacher. He showed both Claire and Aiden each piece of equipment and its purpose. He explained the how and why of it so clearly that there wasn't a doubt in either of their minds about the level of respect a man had to carry into the back lot to prepare. *Intention.* He used that word repeatedly so that it took on the clarity of a mantra, and Claire found herself examining the rope and buckle and leather of it all scrupulously, envisioning each static piece hung on the rails as alive, taut with purpose, made kinetic by intention. It was a world. It was a new and strange and wonderful and scary territory. For Claire it was a geography whose trails were blazed by will, and as she watched Joe Willie lead her son through the range of gear she sensed the toughness it asked of men, the grit, the determination, the sheer courage it took merely to intend, and at the bottom of it all, the soulfulness, the awareness of the animal, the relationship with it and the respect that mapped it all. She saw that in Joe Willie as he talked. She admired it. She wanted it for her son.

"You tie your boots on with this," he said, handing a long length of thong to Aiden, who watched with a grave expression.

"How come?" he asked.

"Bull hide's tough as hell," Joe Willie said. "When you come to spur it that hide'll rip your boots right off your feet when he's bucking."

"Jesus."

Joe Willie handed him a thick roll of padding. He showed him how it attached to the Kevlar vest. "Vest's for your gut. You can always break a rib. That's nothing, really, but you can get horned in the belly or the back. The roll's for the back of the neck on accounta your head'll be slamming backwards some on these bulls."

"Some?"

"Reckon about eighteen times or so in eight seconds."

"What's the helmet for?"

"You kidding me?"

"I was hoping so."

They laughed. It wasn't a nervous laugh, and Claire marvelled at it. Instead it was convivial, casual, the danger imminent, accepted and welcomed. It was the laughter of men joined by purpose and she found herself somewhat jealous of that, as though risk keyed a latent gene in men that allowed them levity and solidarity, a slouching, off-handed candour a woman could only wonder at.

"They get like children, don't they?"

She turned to see Johanna smiling at her and at the sight of Joe Willie and Aiden going through the rote of preparation. "Yes. In a way," Claire said. "I always wondered at ballyhoo and bluster, though."

"Me too," Johanna said. "When you're around cowboys long enough you come to see it's what they have to do to get ready. You eventually see the little boys inside the men. Good boys. Gentle, kind. Genuine."

The wranglers were shunting a big brownish-red bull into the chute, and it clunked and thumped and rattled the wooden rails as it passed. The bull bawled loudly right beside her and Claire started. She could see the horns of it raking the air above the top rail.

"You ever worry?" she asked.

"All the time."

"Do they?" She watched Aiden, the mother in her watching her son wander off alone into the schoolyard with the big boys, knowing she could never call him back and even if she did, he would never be able to look at her the same.

"Birch always said there was never no percentage in it. A bull's gonna be a bull regardless, was his reckoning."

"That's not too comforting. Look at them," Claire said.

"A little on the large side, wild, hairy, live too much in the testicles. Hell, we've had *men* like that, Claire. Why sweat a bull?"

They laughed.

Climbing the rails was like scaling his anxiety. Birch and Joe Willie waited for him, and Aiden stepped carefully, feeling the slats on the instep and pushing purposefully, reaching tentatively with his other foot until it found purchase on the next rail. The trepidation increased with each rail. Unlike the smaller bulls he'd ridden so far, Aiden didn't have to step down as far to reach the animal's back. This bull filled the chute. There was barely room for his legs on either side, and he eased them carefully down around the bull's great girth. Its stillness unsettled him. When it felt his legs along its ribs it shimmied, and the loose wobble of skin made it hard for him to feel, to grip with his thighs. He stepped up onto the rail again to settle himself. He looked at Birch and Joe Willie for some kind of signal or comment, but they were busy with the bull rope and the clank belt.

"Aren't you gonna say something?" he asked.

"Like what?" Joe Willie asked.

"I don't know. Advice."

"Advice. Hmm. Don't have any."

"Birch?"

"Son, you earned the right to be here." Birch handed him the end of the bull rope. "You rode bulls, worked your butt off, faced off against a grizzly. Any advice I give you now's gonna be minor."

"Go ahead."

"Son?" Birch said, looking at Joe Willie.

"All right. When that chute opens he's either gonna blow or buck. He blows, he runs out flat a few steps before he explodes. He bucks, he's taking air right off. You gotta be prepared for either."

"How?"

"Grit your teeth. Feel him. Don't let go."

"That's it?"

"Anymore'll busy your head too much. You know what to do. If you didn't you wouldn't be here. Trust me."

"Okay," Aiden said, and Joe Willie clapped him firmly on the back.

He stepped down and sat. His legs felt stretched way too wide. The bull was enormous. The top of its head between the horns was as wide as a small table, and the pocket behind its shoulders seemed ridiculously small now—the safety zone he would claim as his own when the chute opened was a postage stamp of hide. He settled into it, placed his gloved hand into the rigging, and Birch began to haul on the rope. He felt the tension, the joining to the bull intensified as the rope tautened. "More," he said through clenched teeth.

He flexed his fingers, felt the downward strain of the rope and the feel of the bull against the flat of the back of his hand. "More. More," he said, and the rope felt like it welded him to the bull. He flexed his fingers again and nodded sharply. Joe Willie leaned down and Aiden could see his face at the periphery of his vision. He stared intently at the back of the bull's horns. He felt a hand on his back and one on his chest and he straightened, pushing his seat inward and scrunching the helmet down tighter on his head before raising his free arm high and to the side.

"Everything," Joe Willie whispered hard in his ear. "Everything now. Pull everything you ever felt down into your gut. All the anger, the hurt, the fucking joy, the tears. Pull it down and feel it. Feel it. When that chute opens, let it fly. Let it fucking fly with this sumbitch and you'll be his equal. Got it?"

"Got it," Aiden said, seeing the pale green walls of the joint, the blood, the tears of his mother, the bruises and cuts on her face, the crumpled form of Cort Lehane, and the empty black of prison nights. He leaned his head back until he felt the cords in his neck stretch tight as he grimaced into the clear blue of the sky, then he nodded sharply once, hard, let it all go with a huff and the chute opened.

Detonation.

He felt propelled upward and outward at the same time. The bull launched itself from the chute, and the jarring impact as it landed slammed his head back hard against the padding at his neck and he saw nothing but a flare of sky and felt the incredible tear of his arm in the rigging. His legs thrust out automatically to touch the shoulders with the rowel of the spurs and he felt himself thrust forward over the shoulder. The ridge of horn across the top of the bull's head seemed inches from his eyes, and he pulled with all his might with his lower back to get into the pocket again just as the bull kicked and spun at the same time. It spun quickly. Like a dervish. He flew off the rigging and felt himself spinning flat, spread-eagled, counterclockwise, once, twice, three times, four, before the hard dirt of the corral slammed into his back and his breath huffed out of him completely.

He lay there stunned. The wranglers chased the bull off to the exit chute, and he groaned as Lionel then Birch and finally Joe Willie arrived in a clomp of boot heels to help him up. The horizon tilted crazily. He leaned on their arms and his breath returned in a cool blue wash.

"Damn. That was a hot three seconds," Birch said.

"Sumbuck could jump," Lionel said.

"Kicked like a bastard too," Joe Willie said. "That spin was crazy."

Aiden tore the helmet from his head and when he looked at the three of them they could see the fire in his eyes. He shook his head hard, spat into the dirt, then wiped at his mouth with his gloved hand. "Again," he said and stomped off toward the chute.

She took the engine into her like an ear takes a song. When they eased the block down onto the frame the old truck settled some on the revamped springs and then sat proudly, the heft of the engine borne easily. Joe Willie stepped back to look. It didn't look like much to him at that point, just the frame and the new block with the drive shaft and other vital workings still to be installed before the freshly painted body went on. Still, she looked strong.

Aiden slipped down into the pit to look things over and pushed a circled thumb and finger out at him. Joe Willie nodded. Aiden had talked him into allowing a mechanic from town to do the nitpicky work of installing everything, and he saw the sense in it. He was surely lost when it came to this, and Aiden was plum tired from the effect of four bulls on the first day. Besides, he'd sooner have it done right once than mucked about with a dozen times. Getting her on the road was what mattered to him now, and his pride and the anger that drove it in the early days with her had been replaced with a quiet devotion, a yearning to see her free, wide open on another road, gathering another generation of stories into her steel-and-leather bosom. If he had to step aside for a real truck guy to do the intricate work, so be it. He'd be there to watch, to learn, to come to understand how to care for her once she was ready, how to keep her moving. It was a settled feeling in his chest when he thought of it. He reached out a hand to touch the steel of her frame and felt the cool hardness like the granite and iron it had sprung from. She was a marvel. Sitting there, skeletal, the engine shining at her front end, the heart of her waiting to beat.

Aiden climbed out of the pit and stood beside him. He handed him a smoke and they stood there awhile casually examining the work they'd done together. Four bulls, twelve seconds. That's what Aiden's first day on the rodeo bulls had earned him. Twelve seconds. They'd been a handful of ornery and Joe Willie wondered how he might have made out. The smell of them set off pangs of something like jealousy in him, the fight still in him, the reaction to the challenge still able to flare. But watching the kid satisfied that too. He was a rider. Joe Willie could see that. There was a fraction of a second of adjustment each time, a minor shift in approach that told him the kid was thinking it through, learning to see himself out of the chute long before it opened, learning to anticipate, to read the animal beneath him and prepare himself. When the bull erupted he saw the shift play out, saw the kid try another trick, saw him fly out of the rigging, land roughly in the dirt and stand up quicker, angrier, ready for another go. A rider. He looked at him out the corner of his eye. Slouched. Easy with his body. Hurtin' for certain. But taking it, accepting it, learning from it.

"She's gonna be hot," Aiden said.

"Yessir. I changed the order on the paint job, though."

"What? Thought we agreed on deep metallic blue. Like the sky above the peak."

"We did. I just added a little something."

"Jesus. I can't wait to see what the cowboy mind came up with. Flames and shit. Maybe a cartoon bull? Pinstripes like a lasso curled around the whole body?"

"Never thought of that. Maybe I'll call back and add some of that. Just wait. You'll like it." He punched him lightly on the shoulder. Aiden winced and arched the shoulder around. "Hurt?" Joe Willie asked.

"Some," Aiden said. "That last bull. Caught me leaning, couldn't adjust in the air and landed pretty square on it."

"Could be worse."

Aiden looked at him. He took a long draw on the cigarette, held it deep in the lungs, then let it go slowly, head tilted back and watching the smoke plume toward the roof of the shed. "Yeah," he said. "You still hurt?"

"Some," Joe Willie said. "That last bull. Caught me leaning."

They snickered. Aiden scratched at his ear and when he looked at Joe Willie again there was a grave expression on his face. "Was it worth it? Getting busted up like that?"

Joe Willie pinched out the smoke and put the butt in his chest pocket. "Love'll bust you up sometimes," he said. "Hurts like a bitch for a spell. Long spell. But in the end you come to prefer it. Knowing that it was love done it to you. Not something else. You can get by knowing that."

"It was worth it, then?"

Joe Willie looked at him. "Damn straight," he said.

He ran across the wide stretch of pasture to the road, climbed through the rails of the fence and continued trotting casually along the shoulder. The dog followed him but turned back once he'd ventured down the road a ways. He waved to it and picked up the pace. The muscles in his legs were tight and sore, but as he loped through the first mile they became more elastic and he held the pace easily. Around him the valley was like a postcard, bathed in an impossible morning light. There were shades of green around him that Aiden had never seen, never known were possible. Against the sky a hawk circled, and he caught the flare of brown at the edge of a hill that marked a coyote's quick escape from sight. Ground squirrels chattered in the pastures on each side of him, and here and there was the small smudge of cattle or horses against the green. The land was full. He breathed it deep into him and felt his heartbeat in his chest, strong and hard. When he got to the turn toward town he stopped, jogged in place a moment and then turned back down the road toward Wolf Creek Ranch. The valley plowed an elongated V toward the far horizon, and as he ran he closed his eyes now and again to seal the image of it in his mind. He was sweating now and he rubbed a hand across his brow and back through his hair. He felt the keen sense of his own blood hot in his veins, his breathing hard in his ears and a clarity of vision and thought he'd never had. He shadow-boxed as he ran, flicked out the right and then the left in imaginary jabs and smiled at the feeling of freedom in his limbs.

He'd ride again today. Another four bulls anyway, maybe six. He wanted that feeling back, the feeling he got in the chute when everything had been done that could be done and it was just him and the animal. Waiting. Waiting for the release, the challenge, the answer to the call. He felt alive then, fully and completely alive, and even though the rodeo bulls were winning these initial battles, he got up off the ground with more determination and intensity than before, the ground pounding an education into his bruised muscles. Nine more to ride. Nine more challenges. He sent his mind through the ritual of preparation, seeing himself rubbing rosin into the bull rope, the elaborate pantomime of the ride, lacing his boots to his feet, pulling the chaps snug to his legs, and the weight of focus in his eyes. He ran faster. When he got to the driveway he sprinted full out, kicking up puffs of dust, his arms churning, knees raised high with each stride and the feeling in him, rich and steeped by the run, of aliveness, readiness, certainty. He sprinted all the way to the main barn, where he towelled off some, caught his breath and then picked up the first of the weights Joe Willie had bought for him. He lifted them. Filled with intention.

They were on the veranda shelling peas when they saw him run by. Claire watched him until he disappeared into the black of the barn and then she shelled solemnly, letting the small marbles roll off her fingers and drop into the bowl at her feet. The Wolfchilds let her be, and for a long while there was nothing but the sounds of the ranch in the early morning and the skreel of hawks in the wind.

"This place has been good for him," she said.

"Yes. He's lighter now," Johanna said. "He doesn't fill space the same way."

"I've never seen him look so determined."

"When you find a dream it changes you," Birch said.

"What do you mean?"

"Bulls," he said.

"Bulls?"

"He's a rider. He can feel it. He knows it and he wants it now."

"We're only here a short time," she said. "After that I don't know what he'll do. In the city there's nothing like this."

"I don't expect you'll find that he wants to be back there so much," Birch said. "There was a cowboy in him waiting to be born, and now that he is there won't be nothing less than that for him. Can't be."

"He's not a cowboy."

"Try telling him that."

"Bill Pickett," Lionel said. He looked at Claire and leaned forward with his elbows on his knees. "He was black. He was the one invented bulldogging."

"What's bulldogging?"

"When a cowboy jumps off a horse in full gallop to wrestle a steer to the ground."

"Why?" she asked, and they all laughed.

"Part of the life," he said. "Part of the tradition of rodeo now. Probably didn't look to Bill Pickett's mama that he was cut out to cowboy either. But he was. Gave the sport a whole new look."

"Black cowboys? I had no idea."

"Been many a good man I knew was black," Lionel said. "Damn good riders and some damn fine men. Got a book in there tells all about it. There's a whole history, a whole tradition of black cowboys. He should see that."

"Truth is," Birch said, "was black men that settled the west. Did all the hard work leastways."

"Are you kidding me?"

"No, ma'am," he said. "When he's riding the boy's coming from a rich past, a rich history."

Claire looked at him a long moment. "A tradition."

"Yes," Lionel said. "A damn good and proud one."

"I'll look at that book," she said.

He found it on the tenth bull. There was a moment, just before he was launched into the air again, when Aiden sensed the pocket behind the bull's shoulders, felt if he closed his eyes he could see it, begin to work it like the bull worked it, energy against energy, force against force, that small area the centre of everything. It was a brief intuition. The moment he focussed on the sensory perception of the pocket he lost it and the bull spun into his rigging hand. Picking himself up off the ground and watching the bull kick its way into the exit chute he shook his head and turned to prepare to remount.

"What happened?" Joe Willie asked him when he got to the fence.

"You saw what happened. He spun into my wrap hand and I lost it."

"That's not what I meant. You looked different up there."

"When exactly," Aiden asked with a grin, "in the three seconds I was up there?"

"It was six."

"Really?"

"Really. I thought you were gonna break it."

Joe Willie had limited him to three bulls a day with a day's rest in between. Five days had passed since he rode the first four bulls. In that time Aiden calculated that he'd spent a grand total of twenty-seven seconds rigged up. The bulls were wild. They blasted out of the chute and into paroxysms of spins and kicks and bucks that had been impossible for him to read, gauge, predict and hold through. For the brief time he was mounted he paid attention to the fine points of riding, the free hand high and wide, the legs spurring the shoulders repeatedly and his upper body leaned with his perception of the bull's movements. And he paid attention to his landings in the dirt. Each time he sat on the top rail, alone, far away from the Wolfchilds, the wranglers or his mother, whom he could see watching him nervously, checking his condition from a distance, worrying. In those moments he replayed the ride in his mind. He tried to recollect the twists and yanks and crazy elevations of the bull. But now as he looked up at Joe Willie straddling the top rail, he forgot the animal's moves and imagined the pocket, saw it clearly, felt it in his seat, hips and thighs through the six seconds of recollection. "I'm gonna break it," he said.

Joe Willie studied him. "Yeah," he said.

"Can I ask you a question?"

"Fire away."

"If I do it, if I make eight on the last three, all of the last three, will you get me my permit?"

"You want to rodeo?"

"Not exactly," Aiden said. "I want to ride bulls. I want to join the professional circuit."

"The Professional Bull Riders Association? You want to tour?"

"Yes. More than anything."

Joe Willie shook his head. "Those boys aren't even cowboys. Not all of them. Hell, they go to school for it. They go to college and then join up. For the TV. For the lights, for the money. It's all for the money, Aiden, not for the sport, not for the tradition."

"Still."

"Still nothing."

"Joe Willie, I'm not even a cowboy," Aiden said. "I'm a city kid. But I know how it makes me feel when I'm up there. I know how it makes me feel even when I'm spitting dirt. When I limp around after and every muscle in my body is crying out for me to stop the insanity, I still love it. It's the only thing that makes sense to me."

Joe Willie climbed down off the fence. He pushed his hat back on his head, put his hands in the back pockets of his jeans and leaned against the fence. He looked over at Claire, who watched the two of them closely. "If you do it," he said, "I'll get you your permit. But to rodeo. You want to tour, you tour the rodeo circuit just like I did, like my daddy and my grandfather did. Like my great-grandfather. You respect the tradition that gave this to you. You respect the tradition that woke up everything you feel inside of you. It ain't worth it to me any other way.

"Because it's not just about the ride. Hell, that's only the smallest part. It's all of it. Everything. Hitting the road in an old jalopy and watching those miles spin over horizon after horizon. Waking up in a rodeo motel with eight other cowboys and their women, the room ripe with feet and liniment and bulls and beer. The colour of the talk. Everything coming out like songs. Walking into a back lot and knowing that you know the people you prepare with. Knowing that no matter what happens out there you already won, you're already safe, you're already home. Feeling like you're living in something bigger than bulls, bigger than competition, bigger than you. You live like that and it becomes your heart, Aiden. The way you breathe. You owe it to yourself to discover that." He turned away. "And you owe it to me."

He walked a few steps off and then turned quickly on his heel. "One other thing," he said, so quietly Aiden had to strain to hear. "The ache I felt when it was gone? It wasn't in my bones. You owe it to yourself to feel that too someday. Busted or just plain old, you owe it to yourself to feel that."

Aiden watched him walk away. When Joe Willie reached the end of the corral, he shouted after him, "You got a deal."

Joe Willie walked through the gate, one fist raised high in the air.

She found him in the small room at the back of the barn. It was evening and he was washing the dust of the day from him and whistling. She stood in the doorway and watched him. He had a bowl set on a small table and he sloshed his hands about while he lathered the soap and then raised his palms to his face to spread the lather around and then slopped water over his face and hair. Shirtless, he looked lean and lithe from her vantage point, until he turned and made a grab for the towel that hung off the back of a chair. The arm. It still shocked her. Against the rest of him it hung like a crooked afterthought and she stared at it until she felt his stillness and realized he was watching her. He slowly draped the towel over his left shoulder and and waited for her to say something.

She carried the book Lionel had given her and she walked to the table and laid it there. Then she turned to him and very slowly reached for the towel. He let her. It slid off his shoulder and she hung it off the chair back. She pressed her lips together and reached her hand up to his left shoulder and traced the narrow blade of bone to where it dropped off at the ruined joint. She let her fingertips slide into the small depression between the nub of the upper arm bone and the pocket of the shoulder and then traced the line of his arm over the region of the bicep down to the elbow. He didn't move. She formed a cup with her palm and fingers and rubbed the length of it down to the wrist and back up again, and when she reached the shoulder joint again, she looked at him and smiled softly.

"It's beautiful," she said.

"Never much thought so," he said.

"It is," she said. "It makes you beautiful."

He laughed then, one short, sharp bark of laughter, and then he reached for the shirt that hung against the back of the door. "Most women wouldn't think so," he said.

"Most women aren't me."

He slipped into the shirt and looked at her carefully. "What do you mean?" he asked.

"I mean we all have flaws. But most of us keep them a secret, or at least we spend an awful lot of time and money learning how to hide them. The men I've known have all kept the dark parts of themselves away from me—their hurts, their pain, their rage, their shame, their shattered dreams. I never knew who I was dealing with until it was too late.

"But your arm is a testament, Joe Willie. It speaks of everything you've gone through and it's a plain and direct and honest voice. That's what makes you beautiful," she said and rubbed his arm through the shirt again.

"Always seen it as a testament to failure," he said.

She laughed now. "You couldn't fail anything if you tried."

"You neither."

"I failed my son."

"Bullshit. Where do you think he got the gumption?"

"He went to prison, Joe Willie."

"He walked out whole, Claire. He got that ability from you. He got that from watching you tussle with all the crap you endured. You taught him how to carry on, no one else."

"And the anger?"

"Same place."

"Me?"

"Yeah. But you took it to eight. You rode it out. You made it work for you. He saw all that and it made him different."

"You're saying that I'm a good mother?"

He started to button the shirt. He watched his hands while he did and made the fingers of the left do the delicate threading of the button through the hole. When he finished he gave her a tight-lipped little grin.

"Can't say about that," he said. "I was just saying that you're a real good woman. Most times they're one and the same. From my experience, anyhow."

"Thank you," she said.

"No," he said. "Thank you."

It was a brindle bull with a full rack of horns, and Aiden could feel it before he lifted a leg to the rail. It filled space like a mountain, seeming to pull all available light into it so that it drew your eye even from a distance. It stood quiet in the chute, and when he did begin to climb he could feel it pull its own energy tight, draw itself down into its centre, gather itself like a storm front. Readying itself. He pinched his lips together, flexed his shoulders a tad and began to focus his own energy so that when he straddled the top rail, then stepped over and crossed his leg over top of the bull his face was composed, stern, hardened, like a mountain.

Birch and Joe Willie spoke to him but he nodded out of rote, not really hearing their words. Slipping down onto the bull, he felt a quickening in his blood, and when it shimmied he was ready for it and had his heels on the rail before it moved. The bull bawled, clacked its horns against the rails and clomped its hooves in the dirt. Aiden allowed himself a small grin and then settled in the rigging. He felt Joe Willie haul on the bull rope, and when he flexed his fingers the pressure in his palm was heavy and with his free hand he tugged on the top of the glove, slipping any wrinkles flat, the rope imprinting itself into his hand. He flexed again and nodded. When Joe Willie's shadow cleared his field of vision he saw nothing but the bull, the ridge of horn across its head like a long, flat fist. He stared at it. Hard. As he did he drew himself forward, straighter in the rigging, putting himself deep in the pocket and feeling the cleft of shoulder bone with his pelvis, thighs and knees. He slowly raised his free hand up and away, curving his spine and pressing his groin tight to the wrap of the rope. When he felt positioned he scrunched the helmet low on his head so that the edge of it was like an eyebrow, then raised the hand back up clear of the top rail.

He nodded sharply, and Lionel pulled the chute open.

The pocket flattened into a run and he spurred the bull out hard into the corral. It launched itself into a wild series of running kicks, high, explosive, the back end of it almost perpendicular to the ground so that when he arched his back into it Aiden lost contact with the horizon. But he held the pocket. The bull spun first left then right in a dazzling change of direction that Aiden felt coming with his knee. It

bucked, all four hooves clearing the ground, the impact jarring him, driving his head back into the fat roll of padding,
the strain at the shoulder of his wrap hand immense, the
weight like pulling up a piano on a rope. The percussive clank
of the cowbell filled his ears. The bull gyrated wildly, kicking
its back legs and twisting its hindquarters right, left, right,
left, and Aiden felt the whip of it on his neck muscles, the
helmet slipping down partly over his eyes. There was a slip in
the wrap and he squeezed his rope hand tighter, feeling the
burn along the cords of his forearm and wrist, the bull kicking out and into another wild spin to the left, and he heard
Joe Willie yell, "Time!"

The pickup riders appeared suddenly, and Aiden reached
out with his free arm, snaring the rider's shoulders and leaning
himself out and away from the rigging. He felt himself separate
from the bull, and the clanking of the cowbell ceased as the
clank belt tumbled to the dirt. Aiden started to run in mid-air
as the pickup rider slowed, so that when his feet hit the ground
he ran easily, catching his balance with a few strides and jogging
to a stop in the middle of the corral. The Wolfchilds were all
running toward him, even Joe Willie clumping along at full
speed. They swept him up in a full embrace and Aiden lost himself in the hard squeeze of men, the smell of them rich and
warm with tobacco, sweat and leather, the hardness of their
muscles comforting in their taut joy, and they leaped about
yelling in triumph and when they finally let him go he looked at
them, their faces shining with a glow in the eyes a part of him
knew as respect. Joe Willie stood nodding, tight-lipped, proudly,
and he stepped aside to allow Claire to approach him.

His mother was crying. He reached out to her and she
fell against his chest, squeezing him tighter than he could ever
have imagined her small body held the strength for.

"It's okay," he said, combing her hair with his ungloved hand. "I'm all right."

"I know," she said. "That's why I'm crying."

When Joe Willie stepped forward to them Aiden looked at him a moment then took his hand from his mother's head and held his arm out to him. Joe Willie put his arms around the two of them and they stood together in the middle of the arena and let the feel of it touch them.

"Look at this," Joe Willie said.

"What?" Lionel asked.

The truck was draped with a tarpaulin, and in the shadow of the evening it resembled a sweat lodge. Lionel couldn't shake the image of it even as Joe Willie lifted the edge of the tarp from the front end and a flare of sunset caught the new chrome bumper. As he eased it up over the grillework the old man raised a hand to his chin in admiration. The metal on the grille was chromed, and he watched as Joe Willie skimmed the tarp back, revealing more of the front end of her. When he'd gotten to the hood he folded the tarp along it and stepped back for the old man to see. "Come look now," he said.

Lionel stepped forward. The hood was a deep metallic blue, venturing close to purple but holding itself to blue so that you almost could feel its energy, its wish to linger there, to remain, to not fade or alter, like the line of the sky rich with encroaching darkness. He saw his reflection in the chrome and paint, elongated, so that the fingers he held out to touch her were spindly and long like vines. The metal skin of her was cool, and he closed his eyes as the nub of his fingers grazed her surface. The dog sniffed eagerly about the edge of the tarpaulin, curious at the sharp smell of epoxy and new paint. In the dying light, the chrome took on the orange of the setting sun, and Joe Willie lit the old hurricane lamps while the old man stood silently looking at the hood of her. As the sun lowered even further the shed took on an antiquated light, the rustic warmth of a barn, a stable, a work shed where pioneers, settlers, ranchers laboured, the fruits of their efforts carried within them, borne into everything they touched—a simple, elegant light. Joe Willie put a hand on his shoulder and his grandfather grinned at him and covered it with his own, patting it gently. Then Lionel stepped closer to the truck and placed his palm on the words curled across the nose of her in unobtrusive burnt-orange script. He traced the edges of the letters with one finger.

"Dream Wheels," he said.

"Yeah. Look at the rest of her."

He lifted the edge of the tarp and began to pull it back. They could see the dark blue of it, shiny in the light. He walked toward the cab and pulled the tarp along behind him. It slid up over the cab and dropped along the box, gradually revealing the back end of her, the new tires suddenly squat and firm beneath her, resplendent with flashy aluminum rims. She sat low on the tires, closer to the ground than before, and the tires themselves were wider and Lionel could see how the wheel wells had been scooped out to allow them to fit, the fenders bubbled out impressively. There were lacquered stakes along the length of the box, three high, the thick, round heads of bolts lending it a solidity that spoke of the times it had come from, a craftsman's time, a time when hands fashioned everything, made them firm, strong, able.

"Birch," Joe Willie said, laying a hand on one of the stakes. "Like a talking stick. Like the Teaching Scrolls of the Ojibway."

He opened the door to the cab and they stepped forward to peer inside. He hadn't changed anything, but it had all been retooled, refinished so that the seats were plump and full, the dashboard showed all the original gauges in clear, glossy metal and glass. The upholstering was repadded and polished. "Still got all the scars," he said. He looked at Lionel and smiled. "Scars and breaks make us what we are. Give us character. Make us unique. Make us beautiful. She taught me that."

They moved from inspecting the cab to look at the new front end. The fender skirts were flared some to accommodate the matching tires to the back. They rose in a sweeping line upwards then downwards to the bulge of the headlamps. As they walked along they could feel the swell of her, the flow created by the chopping, the trimming, and the truck felt even more and more like it wanted to roar along a highway, like it would rear at any moment on its back wheels. Each of them lay a hand on the lacquered metal and felt its cool promise.

"The sum of us," Joe Willie said and looked at his grandfather. "No matter where we come from, the stories we carry are the sum of us. That's what Grandma said. I lost that for a while. Lost that tie to tradition. Figured the line ended with See Four. But you know what I learned?"

"What?" Lionel asked quietly.

"I learned that tradition is like the old girl here. She's got a new heart and a new body but she still carries the stories. She can't help but do that because we lived in her, all of us, she's got the juice of our living all over her, in every crease and dent and scar. Our story. Don't matter that she looks different now. Don't matter that it's a different world. Hell, it don't even matter that I'm different now. Because it's still the same story. Our story.

"I thought I had to protect her, keep her the same, the way she always was. I thought that if I changed her I'd lose her somehow. Lose me. Lose me even more than I felt like I had after See Four. But the strange thing is, the change let me keep her. The alteration let me reclaim her, let me reclaim myself, my story, add it to her like a coat of new paint and chrome. Strange, huh?"

"Not so strange," Lionel said. "Your mother and grand-mother knew all along."

Joe Willie nodded. "They would," he said.

He handed Lionel the keys. They were held in a small replica of a rodeo buckle. "You told me that she would take me wherever I wanted to go."

"And where is that?" Lionel asked.

"Here," he said.

They held each other in the antique light of the lamps. They held each other and breathed deep, slow breaths, patting each other between the shoulder blades and rocking on the balls of their feet, their faces pulled tight. When they separated they looked at each other a moment, then turned to look at the old girl again.

"We need to show the others now," Lionel said. "And we got a bull rider to train."

"Amen to that," Joe Willie said.

EPILOGUE

he Old Ones say that the path of a true human being is a Red Road. It's a blood colour. Like blood it flows out of our histories, bearing within it the codes and secrets that shape us, invisible urgings and desires spawned in generations past. Because of that it is a difficult path and only the most courageous and purest of heart have the humility to walk it. It takes great strength, warrior strength, to court doubt and darkness as the cost of knowing, to wield the power of choice like a lance and probe the way forward to the fullest expression of who you were created to be. To walk the Red Road asks the utmost of us, and there are few who choose it. Those that do are rewarded in the end, they say. They come back as Animals. They return as pure spirits born without question, arriving here knowing wholly and completely who they are. They are spared the agony of the search.

Joe Willie stood next to the chute and pondered that old teaching. He wondered who the bull might have been in a previous life, what sort of questions he might have struggled to answer, what battles he fought, what troubles rocked his soul. He was a great beast. Probably the biggest bull Joe Willie had ever seen, and over the course of a life in rodeo he'd seen a great many. Tall at the shoulder, muscles in sheets like armour, head as broad as a talus boulder, and the hard nub of horns bunched liked petrified wood at the sides of its head giving it an ancient, brooding look that was magnified by the deep, dull pools of its eyes. The great bull shivered. Joe Willie recalled the feel of that against his thighs. "Hello, old friend," he said. "Remember me?"

Behind him he could hear the sounds of the arena. Somewhere in that garbled sea of voices Aiden went through the ritual of preparation. The stock could feel the coming contest, and there was an agitated energy in the chutes and pens. The cowboys had shifted from the garrulous babble of taunt and tease downward into a sombre, reflective half silence punctuated only by necessary speech, the terse language of readiness. The bull sensed it and clomped its heavy feet in the dirt.

"You do remember, don't you?" Joe Willie said to it, leaning his face close to the rails. "Well, I sure remember you. I surely do."

He rubbed his shoulder, letting the good hand squeeze and massage the ruined joint. The bull cast a look at him out of the corner of its eye. It was a baleful look, the threat of it cool, measured, tempered with the knowledge of power. Joe Willie nodded. He put a hand through the rails and touched the bull's flank. He heard its voice, low and rumbling, and when it cracked the horns against the sides of the chute, Joe Willie smiled and slapped it firmly, then patted it three or four times. "You're still a big cuss," he said. "Still a handful of mean. Still the best damn bull I ever rode. Or almost rode."

The P.A. was announcing the final qualifying ride. There was a stir of activity everywhere as people headed for their seats, and the cowboys, rope men, bull fighters, pickup men and clowns made their final adjustments to gear and attire.

Joe Willie stepped back and assessed the bull. He nodded. "Damn," he said. "I'd give anything for another go. You asked the best of me and I gave it. I'll never forget that."

He looked up from the bull and off into the background. The arena was lit in the hard glare of spectacle, and he realized how much he'd missed it, how much he'd carried it around within him all that time and how he'd mistaken the weight for loss. He grinned at the folly pain caused him.

"You ready, boy?"

Lionel and Birch were standing behind him.

"Aiden's about ready," Birch said.

"Just renewing acquaintances," Joe Willie said. "I think I make him nervous."

Lionel laughed. "I imagine. He tell you that himself, did he?"

"Not in so many words."

"He's a big cuss," Birch said. "Aiden's got his hands full."

Joe Willie turned and looked back at the bull in the chute. It stood there proud and unquestioning, readying itself for the contest it could sense coming, its nostrils flared at the smell of the primal call in the air, the challenge. Joe Willie smelled it too. As he turned to walk with his father and grandfather he could swear the bull looked like a bear in the periphery of his vision.

Aiden perched on the top rail and watched the action in the arena. There was always such excitement and energy in the air that he swore it rubbed against his skin. When he arched his back and stretched he could feel it press against his muscles, compress nerve and sinew so that the feeling of readiness was a coming together, a gathering, a mélange of light, sound, colour, smell and the faintly metallic taste of dust in the teeth. Another cowboy plumed into the dirt. The crowd groaned and the applause lapped around the fallen rider like surf and bore him up onto his feet again. He lifted his hat and waved his appreciation. In the background the bull fighters chased the bull off into the exit chute and there was a brief respite of calm in the infield. He loved that moment, that lull, that break in the sheer exuberance everyone came together in and that made rodeo less a true spectacle than a communal joy. The let-up of energy punctuated all of it, and he breathed it in, filled his lungs with it and felt it enter his blood, enliven and become him.

He'd been bucked off his share in his rookie year. There'd been a dry spell of a month and a half when he couldn't buy eight seconds, and if not for Joe Willie he might have given it up, surrendered to the shame of slapping the dust from his chaps and hobbling to the rail again. But there was no quit in Joe Willie. Together they'd go over the tapes of the rides and Joe Willie was able to give him a vision of it he was incapable of discerning for himself. He played them over and over in his mind and he sharpened his intuition, his feel of the bull. Soon, he'd begun to appear in the money rounds and he had a handful of buckles now. The cash wasn't great, it wasn't a living, not yet anyway. But the payoff was the indisputable feeling of rightness he carried slung across his shoulders with his rigging. He jumped off the rail and walked over to the chute area.

He'd drawn See Four. When they told him, he could only stand and look at Joe Willie, who nodded grimly, squeezing his hands together. Now he could see them shunting the great bull into the chute, and the size of him was shocking. Aiden had

seen him before but he'd never had to look at him as a chal-
lenger. That perspective changed everything. He went over his
gear one last time, checking the bull rope especially for tackiness and grip, retying the thongs around his boots and tightening the Kevlar vest around his ribs. Then he made his way
to the chute, where Lionel would act as rope man and Birch
and Joe Willie would be in the chute with him.

"Ready?" Joe Willie asked.

"Guess."

"No time to guess. This is a mean mother."

"You should know. Anything you wanna tell me?"

Joe Willie turned to look at See Four. "He kicks hard. He'll
go high and kick out and you're gonna feel like you'll backflip
into the crowd. When he does that you push hard into the
pocket with everything you got because when he lands he'll spin
into your latch hand. It'll be fast so you gotta be square when he
lands because he'll spin away from it just as fast. Got that?"

"Yeah," Aiden said. "Anything else?"

"Yeah. This sumbitch only been rode three times. But
you don't think about that. It takes the best to beat him and
you gotta give him your best. All of it. Right now. No holding
back. If you do that you're his equal. But it takes everything."

Aiden looked at the bull in the chute. See Four stood
there quietly, and Aiden could see him breathing, could hear
the great bellows of his lungs hauling air. "Did you?" he asked.
"Did you give him everything you had."

Joe Willie looked up into the arena and scanned the
crowd. He put his hands on his hips and turned to face Aiden.
"I still am," he said.

The great bull stamped his feet in the dirt. The men at the
top of the chute were moving deliberately now, their voices

carrying that sharp edge of nerves. The sound of the arena was like a giant waterfall, the voices of all the men beings gurgling over top of each other so that the bull became agitated, anxious, wanting this over with and yearning for the quiet and the shadow of the stock pens. There was a slithering along his flank as one of the men attached the heavy rope bearing the noisemaker, and another at his shoulder when the thick rope scratched his hide and was pulled tighter and tighter around his girth. Then the feet stepping cautiously down on each side. This would be the young one, the one who stared fixedly when the bull had entered the chute. As the cowboy eased himself down onto his back the bull stepped from side to side, trying to press the man's legs against the rails hard enough to convince him to climb off. There was a short clamour of voices and the man on his back scrambled up quickly but settled back down again once the bull ceased rocking. The bull bawled and rattled the sides of the chute with his horns. He could hear the crowd in the arena grow excited and he rattled the chute again in excitement. The men above him shouted quickly at each other and the one on his back rocked into position. The bull settled.

He felt the slap of a hand on his back and he reared a little. He caught the high, ancient smell, like blood but older, more insistent. It had been some time since the bull had sensed that irrevocable call and he bawled again, louder, and rattled the sides of the chute hard with his horns. The manspeak above him cut the air like knives, and the bull was pleased. He could sense their sharpened unease. He could feel a slight tremor in the legs of the man on his back and he knew what he would do once the chute blasted open. He would run. He never ran. He had always exploded out of the chute in a billow of strength. But this time he would run out fast and straight, and when he felt the man weight shift with the charge he'd wheel into a spin to find the pressure point that would tell him which side the man clung to him from, and he'd spin into that point, making it harder for the man to sit there. Then he'd buck. Once he felt the weight shift he'd buck high and hard and land in a tight spin into the hand. The bull shimmied, felt the man's legs grip for him and prepared himself for the battle.

Joe Willie pressed a hand to each side of Aiden's chest to steady him. The young man's face was set in a determined scowl. In the background they could hear the arena announcer.

"Coming out of chute number three, a young cowboy who's been lighting up the rookie circuit this year. Aiden Hartley. Trained by the legendary Joe Willie Wolfchild. There's three generations of Wolfchilds in that chute tonight, ladies and gentlemen. That's granddad Lionel on the chute rope and daddy Birch in the chute along with Joe Willie. That's a ton of experience in there with him and Aiden Hartley is a cowboy to watch. Chute number three, Aiden Hartley, ladies and gentlemen, boys and girls."

"Guy's got a lot to say," Aiden said through clenched teeth.

"That's why they pay him the big bucks," Joe Willie said. "You ready?"

"Almost."

"Almost?"

"Yeah. There's just one thing."

"What?"

Aiden looked up at him and pinched his lips together. "This ride's for you."

He pressed his hat down low on his head and stretched his head back until he was staring at the beams and struts of the ceiling. He felt the hard pull of tendons in his neck and the scowl on his face felt gruesome as he slowly raised his free hand up above the rails and nodded sharply to Lionel, who pulled hard on the chute rope.

And the world exploded.

about the author

Richard Wagamese is an Ojibway from the Wabasseemoog First Nation in northwestern Ontario. After winning a National Newspaper Award for Column Writing, he published two novels in the 1990s: *Keeper'n Me* and *A Quality of Light*. His autobiographical book, *For Joshua*, was published in 2002. Wagamese has also lectured and worked extensively in both radio and television news and documentary. He lives outside Kamloops, British Columbia.

a note about the type

The text of *Dream Wheels* has been set in Adobe Jenson (aka "antique" Jenson), a modern face which captures the essence of Nicolas Jenson's roman and Ludovico degli Arrighi's italic typeface designs. The combined strength and beauty of these two icons of Renaissance type result in an elegant typeface suited to a broad spectrum of applications.